It was a soft sound, a whisper of air. It rippled the darkness like a stone thrown into a pond, radiating outward from its source in concentric circles. Quin, still drowsy, thought it was Grant, that he'd just gotten home. Any minute now, she'd hear the fridge sigh open, Saran wrap or aluminum foil crinkling as he found a snack, then his footfalls on the stairs.

She lay back, closing her eyes, drifting . . . GRANT?

She bolted forward and tried to remember where she'd put her gun. Someone was downstairs and it sure as hell wasn't Grant.

Grant was dead. . . .

DARK FIELDS

T. J. MacGregor

BALLANTINE BOOKS • NEW YORK

Copyright © 1986 by T. J. MacGregor

All rights reserved under International and Pan-American
Copyright Conventions. Published in the United States by
Ballantine Books, a division of Random House, Inc., New
York, and simultaneously in Canada by Random House of
Canada Limited, Toronto.

Library of Congress Catalog Card Number: 86-91309

ISBN 0-449-33756-5

Manufactured in the United States of America

First Edition: January 1987
Third Printing: December 1992

To my sister Mary, Linda Griffin, and Diane Cleaver, who believed

Prologue

June 21
Miami

I HAD WRITTEN out the scene in my mind, rehearsed it. I knew who would stand where, what I would say, what he would say. I'd even imagined what I would wear, how I would fix my hair, the purse I would carry. And of course I knew how it would end. That was the important part. Success, after all, begins in the mind. It's as true of murder as of anything else.

I paused at the door, making sure the purse slung over my shoulder fell exactly against my hip. That way, my fingers could hold lightly to the straps and, when the time was right, could dip inside it with the speed of light. I touched the knob with a piece of Kleenex, the door was open, I walked in.

"Hello," I called out, sticking the Kleenex back in my purse.

He appeared in the kitchen doorway. The red apron he wore with the giant pitchfork on it sort of threw me. That hadn't been part of my mental picture. "Well, hi," he said with a grin. "Come on back."

My shoes whispered against the carpeting, clicked across the kitchen tile. He kissed me hello, quickly, then plunged his hands into the suds that filled the kitchen sink. I had visualized it taking place in the kitchen, but not as he washed dishes. That meant I would have to wait. If I offered to dry the dishes, we could get the whole thing over with that much faster. But he would notice if I didn't set my purse on the counter, and there was no way I was letting go of it. I remained where I was, leaning against the edge of the fridge, and asked if he had any Scotch.

"I thought you gave up drinking," he remarked.

How predictable he was. I had imagined this very response and felt certain now that everything would fall into place just as I'd planned. In fact, the precise words either of us spoke from this point on didn't much matter, as long as the mood was maintained.

"Whatever gave you that idea?" I replied.

"Oh, the last time we talked, I thought—"

"You thought wrong." My voice was quiet, even pleasant, but held a sharp edge that indicated I didn't want to discuss it.

"Well, I'm all outa Scotch, sorry. There's beer in the fridge, if you want one."

Pedestrian tastes, all right. And I knew from the tone of his voice that he considered beer less alcoholic than Scotch. Where'd he ever get such an idea, anyway? I helped myself to a can of Coors and made a mental note to take the can with me when I'd finished.

"Grab me one too, will you?"

I hesitated. That part wasn't in the scene. Of course, I could always take *two* empty cans with me. But it bothered me. I feared getting careless and leaving fingerprints all over the house. Besides, it was the unexpected things that fouled me up last time.

As I handed him the beer, his soapy fingers brushed mine and I wondered if he thought much about the night I came after him with the knife. Probably. There were still times when I could hear his voice, taunting me with, *You can't use that on me, you know you can't. You care too much.* But I wouldn't think about that now. It wasn't prudent to contemplate past failures when you were striving for success. And this time I had a gun—my pretty little pearl-handled gun—which was less personal. You aimed it, you fired. No mess and it was quick.

He popped open the beer, took a swig, then dropped his hands into the sink again, rinsed one more dish, pulled the plug. The water made a sucking sound, he wiped his hands on the apron, reached around to untie it. *In a minute, it'll be over.* My tongue suddenly felt as brittle as glass. I wanted a Scotch on the rocks or a Scotch and soda, like the song. I wanted something cold and wet to vanquish the drought in my mouth and wash away the summer nesting in my bones. I couldn't remember who was supposed to say what, where we should've been standing. Now that the moment approached, I seemed to be suffering a temporary fugue.

"Something wrong?" He tossed the apron over the back of a kitchen chair.

Wrong? I nearly shouted. *Everything's wrong.* He wasn't supposed to have asked that, he wasn't dressed the way I'd imagined. I could feel the scene getting away from me, scampering like some disgusting bug toward an unimagined future, a future over which I would have no control. "No, no, it's just the beer on an empty stomach," I stammered.

"I think we should talk," he said, and touched my shoulder.

Oh yeah, I knew the kind of talk he meant. He would promise to get me help, to take care of me as though I were some stupid Cinderella. I'd heard it all before. I'd heard it the night I'd come after him with the knife. I stepped back, his hand fell away. He shouldn't have touched me: it wasn't in the scene. But my skin burned where his hand had been, and the weight of the gun in my purse, against my hip, hurt my side. I felt its heat, its pulse, its unsullied demands, reminding me that he *knew,* he knew my secret. "Don't touch me," I hissed, and stepped back.

"*What* is your problem?" He laughed, a quick, almost startled sound, and moved toward me again. I stumbled back, my heel connected with the edge of the rug. The scene had to take place in the kitchen, and here I was in the living room once again. But he was taller than me, and larger, and I couldn't expect to rush him without the gun. My fingers dipped into my purse, dug down, stopped, dug again like tiny dogs intent on recovering a bone. He said something in that soft, intimate voice I knew so well, that trickster's voice. He was still in the kitchen but continued toward me, and I kept retreating, as though we were chess pieces locked in repetitive patterns on a board. Then my fingers touched the gun.

I brought it out, aimed it carefully at his chest. He stopped. His eyes fixed on the weapon, then hopped along my hands, wrist, my arms, to my face. Wherever his eyes had touched, my skin tingled. "Why don't you just give me that, okay? You really don't want to use it, now do you?" What a controlled, cool voice. If it were edible, that voice, it would taste like chilled papaya, sweet, succulent. "We'll get you help, honey, I don't care what it costs, I've got money, lots of money, we'll get you the best of help." And what that mesmerizing voice didn't say was, *I know your secret, I now control you.*

But oh, how that voice mesmerized me. A part of me wanted to believe his lies. But the other part saw that in another step he'd be in the living room with me. "Get back," I told him. "Just get back." But he lunged and my finger squeezed the trigger and everything seemed to slow down. His body swayed, began to fall, and his arms pinwheeled as if he were doing the backstroke through a vat of molasses. His face registered astonishment, he grunted, the front of his shirt quickly turned red. He smacked the floor. As I stepped around him to reach for the two cans of beer, I noticed a faint stain like cranberry juice on his upper lip and giggled. *I told you your mouth was stained with blood.*

I grabbed the cans of beer so quickly, one of them spilled. Beer spread across the counter, dripped onto the floor. I ignored it, shoved both cans in my purse, yanked a paper towel from the rack on the wall so I wouldn't leave prints on the knob or the light switches on my way out. I thought about kneeling beside him, performing some quick obsequy. But what would be the point?

It wasn't in the scene.

PART ONE

Secrets

"All cruelty springs from weakness."
——SENECA

1

IT WAS DARK when Quin stepped outside. The hot air tightened around her and seemed to pucker like skin on a fat, ripe grape. The swell of humidity had captured the redolent scent of jasmine and gardenias from the cluster of plants at either side of the stoop, and the fragrances smelled good enough to eat. Her stomach growled as if in agreement, reminding her that despite dinner three hours ago, she was hungry.

She locked the front door of the office, then carefully stepped around the welcome mat on the porch that said FORSYTHE & ST. JAMES, PRIVATE INVESTIGATORS. It was one of her small superstitions that if she treaded on Trevor's name or her own, the firm would go bankrupt or some other tragedy would strike them. Okay, it was silly. But she'd been following it like a tradition for two years, ever since she'd become a partner, and the firm had flourished, so why tempt a good thing?

She'd no sooner finished locking the door than she realized she'd forgotten her briefcase, and the Dodge file was inside it. The case involved a multimillion-dollar suit against the company for a faulty steering mechanism, and because she'd spent most of the day working on it and still had notes to review, she returned to get it.

She was in such a rush on her way back out that she neglected to step around the mat, and when she looked down—the tips of her shoes covered her name. She wanted to laugh at the way her stomach tightened, at the way she hopped to the side, but somehow the laugh wouldn't come. She heard Grant's voice chiding her one day a few months ago when she'd refused to open an umbrella in the house. *I bet you even throw spilled salt over your shoulder, don't you, Quin.*

As a matter of fact, she didn't. She was rather selective about her superstitions. But she hadn't bothered telling *him* that.

She hurried down the walk to her car, refusing to think about stepping on the mat. In the glow of the street lamp, the Toyota's beige metallic finish made it look like a whale that had been rubbed down with baby oil. She ran her hand over the roof, knocking off the dried leaves and twigs, and considered going by Grant's townhouse on her way home. Her stomach rumbled again as if to say *not before you feed me,* and she wished she could remember what she'd done with the apple she'd packed with her lunch this morning.

She unlocked the door, annoyed that she was the only person she knew whose life seemed to be ruled by the whims of her appetite. If she were fat, she might've felt kinder toward the compulsion. But she ate constantly and couldn't gain an ounce over the one-oh-eight she'd weighed ever since she'd hit her full height of five-ten when she was fifteen. Nineteen years of gluttony could be depressing.

She slid into the car and saw the missing apple. It was on the dash, and the brutal June sun had baked it. The thing oozed juice and bits of mush, and the inside of the car smelled as sweet as an orchard. "God," she groaned, plucking it from the dash and dropping it into the trash bag on the floor. She went through the glove compartment, looking for gum, mints, peanuts, anything to stave off her hunger. Ever since she'd quit smoking a couple of months ago she'd made a point of carrying munchies around with her. But her stash was depleted. There wasn't so much as a gum wrapper to suck on.

Well, she would still drive by Grant's, and for once her stomach could just wait. She headed south to the Gables, knowing already he wouldn't be home. He wasn't due back from his trip until later this week and if he *had* returned early, he would've called her from the airport.

But just the sight of the townhouse would somehow diminish the emotional gap of his absence. It made no more sense than not stepping on the welcome mat at the office, but she didn't care. Sometimes irrational acts were justified.

Right before she and Grant had bought the house and moved in together, the people who'd been renting his condo had moved. Instead of finding new tenants, he'd started using the place for work. He maintained his darkroom there, his files of slides, professional addresses, some of his cameras and other equipment. If nothing else, she could make sure the place hadn't been broken into and robbed.

And suppose he's back? Then what?

"Oh, stop." She'd become so accustomed to intrigue and duplicity in her work, it was a wonder that everyone closest to her wasn't under suspicion for something.

As she pulled into the lot in front of Grant's condo, the still summer air screamed with silence. It plucked at Quin's uneasiness as she stepped out. She glanced toward the row of acacia trees across the lot from her, frowned, ran her hands against her skirt, shook her head. She thought she saw Grant's car parked in the deep pocket of shadows at the corner of the lot, but that wasn't possible.

Her shoes tapped hollowly against the pavement, her hunger ebbed, she wanted to turn away and pretend she hadn't stopped here. It was Grant's Escort, all right, melting into the shadows, thick as a lump of bitter chocolate. The rising gibbous moon blinked like a great singular eye in its back window. Pale light splashed across its trunk, illuminating a bumper sticker that said BEAM ME UP, SCOTTY.

She peered into the side windows, eyes combing the interior as though she expected it to cough up answers. But the car was empty. She turned and hurried toward the townhouse. The dark windows, the walk littered with gardenia buds, the weeping willow that sagged pitifully beneath its own weight gave the place an empty, hollow feel. She kept waiting for the front door to open, for Grant to appear. Instead, the heat seemed to suck at her, robbing her body of moisture. Her mouth turned dry, her eyes burned. The mournful whistle of the nine o'clock train from Miami to Jacksonville, half an hour late as usual, cracked the stillness. Through it rushed the bark of a dog and the sound of a car racing over the cobblestone road that wound through the complex. The noises were no more and no less than she'd heard dozens of times, but now riddled the air with foreboding.

Quin paused at the front door. A muscle twitched beneath her eye as she glanced at the windows where darkness swam thick as ink. If he were home, why weren't there any lights on? She rang the bell, waited, knocked, waited. The dryness in her mouth made it difficult to swallow. Her tongue felt swollen. She had a key to the place but didn't want to use it. For a moment, she considered driving up to the corner Seven-Eleven to call him. But her hand was already reaching into her purse for the key, drawn inexorably by the need to know . . . *what*?

She inserted the key and was surprised to find the door unlocked. It creaked as it swung inward, and a rush of cool air dried the dampness on her face. "Grant?"

The quiet tossed her voice back to her and raised goosebumps on her arms. Her hand quickly patted the wall for the switch. Track lights illuminated a cluster of his Amazon photographs on the far wall. The familiar sight attenuated her unease. *See? There's nothing wrong.* Grant had just gotten back earlier than he'd expected and was probably sound asleep upstairs. *But why didn't he call?*

She hit the second switch. When the lamps came on, when she saw the blood smeared across the egg-white wall around the light switch, her breath struck the air in small jerks. Her eyes dropped to the dark spots like squashed insects trailing erratically across the smoky blue rug toward the kitchen. She blinked, whispered, "Grant, it's me, Quin."

The air conditioning whirred in response. A gelid stream of air slipped across her cheek. She shivered, forced herself to move toward the kitchen. Another light, and she grappled for the edge of the doorway to steady herself when she saw him.

Even if there hadn't been so much blood, she would've

10

known he was dead. There was a look of heaviness, of finality in his face, as though his features had drooped beneath the very weight of death. His hand was against his chest, fingers slightly splayed and bloody. His open eyes stared vapidly at the far wall, where the hands of the clock quivered at 9:35. Part of her wanted to rush toward him, drop to her knees, kiss the pink back into his cheeks like some enchanted witch. The other part wanted to run back outside and start over again. Maybe then when she turned the knob, and the door opened, he'd be standing there in his jeans and scruffy shirt, grinning with mischief.

She didn't know how long she remained in the doorway, eyes fixed on the blood as she kept hoping he would suddenly get up, shake himself off, smile. She finally moved woodenly to the phone. But on the chalkboard above it, a word had been scrawled. It slanted downward, its letters oddly shaped, weak, streaked with blood. She stared at it, waiting for the letters to connect in her mind, to form a word, to make sense. But her brain was sluggish and slow as a snail, and now her stomach was heaving. She slid toward the half bath near the back door, nearly fell, made it to the bowl before she retched.

Her breath came in great heaving sobs as Grant's face floated through the sour dark of her mind. She saw him waving at her from his car as he'd backed out of the driveway three weeks ago, en route to the airport. His dark hair, graying at the temples, had fallen across his forehead, his sea green eyes had crinkled at the corners, and then he was gone.

Now he was here.

Dead.

Nothing bridged the two events.

She finally lifted herself up, rinsed out her mouth, grabbed for the nearest towel. She ran it under cold water, pressed it against her face, her eyes, until black stars danced inside her head. She backed out of the bathroom so she wouldn't have to look at him, her knees stiff as planks, her insides in an uproar. Her hand trembled as she lifted the receiver. It wasn't fair. It wasn't fair that she should walk in here and find her life turned upside down in just ten seconds.

She couldn't remember the emergency number, and dialed 0. But when the operator answered, she couldn't speak. The enormity of what had happened had shoved its way down her throat and chopped up her vocal cords.

"Hello? Yes, hello?"

"Police," she said finally, and spit out her address.

"What seems to be the problem, ma'am?"

"Wha-what?"

"The problem, I have to have something to tell the police."

She was staring at the blood-splattered blackboard, the word that meant nothing.

"Dead," she whispered. "Grant's dead."

2

THE TOWNHOUSE BLAZED like a carnival, light spilling
from its windows and flooding the parking lot. Two
police cars and an ambulance were flanked by a dozen
people drawn by the atavistic stirring, McCleary thought,
that the scent of blood created. He almost expected to
see midgets and fat ladies selling tickets to the show
inside. But there was only a woman sitting on the porch
steps, in the shadow of a weeping willow. She didn't
stand as he approached.

"Mrs. St. James?"

"Miss." Her voice was soft, flat.

"I'm Mike McCleary, Metro-Dade homicide."

"Your friends are inside." She pressed her hands
against her thighs and pushed herself to her feet. She
was thin, nearly as tall as he was, about five ten. Her
curly umber hair fell just below her ears and framed her
pale face like a photograph. The haunted look in her
blue eyes disturbed him; it was like peering into the face
of a wounded fawn. "I couldn't stay inside anymore."

"We can talk out here, if you want."

Her eyes swept through the parking lot, and she shook
her head. "The courtyard might be better."

"Okay. Let me check inside first."

She hugged her arms against her. "I'll go around."

The place was about what he'd expected for this part
of the Gables: spacious and expensive. The front room
had a vaulted ceiling, furniture that was mostly glass,

13

chrome, and wicker, and an imprint that was definitely male. Several watercolors adorned one wall, their soft blues and celery greens so tranquil, McCleary felt drowsy just looking at them. On another wall hung perhaps half a dozen framed photographs of various jungle scenes: a dark-skinned woman scrubbing clothes at the bank of a wide, muddy river; an owl with feathers the color of sand and eyes older than time; a shot of an Indian village; kids with dark liquid eyes and distended bellies in dugout canoes, splashing in the river, sitting listlessly.

Then he saw the blood on the wall, trailing across the rug to the kitchen like scattered roses. It seemed as misplaced in this expensive room as the jungle photos. When he looked up, Tim Benson stood in the doorway, the reflection of the overhead lights captured in his glasses like tiny suns. He didn't look any too pleased about being here either, McCleary thought. Behind Benson, in the kitchen, were several cops, a police photographer, two paramedics.

"Mike, what kept you?"

"I didn't get your message until I was on my way home."

Benson, a tall, gangly man in his late forties, ran a hand through his short black hair. "From the looks of it, the guy was shot with a .45."

"Have you talked to the woman?"

"Just for a few minutes, then she got sick." He jammed his hands in his pockets. "Hell of a mess in there." Tim Benson was actually with the robbery division, but he'd been McCleary's partner for the last couple of weeks, while Robin was on vacation. He was a reticent, self-contained man, and McCleary had learned that when he said something, he was usually right. So he braced himself as they walked into the kitchen.

McCleary's decade in Miami homicide had innoculated him against most of the horrors of violent death. But even so, the sight of Grant Bell brought urgent flutters of his own mortality. It wasn't the blood, although there was a lot of it, or the hole in the man's chest. It was the proximity in their ages. Bell looked to be in his early forties, maybe four years older than McCleary, and had evidently lived awhile after he'd been shot—long enough to stumble from the kitchen to the living room and back again.

"He was a freelance photographer," Benson explained. "Weddings, some travel stuff, and promotional brochures for local companies. This is his place."

"What was the woman doing here?"

"She said she stopped by on her way home from work. She thought he was still out of the country, on assignment. They lived together in a house across town. She says he used to rent this place, but when his tenants moved, he kept it as a place to work. You oughta see the darkroom. There must be thousands of dollars of equipment in there." Benson nodded toward the courtyard, where Quin St. James was sitting. "You know who she is, don't you?"

He shook his head. "Should I?"

"She's *the* St. James, as in Forsythe and St. James, the private eyes."

McCleary nodded; he'd heard of them. The firm, one of the top PI outfits in South Florida, employed more than thirty investigators. It dealt almost exclusively with medical malpractice cases and insurance claims against major manufacturers. From what he remembered, Forsythe's old man had started the company back in the early forties, when Miami was little more than an enchanted, sun-kissed village.

"Where was Bell supposed to be?"

"The Amazon. It was his fourth trip this year."

That explained the photos. "You think she killed him?"

"Naw, Mac. Besides, her story'll be easy to check because she says she and another investigator were working late." Benson pointed at a small chalkboard over the phone. "Take a look at this. 'Greenfire.' She says she doesn't have the foggiest notion what it means."

"So he lived long enough to make it from the kitchen to the living room and back into the kitchen to scribble this."

"Apparently." Benson shrugged as if to say that the vagaries of the dying were an oblique mystery, impenetrable. "Damned weird, if you ask me."

"Any sign of breaking and entering?"

"One of the guys is still checking, but not so far."

Benson motioned to a neat pile of things on the counter. "I went through his pockets. He was carrying his passport, and according to the exit stamps he left Peru nearly a week ago."

"How much money was he carrying?"

"Couple hundred dollars. I don't think it was robbery, Mike."

Probably not. These days, homicide in Miami was rarely for something as simple as robbery. McCleary looked slowly around the kitchen, which wasn't very big. A red apron with a pitchfork on it draped the back of a nearby chair, dishes were stacked in the rack, something sticky coated the counter. He ran his hand over it, then sniffed at it. Beer? He glanced in the garbage can under the sink, but the bag was empty. He strolled into the adjoining breakfast nook. The chain was still on the door that led from it to the courtyard. He stood at the jalousie windows a moment, gazing into the courtyard where Quin St. James sat. Her back was to him, but from where he stood, he could see her profile.

She didn't look like a private eye.

She looked like a teacher or maybe a computer programmer who'd never seen a dead person in her life, except on TV.

He turned away from the window and proceeded down the hall. It was a virtual gallery of photographs, and most of the scenes depicted were foreign. In the den, he noted the oddities on the walls: headdresses made from colorful feathers, blowguns, a shellacked piranha mounted on a piece of wood, a hand-carved wooden paddle with the broad part shaped like a teardrop. There was an electric typewriter on the desk, a stack of folders; next to it were filing cabinets. In the room off the garage he found the darkroom. It was beautifully equipped: a Nikon enlarger, an electric drum dryer, an aluminum counter that drained into an aluminum sink, bottles of chemicals stacked neatly on shelves against the wall. Negatives hung from a pair of clotheslines strung from one end of the room to the other.

McCleary glanced at some of the unframed photos clipped to the line with clothespins. Some were straight black and white or color photos, others were the result

16

of darkroom magic: blacks where whites should have been, pink skies, phantom images burned into green waters. The man, he thought, had been not only a photographer but an artist as well.

When he returned to the kitchen, he and Benson walked out into the courtyard. It was lit by several lampposts that sprouted from the foliage like mutant plants. Magenta blossoms from the acacia trees that shaded the area were strewn about like dyed rice after a wedding. They joined Quin St. James at an aluminum table covered with bits of dried leaves.

"You feel up to answering a few questions?" Benson asked her.

"Not really, but go ahead."

McCleary silently congratulated her on her frankness, and let Benson start. His soft, easy voice usually put people at ease, and the paternal air about him encouraged trust. McCleary noticed it didn't take long for her to succumb to Benson's spell. Her thin shoulders seemed to sag, as if with fatigue, the muscles in her face loosened, she sat back in the chair. She spoke with an ersatz calmness, as if she were relating something that had happened to someone else. Only when she got to the part about opening the door did her voice falter.

"Do you know about what time you got here?" McCleary asked.

"Nine-thirty. The nine o'clock train from Miami to Jax was just going through, and I remember thinking it was half an hour late." Her eyes, fixed on something beyond McCleary's shoulder, were an Aegean blue, almost transparent. The kind of eyes, he thought, that penetrated and made you squirm if they watched you too long. The long, dark lashes clustered together and shadowed her cheeks. For a moment, there in the dim light in the courtyard, her face had a soft-focus beauty that Monet might've painted. She wasn't pretty, not like Robin, but there was something about her he found oddly appealing.

"Who was he on assignment for?" Benson asked.

"For Wishod Pharmaceuticals, in Lauderdale. He was doing promotional stuff for them. He may have had an assignment with one of the travel magazines too. That's how he used to try to work it. He'd get a company to pay his way down, do what he had to do for them, and gather stuff for other assignments on the side."

"Why would he need to travel for Wishod if he was just doing promotional brochures for them?" McCleary asked.

The resignation in her expression indicated she knew exactly what line of questioning they were following. "They're supposedly setting up some sort of research lab in the area. I think they're working in conjunction with botanists from a couple of different universities. Grant's job was to get pictures of people on site, that sort of thing."

"What kind of research?" Benson prodded.

"Look, I'm not real sure on the details." She sat back, her fingers tapping the edge of the table. "Would either of you happen to have gum or mints? My stomach feels like there's a hole in it."

Both men patted their pockets. Benson brought out a roll of Lifesavers that looked like they'd gone through the wash. "Thanks," she said, and popped one in her mouth. "The way Grant explained it to me," she continued, as though there'd been no interruption, "the deforestation that's going on in the Amazon now is a threat to a lot of the plant life, including stuff that's never been identified. The botanists hired Wishod to test some of the plants for their possible usefulness as drugs. Or maybe it was the other way around. I don't remember." She bit into the mint, and McCleary winced as it cracked.

"What does Wishod manufacture?" he asked.

The illumination from the posts bled into her hair, lightening the color. "Generic drugs and vitamins for companies like K Mart and some of the drugstores. I imagine they have other products, too, but I don't know what they are." She came forward again, arms resting along the edge of the table. Her gaze, when it paused on him, made him fidget. "I don't know who would want to see him dead—isn't that how the line goes? But it's true. We'd only known each other about a year, though, so maybe he had enemies. Maybe there were reasons for him to have enemies. Anything's possible." The bitterness in her voice bit like acid into the hot, humid air.

"Were you in the habit of dropping by here?" Benson asked.

She shook her head and explained she hadn't been in the townhouse for nearly a year. "I worked late and my stomach was trying to boss me around and I got fed up and decided to show it who was in charge."

McCleary and Benson exchanged a look. Funny, he thought, she didn't look like a nut. Then he decided that maybe he'd missed something. "I don't follow."

Her expression loosened, as if she were about to cry. "If I'd had my apple, this wouldn't have happened, I mean, it would've happened, but I wouldn't have been the one to . . . to find him. But my goddamned apple baked on the dash in my car, and then there weren't any mints in the glove compartment, and . . ." She stopped and made an impatient gesture with her hand. "Oh, forget it. I don't know why I dropped by. I did, that's enough."

McCleary glanced at Benson again. He shrugged as if to say that the vagaries of people who were close to homicide victims were perhaps as odd as the victims themselves. McCleary decided not to try and figure out what her little story had been about. He'd made it his business over the years to observe details, nuances, and he suspected that despite her quirks, she probably hadn't killed Bell.

"When were you expecting him back?" Benson asked.

"Any time after the twenty-fourth, three days from now."

"Did you know the upstairs has been ransacked?"

That was another thing Benson was good at: surprises. And they were always uttered in that same calm, *aw shucks* voice. From the expression on her face, though, McCleary realized she didn't know about the upstairs, that it probably hadn't even occurred to her to check. "No, I didn't." She ran her hands along the sides of her slacks, looking at her hands. She was quiet for so long, he thought she'd forgotten their presence. "Look, I'd like to get out of here. I think I'm going to stay with a friend tonight. Would it be all right if I called you tomorrow and arranged to come by the station?"

McCleary nodded. "Yeah, I don't see why not."

Benson excused himself and went back inside to see if the other men were going too be winding up shortly. "Besides the companies you mentioned, is there anyone else we should talk to?" McCleary asked.

Her head bobbed. She reached for another mint. "Sure. But I'll be talking to them as well."

"I'd rather you didn't."

A corner of her mouth turned down with what he thought was contempt. "I conduct investigations for a living, Mr. McCleary, and I'm going to find out who did this. It may take me a while, but I'll find out."

"You don't conduct *homicide* investigations for a living."

"So what. It can't be that much different than a malpractice investigation. In both, you're looking for the guilty party."

Her calmness had sloughed off like an old skin, and the tenacity beneath bothered him. The last thing he needed was her messing up his investigation. "Are you licensed to carry a weapon?" he asked.

"Yes, why?" Her tone turned defensive.

"Have you ever shot anyone?"

"No."

"Then I suggest that if you're planning on solving this yourself, Ms. St. James, be prepared to use the gun, because whoever shot your friend in there isn't going to give a damn whether you're a private eye or God."

"What makes you think *you're* immune?"

Okay, McCleary thought. It's late and I'm tired. She's a bitch, but she's hurting. Be patient. "Nothing. My point is that you're still a private citizen, and if you use a gun on someone, be damned sure you can prove it was self-defense."

"I might be able to find out things you can't. And besides, I can't just sit around and do nothing." Her expression was somehow plaintive, as though she wanted him to understand as much as she herself needed to understand. Okay, he didn't blame her, but he still didn't like it. There were idiosyncrasies that rode tandem with this business, and one of them was a kind of possessiveness about cases. The few times he'd had dealings with PIs, facts had gotten muddled, suspects had inadvertently been tipped off, everything slowed down. And since she'd been living with the man, it would just be worse.

"Suit yourself. I need those names and also the names of any members of his family."

"No immediate family. Just an ex-wife, who's remarried. Treena Bell Esposito." More energy seemed to hiss out of her by the second as she gave him half a dozen names.

A little while later, he walked with her to her car. The bystanders were gone, the paramedics had left with the body, and ahead of him lay the tedium of taking statements from neighbors. *You're getting too old for this shit, Mac,* he told himself, watching the receding taillights of Quin St. James's Toyota leaving the complex. At this point, one more murder was one too many.

Besides the usual drug-related homicides, he had five unsolved murders on his hands, the last a month ago, that were beginning to look like serial killings, the bane of any homicide department. The victims, single men between the ages of twenty-five and thirty-five, had been knifed—two in their homes, one in an alley, one in a hotel, the last in his car. There were pitifully few clues, and so far no fingerprints.

He stood in the sultry stillness, rubbing the back of his aching neck, and stared at his shadow against the ground. His shoulders stooped with fatigue. He knew if he looked in a mirror right now, he would see circles beneath his sharp blue eyes, a subtle sag to his square, stubborn chin, and gray laced through his cocoa-colored hair and mustache. Gray, at thirty-seven: ridiculous. Homicide was aging him, aging him fast.

But what were the options? Before Miami homicide, he'd worked homicide in Syracuse, New York. Before that, for several years after he'd graduated from college, he'd been selling insurance. No way he was going back to that. *How about used cars, Mac? There's always a need for used cars.*

"Mac?" Benson walked up behind him.

McCleary turned. "Yeah, I was just coming back in."

"No need, man, I forgot to tell you we took statements earlier. There are only two other apartments in this building."

"Did anyone hear anything?"

"One family was out, and the woman in the other apartment was home with her kid, upstairs watching TV. She claims you can't hear anything from there. I didn't get to speak to the kid; he was sleeping."

So what had he expected, anyway? That it'd be easy? "Maybe a silencer was used."

"Maybe."

Variables, McCleary mused. There were always so many variables. Solving a murder was a bit like trying to fit together a Rubik's cube. Unless you perceived the overall pattern, you could shuffle the pieces around until you were blue in the face and still not find your answer.

"Got any burning hunches?" asked a smiling Benson, who didn't believe in hunches.

"Nope," McCleary replied with a grin. He'd gotten used to Benson's ribbing about hunches.

A car drove into the lot, a Buick, a beige Buick Regal. The tension in McCleary's neck dropped away. Benson nudged him. "Hey, it's Robin. I didn't know she was back."

"Neither did I."

"You go on, Mac. I'll have one of the guys drive the cruiser back to the station."

"You sure?"

When Benson smiled, the lines at the corners of his eyes cut deeply. "Yeah, don't worry about it. You haven't seen her in two weeks. You think I don't know what that's like?"

"I owe you one, buddy."

Robin's head poked through the window, her smile like a burst of sunlight. His heart quickened. Perhaps tonight would be salvageable, after all.

3

1.

SHE TASTED OF cinammon, and the familiar scent of her perfume wafted around him like smoke. "Shalimar or Opium?" he asked, pulling away from her a little.

"A squirt of each," she laughed, hugging him again. "God, I missed you, Mac."

He held her for a moment, there in the shadow of a townhouse where a man had just been murdered. This was what homicide taught you, he thought: divide your mind or go nuts. "Let's get outa here."

"We're off."

"How was Chicago?"

"Windy. How was it having Benson for a partner?"

"Okay, but not like having you."

"Flatterer."

Her voice was throaty. He called it her Bacall voice and liked to imagine she used it just with him. It fit her sleek, good looks—high cheekbones like an Indian, that expressive mouth, eyes as dark as coffee. Her hair, a rich auburn, tumbled to her shoulders in loose curls. They'd been partners for two years and lovers for about half that, and it hadn't all been as easy as it was right now. This was different; this was the result of her two-week absence. "I would've picked you up at the airport, you know. If you'd told me when you were getting in."

"I wanted to surprise you."

"How'd you know where I was, anyway?"

"I stopped by the station thinking you might be around. The dispatcher told me where you were. Who was he?"

McCleary told her briefly what he knew, then quickly changed the subject. He didn't want to talk shop; he wanted to talk marriage. "How about if you stay at my place tonight?"

"Exactly what I had in mind."

"Let's get a place together, Robin. Let's get married."

She was smiling when she glanced at him, but smiling in that thin, restrained way that said, *Please, not tonight, let's not argue tonight.* "Oh, you."

He gave an exaggerated sigh. "I may stop asking. Then what're you going to do?"

A quick laugh: "Then it'll be my turn to ask you."

Although McCleary smiled, he wished she wouldn't joke about it. He knew she cared for him, he didn't think there were any other men in her life, and she'd as much as said they were good together. But she wouldn't marry him. *It isn't as clear-cut for me as it is for you, Mac,* she would tell him when they discussed it seriously. But *what* wasn't clear-cut? Her feelings toward him? The relationship? *No, my feelings toward marriage,* she'd say.

In the beginning, he blamed her reluctance to marry him on her parents' divorce when she was in her teens. Then he thought it was because they were both cops, and partners, which threw them together most of the day. But a few months ago, when he suggested they request new partners, she argued that he was playing unfair, dragging work into it when that didn't have anything to do with how she felt toward marriage. *If you don't love me, then just say so, Robin.* But her response to that had been an exasperated sigh, as though the entire discussion were futile. *Loving you has nothing to do with it.* And since then, he mentioned marriage less frequently, and always with a soft banter in his voice, to let her know he was just asking, after all, and she had the right to refuse. Of course.

McCleary, whose secret passion was art, sometimes felt the way Van Gogh must have when he'd cut off his ear and had given it to the woman he'd loved. Not that

24

he would cut off his ear for Robin, but it was the same desperate sort of love, he thought, and he wished he knew how to shake it.

They stopped by her place first so she could pick up clothes for work tomorrow. "Be back in a jiffy, Mac."

"Okay, I'll wait here."

He watched as she hurried up the walk, moving with the grace of an angel. It was Benson who'd first called her that, McCleary remembered. They'd been standing outside the chief's office and she'd walked by, smiling rather shyly at them. "If Izzo hires any more women who look like *that*," Benson had murmured, "the divorce rate among cops is *really* going to soar. She's an angel, Mac."

"Who is she?"

"Robin Peters. She was supposedly an attorney in the Midwest somewhere, I think. Chief Izzo said she was really successful, then got disgusted with the law, came down here and went through training, and graduated top in the class. She wants to be a cop."

"We'll see how long *that* lasts," he'd remarked.

The next day, Izzo had informed McCleary he had a new partner. "I don't want a female partner," he'd argued.

"She's good, Mac, very good."

"Training classes aren't real life, Bob, you know that. I need someone who can back me up."

Izzo had shrugged nonchalantly, indicating the subject was closed. "Try her for a month, and if you're not satisfied, then we'll talk about a replacement."

Within two weeks, she'd solved a homicide he'd been working on for five months. When he'd asked how she'd fingered the killer, who wasn't even a suspect, she'd said she had a hunch, that was all. "And I always follow my hunches."

Even about men? he wondered.

He saw her come back out after a moment and head around the side of the building. Robin was always forgetting her keys. She kept a spare house key under the doormat at the rear door of her apartment and an extra car key taped to the inside of the Buick's bumper. She was not, he thought, the most organized person in the world, a trait she claimed was a rebellion against the strictures the practice of law had imposed.

Her disorganization had bothered him in the beginning. She'd misplaced files, reports, her notes, and had neglected to give him phone messages. But after the first few months, he stopped noticing her disorganization. Instead, he'd grown to rely on her keen intelligence. She'd added a new dimension to his life as a cop. Of course, by then he was so much in love with her, it wouldn't have mattered if she'd misplaced every case he'd worked on in the last ten years.

It had taken him nearly the full twelve months of their first year as partners to muster the courage to ask Robin out. She'd never given any indication that she was aware of how he felt or that she saw him as anything other than the man she worked with. But once he'd taken the first step, everything had happened quickly. And then begun to sour when he'd started making noises about marriage. There was a moral to the story, but at the moment, he couldn't think what it was.

He waited five minutes. Then ten. The lights in the apartment were still on. He got out of the car, stood against it for a moment, his thoughts wending around again to Robin's hunches. Maybe a hunch was what stood between them and marriage, a hunch that he'd be a lousy husband. But hell, if she'd give him half a chance, he'd prove her wrong.

Pick, pick, pick, you're always picking things apart, Mac, overthinking everything. Was it true? Is that what he did?

Yeah, he supposed it was true. But so what. He picked, and she wasn't organized, and in McCleary's mind it was an even trade.

Crickets cried out in the still dark, singing for rain. A mosquito buzzed around his head. McClearly glanced toward her window, then shut the car door and went around to the back of the building. It was an old place that had been recently renovated, and the air held the faint scent of paint, varnish, and, of course, Robin's perfume.

In the hall, he heard the drone of a TV in the next apartment. Robin's door was open a crack; she was laughing, a soft flirtatious laugh. "I know, sweetheart," she said. "I know, I feel exactly the same way. . . . Right. Sunday. I love you."

Who? Who does she love?

The phone clicked as she hung up, he heard her footsteps receding. He waited a moment in the warm hall, wondering exactly who it was she loved, who she was seeing Sunday, then he knocked on the door. "Ready?" he called out.

"Almost. Come on in."

McCleary stepped into the hall, past the den, the bedroom, the bathroom where water was running. He continued into the living room. It was large but crowded with books, an expensive stereo system, a hodgepodge of furniture that fit no particular color scheme. It was as if Robin had made the rounds of the flea markets when she'd moved here and had purchased whatever struck her fancy. The tiled floor reflected the glow of the lamp by the phone. He caught the fragrance of her perfume again. Sometimes the scent lingered in his sheets after she'd stayed overnight, and he would drift into sleep the next night and dream he was in a field of flowers.

She came out, her face freshly scrubbed, her mouth etched in a smile.

"Got all your stuff?" he asked.

Her smiled faded like a tan. "What's wrong, Mac?"

She reads you like a comic, McCleary.

"Who was on the phone?" he asked, trying to keep the defensive edge out of his voice.

A frown drew her dark eyes closer together. "My mom. She was just calling to make sure I got home."

There, see? A perfectly reasonable explanation. And he, with a mind poisoned by the intrigue and suspicion of a decade in homicide, had assumed the worst. Naturally. Professional hazards.

Robin rocked forward on the balls of her feet, brushing his mouth with her own, her perfume spinning webs around him again. Then she touched him between the legs. "Home, Mac. So I can ravage your bod."

On the way across town to his apartment, Robin chattered: Chicago had changed since she'd last visited a year ago; all her cousin's new baby did was shit and

27

nurse; wouldn't it be nice if they had a million dollars and didn't have to go into work tomorrow; two weeks was too long to be away from him. She knew the right things to say. She knew he needed to hear them. But in the back of his mind, the old doubts were re-rooting. He wanted to ask her why she'd lied about the call, wanted to know who she loved, who she was going to see on Sunday.

Nothing has changed, he thought miserably. Things had only been postponed.

2.

Quin felt like an eight-year-old who'd had a nightmare and was now safely ensconced in the family room with the baby-sitter. Any minute now, her parents would come home and her mother would pick her up, whispering sweet assurances that vanquished the terror of bogeymen. And in the morning, she would no longer remember what had frightened her so terribly.

A lovely fantasy, Quin thought. So what if it was twenty-six years later and her parents were living in Europe and the woman in the family room was Nikki Anderson, not a babysitter. So what if the nightmare was just beginning and would probably be worse in the morning. For this moment, she felt safe, protected.

In fact, if there were tips on what to do in the aftermath of a violent crime, among them would be seeking the company of a close friend. Quin knew it didn't matter to Nikki whether she wept, yelled, beat her fists against the wall, or just sat in a stupor and stuffed her face with cheese and crackers from the plate on the coffee table. Nikki would be here regardless.

They'd been sitting in the family room for a long time now, light from the stained-glass lamp melting around them like pats of butter. Quin had related what had happened, had even told Nikki about stepping on the welcome mat outside the office just before driving over to Grant's, and now she was all talked out.

The noises in the room acted on her like a tranquilizer: the occasional click of the air conditioner as it came on, the drone of the TV in the background, the cats' purring, the murmur of Nikki's voice saying something Quin was too weary to hear. She wanted to capitulate to fatigue and close her eyes, but every time she did, she saw Grant, bleeding on the kitchen floor. Or she saw the inside of the house when she'd gone by there to pick up Merlin, her cat, before coming to Nikki's. Yeah, the house had been bad, she thought.

It was one thing to enter the empty rooms when she'd known Grant would be back. But this had been different. Permanent. Her footfalls had echoed in the tremendous living room. Grant's Amazon photos on the walls had stared back at her like grotesque parodies of the life he'd lived away from her, the life she'd known so little about. Everything in the house had reflected her sudden isolation, and now, less than a mile from home, it loomed like a wall between her and Nikki, despite the nine years of their friendship. After all, *she* hadn't found Grant. And although Quin could talk until morning about what she felt and Nikki would nod with sympathy, the experience had been Quin's and Quin's alone.

"Hello, Earth to Quin." Nikki leaned forward, her face swimming through Quin's vision, lovely as a portrait. She wondered vaguely how anyone could look so good this late at night, so unsullied.

"Hmm."

"I don't think you've heard a word I've said." Nikki topped a cracker with a slice of cheese and nibbled at it, her movements slow, careful, fastidious.

"Yes, I have. Every word."

Nikki smiled. "You were always a lousy liar, Quin. What I was saying is that I think it'd be a mistake for you to get involved in this. Let the cops handle it."

The cops: Benson was okay, she wasn't so sure she liked McCleary, and she couldn't remember any of the others who'd been scouring the house like bloodhounds. But even if she'd known them all personally, it wouldn't have made any difference. While Grant's murder was just another case to them, she wouldn't be able to get on with her life until the killer had been caught and sentenced to rot in prison for the next twenty-five years. She couldn't depend on them to solve it, so she would have to do it herself.

"I'll be collecting Social Security by the time they figure out what happened. Besides, I *am* involved. I found him. And even if I hadn't found him, I'd be involved."

Nikki's blond head bobbed to say she understood, even if she didn't agree. "But you've never done a homicide investigation," she said, echoing McCleary.

"So I'll learn."

Or die trying, her expression shouted.

Quin popped a cheese-and-cracker in her mouth, thinking that when she'd started working with Trevor she'd known zip about insurance and malpractice investigations. But she'd been so desperate to get out of teaching, to get away from adolescents, she'd learned the ropes in a few months. Well, she felt the same kind of desperation now, and said as much to Nikki.

"Look, I know how stubborn you are, Quin. Remember? This is me you're talking to—Nikki. I just don't want to see you hurt anymore." She ran her long fingers through her Persian cat's fur, her raspberry nails like drops of blood against the white. Quin looked away. "You aren't equipped to deal with a maniac."

"Who says it was a maniac?"

"Who else but maniacs commit murder?" Nikki retorted.

"People who know the victim."

Nikki shook her head. "Not in this case." She got up, added, "I'll be back in a second."

Merlin leaped into the chair and settled down alongside Quin. She stroked him absently, remembering she'd read somewhere that these days seventy-five percent of homicides were committed by people who knew the victim—not by strangers, not by Manson-type maniacs. Sooner or later she would have to go through a list of people Grant had known. A list that was longer than what she'd given McCleary, she thought. But at the moment, she just wasn't up to it.

Nikki returned and wagged a joint in the air. "Just to make sure you sleep, kiddo. Two tokes on this and you'll be out for at least eight hours."

They smoked half the joint, and for a while their conversation turned away from Grant to the year they'd met while teaching in the same school. It astonished Quin that the past could distract her. Were those misfits Nikki described really the two of them? Had they spent so many lunch hours in the staff room, bitching about teaching and plotting out their options in other professions? That younger Quin, possessed by an indomitable optimism, had dreamed of seeing the world, of recording her travels as Grant had done, through the eye of a camera. What had happened to the dreams? Now, in the murky aftermath of Grant's death, they became planets whose elliptical orbits swung toward her again, mocking, challenging, shouting, *Remember*.

Oddly, she recalled the point where her life had diverged, taking shape like an artist's dimly conceived idea for a painting. It was a spring day eight years ago, when Trevor Forsythe had visited Quin's class during career week at school to talk about private investigating as a profession. Quin—not her students—had approached him afterward and asked where she could sign up. Two months later, at the end of the school year, she resigned and began working for Trevor.

And because of her job in the firm, she'd met Grant, when she first investigated his insurance claim for the theft of photography equipment. But for that, she wouldn't be sitting here now, feeling numb as a molar that had been injected with Novocain. For that matter, Nikki wouldn't have met her fiancée, Steve Killington, since it was Grant who'd introduced them. And if it weren't for Killington, vice president of Wishod Pharmaceuticals, Grant wouldn't have gone to the Amazon and might still be alive. After all, the only clue, "greenfire," had to be connected to his traveling, didn't it?

Her head began to ache—from hunger, fatigue, from loss, and she wondered if years from now she and Nikki would be sitting in another room, *remembering when* about tonight. Maybe they would recall it in much the same way they did Nikki's marriage and divorce and her departure from teaching for fashion and color consulting. Maybe they would discuss it in the same wizened tones as they did relationships gone sour and the ups and downs in their careers. Maybe. But before that could happen, Quin thought, before she could dig out her old dreams from the trunk of the past and steer her life in another direction again, she had to know who had killed Grant and why.

Then, as if this thought had triggered some vital synapse in her brain, time screeched to a crawl and she was inside the townhouse again, staring down at Grant's body, at all the blood, and then at the word on the chalkboard. In slow replay, she seemed to view the horror as she might an event in her childhood. What nagged at her were the whys. Why did he stumble into the living room and then back to the kitchen to scrawl "greenfire"? Why hadn't he scribbled the name of his killer instead?

No, that was something *she* would've done, not Grant. Right until the last, he'd probably believed he wasn't going to die.

Die, dead, death.

"I've got to go to bed," she said suddenly, and stood.

When Nikki hugged her good-night in the hall and reminded her she was just a shout away, Quin wanted to clutch her shoulders and confess there was something wrong with her mind. Grant's body was cold and stiff in the morgue, and she should've been prostrate with grief. Instead she seized interrogatives like the English teacher she'd been: *Why, who, what, where, how?* The words revolved in her head like a department store credit card, each question a purchase she couldn't afford.

She crawled into bed, snuggled down between the clean sheets, into the clean scent of Arm & Hammer detergent and spice, into a pool of moonlight. She began to cry and realized with a certain horror that the tears were for herself, for the swirling lacunas his death had left in her life. When she could no longer breathe, she sat up, a vagrant sob scratching her throat, and threw back the covers.

You're sick, she thought as hunger drove her out of bed to raid Nikki's fridge. She helped herself to a piece of kiwi fruit and more cheese, then sat in the dark of the family room, picking apart the riddle. Why didn't he call? Why had he returned early from the trip? Why did the town house look so lived in?

Despite statistics, it was possible a stranger had killed

him, maybe some recently released inmate of a mental institution or a prison. It would've almost made his death cleaner somehow, more manageable. But it didn't feel right. And if a stranger hadn't done it, then a person who'd known him had.

Slowly, hesitantly at first, then faster and faster, she flipped through a mental Rolodex of Grant's friends and acquaintances. But her conclusion was the same she'd drawn with McCleary: she didn't have any idea who would want to see him dead. Yet, if she ruled out a stranger as his killer, then it had to be someone who'd known him. And if that were true, then chances were good she knew the person as well.

4

SOMETHING HAPPENED LAST night. I could feel it, the event, like a tumor inside me, or a child. But I couldn't reach it. This was the same sensation I experienced when I'd been writing a particular scene, knew I'd nearly gotten it the way I wanted it, then suddenly the whole thing just slid away from me.

Sometimes these incidents I'd forgotten would surface abruptly, like small epiphanies, stopping me dead. My knees would weaken, my heart would thud like an old engine, and in my mind I would see men I couldn't remember meeting. I would see them bleeding, I would see them dead, and I would think: *I did that.* Then oblivion would sweep over me again.

Or so I liked to think, anyway. Actually, I had an excellent memory. It was just this circuit breaker in my head that clicked sometimes and suddenly details would blur, I would confuse names, faces, events. Things would melt together like cheese. But I knew Grant was dead and that I had killed him: that was fact. I knew I'd shot him, but I couldn't recall the precise moment when my finger had squeezed the trigger or what, if anything, we'd talked about before he stumbled back, clutching his chest. But I vividly remembered the shape of the bloodstain on his shirt—like a flower, a rose. The circuit breaker, see, was selective in its effacement of memories.

In a way, I wished he'd never told me he knew my secret. I wished he'd kept it to himself. But oh no, he had to flaunt his knowledge, he had to wave the evidence in my face, then had the audacity to assure me it didn't matter, that he would get me help.

Help: ha. I knew what kind of help he had in mind—control. First by him, then by some fat shrink who would've tried to fit me into a neat category labeled "Manic depressive" or "paranoic" or "schizophrenic." I wanted none of it. There was nothing wrong with me. Grant had left me no choice.

I would have to place flowers on his grave; it was the proper thing to do. But maybe he was the sort of man who stipulated in his will that he preferred cremation. In that case, his ashes would go into a jar on someone's mantel.

Whose mantel?

Quin's. She would keep his ashes, just as she would keep his town house, his belongings, his photography equipment. Yes, the camera bothered me most of all; they belonged to me. *Quin, you hear me? Those cameras are mine*. It wasn't greed. I wanted them as reminders that I'd never let him take my picture. In fact, if I ever had the opportunity to introduce myself to Quin as Grant's killer, I would explain how it was possible for a photographer or an artist to control your soul, your essence, by capturing your image on film or on canvas.

Once, I told Grant that my mother lost her mind shortly after my father had bought a camera and went around snapping pictures of her like a madman. He scoffed and said it was an old wives' tale. *If your mother went bonkers, kid, it was probably because of you,* he'd said, and laughed.

But the bastard wasn't laughing now, was he.

5

1.

QUIN TOOK A savage pleasure in the warmth of sunlight streaming through the car window. *The dead don't feel this,* she thought, noting the way the light sliced across her arm. It tipped the blond hairs near her wrist with fire, then splashed into her lap, where Merlin sat, its brilliance sucked into his black fur.

She parked in her driveway, opened the door, and Merlin leaped out and streaked up the walk. Quin stood there a moment, staring at the house. Built from redwood and pine, it was the kind of place more common in California than Florida. The banyan trees on either side seemed to be embracing it, comforting it, as if both house and trees possessed an elementary consciousness that understood Grant had died. Even the sag in the porch, which had existed when they'd bought the house, now seemed weighted with the knowledge of his death. It spooked her, and she hurried inside.

The isolation she'd experienced in these rooms last night was lessened somewhat in the daylight. Her relief immediately manifested as hunger. She got an orange out of the fridge, sliced it into quarters, opened a drawer for a baggie into which she could put other fruit to take to work with her. But when she opened the drawer, she found the butter container squeezed in between a pack of aluminum foil and the baggies. Butter had oozed over the sides and covered everything. A batallion of ants swarmed with impunity across the mess. "Great," she muttered and reached for the dishrag.

In her mind, as she wiped and removed everything in the drawer, she heard Grant's complaint that she was absentminded. *I find a glass of milk in the cupboard and the pack of aluminum foil inside the microwave and a warped spoon in the garbage disposal. What's wrong with you, anyway, Quin?*

The problem, she'd tried to explain to him, was that her thoughts were always two hours ahead of her body, as though she suffered from some weird kind of jet lag. When she finished cleaning the drawer, some of the ants had escaped and scurried toward the sections of her orange. Quin grabbed the dishrag again, slapped it once across the counter, and washed the tiny corpses down the drain. "Sorry, guys." She scooped up the remainder of her orange and sucked on it as she walked over to the window.

Sunlight cut through the bamboo blind and fell unevenly across the tile floor. She raised it, glanced out into the yard. Either her own sorrow was tainting everything she looked at or the two acres of ficus trees, pines, citrus, and the lush canopy of Grant's intricate garden actually drooped in mourning.

How could this have happened? An inchoate yearning swept through her, and she moved quickly from the window, blinking rapidly, as though the view had blinded her. *These things happen to other people, not to me.* She hurriedly fed Merlin, trying not to think of everything she had to do, of the details death imposed on the living. When she realized she was failing utterly and miserably at that, she fled upstairs to shower and dress for work.

On her way toward North Miami an hour later, memories marched through her skull like little tin soldiers. She thought of the morning she'd met Grant a year ago. He'd filed an insurance claim for the supposed robbery of about $5,000 worth of camera equipment and lenses which the insurance company wanted investigated. Trevor had dumped the case in her lap. His theory was that in an investigation, she was better with the men and he, with the women. It wasn't always true, but in this case it had been.

Annoyed at herself for not having told Trevor to assign the minor case to one of the other investigators, she arrived at Grant's condo in a stew. They sat on his back porch, she remembered, surrounded by a veritable forest of plants: orchids, dracaena, flaming vine, aralia, long, graceful shoots that were bird of paradise, and dozens of other plants she couldn't identify. She was brisk and formal about why she was there, and he answered her questions with a half smile on his face that increasingly irritated her. She finally asked what was so funny.

He drew an X over his heart with his finger. "I didn't sell the stuff. I promise."

"I'm just doing my job, you know."

"Yeah, I realize that. The funny thing is, I'm pretty sure I know who took it. The kid next door."

"Didn't you tell the police?"

"No, I don't have any proof. He's just been different toward me. It used to be, 'Hi, Grant, what's happening?' or 'Hey, Grant, where're you off to this time?' Now I'm lucky if I get a nod."

"How'd he get in?"

"Through here, probably." He thumbed the air behind him, indicating the porch door. "Any jerk with a penknife can get in. And he knew where I kept the stuff, because sometimes when I'm gone he waters the plants for me."

She glanced at her notes. "Two camera bodies and five lenses, right?"

"And a couple flashes, a tripod, and a suitcase filled with film. And two camera cases."

"I suppose you have clips to back up what you do."

That half smile returned; a dimple appeared in the corner of his mouth. This time it wasn't the least bit annoying. It wrinkled his sea green eyes that seemed to float as serenely as twin islands in his face. "Here I pay my homeowner's insurance on time every month, year after year, then I make one lousy claim and look what happens."

"If the insurance company ever comes back to us and asks why we found your story reasonable, then I'll have my proof."

"So I've passed your test?" he laughed.

"You passed."

"I'll get you some clips."

By the time he returned with a file of clips, she had walked around the room, looking at the plants, touching them, entranced. "Where'd you get all these?"

"A lot of them are from the Amazon. Plants are sort of my hobby. C'mon, I'll show you."

He took her upstairs, to the porch on the second floor. It was a miniature rain forest, a self-contained world of deep, rich scents. He'd knocked down a bedroom wall to widen it and had built a stone path that inched and twisted through the labyrinthian greenery. Vines and flowers billowed from ceramic reptiles, birds, and pink dolphins.

"Pink dolphins instead of flamingos, huh?" she remarked.

"There really *are* pink dolphins." She watched his face in the diffused sunlight, beaded with dampness like the leaves, as he leaned toward a three-foot ficus tree and plucked off several dry twigs. "There's a certain mystique about them. Natives believe pink dolphins have the power to transform themselves, to become human. Sometimes, if they hear music from one of the villages, they come up out of the river as men, dressed completely in white. They dance with the prettiest women, lure them to the river, then pull the water over them like a blanket, and the women become dolphins."

His voice, she remembered, became a murmur, touching her like a summer heat, like moonlight. She felt as if she were four years old again, listening to one of her father's stories, the tale unraveling in her head, swift and clean as a movie. Then he smiled, and there was something infinitely sad in his eyes that the smile couldn't touch. "Nice story, isn't it?"

"Tell me another."

"Really?" His eyes lit up.

"Really," she said.

They remained in the little rain forest for nearly an

hour, Grant weaving a mosaic of colorful superstitions that ruled the lives of the *rivereños*, the Amazon River people. There were tales of club-footed jungle characters, of love lost and gained, of giant anacondas. But always, his stories twisted back to the mystique of the pink dolphins, almost as though he were telling her that his life, too, was veiled. Before she left, he asked her to dinner.

That was how it had started, she thought.

And last night it had ended.

Ended.

She jerked the wheel to the left and drove into the parking lot behind Forsythe & St. James. She parked next to Trevor's Mercedes and sat there trembling, gripping the steering wheel. *Ended. Dead. Zip. Nothing.* Then her mind flattened out in a long thin line, and at the end of it, like punctuation at the end of a sentence, was the word *murder*, not *death*.

He was murdered, and that meant there was a murderer whom she could track down. One way or another, she would vindicate Grant's death.

As she got out of the car, her mood possessed an unexpected levity; she felt as if she had purpose again. Then she was beneath the shade of the ficus trees that flanked the building. Birds fussed in the tangle of branches where a breeze stirred the emerald leaves. The air smelled hot, fecund. *Business as usual,* Grant had said to her before he'd left, standing here in this very spot. *I should be back within three weeks.*

The brim of his Indiana Jones hat had partially hidden his eyes. *Again? You're going down there again?* she'd asked, peeking under the brim.

And he, ignoring the remark, had grinned and said, *Do you like my hat, Quin? You didn't say anything about my hat.*

She walked quickly through the back door and into the building. The tap dance of computer keys rang out in the cool air. She heard voices, typewriters, the low hum of the copy machine: familiar sounds. Rusty Johnson, with whom she'd worked late last night, greeted her with his usual, "Hey Quin, what's tricks, sweet lady?"

Then he snapped his fingers, shuffled his feet in a break dance, spun once in the hall, and was gone.

He didn't know, she thought.

But Trevor did.

She saw it in his face the moment she peeked into his office and their eyes met. He was on the phone, the receiver propped between his ear and shoulder. "Listen, I'll call you back. . . . Right." Then he dropped the receiver in the cradle, just looking at her, his dove gray eyes like warm mounds of earth in his plump face. "Christ, Quin, I heard," he said softly.

There wasn't much to say to that besides, "Oh." She plopped down in a nearby chair just as Trevor rose.

His jowls seemed to bounce, and she wondered when Trevor had gotten so fat. No, fat wasn't the right word. He was at the hairline juncture between plump and obese. Another five pounds would do it. Another five pounds would send his stomach dragging over his belt and his blood pressure shooting for 220. "You didn't have to come in to work. You could've called me last night, Quin. You could have."

"I just wanted to get away from there, Trevor. I stayed with Nikki. How'd you hear, anyway?"

"On the news this morning on my way in. Then when I got to work, a homicide detective named Mike McCleary was here. He asked me if you worked late last night. I told him I wasn't here, that you'd been working with Rusty, who wasn't in yet. So McCleary's going to call him later."

He poured two cups of coffee from the pot on the bookcase and handed her one. She gazed at a point just over his shoulder, at the photo of his father that hung on the wall. When old Sammy Forsythe had died two years ago, he'd willed forty-nine percent of the firm to her. It had surprised her more than it had Trevor, who'd expected to inherit the whole thing. But in retrospect, she understood why Sammy had done it: she was the investigator, Trevor the businessman with a nose for good land deals.

Their offices, for instance, were located in a refurbished house on a tree-shrouded road in North Miami which Trevor had purchased for a song shortly after

Quin had become a partner. They'd already outgrown it, and now he was negotiating to buy the house next door. She supposed that within five years he would own the entire block; that was how he operated. He had a talent for investments, and most of those included property, lots of it. At last count, Forsythe & St. James owned four duplexes, an office building, and a large tract of commercial property in Boca Raton that IBM was bidding on. Even if they never took in another case, she thought, the company would flourish.

"Quin?"

Her eyes slid back to him.

"You okay?"

"Hmm. What else did McCleary say?"

Trevor leaned against the edge of his desk and lit a cigarette. The aroma of the smoke made her mouth water for a Marlboro Light. She reached into her bag for a mint or something to suck on, then remembered she'd neglected to replenish her stash. "Oh, the usual stuff cops like him ask: Did I know Grant? How well did I know him? How long have you worked here? How long have you been a partner?" He paused, ran a finger alongside his nose. "He also asked me to try to persuade you not to work on this case, to let them do their jobs."

Quin smiled; she'd expected something like that. "McCleary's got a hang-up about PIs, that's all."

"You mean you *are* going to investigate?" The words rolled out in a puff of exhaled smoke.

Why was it, she wondered, that people were trying to discourage her from doing exactly what they would've done in her place? McCleary, Nikki, now Trevor. "Of course I am."

"But Quin, we don't do homicide investigations."

Again? McCleary, Nikki, now Trevor? "This isn't just any homicide, Trevor. And don't worry, I'll do it on my own time."

"Quin, honey, that's not the point. It might be dangerous. You don't have any experience in dealing with lunatics."

Quin was beginning to think that McCleary, Nikki, and Trevor had conspired on their responses. She felt like informing Trevor that half their clients were lunatics; they just weren't violent. "I can't believe I'm hearing this. What would you do if it had been Winnie? Or one of your daughters? Huh, Trevor?"

"That's different."

"How?"

Trevor sank into the chair next to hers, his expression skewed with earnestness. "Quin, Winnie's my wife, for Christ's sakes. And my kids are my kids. You and Grant, well, you were just living together."

She burst out laughing. "That doesn't count? Only marriage counts? Save the sanctimonious crap for your Sunday-school class, Trevor." Quin stood, brushed a hand along her slacks, smoothing out the wrinkles. "I've got work to do."

Trevor followed her to the door, and when he spoke again his voice was an asthmatic wheeze. "I'll be here if you want to talk."

"Yeah, thanks." *For nothing.*

She walked into the staff kitchen, yanked open the fridge door, found some crackers. She took them and a cup of coffee into her office and closed the door. Sunlight squeezed through the vertical blinds and ribboned the soft gray rug. Grant materialized in the chair where she dropped her purse. She saw him laughing when she'd asked him, point blank, exactly what was going on in the Amazon that kept drawing him back. And back. Again and again. *When? When did we have that conversation?*

Forget it, don't think about it, she told herself, and eyed the files on her desk. She wouldn't let Trevor get to her either. So far, she'd managed to ignore his Born Again pontificating and the fundamentalist morality that went with it. Why should today be any different?

His religious conversion had come about when his dad had died. He'd been Ripe for the Light, as Grant used to say. Now he tithed ten percent of his earnings to the Church of the Good Faith, taught Sunday school, read his Bible daily. Occasionally, he mounted his soap box to preach the good word to people in the office, but no one listened. To Trevor, they were all a bunch of heathens who were going to rot in Hell, and she supposed she topped his list.

Quin pushed Trevor out of her mind and shuffled through the files. The suit against Dodge took priority. But she also wanted to go through another insurance case for a two-hundred-and-fifty-grand claim in family heirlooms that the company who held the policy wanted investigated. Then there was a five-million-dollar medical malpractice suit filed by a woman who claimed the clamp her physician had left in her abdomen had caused a miscarriage that necessitated a subsequent hysterectomy. *And Trevor said our clients aren't lunatics?* Business as usual, she thought, just as Grant had said.

She worked for a while, noticing that the shock had skittered to a back room in her mind. But in that back room, a part of her picked apart everything that had happened from when she'd walked in the house last night. Why had Grant headed into the living room after he'd been shot? For help? To try to make it to his car? Maybe he'd stumbled after whoever had killed him. Then, weak from loss of blood, he'd made his way back to the kitchen.

She swiveled her chair around to the computer, slipped in a disk to which she intended to add her notes on the Dodge file. When she called up the directory, there was Grant's name among two dozen others. It startled her, seeing it there in small green letters. *GRANT BELL*: one case among many. Her case, from a year ago. She stared at it, then removed the disk, suddenly, quickly. *What good am I doing here?*

She needed leads, clues, a thread that would connect Grant's death to "greenfire" or to something else, and she wasn't going to find it here, in front of the computer.

2.

The air seemed lazily peaceful around the townhouse. A breeze stirred the branches of the weeping willow, where a cardinal sang as though its heart were breaking. The sinuous walk that led to the front door was lined with hibiscus, flaming vines, geraniums, and gardenias. She could almost believe that nothing violent had ever happened here. Almost.

Quin paused at the front door, not entirely certain now that she wanted to go in. *The blood, what about all the blood?*

Okay, there was blood, but no body. The worst was over.

She let herself into the apartment, her footfalls sighing against the rug. She kept her eyes straight ahead, seeing the stains only peripherally, and stopped in the front room that opened onto the balcony facing the courtyard. The curtains were drawn, but pale light speckled the throw rug and the pine floorboards that swam around it like a sandy sea.

She thought of the bright pink exit stamp in Grant's passport which Benson had shown her, the stamp that said, IQUITOS, PERU, and the date, the bloody date nearly a week ago. He'd been living here. *Why the lies? And why does the apartment look so lived in if he was only working here sometimes? Why?*

Quin walked down the hall to his study. His electric typewriter was set up on the desk, and beside it were several stacks of slides. His file cabinets were crammed with stuff. Even the walls were decorated. The condo didn't just seem lived in, it was as if he'd had two separate and distinct lives—one with her and one here.

She backed out of the den and headed for the stairs. The second floor had been ransacked, just as Benson had said. In the master bedroom, drawers seesawed from the bureau, clothes were strewn around the room, shoes had been tossed out of the closet. But it was the sight of all the clothes in the closet and tossed on the bed that made her suck in her breath. Shirts, slacks, coats, jackets, jeans: *Two wardrobes, one at home, one here*. *Why?* And in the bathroom, in the linen closet, she found towels, all relatively new, and beneath the bathroom cabinet were supplies: toilet paper and cleansers, razor blades and soap, all the necessary household accoutrements.

Would she find plates in the kitchen cabinets? Glasses and silverware? Were there sheets on the bed? Had he ever really rented the place? How much time had he actually spent here? Quin sat at the edge of the bed, wondering if some of his trips had never been taken. Maybe, instead of leaving, he had sometimes come here to . . . *to get away from me?* Maybe he'd intended to end their relationship, but not until he'd had the house long enough to make a profit when they sold it. So in the interim, he'd continued the facade and had been busily building a private life. Here.

A secret life, here.

Had she ever seen him board a plane? No, never. She'd driven him to the airport plenty of times, but because of the airport security system, she'd never seen him leave. And when he'd returned, he'd taken a cab, used the limo service, or he'd driven his own car. But why create such an elaborate deception?

I haven't had much luck with relationships, Quin, but I'm willing to try. When had he told her that?

Did it matter?

Yes, it mattered. It did. She thought a moment. Her brain spit out a close-up image of Grant's mouth, and a moment later provided sound. He'd said it the first time they'd talked about buying the house, and she'd laughed and told him it sounded like a warning. *It's just that I've had problems sticking to one woman*. He'd said that, too, but it was something her brain had censored in much the same way kidneys filtered impurities. Selective perceptions, a form of defense.

Her temples ached, her eyes burned from lack of sleep. She started to lay back on the bed, wanting only to close her eyes and drift into some safer harbor, when she thought she heard a noise downstairs. The door? Was that the door creaking? Had she left it open?

She got slowly to her feet, listening, her hand digging into her purse for her gun. Had Grant's killer returned to look for whatever he hadn't found last night? She scurried toward the porch that had once housed the little rain forest. Her hand touched the knob, turned it. She winced as the door squeaked ever so slightly, then opened it wide enough to squeeze through. She shut it quietly behind her, backed into the corner, both hands holding the .38 as she aimed it at the door. Her thumb knocked off the safety.

The bright sunlight seared holes through her eyes, to the back of her head. The heat quickly brought jewels of sweat to her face. It trickled along the underside of her arm. She waited. Someone was inside. She felt the person's presence as if the rooms were extensions of herself.

Somewhere distant, the cardinal was still singing. She knew if she turned her head she would see the shimmer of sunlight through trees.

The knob turned.

Blood rushed to her head. *Better be prepared to use it*, McCleary had warned. She was. Yes, she was.

The door swung open. Her hands trembled as her finger rested uneasily against the trigger. A man stepped out, and his face came into focus in sections, like an orange: dark mustache laced with gray, dark hair, eyes like chips of steel. When his face was whole, when it clicked into place, Quin lowered her arms and laughed.

"You. I should've figured," grumbled McCleary, and walked back indoors.

6

1.

McCLEARY SAW RED. "Suppose it hadn't been me?" he barked.

"Then I guess I would've pulled the trigger."

"Great, that's great. Which is exactly what I was talking about when I asked you not to get involved."

Her eerie blue eyes regarded him cooly, then slid to the floor, at the orphaned shoes that surrounded them. Shirts, coats, and slacks created erratic patterns across the foot of the bed. Some items had slipped to the floor, where streaks of light from the porch ran like oil over the wood and cut across the tips of McCleary's shoes. Silence stretched uneasily between them, and he began to regret the brusque tone he'd used with her.

She dropped her gun in her purse. "I'd appreciate it if you'd stop trying to give me advice about what to do and not do, all right?" She swept past him, her purse hitting her at the hip as she moved. McCleary stared after her, then followed her downstairs.

"Look," he said as he came into the kitchen, where she was opening cabinets, slamming them, evidently looking for something. "I don't want you getting hurt."

"Thanks for the concern, but I can take care of myself." She grabbed a can of coffee from one of the cupboards, pried off the top, filled the coffee maker. Her movements were jerky, and after a few moments coffee grounds covered the counter like an army of ants.

48

He noticed the floor had been cleaned and wondered if Benson or one of the men last night had done it. Probably. He couldn't imagine Quin tackling the job.

"How'd you get in, anyway?" He spoke to her back.

"I broke in, what do you think? Stop giving me the third degree, will you? I had a key. I wanted to look around. Is that a crime?"

He decided it wouldn't take much to dislike this woman. "Next time call me and I'll meet you here."

"Stop patronizing me, Mr. McCleary." She spun around, glaring at him, then began yanking open the cabinets at random again. "Well-stocked pantry, for someone who didn't live here. But no sugar. Grant didn't use sugar. But maybe in *this* cabinet"—the door slammed open—"I'll find sugar, five pounds of it, and realize I was wrong. About the sugar. Wrong about everything," she finished with a whisper.

He felt like a Peeping Tom. He wanted to dig a little hole for himself in the floor until the rawness of her emotions had fled underground again. Okay, murder wasn't the most gentle way of being confronted with the truth, but this morning he was short on words, patience, on just about everything.

The phone call he'd overheard last night at Robin's had worked away at him like an obsession, robbing him of sleep, marring her homecoming. It hadn't changed the sex between them—nothing ever seemed to do that—but it had altered the texture of everything else. Then this morning, when they'd gotten to work, Izzo had assigned Robin and Benson to a training seminar for the next two weeks, which left him pounding sand alone.

McCleary finally walked over to the counter, poured coffee into the mugs Quin had set on the counter, held one out to her. When she looked up, he saw lines of exhaustion in her face. Steam from the mug drifted toward her hair.

"Thanks."

"Let's sit down," he suggested.

"Not in here. Outside."

She unchained the door in the breakfast nook which led into the courtyard. They sat at the same aluminum table where they had sat last night. "See, I was going to put some files on the computer," she said, "and I inserted the wrong disk and came across Grant's file."

"Your firm investigated him?"

The frenzy had left her now, the raw feelings had been hastily sheathed. As she told him the story, there was some quality to her voice that led him to believe she'd handled the investigation, that it was how she and Bell had met. ". . . so I came over here to look around and discovered that Grant was apparently spending a lot more time here than I thought."

"Was he away from home a lot when he wasn't traveling?"

Her expression tightened; some of the bite returned to her voice. "Is that a tactful way of asking if there were other women, Mr. McCleary?"

"Yeah, maybe it is." Then, because "mister" made him feel old coming from her, he added, "I wish you'd call me Mike or Mac or Michael or anything other than 'mister.' "

This made her smile. "Okay. McCleary." He laughed, and the tension between them eased somewhat. "Maybe there *were* other women. Maybe that's what this cozy little hideaway here was all about. I don't know."

Duplicity: it was insidious in this town, like a virus that wouldn't quit. "That Ford Escort in the lot is his, isn't it?" McCleary asked.

"Yeah, I'm going to drive it back to the house. The thing's a junker, but I don't want it just sitting out here."

"Did you look through it?"

"Sure. There's a bald spare tire and Grant's huge toolbox in the trunk and maps and stuff in the glove compartment."

"You don't have any idea what 'greenfire' meant to him?"

She shrugged. "The only thing I can figure is that it's one of those Amazon folktales he collected. Whenever he traveled, he got into the local mythology, and he usually managed to work it into his photos somehow."

"That's it?"

"That's not enough?"

"Look. Your friend was shot in the kitchen and stumbled into the living room, maybe hoping to get help, and then he made it *back* to the kitchen just to write that word. A story isn't enough. There's got to be something else."

"His name was Grant, and he was not just my *friend,* McCleary, I think we should get that straight right now."

Here we go again.

"And you're wrong about a story not being enough. Grant was a romantic. It's exactly the sort of thing he'd do."

"Not with a bullet from a .45 in him, he wouldn't."

Her eyes weren't kind, but there was no anger this time, just a nakedness that made him want to reach out and gently close her lids. "God, first I have to deal with Trevor's moralist crap and now your cynicism."

"If you intend to keep pursuing this, then don't cringe at the facts. A man bleeding like a stuck pig does *not* make a point of living long enough to write something because it's a *nice* story. It's a lovely thought, but it just ain't so."

She looked away from him and concentrated on her coffee. Dried leaves, shaken loose from the trees by the breeze, floated through the June air. One landed on the table. She reached for it, bent the tip with her thumb. It cracked and broke off. She crushed it in her hand and poured the tiny bits onto the table, watching them fall like grains of sand.

When she spoke, the fierce determination in her voice startled him. "You're not going to intimidate me. You're not. I'm going to find the shit who did this."

All right, she was pigheaded and didn't intend to back down, and he didn't feel like arguing. Fine. And since he was minus a partner for the time being, maybe they could work something out.

"Yeah, you'll probably find him," McCleary said.

The bits of leaves had stopped falling from her hand, but she still held it in the air, fingers bent in a loose fist. "What? A change of tune?" She smiled as she said it.

"I think we'd get farther on this if we worked together instead of against each other."

"Like partners."

"Right."

"I thought you had a partner."

"I thought *you* did."

She laughed; it brought a touch of color to her cheeks.

"Trevor's a Born Again. His partnership's basically with Christ."

"Well, Robin's in a training seminar for two weeks."

"So we'd be partners for real on this case?"

"For real. And unofficially."

"With you giving the orders, I suppose."

"No, equitable all the way."

"No offense, McCleary, but I have trouble believing that."

He laughed. "You aren't exactly the most subtle person I've ever met."

"You try working with Trevor Forsythe for eight years and see how subtle *you* are at the end of it."

"He seems pretty fond of you."

"He's fond of my forty-nine percent and still resents the hell out of me because his father willed the stock to me, not him."

"Why you?"

She sighed, brushed strands of hair from her forehead with the back of her hand. "That agency was a dream old man Forsythe had ever since he worked for Pinkerton. I think he knew that if Trevor had complete control, the investigative part of it would atrophy within six months. I had some real doubts about staying. But then I thought about my options. I mean, what was I going to do instead? Go back to teaching school? Sell real estate? Now I'm in charge of investigations and Trevor deals with investments." She finished the coffee. "So where do we start, McCleary?"

McCleary removed his notepad from his pocket and glanced at the list he'd made earlier this morning. "The man I want to see at Wishod Pharmaceuticals is out of town until Monday. I'm going to be talking to Grant's ex-wife this afternoon."

Quin made a face. "Oh. Treena."

"You've met her?"

"Once. She stormed in here one night, and it was like a Grade B movie. I hid behind a door. But maybe she's not as crazy now that she's remarried."

"How about if you find out as much as you can about Wishod?" He quickly added: "That's not an order."

She smiled. "Okay. A rundown on what products they manufacture, that kind of thing, right?"

"And a list of corporate officers."

"Who're you going to be seeing there?"

"A guy named Steve Killington."

"Oh."

"You know him?"

"He's engaged to my friend Nikki, the woman I stayed with last night. Grant knew him for a long time."

"What's he like?"

"Okay, I guess. He's the Wishod Wonder Boy, you know. The visionary. He's been written up in dozens of magazines."

"But you don't like him."

"I like how happy he's made Nikki," she said, then changed the subject. *Cagey*, McCleary thought. "I was going through names last night of people who knew Grant, and I thought of one I hadn't given you. Paul Holmes."

"As in Holmes the DA?"

"Yeah. He and Grant had been friends since college."

Terrific. First he had to deal with a private eye and now Holmes the Whore, as he was known in the homicide department. The name had come about when he was in private practice, defending anyone who had the money to afford him. He'd gotten two of McCleary's arrests off absolutely free on "technicalities," which McCleary suspected—but had never been able to prove—were the results of bribes. There were probably half a dozen or more similar cases. Two years ago, the man had run for DA and won, largely because he'd wooed the female vote in the county by running on a platform that advocated mandatory castration for rapists.

"I think he's probably Grant's attorney."

McCleary nodded.

"You don't like him," Quin said with a smile, borrowing his own remark from several moments ago.

McCleary smiled. "You're right. I don't."

2.

McCleary's office, a small corner room on the third floor of the station, was shaped roughly like a triangle. The two walls that formed the point were darkly tinted glass that seemed to jut out over the city like the bow of a ship. He'd inherited it the year before when he'd been promoted to chief of homicide, and still experienced moments of disorientation whenever he entered. He felt as if he should brace himself for a sudden movement that would toss the bow forward, into the sea of light and concrete below.

A dozen plants in ceramic pots basked in the filtered sunlight. Those were Robin's touch, to temper the view, which was nothing to brag about—just traffic and more traffic and, in the distance, I-95, snaking off into the white blaze of concrete. On the far wall were half a dozen paintings that McCleary had bought at local art fairs. None was a masterpiece. But each evoked a particular emotion through some trick of shape, color, or symmetry that had the power to transport him out of homicide and into a softer world.

He found the notes Benson had left on his desk and entered them and his own in the computer. He usually did the paperwork on cases, since Robin didn't type and he could never read her handwriting. Benson had sure been an improvement in that respect. In fact, had it not been for Robin, he would've asked Izzo to assign Benson to homicide, as his permanent partner. Unless things improved between him and Robin, he might end up doing that anyway. Which was probably why most cops didn't get involved with other cops.

"Hey, Mac." Benson had popped his head in the door. "How goes it alone, buddy?"

"Slow. I thought you were in the seminar."

Benson came in and shut the door. "We broke for lunch. It's *baaddd*, Mac. You know who's teaching it? The Whore himself."

"Holmes?" McCleary laughed. "Better you than me, Tim."

"You gotten in touch with him yet?" Benson asked, stretching his legs out in front of him, folding his hands at his stomach.

"No. I don't want to spoil my weekend."

Benson chortled.

"I finally gave Wayne O'Donald the facts on the five knifings and told him we thought they were linked. So our illustrious shrink in residence is going to draw up a profile on the guy," McCleary said.

"You know, Mac, I've been thinking that maybe this serial killer isn't a guy."

McCleary wished everyone would stop using that word, *serial,* until they were absolutely sure that's what they were dealing with. "I know. That's occurred to me, too."

"Or maybe there aren't going to be any answers until we've got another corpse on our hands. Maybe this one's in the dark field."

McCleary hoped not. The term referred to a sort of myopia or blindness that sometimes occurred among investigators, particularly homicide investigators, when they got too close to a case to see the obvious. In instances like these, it was often someone with distance from the case who ended up solving it. He suspected that was what had happened two years ago when he and Robin had first started working together and she'd solved his months-old homicide in a matter of weeks.

"Well, if I can help you out in any way, let me know." Benson glanced at his watch. "Gotta grab a bite to eat and head back to the courthouse. You eaten yet?"

"Yeah, but I'll walk out with you. I've got an appointment with Bell's ex-wife."

When he and Benson walked outside the heat struck him like a blow. The bleached sky was a scrim behind which the sun quivered, huge and white like an alien craft. Heat rose from the pavement in waves. Benson groaned. "If I ever get rich, I'm going to be a snowbird, Mac. Florida in the winter and someplace like the North Carolina mountains in the summer."

"What's this seminar on, anyway?" McCleary asked as they continued toward the parking lot.

"I haven't figured it out yet," he replied, and McCleary smiled. "It's just blah blah this and blah blah that. You know how that turkey is, Mac."

Yeah, he knew. Holmes was the courtroom marvel who could talk circles around God.

3.

Treena Bell Esposito lived in a neat little box house in Kendall, southwest of Miami. Thin and pale, she looked as though she'd been living underground for the last few years. Her tousled blond hair seemed almost boyish, but it accentuated her sweeping forehead and startling emerald eyes, which created an eccentricity about her appearance. What struck him most of all was just how different she was from Quin—a difference that was perhaps a comment on some dichotomy within Grant Bell himself.

They sat on the porch, and she answered his questions easily, willingly, filling in some of the gaps in his knowledge of Bell. Although they'd been divorced three years, she said, they'd remained friends. "Oh, I was plenty hurt for a while after the divorce, but I understood Grant. I liked him in spite of everything. Maybe that was really his problem. He was such a damned likeable man. Bright, too. He was a member of Mensa. Did Quin tell you?"

"Mensa?" It sounded like a kind of soup.

"Yeah, the high-IQ society. The members supposedly place within the upper two percent of the population in terms of intelligence."

So what we have, McCleary mused, is one dead genius. "No, she didn't mention it." He suspected she probably didn't even know. "Why were you two divorced?"

He could tell it wasn't something she particularly wanted to discuss, especially with a stranger. "That really isn't any of your business, Mr. McCleary."

"Look, I'm just trying to piece the puzzle together, Mrs. Esposito. Anything you can tell me might help."

She ran her fingers through her hair. "I'm sorry, it's just that some things are hard to talk about." She paused, and McCleary waited. "Between the traveling and the other women, I got tired of it all. Grant's women . . ." She hesitated again, drawing in her breath, stirring her iced tea with distraction, then continued. "His traveling, his photography and plants—it was all part of the package, you know? I mean, you couldn't just slice away a part of him and say, Okay, this is the part I want. The only part. It was all or nothing. And the women . . . they were his diversions, his vices. It wasn't like he flaunted them or anything. He seemed to pigeonhole his life, if you know what I mean." She glanced up. "I'm sure Quin could tell you more in that respect than I can. Like I said, I hadn't seen him for a while."

"Do you know any women in particular I could speak to?"

"No." Her tone was curt, and she lowered her eyes. They may have been divorced for three years, McCleary thought, but there were still scars, plenty of them. He turned the conversation away from Bell's infidelities and asked what she knew about his association with Wishod Pharmaceuticals. Her story was much the same as Quin's.

"I'm not sure I understand what their interest is in the Amazon," he said.

"Plants, Mr. McCleary. Plants that might have potential uses as drugs—painkillers, antibiotics, you name it. Anyway, he'd always had a tremendous interest in plants—our house used to look like a botanical garden— and this gave him the chance to bring stuff back home. He used to collect local folklore and mythology, too, that was another one of his passions. I think he was planning on compiling all these stories into a book someday. His Spanish was flawless, which made it all that much easier."

"Does the word 'greenfire' mean anything to you?"

"No, not offhand. Why?"

McCleary told her about finding the word on the blackboard in the townhouse kitchen. "After talking to Quin, I thought it might be related to something in Amazon folklore."

"That's probably a good guess. And it wouldn't surprise me if it was a myth about hidden treasures, a lost city, or some herb that's supposed to be a cure for cancer. That'd be the sort of thing that would've appealed to him. Whatever it is, if he struggled to keep himself alive long enough to scribble it, then there was a damned good reason for doing so."

"You must know Steve Killington, then."

She nodded. "Sure. He's an okay guy. But if I were you, Mr. McCleary, I'd be taking a real close look at his organization— not him so much as the people Grant was working with in the Amazon. I mean, it could be that this greenfire thing involved some sort of plant down there with a potential use in the millions of dollars. Maybe he got killed for what he knew."

Or maybe one of his women got pissed off, and maybe you watch too much TV, McCleary thought, trying to imagine this woman bursting in on her ex and Quin. Hell, maybe she killed him. There had certainly been less likely motives for murder. In fact, maybe greenfire was a nickname for those eyes of hers.

In the early days, digging around for motives had fascinated him. He'd considered himself a sort of archaeologist, shuffling through the detritus of a victim's life as though the clues he found would answer some arcane riddle. But over the years, he'd realized there were no riddles, only labyrinths carved by lies and deceptions. A cynic: that's what Quin had called him. She was probably right.

As he was leaving a few minutes later, McCleary paused on the front walk. "Oh, Mrs. Esposito. Just for the record. Where were you last night?"

"At school. I'm going to be teaching summer school, and there was a faculty meeting last night." She folded her tiny arms, her bird arms, at her waist. "That's Kendall High School, Mr. McCleary. I teach Social Studies. The meeting got over about nine-thirty. You can check. And no, I didn't kill him. If it were ever going to happen, it would've happened about four, five years ago."

"Just asking," he said.

"Well, I'll tell you something. I can't say I'm surprised, considering how he lived. Sad, yes, but not surprised."

7

I LIKED THE music, the twilight, the smell of the smoke. The first sip of Dewar's burned going down, and I liked that, too. In the mirror over the bar, I could see the man watching me, a typical South Florida type with a tanned, rugged face and oh yes, I liked that very much. In a moment, he would get up and come over to me and he would say something predictable like, *Can I buy you a drink?* But this really wasn't the sort of place where a man would speak like that. He was more likely to bum a cigarette or ask my name or just say, bluntly, *You wanna fuck?* It had happened once, but I could no longer remember what that man had looked like.

Now Mr. Macho rose, came toward the bar, signaled the bartender. He glanced at me as if I were incidental, as if he weren't interested. Okay, I could play that game too. There weren't many games these guys played that I couldn't beat them at. Even Grant had learned that in the end.

"Mind if I sit down?" he asked.

"It's a free country." *What movie had I seen that in?*

"What'll it be, Tom?" the bartender asked.

"Another Miller for me and another of whatever the lady's drinking, Henry."

"Dewar's on the rocks," Henry the Bartender said. "Coming up."

"Thanks." I flashed a smile that was friendly—but not easy. I liked what I saw. He was taller than I'd thought, with broad, muscular shoulders. Probably a weight lifter who figured that since he worked out two hours a day he could consume two six-packs of beer.

"No offense, but what're you doing in a dive like this?" the man—Tom—asked.

"Research."

He laughed. "Yeah? On what, Miami dives?"

"For a novel."

"You write books?"

"I try."

"Have I ever heard of you?"

I laughed. "Doubtful. I'm Kara Newman."

"Kara Newman." He said my name pensively, like he was really trying to place me.

"See? I told you you'd never heard of me."

"Well, have I ever got a story for you, Kara Newman," he said with a smile, straddling the bar stool like a saddle, his eyes scrutinizing me without seeming to do so. "An honest-to-God writer, huh?"

The magical word: something subtle had shifted in his expression. That word, *writer,* acted on men like a drug. For some it was a stimulant, catapulting them into weird and fantastic tales of heists or corruption or the best fuck they ever had. For others the word was a depressant that stirred stories of love lost or a mother who died of cancer after a valiant struggle. Each man told his story with a bright flame of hope that I might use it, thus immortalizing him. It was enough to make me puke.

His story was about a tennis pro from Wisconsin who came to Florida and made it with all the lah-de-dah rich women at the country club where he taught. It was a variation on the movie *Shampoo*. But instead of Warren Beatty running around with a bottle of perm lotion in one hand and a boob in the other, there was the Wisconsin pro who did it with his socks on.

And so it started, the familiar dance, the rituals of my research. He asked me about my books (two so far, I said, but only one published); I asked if he was the tennis pro from Wisconsin (sure, he said); and then we swapped stories about Miami. Whoever said New York was the naked city?

When I looked at the clock again, it was 1:30 and I

was feeling high from the Scotch, and Tom, bless his heart, had his hand high on my thigh and kept kissing my neck, nuzzling my ear, saying sweet things to me. He asked me back to his place, and naturally I demurred at first, but then he said something that made me laugh, that excited me, and I told him I would follow in my car.

He lived at a place called Tennis & You, a complex with thirty-five tennis courts and a clubhouse, surrounded by a pink wall. The guardhouse at the gate almost caused me to turn around, until I realized it was empty. He stopped in front of the fourth building and I pulled into the spot beside his. In the courtyard, he pointed at the six-foot mosaic of a tennis player in white knickers that was embedded in the pink wall. "That's Mr. Brooks," he said, like I was supposed to know who he was.

"Oh."

"All the buildings are named after tennis players."

"Do you teach here too?"

"No. I just practice here."

The apartment was pretty comfortable—a huge living room with a dramatic black iron spiral staircase that led to three bedrooms on the second floor. I wondered if maybe he was dealing drugs or something on the side, since the place seemed a bit too luxurious for a tennis pro.

After he'd shown me around and poured me a Scotch—not Dewar's, he apologized—we settled in the living room. He put on music that seemed to make the air quiver, like it does on hot, breathless summer days. He took me in his arms, and we moved slowly and rhythmically in a small, tight circle. He kissed my neck; his hands lit a fire across my back and ribs and breasts. "Kara Newman, Kara Newman, I'll read every single one of your books for sure," he whispered, and I laughed and wiggled away from him.

"May I have some more Scotch?" I thrust my glass toward him and ran my fingers through my hair, feeling good now, very good.

"You sure can put that stuff away."

"We've all got our vices."

I kicked off my shoes and glided around the room. I glanced at myself in the wall mirror. Pretty, I thought, you're pretty. Men had always told me this, and I knew it was true, but why did I feel so ugly so much of the time? Why did I feel like there were little gremlins living inside me, whispering things to me?

Nonsense. It was what Grant had wanted me to think. I was normal. The whispers were my muse. This was just part of my research, where I climbed inside my characters' skins, where the lines were written as they were spoken.

"Here you go." He handed me the Scotch, dimmed the lights, then sat beside me on the floor. "You didn't tell me what kind of books you wrote."

You never gave me the chance, dork. "Murders."

"No shit," he murmured, his mouth seeking my neck again, like a vampire.

"My first book was called *Black Bird*."

"Hmm. *Black Bird*." Another kiss, at the throat. I dipped my finger in the Scotch, humming softly to myself, humming even as I touched my wet finger to his mouth and he licked it off. Then everything seemed to slow as he took the glass from my hand, set it on the coffee table, and urged me gently back against the floor. A long kiss this time as his fingers fumbled at the buttons on my blouse.

"Hey, not so rough," I said, pushing his hand away and sitting up. "I can undress myself, you know. I'm perfectly capable of undressing myself." I wiggled out of my blouse. Better, much better. Now I could breathe.

"Kara, Kara," he said softly, touching me. A wave of heat flashed across my skin and seemed to strike into the core of my brain, hitting some dim memory, an uneasy memory.

Billy was his name, Billy Hendrix who lived down the street, Billy who . . . Bad Billy. Billy had touched me in places boys weren't supposed to touch and I'd screamed and he'd pushed me to the ground and . . .

My eyes flew open. The man was on top of me, grinding his hips against mine, trying to get my jeans off, saying, "C'mon, baby, c'mon, let's get these things off and I'll—"

"No. Cut it out, Billy." I shoved him away and bolted forward. "Stop it." *Naughty, Billy.*

"Billy? What're you talking about? My name's Tom. Tom Darcy."

My head pounded, I reached for my blouse, slipped it back on, buttoned it. I couldn't breathe in here. He was going to do something to me, I knew he was, something bad, and then the Devil would come and I'd fry in Hell. Mama had said so.

"Hey. Hey, what do you think you're doing? You little tease, hey . . ." He grabbed my hand as I got up, twisting my fingers until I cried out, yanking me back to the floor. His cheeks were pink. His hands groped, trying to tear off my blouse now.

"Stop it," I hissed. "Just stop it." I lashed out, scratching his face, and he slapped me. The sound stung the air and sent shoots of hot pain through my cheek. Then he shoved me back to the floor, straddling me so I couldn't get up. He was saying something to me, something ugly and mean, and suddenly I began to laugh. "Okay, okay, I just . . . you know . . ."

I just want to know how my character is going too feel before she does it, Tom Darcy. That's all.

The force of his body against mine lessened. "Oh, I get it," he said, his voice quieter now, his head bobbing up and down. "You like to be roughed up a little, right?" He laughed. "God, this town's got all types, you know? But that's okay with me, Kara Newman, who writes murders."

"Let me get my purse. I've got some great oil in there. You know, to rub you down."

"Oil? You carry it with you?" He laughed and shook his head as though he couldn't quite believe it. But he moved off me. *Naughty, Billy.* He shouldn't have done that. Shouldn't have been mean to me. As I reached into my purse, wondering what I was doing, I heard the circuit breaker in my brain click. A dark pool flowed over my thoughts like greasy water, and the uncomfortable memory thumped against the inside of my skull, hurting me, reminding me . . .

There was a field in which Billy lay, Billy bleeding because I'd cut him, because I'd had to cut him for hurting me, and then there was the lake and . . . Billy was the black bird, the dark face of death, the . . .

My throat constricted as my fingers closed around the knife. The pearl handle was cool against my skin. "You just lay back now." I spoke softly, brushing my mouth against his neck, his beautiful neck. There was something wrong with this scene, with the way it had nearly veered out of my control, the way it kept getting mixed up with something else. "Is this in the book now?"

"What?" he asked.

Is it?

"Nothing."

"You are one weird chick, Kara Newman." He was still smiling as his eyes closed, as I brought my hand from my purse. His smile lingered even as I pressed the cold blade against his throat and drew it in a clean, swift motion from ear to ear. He let out a strangled cry, his eyes bulged, blood ran in rivulets down his neck, onto his shoulders. I leaped back, shaking a finger at him, backing away. "You shouldn't have been mean, Billy. You shouldn't have hurt me."

Is that what my character would say?

But there was no time to think about it, because he was trying to get up, scrambling to rise, his hands holding his throat. Blood pumped between his fingers. He stumbled toward me, gurgling, his stricken eyes paralyzing me. *It isn't supposed to happen like this.* I couldn't move, and he just kept staggering toward me, making that terrible gurgling sound. Now one of his arms shot out, the fingers flexing grotesquely, clawing the air as though it were my eyes.

Then suddenly I came loose from the floor and rushed him with the knife. It sank deeply into his chest. Blood spurted, God, there was so much blood, and I stumbled back and saw him falling. He slammed against the floor. His left arm flayed, once, hitting the edge of a table. The lamp on it toppled sideways: the bulb popped and went out.

The quivering music filled the sudden quiet.

I stood there for nearly a full minute, looking at him, shaking, expecting him to leap up, lunge for me. But when he didn't move, when I could see he wasn't even breathing, I sank to my knees, wishing he hadn't made me hurt him, wishing . . . Oh God, I didn't know. Just wishing.

I finally scooted toward him. His eyes were wide open, hideous. *This is the mask of death. Remember it.* Right, the details were important. I reached for my knife, wiped it clean on the rug. The music had ceased, the stereo had stopped automatically, the quiet swelled with the stink of blood. I looked frantically around the room, trying to remember what I'd touched. The glass. Okay, I would wash the glass. Had I touched anything else? No. Nothing.

I slapped the knife against the rug again, reached for the glass, saw that he'd died with his socks on. The thought brought on a spasm of laughter. It coiled and bubbled inside me, then shoved its way into the air. I scrambled up and hurried into the kitchen. Paper towel, water: I scrubbed the glass with one hand as I held on to it with a paper towel in the other.

The cops in my book would never figure this one out. No fingerprints, everything squeaky clean like in one of those TV commercials. I returned to the living room and looked down at Tom Darcy, tennis pro. *My character would* . . . be sorry he hadn't died immediately. And I was sorry too. I was. I hadn't wanted him to suffer. Not like he'd made me suffer. No one should hurt like that. I wet the tip of my knife with blood from his neck, and made a tiny sign of the cross on his forehead.

"You're forgiven," I whispered. I forgave him even though he was naughty.

buff, and now another knifing. What else could occur to make...

There were, anyway, at a few months, with a kill

8

1.

AT 7:00 SATURDAY morning, the neighborhood where McCleary jogged nestled deeply in slumber. Sunlight winked against windows, squirrels scampered furtively through empty yards and pilfered from mango trees, birds trilled in treetops. He'd been running for nearly eight months, since shortly after the serial killer, if that's what he was, had first struck. It was almost as if his body had known then what his mind had not: that he would need a buffer against the stress the subsequent killings would create.

He moved at a comfortable pace, enjoying the quiet. There was far too few mornings like this in his life. So few, in fact, that it had been months since he'd even had time to fiddle with his paints. Before the knifings had started, the hobby had taken second place only to Robin in his off-hour pursuits. But now that Robin apparently had other amusements, he thought bitterly, maybe there'd be time for painting again. In fact, maybe when he got back he'd dig out a canvas and his paints and work on the porch.

Four miles later, McCleary reached his apartment winded and sheathed in perspiration. Anticipating a few hours of artistic indulgence, he showered quickly, had a bowl of cereal and a cup of coffee, then set up his easel and paints on the porch. He usually worked from sketches or photos—in this case, three eight-by-ten colored photographs of a cabin on Lake Cazenovia in upstate New York. The pictures had been taken more than two years ago, during his last visit to Syracuse. *Before Robin*, he thought, marveling how their affair had neatly divided his life into *before* and *after*.

The phone rang just as he was beginning a preliminary sketch. And at 8:19 on a Saturday morning, a call portended only one thing: trouble.

It was the dispatcher, apologizing for disturbing him at home. "But Mike, I've got a raving woman on the line who says she just discovered a body. A, uh, stabbing. You said you wanted me to let you know if any more of these came through."

So much for the pursuit of art, he thought, and scribbled the directions on the back of his sketch pad.

Apartment complexes like Tennis & You furthered McCleary's contention that beneath the loose easiness of South Florida living, paranoia ran rampant. The complex was like a throwback to the days of enclaves, of tribes, with its bright pink wall and guardhouse screaming, *There's safety in numbers.*

He spotted Doc Smithers's clunky old Mercedes in front of the fourth building and wondered how the doc nearly always managed to make it to the scene before he did. There were a few people in tennis outfits mulling about in the courtyard, and the arrival of the ambulance would draw even more. Then they would wait patiently for a glimpse of the dead man, and for a few hours they would move through the rituals of their lives thinking, *Better him than me.*

Smithers and several men from forensics were methodically going about their business as McCleary stepped into the apartment. The doc greeted him with a rather weary smile. "I always listen to the police band when I'm shaving in the morning, Mac," he said without preface, as if impelled to explain how he'd arrived here first.

McCleary chuckled. "By now, Doc, I'm used to your being first."

Smithers was a short, plump man with a head as bald as a radish, except for wisps of hair around his ears. He reminded McCleary of Tweedledum. He'd been coroner for Dade County as long as McCleary could remember, and seemed to have a preference for the scene of a crime rather than its aftermath in the lab.

"Who found him?" McCleary asked.

"Neighbor. She saw his door open. Name's Tom Darcy. He's a tennis pro at the Coral Gables Country Club." A corner of Smithers's mouth turned down, and he jerked a thumb toward the front door. "The neighbor was hysterical, so I sent her home."

Darcy was lying on the living room floor on his back, his head propped at an odd angle against the foot of a chair, his throat slit. He was shirtless, the fly to his jeans was open, he had his socks on, but no shoes. An inordinate amount of blood splattered around him left McCleary slightly queasy. Less than a foot from Darcy lay a lamp that had been knocked off the coffee table. McCleary noticed a tiny mark on the man's forehead and crouched to look at it.

"A cross?"

He gazed across the body at Smithers. "That's sure what it looks like to me, Mike."

"In blood."

"Yeah."

"Same kind of knife as the other five, do you think?"

"Won't know for sure until I 'xamine the body, but I'd say so. Thin blade." He gestured toward Darcy's throat. "And a cut as clean as a whistle."

"Does it look like anything's been stolen?"

Smithers ran a hand over his smooth head, and for a moment McCleary thought he was going to crack a joke about how police work had made his hair fall out. Instead, he shrugged. "Hard to say for sure, but I doubt it. I think it's a woman. I don't know why I think that, but I do."

Which was exactly what Benson had theorized, McCleary mused. He got up and walked slowly around the downstairs. There were water marks on the coffee table, ashes on the rug, and two glasses in the sink, both filled with water. Except for a paper towel and cup, the garbage can was empty.

"I don't suppose the neighbors heard anything," McCleary remarked as Smithers came into the kitchen.

"I don't suppose so. Except for the woman who called, we haven't heard a peep from any of them. I already sent someone over to the Coral Gables Country Club, Mike, to see what they've got to say."

"Let's take a look upstairs."

"I've already looked. You go on."

The master bedroom had a door that led out onto the porch that ran around the second floor of the building. The chain was still on, and it didn't look as if it had been tampered with. On the bureau were several photos of Darcy on a tennis court and a letter postmarked Madison, Wisconsin. McCleary opened it. Darcy's mother said it had been only six weeks since he'd left, but she and his father missed him terribly and hoped he'd gotten settled. Did he think he'd be able to make it home for Christmas?

McCleary slipped the letter back in the envelope and set it aside. Later, when he was in a better frame of mind, he would call the Darcys in Madison. It was the one responsibility he'd inherited with his promotion that he could've done without. He thought momentarily of the raw pain in Quin's face yesterday and felt grateful that at least he wouldn't have to look at the Darcys when he told them their son had been murdered.

The other two bedrooms had no furniture, just cartons of belongings stacked against the wall. Two tennis rackets and a cylindrical container with tennis balls in it leaned forlornly against the closet door. Right here, McCleary thought, is the summation of Tom Darcy's life. It depressed him, and he went back downstairs.

"I guess I'll start knocking on doors."

Smithers put a hand on his shoulder. "Hey, son, don't sound so defeated. I'll give you a hand. You start at one end of the building and I'll start at the other."

McCleary smiled. "I appreciate the offer, Doc, but you really don't have to."

"I know I don't have to, Mike. But I'd rather do that than head back to the lab."

They walked outside, and Smithers inhaled deeply. "Now *this* is preferable to the smell of formaldehyde,

Mike. Don't ever let anyone tell you different." They stood there a moment longer, then turned their backs on each other and headed off in opposite directions like two men pacing distance before a duel.

2.

In the dream, Quin was standing in the house with an armful of groceries, looking around, waiting for blood to seep from the walls, for Grant's body to materialize. Merlin was plopped back on his haunches, howling like he was in pain, and then he became a dolphin, arching across the blue of the rug as though it were water.

She dropped the groceries. Cans and bottles rolled every which way. A bottle of catsup popped open, spraying the rug, the furniture, and she dropped to her knees, sobbing, clawing at the rug to get out the red. The dolphin dived for a head of lettuce and slammed into the far wall, becoming a howling Merlin once again. Grant appeared naked in the hallway, scratching his head, blinking his eyes like he'd just gotten out of bed. *What's all the racket, Quin? I've got company.*

Then she was running down the hall after him, the floor moving like an escalator under her feet so that she had to struggle for purchase. She heard Grant's voice from behind a closed door, a soft, persistent voice, and then the rachitic song of the bed. She burst into the room. She saw the painted fingernails against his spine, flexing, straightening, the woman's hands, her arms, part of her legs, her feet. Grant was on top of her, straining, whispering, and then suddenly his head jerked around. *What're you doing in here, Quin? I told you I had company.*

She began to cry and awakened with the sheets tangled around her legs. Light slipped through her bedroom shutters. A cool hiss of air from the overhead vent caused her to shiver. She threw back the sheet, disgusted with herself, and went downstairs for a drink of water. Merlin padded behind her, anticipating a spot of breakfast. "Did he ever do that, Merl?" she said, looking down at the cat as she opened a can of his food. He

70

arched his back and meowed in response. "Yeah, right. Too bad we don't speak the same language."

She glanced at the calendar tacked to the corkboard near the phone. Saturday: she could sleep in, go to the beach, read, watch TV, clean, do nothing.

Nothing: death is nothing.

The thought galvanized her away from the counter toward the fridge. *You've got to keep busy, Quin,* Nikki had said yesterday when she'd brought her cleaning lady to Grant's to restore the upstairs of the townhouse. *Busy,* as in making breakfast and fixing coffee, and missing her first cigarette of the day. Busy as in sweeping and mopping the kitchen floor. There was comfort, again, in rituals. They offered her a structure of defense against the ineluctable marching of her thoughts to the ample opportunities Grant had for seeing other women: while she was at work, when she was out of town on a case, when he traveled. Then, of course, there was the townhouse.

She hadn't remained long after McCleary had left yesterday because she was afraid of what other secrets she might uncover. She'd driven Grant's Ford to work, the damned thing sputtering and coughing the entire way, then she'd run a check on Wishod Pharmaceuticals. She'd left the Ford at home and had taken a taxi to the townhouse to meet Nikki there. But today she'd return, today she wasn't afraid. He was dead, and what could be worse than that?

The phone rang as she was fixing bacon and scrambled eggs, muffins and a bowl of fruit. It was Ellen, her sister, calling from Ashville. Ellen, who taught nursing at the University of North Carolina and had a three-year-old daughter and whose life had progressed along the most traditional lines. Ellen, who'd never liked Grant.

"I thought maybe you'd left the country, Quin. I've been trying to get in touch with you for two days."

"Things have been a little crazy around here. I was going to call you today." *To tell you about Grant.* But now that Ellen was on the phone, she didn't know what to say, so Quin let her talk. Her classes were finished for the summer, Jeff would be doing a lot of traveling for two weeks in late July or early August, she said, and how would Quin like some company?

"It'd just be the two of us, Quin, because Jeff's parents are going to keep Samantha. I mean, if you and Grant don't mind having me."

"Grant's dead," she blurted, and before Ellen could say anything, Quin told her what had happened. Each time she related the story to someone, she thought, the horror lessened.

"I'll get the first plane down there, Quin."

"You don't have to do that. I'm okay, really."

"*Okay?* How the hell can you be okay?"

"Because I'm going to find whoever did it."

A brief silence ensued. A judgmental silence, Quin thought, and wished she'd said nothing at all. But then Ellen surprised her. "Good for you, Quin. I'd do exactly the same thing. You almost have to, given the crime rate and everything the police *don't* do."

Quin smiled. The words were an anodyne after opposition from the very people who should've been supportive. "Well, by the time you get down here, the bastard's ass will be in prison."

"Just be careful, okay?" Ellen said softly.

Amazing what a little unexpected encouragement could do for her appetite, Quin thought when they'd hung up and she polished off breakfast. *Ellen, of all people.* But then, Ellen had the best of both their parents, Quin decided, guts without turmoil, looks without vanity, and a tenacious intellect that honed in on a goal and shot straight toward it.

As Quin cleaned up, she peeked in the drawer where the butter had melted. Several dozen ants scurried back and forth along the bottom. In college, she'd known a woman who claimed she could communicate with ants and convince them to leave her apartment so she wouldn't have to kill them. Quin had actually watched her talk to the ants one day as if they were sentient beings. To her astonishment, the insects had retreated. She wondered if it would work for her.

"Okay, guys. I don't want to squash you. But I would appreciate it if you would leave the drawer, all right?" She leaned close to the drawer as she said it, watching earnestly for any change in their direction. But the ants continued their trek across the bottom of the drawer. So much for ants as sentient beings, she thought, and brought out the jar of honey. She removed everything from the drawer, dripped honey onto a paper towel and set it inside. Within seconds, the ants swarmed over the honey. She picked up the towel carefully, opened the back door and carried it across the yard. In Grant's garden, she set the towel down as if it were an oblation to the sun god, and felt a certain smugness that she hadn't squashed them. "Now stay outa my kitchen," she said and went back inside.

Before she departed, she called McCleary and left a message on his machine that she wanted to talk to him. Then she realized it was Saturday and early. He was probably still asleep and most likely not alone.

It only took her fifteen minutes to get across town. There were few cars, no overturned semis, no traffic jams, no roving gangs of kids shattering car windows and robbing motorists—the newest of Miami crimes. She stopped in front of Grant's condo, started up the walk, changed her mind, and went around to the courtyard first, where the mailboxes were. She'd lived here with him for a couple of months when they'd started looking for the house, and she still had the mailbox key.

The box was jammed with stuff. She carried it over to the table where she and McCleary had sat and started going through it. A kid who was maybe twelve or thirteen came into the courtyard with a cocker spaniel, a bucket, and a hose and began bathing the dog. He glanced at Quin, said, "You a friend of Mr. Bell's?"

"Yes."

"He's not home."

"Yeah, I know."

"I mean, uh, he's not coming home. Ever."

Ever: the finality of death. "Right, I understand. You live in the building?"

He pointed with a soapy hand at the apartment directly across from Grant's. "In one-oh-four. I'm Pete Gilbert."

"I'm Quin." She wondered if he was the kid who'd

stolen Grant's camera. "Did you know Grant pretty well?"

"Sometimes we shot baskets on the court across the street. And after Karl left—he used to live next door to Mr. Bell—I ran errands for him when he was busy working."

"This was recently?" she asked.

He squirted more shampoo onto the cocker and ran his hands along the dog's tail, soaping it. "I've been doing it for a couple of months, and then a few days before he was killed, too."

You mean a few days ago when he was supposed to have been in the Amazon. "What kind of errands did you do for him?"

"Depended. Sometimes I mailed letters and stuff for him or ran to the store if he needed something. Usually there'd be a couple things to do that would take an hour or two, and he paid me five bucks an hour, so it was a good deal for me." He paused. "He was a pretty neat guy. He got shot in the apartment, you know. I was asleep when the police were talking to everyone. Were you one of his girlfriends?"

One of. "No, I'm a private eye."

"Really?" His eyes widened, he squirted the cocker once more, rinsing off the soap, then whipped a towel from a nearby bush. "Someone hired you to investigate his death, huh."

She nodded. "He had a lot of girlfriends?" The words left a bitter taste in her mouth. She saw his dark head bob, and an ache ripped open inside her.

"He dated a lot of girls, but I don't know if they were all girlfriends, if you know what I mean." *At twelve he knows the difference?* she wondered. "I hardly ever saw him with the same girl." He finished drying the dog, who scampered away, shaking himself, water flying off his back, and turned off the hose. Then he came over to the table, wiping his hands on his jeans, and sat down. "You know what I liked about him? He was real easy to talk to."

Because he listened, Quin thought. Because when you had his attention, you possessed it completely. That had been part of his charm. "Did he ever tell you about the pink dolphin?" she asked.

"Yeah, you bet. That's some weird story. The dolphin that turns into a man."

"Pink dolphin," she corrected. There was, after all, a difference, as Grant would've been quick to point out.

"Right."

"How about greenfire? Ever hear that story?" she asked hopefully.

He thought about it. In the sunlight, she could see the fuzz on his upper lip. A cute kid, she decided, the sort Grant would befriend. "Nope, I don't think I remember that one."

"You know what I'd like you to do for me, Pete?" She brought a card out of her purse and handed it to him. "If you remember anything else about Mr. Bell or his girlfriends or something you think might be important, would you give me a call?"

"Yeah, sure." He looked at the card. "You really *are* a private eye. How neat." As she got up, the stack of mail in her hand, he said, "I do remember one thing. And I didn't get to tell the cops, since I was asleep."

"What's that."

"Well, the night he was killed, I was out walking Gypsy and there were lights on in his place. I didn't know he was back till I saw the lights."

"Did you see anyone?"

"Uh-uh."

"You remember what time it was?"

He ran a finger under his nose sniffled. The freckles on his cheeks seemed in danger of sliding off. "Yeah, around eight-thirty or a little before. My mom and I were going to watch *The Last Starfighter* on TV and I 'member she was nagging me to take Gypsy for a walk before the movie started."

Probably right after he'd been killed, Quin thought. "And you never heard any shots or anything."

"Nope."

"Like I said, if you remember anything else, give me a call, okay?"

"Sure thing."

She let herself into the apartment, made herself some

coffee, then began sorting through the mail. Most of it was professional stuff, checks, bills, and three personal letters. The first was postmarked Holland, sent by a woman Grant had evidently met on a boat in Peru. There were several references to a three-day trip up the Amazon, which she claimed were the most romantic she'd ever spent with a man. Her English, Quin noted, was atrocious. *But on a romantic Amazon trip, who gives a damn about a little problem like English, Quin?*

The second, postmarked Iquitos, Peru, with just a post office box for a return address, was written in Spanish and was signed "Felix Mendez." She had no idea who Felix was, and she didn't read Spanish, but she would find someone who did.

The third letter, printed neatly on yellow paper, said:

Sweetie,
  I know you're home. Let's talk. Greenfire, if you remember, is part mine.

                                        Ginger

The letter was postmarked Miami on June something; the day was smeared. There was no return address.

Ginger: a spice for a name. But she knew about greenfire, which was more than Quin knew. She tossed the letter aside, opened the envelopes with the checks to see who they were from: travel magazines and Wishod Pharmaceuticals. The check from Wishod alone amounted to $5,500.

Quin stacked everything, slipped it in her purse, decided to check the upstairs first. She and Nikki had put the room back in order, and now Quin went through Grant's closet, identifying shirts, slacks, several jackets that she'd wondered what had happened to. She'd even asked him about the corduroy jacket, she remembered, and he'd told her he'd dropped it and some other stuff at the thrift shop.

There were several flat boxes stacked on the closet shelf under half a dozen sweaters that she'd missed yesterday. When she went through them, she found negligees in assorted colors, sizes, and cuts; two designer-label satin blouses, a size 8 and a 10; a silk robe the color of plums. Everything was new. Gifts for his ladies?

A secret life, whispered a voice in her head.

In his bottom drawer was a shoebox with garters, several pairs of silk panties, one a size 3, and a black lace bra, size 34C, one of those things from someplace like Frederick's of Hollywood with the nipples cut out. These things were used. She threw everything on the bed, only dimly aware that some other part of her had taken over, that the Quin who should have been reacting with incredulity, maybe despair, had taken leave. Gone on vacation.

On the back of the bathroom door, hanging beneath his chocolate-colored terry-cloth robe, was a woman's robe, floor length, a pale yellow, a small. Quin draped it over her arm, carried it into the bedroom, and dropped it on the pile with the other stuff, which she then carried downstairs.

Next, she went through the den, setting aside notebooks, files of slides and correspondence which she would go through later, and anything else that looked even remotely promising. She carried the stuff into the living room, set it on the pile of his other belongings, and thought: *All right, it was official. Grant definitely had a secret life.*

Just then the door opened, and she thought, *Oh God, not again.*

9

"QUIN."

She stared at Paul Holmes and didn't realize she'd been holding her breath, that her hand was balled at her heart. She sighed and her arm dropped to her side. "God, Paul. You nearly gave me heart failure."

"What're *you* doing here?"

"I could ask you the same thing, you know."

Holmes came inside, shutting the door behind him. He was carrying a clipboard. "I got a call last night from Grant's attorney, and since he was going to be out of town this weekend, he asked me to come over here and inventory the stuff in the townhouse."

"I thought *you* were his attorney."

"*Was,* Quin. When I was elected DA, I recommended that he find someone else." He eyed the pile of things on the chair. "You can't take that stuff with you. The condo and everything in it is going into probate."

"Screw probate," she said.

They stood for a long moment, saying nothing. Quin waited for Holmes to pull his I-am-the-DA routine on her. "Well, what *is* that stuff?" he asked finally, going over to the chair.

"Lingerie."

"That you left here?"

"Yeah, sure, Paul." She whipped the lid off one of

the boxes, held up a pair of underwear. "I'm thin, but I'm not a size 3."

"Yeah. I see what you mean." He ran a finger across his upper lip and didn't seem to know what to say.

"But I suppose you knew about this."

"Look, Quin, Grant and I were friends, yeah, but it doesn't mean he told me everything. We weren't as close as we used to be. So there were women other than you. So what. You're the one he lived with. That's what counted."

Which told her something about Paul Holmes's marriage, she thought. "Well, I'm taking this stuff. The cop who's investigating Grant's death may be interested."

"You mean McCleary."

"Yes."

"I suppose you gave him my name."

"Any reason I shouldn't have?"

"Only that I probably know less about Grant's personal life than anyone else." He set his clipboard on the coffee table and sat on the couch. "Anything cold to drink in the fridge?" He locked his hands behind his head and lifted his feet onto the coffee table. He seemed to think she was going to wait on him.

"Juice. Help yourself. The kitchen's well stocked."

She sat on the arm of the chair where Grant's things were, realizing she'd never liked Holmes very much. Oh, he was personable enough, but she always felt as if she were in the presence of an image rather than a man. Everything about him—from his designer clothes to the way he looked and moved—seemed to have been created for effect. His thick salt-and-pepper hair was combed just so, his mouth that was a shade too wide smiled enough to show off his perfectly white and no doubt capped teeth, his slate blue eyes were set deeply in a face that had just the right touch of a tan. He might've been one of those male models grinning from the slick pages of an ad for Christian Dior shirts, she thought. A man without a soul, a man who'd lost himself completely when he began believing his own PR.

He brought two glasses of juice back into the living room, handed her one, and sat on the couch again. "I've got some theories on who killed him, you know. If you're interested in hearing them."

"Sure."

"About a year ago, Grant told me he believed he was onto something big, real big, in the Amazon, and needed investors for a project he figured could quadruple their money within six months to a year."

Are we talking about the same man? "Quadruple? That's some promise. How much did he need?"

"A bunch, that was all he said."

"To do what?"

"I don't know, he never told me."

"He was asking *you* for the money?"

"No, he was just saying that he was looking for investors. I pressed him for details, but he wouldn't tell me what it was about. I told him he should go to someone at Wishod, since they're the people with the big bucks." Holmes paused, lifted his legs, and rested them on the coffee table, making himself right at home, Quin noted irritably. "But he didn't want to do that, because then they'd get a piece of the action." When he hesitated again, Quin sensed it was for dramatic effect and not because he was at a loss for words. "I think he went to someone at Wishod, Quin, and I think he probably got the cash, and I think he was killed for whatever this involved."

"You're making a lot of suppositions."

"Maybe. But he said this involved millions in profit."

"Drugs?"

He ran a hand over his hair. "Hell, I don't know. But he'd been down there often enough to make the right connections."

She started to tell Holmes that Grant wasn't involved in drugs, but she could no longer say with any certainty what Grant had or had not been involved in. "I just can't see a company like Wishod in the drug trade."

Holmes rolled his eyes. "Oh, Christ, Quin. Don't be naive. That company has had its share of crooked dealings, take my word for it."

"Your word as DA?"

"Yeah."

"Can you be more specific?"

He flashed his number-one smile, teeth lining up like a white picket fence in his mouth, eyes crinkling a bit at the corners. "Sure. An attempted payoff to a group of independent researchers to falsify reports on a certain drug they were trying to get approved by the FDA."

"How do you know about that?"

"Never mind how I know. The point is, it wouldn't surprise me in the least to find out they were responsible for Grant's death."

"I've got a question for you. Who's Ginger?"

"Ginger?" He uttered it as though the word weren't in his vocabulary, but his voice, which was a shade too high, betrayed him. So she bluffed.

"Ginger, yes. G-I-N-G-E-R. I know she was a friend of Grant's. A good friend. But just how good a friend, Paul?" She gestured angrily toward the box of lingerie. "*That* good?"

"Look, the man's dead, Quin. He loved you, whether you care to believe it or not. These other women were just—"

"Who is she, damn it."

"Christ," he sighed. "Okay, okay. Her name's Ginger Hale and she owns a jewelry store in Lauderdale called Ginger's. I don't know what difference it can make now."

"Where'd he meet her?"

"I don't know. But he was seeing her a long time before he ever met you, Quin."

"And still seeing her afterward, too."

"But it wasn't the same, that's what I'm trying to tell you, kiddo. You were it for him."

She laughed; the bitterness balled inside her like an undigested meal. "Sure." She waved her arm toward the lingerie. "And all this stuff was for me, right?"

He pressed his hands against his thighs, got up. "Look, I've got to get to work inventorying this stuff."

"Did the attorney tell you anything about Grant's will?"

"You got the condo and his interest in the house, naturally, and the car and a few other odds and ends."

"Then you won't mind if I take these things."

He glanced at the boxes and shook his head.

"I'd sure like to know how he had time to squeeze everyone in, what with his traveling and the writing and living with me. Busy, busy man, huh?" She picked up the boxes. Several gowns, a blouse, and lingerie spilled over the sides, colorful as rainbows.

"Quin, just let the memory be, all right? You're going to drive yourself nuts if you start thinking about it."

"You never met any of the others?"

"No."

"But there *were* others."

"Yeah, I think so, from time to time. Women he met when he was traveling, that kind of thing. He alluded to it; you know how vague he could be."

Vague: she almost laughed. Yeah, it turned out he'd been mighty goddamned vague, all right: other women, multimillion-dollar deals in the Amazon, a search for investors, something called greenfire, a townhouse that had proven to be an ideal locale for his double life. Naive? Was that what Paul had just called her? Hardly. Stupid was more like it, stupid and myopic.

"How'd you know about Ginger?" Paul asked as she was starting for the door.

She glanced back at him. "Does it really matter?"

2.

"Hi, Mac. I thought I'd find you here."

Robin stood in his office doorway, smiling and lovely in white slacks and a loose-fitting pale blue blouse with a pocket over each breast. "Hi, stranger." For a moment, McCleary forgot he was annoyed with her, that she'd lied to him about the phone call. He almost managed to forget the three hours he'd spent at Tom Darcy's apartment complex, interviewing the neighbors. He and Doc Smithers had discovered virtually nothing, which wasn't really surprising. In an area of transients, where your neighbors frequently changed from month to month, friendships were rarely forged.

She came in and shut the door. "I thought all seminar participants had the weekend off," he remarked.

"I was studying downstairs in the library. You wouldn't believe the stuff we've got to memorize in this training thing, and at home I just get distracted. Anyway, I needed a break."

"There was another knifing last night."

"Like the other five?"

"It sure looks that way. The MO's similar."

She leaned toward him, cupping her chin in her hands. "Poor Mac," she said quietly. "No wonder you look beat. Look, I'll talk to the chief on Monday and tell him I want out of this stupid seminar."

"For what? During all these months we haven't been able to dig up a clue. What makes you think it's going to be any different this time?"

She sat back. "You're being too negative."

Negative, cynical—what else had he been called in the last couple of days?

"Has anything more happened with the Bell case?" she asked.

"I just spoke to Quin a while ago, and we're at least uncovering a few leads."

Robin slipped off her sandals, pulled the other chair closer and lifted her legs onto it.

"Looks like this Grant Bell character had his share of secrets."

"The dead always do," she said.

And so do the living, he felt like saying, but didn't. He began to explain a few of the inconsistencies Quin had unearthed about Bell, but the story somehow wound back to the murder of Tom Darcy.

"Did they find any fingerprints?" she asked.

"Nothing. It's always the same. It's like the guy goes through the place afterward, wiping everything off. I called Darcy's folks in Wisconsin," he said, but didn't finish the story. He didn't want to think about how Mrs. Darcy's voice had broken or how her husband's voice seemed to just shrivel up like a prune at the other end of the phone. "Shit. Let's talk about something else. This is depressing."

"C'mon, sport. Let me go get my stuff in the library, then we can go to the beach or something."

Much later that afternoon, the patter of rain woke McCleary. He saw a patch of dusky, gray light shaped like a trapezoid, a dip in the middle of his venetian blinds, as though a fat midget had sat on them, then the sleek curve of Robin's head, dark against the white of the pillow.

When they'd left the station, they'd grabbed a bite to eat and had driven over to the beach for a swim. After an hour, the sky had started to cloud up and they'd come back to his place with a bottle of wine and Robin had lit up a joint and one thing had led to another and here they were. He knew she wouldn't be staying the night. After all, she had a commitment tomorrow, and it'd be easier to leave this evening than to make up an excuse in the morning. So there'd be no leisurely Sunday morning coffee, no rifling through the Sunday paper, no rituals of an ersatz marriage as there had been so many Sundays. She would go her way, and he, his.

McCleary went into the bathroom. He turned on the shower, waited until steam was rising, then stepped in with a grunt and let the hot needles drum his back and neck and shoulders. He tried not to think about the night ahead, about how he was going to fill it, but it loomed as vast and barren as a desert. He could go in to work, of course; there was always work. Or he could call Benson or Quin or find some quiet bar where he could shoot pool and get quietly blasted.

The problem with getting drunk was dealing with the morning after; he immediately ruled that out. Well, he would think of something. Hell, this was Miami. If nothing else, he could drive around and wait for a crime to happen.

He felt a draft and reached out to fix the curtain, but Robin said, "Hey, you didn't wait for me, Mac." She stepped into the shower with him. "How come you didn't get me up?"

"You looked too comfortable. I was thinking maybe we could go out to dinner. There's a place on the New River in Lauderdale I'd like to try." *Test her: see if you're right, Mac.*

"The water's perfect," she murmured.

Evasion.

He stepped back, watching her squirt shampoo into her hair and work up a lather. The water deepened the color of her skin, the soap foamed white and ran off her shoulders. Her breasts were small, plump as fruit,

84

with the same smooth flawlessness as the rest of her skin. Her tummy was flat, her hipbones sharp, thighs slender, without an ounce of fat. As she turned sideways, he counted the steps of her ribs. His eyes traced the long line of her neck, and he wished suddenly that he possessed the skill to paint her now, just as she was.

Who, Robin? Who're you going to see? He reached for the soap, but it slipped out of his hands and came to rest against her foot. When he crouched to retrieve it, her painted toenails stared up at him like smiling faces. He laughed and began soaping her ankles, calves, her thighs, behind her knees.

Who says she's not essential, Mac? Huh?

Her fingers ran through his hair, her nails kneaded his shoulders. The hot water drummed against them. *Who? Who?* whispered through his head as his hands lathered, caressed. She made small sounds of pleasure, her back against the wall now, her eyes closed, water slipping over her. Her skin tasted of soap and smelled of perfume. The muscles in her belly quivered as he tasted her, as his tongue darted and teased and persisted until she had slid down the wall and was sitting on the floor of the shower, legs bent at the knees, her hands hard against his shoulders, holding him there.

"You're making me crazy," she whispered.

Crazy enough to stay, Robin? Crazy enough for that? Who? Does he do this to you, Robin? Does he love you like I do?

Did he love her? Sometimes he thought he loved the inaccessible aura about her, that secret remoteness that seemed to promise paradise if he could penetrate it. He slipped his finger inside her and watched her face, and the rippling in her thighs, and how she reached out for him. She kissed him hard, her arms encircling his neck.

The steam filled with the scent of shampoo and sex, water pounded the air, her breath came in soft, urgent pants. "Inside, I want you inside," she said in her husky voice, that voice that excited him enormously. He thrust himself into her. Her legs locked around him, she arched her back, pulling at him, demanding completion. But he moved slowly, ever so slowly, drawing her to the edge, stopping, moving, stopping again, until her body began to shudder.

After, as they toweled themselves dry, he felt little more than vague disgust. For months he'd believed that in lovemaking he penetrated that emotional distance he sensed in her; now he suddenly knew the belief was an illusion. It was the act of sex that she craved, needed, not him.

He walked into the kitchen and made a pot of coffee. He got out eggs, bacon, muffins, orange juice. He would make breakfast for dinner. Robin came out of the bedroom with her purse slung over her shoulder. "I've got to get going, Mac."

Okay, there it is, he thought.

He nodded, dropped several strips of bacon in the frying pan.

"Mac?"

"Who is he, Robin?"

"Who is who?"

He kept his back to her. "The guy you're seeing tomorrow. Or is it tonight? That *is* the rush, isn't it?"

The silence filled with the sound of the rain; thunder cracked in the distance. He felt her eyes on his back but refused to turn around. "I don't ask you what you do when you're not with me," she said finally.

"Because you already know."

Another brief silence: McCleary finally turned. She was going through her purse; she brought out her car keys. "I know only what you tell me. That doesn't necessarily mean it's true."

She started to walk away, but he caught her arm. "I'm not in the market for games, Robin."

She folded her arms at her waist, dropped her eyes to the floor, bit at the side of her nail, looked up at him again. "Mac, everything is black and white for you, whether it's your feelings toward me or homicide or your taste in food. Well, you're lucky. For me, for most people, life is gradations of gray. Can't you just enjoy this for what it is?"

"I think I know what it is for me."

Do you, Mac? Do you really? One minute you love the woman, and the next, you never want to see her again. But he heard himself saying, "The problem is that I don't know what it is for *you.*"

"Maybe I don't know either," she whispered. Two big tears spilled from her eyes. She swiped at them angrily, then spun around. He heard her footsteps receding, heard the front door open and close. Then he was left with nothing but the sound of the rain and the sizzling of bacon in the frying pan behind him.

3.

When the sun went down, Quin found herself listening for noises in the house, footfalls outside, things that went bump in the night. It was ridiculous, really, since she'd certainly spent enough time alone when Grant was traveling. But now he was dead, and a part of her feared that if the killer hadn't found what he was looking for in Grant's townhouse, he might come here.

A face, try to imagine a face for the killer, Quin. But right now, alone at night, the mere thought frightened her, and she finally capitulated to the fear and called Nikki, who suggested they go to a movie. They drove into Coconut Grove and saw *Kiss of the Spider Woman*, a strangely compelling story about the relationship that developed between two men in an Argentinian prison. She cried at the end, and it reminded her of how once Grant had told her she was a mush head. *What's a mush head?* she'd asked.

Someone who cries at the end of a movie or from reading an article about lost kittens or because some old person is crossing the street alone. That's a mush head.

"Am I a mush head, Nikki?" she asked when they were walking through the Grove to one of the bars. The rain had turned to a mist and felt good against her face.

"A *what*?" Nikki laughed.

"A mush head." As she explained, she thought about the way she'd carried the ants outside on a paper towel and realized the memory embarrassed her. *Mush head, for sure.*

"Oh, you mean a softie. Well, if so, then Grant could've been a little more that way."

The tone of her voice surprised Quin. She'd never really thought about it much before now, but she supposed Nikki had never cared for Grant. She said as much, and Nikki nodded. "He wasn't exactly the sort of person I could warm up to, Quin. I think he . . . well, that he had a mean streak. Sometimes he seemed to take a kind of perverse pleasure in other people's insecurities or unhappiness or whatever."

"Like when?"

"Oh, God, I don't know." An exasperated tone, completely unlike Nikki, Quin thought. "Let's talk about something else."

Their subsequent silence filled with music rolling from open doorways, cars splashing through puddles, laughter from couples passing them on the walk. Then thunder crackled overhead and the skies opened up again. They ducked into Richard's, a night spot with tables beneath an outside awning. They sat at the edge of the rain, music fluctuating with the rise and fall of voices, and the susurrous murmur of the wind. It was a place she and Nikki used to frequent in the past, in the days long before Grant and Steve, when Nikki's first marriage was falling apart, and after. For Quin, it brought back memories of a friendship that had seemed young, eager, and somehow closer.

Even yesterday, when Nikki had brought her cleaning lady to the townhouse, Quin had sensed the gulf between them that she did now. Perhaps it was nothing more than the natural progression of their lives into something new—for Quin a result of Grant's murder and for Nikki because of her impending marriage to Steve. But whatever the cause, she missed how things used to be, how one or the other could just pick up the phone and say, Let's go, and away from Miami they'd gone with Merlin and Demian, Nikki's cat, in tow.

"You're mad, aren't you?" Nikki said suddenly, then sipped from her glass and watched Quin over the rim.

"No." Quin helped herself to a potato skin stuffed with cheese and walnuts and realized she was hungry enough for a second dinner. Munchies just weren't going to fill the gaping hole in her stomach tonight. Was perpetual hunger the price of truth?

"Look, Quin, I know you loved the man. I know you're finding out a lot of stuff about him that's hurtful. But I honestly think that in the long run you're better off."

With him dead: that was the part she hadn't said aloud. "Then be specific."

"There were mostly small things, Quin. Like the time you two were over at the house and Demian leaped into Grant's lap and he threw him down on the floor. Threw him, for Christ's sake. That kind of meanness."

Quin had no memory of such an event. "Where was I?"

"In the room."

Another incident her brain had censored. "What else?"

Nikki sat back. "Like I said, mostly small things. But they add up over a period of time. All the times you waited for calls that never came; the rage he went into that night when you and I went out for a couple of drinks somewhere and he happened to come back from a trip and you weren't there."

Quin nodded. That memory was clear enough. She shoved it aside.

"Like the night I ran into him at the mall with a woman about half his age."

Nikki had lowered her eyes when she said this, and now twirled the ice in her drink with the tip of her finger. "You never told me that." God, why was it so hard to say? she wondered. And why was it so bloody easy to imagine?

"What was I going to do, call you up and say, Hey, Quin, guess who I saw?" Nikki shifted uncomfortably in her chair, dropped her head back, and gazed out into the damp courtyard beyond the awning. "Shit, Quin, I could just never find the right moment to tell you."

But if the situations had been reversed, Quin thought, wouldn't she have told Nikki? Maybe. She couldn't say for sure. It would depend. "Who was she? The girl, I mean?"

Nikki drew her finger around the rim of her glass until it hummed—an odd, high-pitched sound, alien. "I don't know. Some little twerp with big boobs in tight shorts and a haltar top. He saw me, too, and pretended he didn't." Then, anticipating Quin's next question, she added, "You were out of town on a case."

When Nikki moved forward in her chair, the tiny gold cross around her neck swung out, away from her body.

Quin looked at her. She was a striking woman, the sort men looked at twice and then once again just to make sure they'd seen what they thought they'd seen. Part of it was the way she dressed. As a color and fashion consultant, she was conscious of the small details, nuances, the miracle of color and fabrics and the lines of clothes. Everything about her always blended—from her jewelry to her bag and shoes. Her almost delicate bone structure was at once vulnerable and strong, innocent and wise, deceptive and sagacious. A face filled with dichotomies, mysteries, secrets. And yet now, in the lambent light from the candle in the center of the table, everything about her appeared distorted, as if Quin were gazing at her through the bottom of a glass.

Her nose seemed shorter, her forehead broader, her mouth fuller, excessive. And for a moment, the change frightened Quin. It was unreasonable, this fear, but it was as if she were seeing, for the first time, a side of Nikki she hadn't known existed: the residual bitterness of her failed marriage, the struggle to establish her own business, the alcoholic trap she'd fallen into briefly, and the men, a number of men, in whom she'd sought refuge before Steve.

"Grant was a bastard, Quin." She uttered it softly, coldly, and Quin knew Nikki wasn't telling her everything. But before she could ask, Nikki glanced at her watch. "We'd better go, Quin."

It's still early, Quin wanted to protest. *I don't want to be home by myself.* But Nikki was already rising, reaching for the bill, and Quin couldn't remember ever feeling so utterly alone.

10

YESTERDAY'S REMINDED ME of an aging matron with a divided life. It rose from the edge of the intracoastal canal, a glittering tribute to Fort Lauderdale, land of skin, sin, and secrets. Its bottom floor was a sprawling restaurant with numerous tucks and nooks and waterfront vistas. The second floor possessed a musky undercurrent, a pulse that throbbed along its twisting bar like an arhythmic heartbeat. My kind of place, for sure.

I arrived at the bewitching hour, prepared to sing the body electric, to slide into the dark, cruel underside of the city's nocturnal beat. My flesh tingled, my eyes roved, recording details: mirrored walls, the huge skylight beyond which the moon struggled from a bank of clouds, and the men. So many men. These were details which would breathe life into this novel. It would surpass *Black Bird* and my second book, which was hidden away in my closet and still needed work. Lots of it.

I squeezed through the crowd to the waist of the figure-eight bar. Someone bumped me from behind. It jarred loose something from the other night, from another bar. There had been a man, but I couldn't recall his face or his name. Well, it didn't matter. This was another bar, another night, and the other chapter had already been written.

I ordered my Dewar's, and within five minutes a man was standing there beside me, lighting his cigarette with a gold, monogrammed lighter. Money, panache: that was what characterized the crowd here.

"Jammed, isn't it," he commented.

Graying hair, older than I normally liked, probably married: I'd learned to assess men quickly. I usually kept away from the married ones; it was too easy to imagine myself in the wife's position, waiting for a call that never came. "Yeah, I had no idea so many people came here." My tone remained cool but pleasant, affable but not eager.

I got the impression he wanted to say something else, but that a sudden diffidence had seized him. I decided he might be recently divorced and was a bit unsure of himself. It softened me. I asked if he came here often. This seemed to bolster his courage, and for a few moments we chatted. Then the band in the other room started, gobbling up his voice.

I leaned close to him, noting the scents that trembled in the air around him: an after-shave lotion, smoke, a tinge of sweat. "What?" I said. "I didn't hear you."

His mouth formed an Oh, and, smiling, he leaned close to me. "Would you like to dance?"

"Are you good?"

He threw his head back, laughing. He had a nice laugh; I liked it. "Yeah, not bad, not bad."

In fact, he was better than good. His body flowed, it rocked, twisted, and later, on a slow number, after we'd had a drink together, it undulated against mine. Which was okay because by then I knew his name (Jake Wilford), what he did for a living (real estate broker), that he was, indeed, divorced and had two kids, that his passion was books (sci fi, in particular). I decided my protagonist would like him.

He asked what line of work I was in. That was just how he said it, too, *line of work,* as if it were a line of cosmetics or perfumes. I told him, and he threw up his hands. "God, how great."

We went downstairs where it was quieter and had several more drinks. We talked books, all sorts of books, and of course I said I would go home with him. I followed him south on U.S. 1. At a red light, I pulled alongside his car and pointed at the Bon Soir Motel with its huge blinking sign that said, WE HAVE CLOSED CIRCUIT TV AND WATERBEDS. "Let's try it," I called out. "I've always had a thing about waterbeds."

It was only partially true. Actually, I had never slept on a waterbed. But my character had. "For real?" he laughed.

"For real."

I waited in my car while he registered. My head ached something fierce; I took three aspirins, closed my eyes. The circuit breaker in my skull clicked. Bits and pieces of that other memory floated in: *A man named Tom who was rough with me, mean.* But I'd already written that chapter, hadn't I?

My eyes popped open. Jake approached, his step quick, light, bouncy. He leaned into the window. "This is crazy." His voice was quiet, breathless. "I feel like a teenager, doing it for the first time or something."

A perfect line: I would include it.

In fact, I could already see this scene in my mind: my character and Jake, walking through the outside corridor to their room, past the peeling walls, beneath naked bulbs where moths fluttered frantically. I could even hear my character thinking about the spidery feel of Jake's hand.

The room was nothing great, but the waterbed was comfortable. It rippled, whispered, sighed, it moved as we moved. Jake switched on the TV, and for a while we sat up against the plump pillows, watching some stupid soft-porn film that had us both laughing until our ribs ached. Now and then he would kiss me tenderly, and later he was gentle with me and touched my body as though it were made of silk. He told me I tasted of chocolate.

Chocolate.

Another perfect line. In the book, I would have the man sample my protagonist's fingers, her mouth and eyes and the backs of her knees, tasting her as though she were a smorgasbord of Swiss chocolate.

When I fell asleep, I dreamed of Billy when he was straddling me, when his friends pinned my arms down. I could smell the dirt and the dying leaves, the cold thrust of autumn, I could feel their fingers digging into my wrists as I screamed and screamed. Then the dream shifted slightly and Billy became Grant and he was laughing at me as I raised the gun, as I aimed, as I pulled the trigger. He didn't stumble back, he didn't fall, he just kept on coming, grinning as his shirt turned bloody. I awakened in a cold sweat, heart pounding, head hurting so much I could barely catch my breath.

I was in . . . *Easy, now, don't panic* . . . a motel. Right.

The man was asleep on his side, his back to me. In the flickering light from the TV, he reminded me of a dolphin, slick and smooth. I began to cry, softly, panic crawling along my sticky tongue. I got out of bed, and the water in it gurgled. I reached for my purse, opened it, took two more aspirin, then got up and slipped on my clothes. Home, I just wanted to go home, where everything was known, familiar, where my brain didn't short-circuit and topple helplessly into fugues.

"Kara?"

"I've got to go."

"*Go*? Now? Where're you going?"

His voice ground my nerves, my fingers flexed, curled into tight fists. But then I glanced over at him, at his beautiful salt-and-pepper hair, his supplicating eyes, and my heart stung with remorse. "I'm going home."

"Now?"

Why was he asking me so many questions?

"Yes. Now. I'm going home. I have to go." I had things to do, a chapter to write. I slid on my sandals, ran a comb through my hair. "Thanks."

"Wait. Hold on." He leaped out of bed. Something in the way he walked frightened me.

"Don't hurt me, please don't hurt me," I whimpered.

"Hurt you? I'm not going to hurt you. I just want you to stay the night. I mean, I don't even have your phone number. I'd like to see you again."

No. There was rarely a repeat performance. It just didn't fit into the book. The exception was Grant, of course, but that was different, Grant wasn't in this book, Grant was a mistake and had nothing to do with my research, not really. "I can't," I said. But his spidery hand reached for mine, the skin damp, cool. I yanked my arm away. "I have to go. Really."

Let me go, Billy, I mean it, let me go.

The pain in my head spread like a brushfire, tightening the skin at my skull, my eyes. He gripped me by the shoulders, tried to kiss me, his breath smelled bad. I'd thought he was such a nice man, a gentleman.

"Please. Let me go, just get away."

But he wouldn't, so I pushed him hard, and he grunted as he fell back, hands clutching his chest, the handle of the knife protruding between his fingers. *When? How?* I had no memory of touching the knife, holding it, no memory at all.

Out of control: this was what had happened the other night with the tennis pro who always did it with his socks on. O-U-T O-F C-O-N-T-R-O-L. The separate letters hurtled between us as blood bubbled in the corner of his mouth, as he hissed, "Jesus, Jesus, what . . ."

He somehow managed to pull the knife out and stumbled toward the phone. "Oh no, no, you can't. Please, you just can't. I'm sorry." I rushed toward him, pounded his back with my fists, kicked him in the small of his back. Weakened by loss of blood, he went down with a shout dying on his lips, and I had to stab him again, I had to, he'd left me no choice.

The knife made an ugly, sucking sound as the blade pulled free. My head hammered, the muse was loose, frantic, shouting at me, and I couldn't remember what all I'd touched in the room.

I rushed into the bathroom, whipped a towel from the rack, cleaned the counter, faucet, doorknob, lock, wiped the blood from the knife. *What happens when you die, Mama?*

A blessing, he needed a blessing.

For an instant, as I approached him, I thought of his soul or spirit or whatever *watching me.* I touched my knuckle to the blood and made the sign of the cross on his forehead. *The dead must always be blessed,* Mama had said when Daddy passed away.

So I said the words, then kissed my knuckle and murmured, "Amen." Everything in the room swirled, his astonished face blurred. *This is only a book. Not real. Never real.*

Right?

I jumped up, a ball of desperation clinging like old gum to the roof of my mouth. Wrong, everything seemed wrong, misplaced. I backed slowly to the door, covered my hand with the edge of the curtain as I unlocked it and slipped outside.

When I was in the car, my tongue slid along my lower lip, dampening it. I realized I'd gotten a spot of his blood on my mouth. I marveled at how salty it tasted.

11

1.

MONDAY MORNING WHEN McCleary was running, he passed a woman out walking her pit bull. The dog growled and yanked on its leash as he loped by. Its ugly features vanished into a mouth that was all sharp teeth. He shuddered, thinking of a kid several years ago who'd lost most of his face in a pit bull attack. A moment later, the woman shouted, "Bingo, come back here!" And when McCleary glanced around, he saw the dog tearing toward him, those teeth snapping at the hot air, its leash slapping the sidewalk.

He tucked in his arms and flew, damning himself for every cigarette he'd smoked, every drink he'd swallowed. He scrambled up a tree, and it didn't occur to him until he was in it that he hadn't climbed a tree since he was ten years old. He clung to the thick trunk, peering down at the dog that leaped and barked on the walk beneath him, wondering why the cosmos seemed to be conspiring against him. This didn't portend well for the week ahead, he decided. And because deep down he believed in portents, he wasn't really surprised when he received a call an hour later at work from a homicide detective in Lauderdale.

As Lieutenant Ron Valencia spoke, McCleary turned toward the bow of his private little ship and stared at the sagging gray sky, his irascible mood worsening. The pit bull, and now another knifing. What else could possibly go wrong today?

Plenty. It was just a few minutes past eight.

This was how homicide aged him, he decided, walking back over to his desk and sinking into his chair. His emotions were like bits of string wound up inside some kid's yo-yo. When the kid flung the yo-yo out with a flick of his wrist, the strings tangled, the motion yanked to a halt, the whole process broke down.

He agreed to meet with Valencia after his appointment at Wishod Pharmaceuticals in Lauderdale. They hung up, and McCleary started to pace, following the worn track in the carpet. Then he glanced at his list of things to do. He had lists for everything, and today a call to Treena Esposito's principal was at the top.

Mr. Plymouth, principal at South Kendall High School, confirmed that Treena Esposito had attended the faculty meeting the night of the twenty-first. But, he added, she'd left early, between eight and eight-thirty. Her husband had evidently arrived home unexpectedly from a business trip, didn't have his key, and she had to let him in.

"Did she come back to the faculty meeting?"

"Yes, about an hour later." Plymouth lowered his voice. "I have to add, Detective McCleary, that it's absolutely preposterous to even speculate that Treena killed her ex-husband."

Right, McCleary thought, then thanked Plymouth for his time and hung up before he could offer any more opinions. He was sick of people's opinions, their dogs, and sick of lies, all the lies— Robin's, green-eyed Treena's, Grant Bell's. And yeah, come to think of it, maybe he was even sick of homicide.

2.

Thunder grumbled like a discontented God as Quin left her car in the lot and walked across the street to Denny's to meet McCleary and Rusty Johnson. The weather seemed appropriate somehow, as though her cranky mood had rolled out into the world, infecting it.

She'd spent most of Sunday looking through Grant's

98

notes and files, searching for something on greenfire. She'd found nothing. In the books on the Amazon she'd checked out of the library, she'd run across the pink dolphin story, but little else that was useful. She was beginning to think that maybe she was wrong about greenfire being part of an Amazon folktale.

As she entered Denny's, she saw Rusty. He flashed one of his Cheshire cat grins as she sat down. "I ordered us coffee, lady." Then he leaned toward her and she had the feeling that at any minute he was going to leap onto the table and dance. He was the only person Quin knew who seemed to vibrate, even at rest, as though his energy were too great to contain. "Now what is going on?"

"I've got something I was hoping you could translate for me."

"If it'll keep me away from fat man this ugly Monday morning, of course."

She laughed.

Rusty Johnson was part Cuban, on his mother's side, and his fluent Spanish was one of the reasons Quin and Trevor had hired him. Quin passed Rusty the letter from Felix Mendez. He glanced at the postmark. "Iquitos, huh. That's in northern Peru. I may never have been outa the country, Quin, but I knows my geo, yes sir. Okay, let's see here. How about if I just read it aloud as I go along.

Dear Grant,

I was relieved to hear you got back to the States safely and pleased that you have already found a buyer. I will pass the word on to Jason. As you know, the rainy season never really arrived this year, and because of it, the river has been treacherously low. Hopefully, by the time you get back here on July 4, we will have had some rain and can check out the oxbow. Imagine, my friend, what will we do with ten or twelve million? I will meet you as planned on the 4th of July in Iquitos.

Last night, we toasted you—and greenfire.
Vaya con Dios.

Your friend,
Felix Mendez

"That's what it says? Ten to twelve million?"

Rusty nodded.

"Well," she said. "Well." She could see the zeros, but the concept of ten to twelve million dollars was like trying to puzzle through a problem in advanced calculus.

"Well? That's all you got to say, lady? What was he doing, smuggling coke?"

"I don't know."

"What's greenfire?"

"I don't know that, either."

Rusty folded the letter in half, then folded it again. He ran his fingertips along the crease several times. "Who's the Felix guy?"

"Don't know." Questions without answers were becoming a way of life.

"You need help, lady. And today I got time, plenty of it. I just wrapped up that Toyota case on Friday and did me some celebratin', and now I'm rarin' to go."

"Trevor won't like it."

"So what. Start from the beginning."

So she did. And as she was talking, Mike McCleary walked in. He hesitated in the doorway, hands in his pockets as he glanced around. Outlined there, the muted light behind him, she noticed a hard leanness to his body that had escaped her before. He nudged his sunglasses back onto his head and scratched once at his mustache. His hands vanished into his pockets again. He seemed self-conscious, which didn't fit her image of him. But it certainly made him seem more human, more approachable. Quin waved and he saw them, smiled—a nice smile, she noted—and hurried over.

"Forsythe said I'd find you here. Goofing off, I think that's the expression he used." He scooted in beside her and Quin introduced him to Rusty.

"The lady needs help, my man," said Rusty.

"She's not the only one." The waitress came over, and McCleary and Quin ordered breakfast. As usual, she was starving and ordered bacon and eggs with whole-wheat toast and a side order of fruit and pancakes.

"You always eat like that?" McCleary exclaimed.

"You ain't seen nothing, my friend," Rusty laughed. "Quin packs away food like no other woman alive, I'm telling you. She's got this metabolism, see, that burns calories before they're even in her mouth. She should weigh a minimum of three hundred.''

McCleary looked at her as though he'd never really seen her before. It made her skin tingle. "It got worse when I quit smoking," she said, feeling compelled to explain.

"Ha. You were always this bad, even before you quit smoking.''

"You're just making me hungrier, talking about food. Let's discuss something else.''

"Okay, how's this for starters on a Monday morning,'' said McCleary. He held up his hand, the fingers splayed. He tapped his index finger. "This is the pit bull that chased me at six-thirty this morning.'' He touched the next finger. "This is a phone call I got from a homicide detective in Broward, informing me the knife lady seems to have struck again. And this''—he wiggled the fourth finger—''is just for a lousy weekend.''

"That last part, my man, sounds like lady troubles,'' remarked Rusty.

McCleary gave a noncommittal grunt and related the story of the pit bull. Quin was pleasantly surprised that McCleary apparently had a gift for painting pictures with words. She could almost see him perched in the tree as the pit bull had conniptions below. She wondered, suddenly, if there *was* a woman, and puzzled over what type of woman McCleary would be involved with.

After they'd eaten, Quin brought out Felix Mendez's letter. Rusty started to translate it for McCleary, but he shook his head. "It's okay, I can read it.''

"You speak Spanish?'' Quin asked, wondering why it should surprise her.

"During the influx of Cubans from the Mariel boatlift, I realized I was probably going to regret it someday if I didn't learn it, so I took an eight-week leave of absence and went to South America. When you have to ask where the bathroom is often enough, believe me, you learn it.''

He perused the letter, then Quin told him about her conversation with Paul Holmes.

"You think Holmes lent Grant money?" McCleary asked.

"It's a good possibility. I just don't trust him. I never have."

McCleary's smoky eyes wrinkled with mirth. "Well, your judgment in people seems to be improving. Personally, I've always thought the man was a crook."

"Asshole, that's the way I hear it," Rusty interjected. "Good buddy of mine works over in the traffic division at the courthouse and he says the dude thinks he's a ladies' man, always struttin' his stuff, you know."

"What stuff?" Quin mumbled, and the two men laughed.

It was drizzling when they left at 9:45. They darted across the street and under the back awning of the firm. McCleary suggested they get together that night to read through Grant's notes and peruse his slides for possible leads. Quin said she'd already done that.

"But we haven't," Rusty pointed out. "And we might pick up something you overlooked."

"Yeah, you might at that."

McCleary smiled. "She would've bitten my head off if I'd said that, Rusty."

"Not true, McCleary." The way he looked at her made her laugh. "Okay, okay, it's true."

He threw out his arms as if imploring the sky. "I can't believe it. She actually admitted I was right."

"He's okay, Quin," Rusty remarked as McCleary honked and pulled out into the street in his RX7.

"Yeah, he is," she said, and realized she meant it.

2.

McCleary had some time to kill before his appointment at Wishod. He went back to the office and dialed Holmes's office number. The secretary informed him that Mr. Holmes wasn't in at the moment. "Maybe you can help me," McCleary said, "I'm calling from Sun Bank. Mr. Holmes asked me to let him know when his wire had cleared and I—"

"Uh, Mr. Holmes banks at Barnett. You must have the wrong Holmes."

McCleary smiled, thanked her, and hung up. Maybe this wasn't going to be such a bad day, after all, he decided. He drove over to the Barnett Bank near the courthouse and headed straight to Adrian Rozelli's desk. Her plump face became a caricature when she winced.

"Oh-oh. Mike McCleary. And on a Monday, no less."

"What kind of hello is that, Roz?"

She laughed; her dark eyes floated in her fat cheeks like tiny black beads. "Have a seat, Mike. What's it this time?" she whispered. "Colombians on the rampage? A jealous husband? A body in a trunk?"

Adrian Rozelli: consumer of mysteries, romances, the soaps. She'd been working at Barnett as long as McCleary could remember, and he'd been banking here nearly a decade, since leaving the Syracuse, New York, police department. In fact, Roz had been a bank officer then, and now she was second VP in charge of operations, whatever that meant, and one of the better contacts he'd developed over the years. Most everyone from the police department and the courthouse banked here. How convenient that Paul Holmes did, too.

"What we've got, Roz, is maybe ten to twelve million dollars at stake, a man dead from a .45 in the chest, possible connections with a pharmaceutical company and the DA's office."

"Too many possibles, Mike."

"I know. That's the problem." He sat back.

"What pharmaceutical company?"

"Wishod."

She shook her head. "Never heard of them. Who in the DA's office?"

"Paul Holmes."

She made a clucking sound with her tongue against her teeth. "You may lose your balls, Mike."

"Thanks."

"Is this about that photographer? The thing that was in the paper the other day?"

"The same."

"Something about the Amazon, right?"

"Some memory you've got."

She sniffled at his implication that she scoured the

obits. "I just read the paper thoroughly. So what do you want to know?"

He told her.

She turned to the computer monitor at her desk, her plump fingers playing the keyboard like a piano. "You have any idea when?"

"No. Wait. Let me think." He tried to remember what Quin had said. "Check back up to a year ago."

"Okay." It took her a while, but she finally tapped the screen, said, "Good instincts you've got, Mike. Here it is."

"How much?"

"Three checks to Grant Bell for five big ones each, hon."

McCleary grinned.

"Maybe he loaned the man money for a car or something," she suggested.

"Maybe." But the maybe would've been a lot stronger if the person in question had been anyone except Holmes. He knocked his knuckles once against her desk. "Thanks again, Roz. I'll be in touch."

She shook her finger at him. "I want to know how *this* one turns out, Mike."

"That's a promise."

He cruised over to the courthouse, intending to make an appointment with Holmes's secretary, but when he walked into the front hall, there was the big man himself, leaning over the drinking fountain. Just seeing him raised McCleary's blood pressure. He was not the sort of man who forgave and forgot, especially not when two of his arrests were involved. And for the last three years, Paul Holmes had been the proverbial thorn in his side.

"Morning, Mr. Holmes."

He looked up, dabbed at his mouth with a monogrammed handkerchief. McCleary saw uncertainty crouched in the back of the man's eyes, as though he'd been expecting this visit, but not this morning. Then his smile snapped into place and he held out his hand. "Mike McCleary. Good to see you."

My ass. "You have a few minutes?"

"A few," he said, still smiling. "Let's sit in the cafeteria."

They settled at a table near the window with cups of coffee—McCleary's fourth for the morning—and Holmes, with typical aplomb, got right to the point. "I want to give you as much help as I can on this Grant Bell murder, Mike. He was a friend of mine."

Mike. No one could ever accuse Paul Holmes of not being smooth. "Good. So where were you the night of June twenty-first?"

Holmes sat back, still smiling, and shook his head. "So I'm a suspect because I knew the man?"

"Who said anything about suspect?"

Holmes ran a hand over his hair, stirred cream into his coffee. "Okay, let's see. The evening of the twenty-first I was in court until five-thirty, Mike, yeah, I remember because it was the first day of summer. Then I went to Friday's for a drink and then I went home and yes, my wife will attest to that and so will our maid."

"What was this project Grant Bell needed investors for?"

"So Quin *is* working with you."

"Considering that she lived with the man, I don't think it should come as any big surprise that she's interested in the case."

"Look, Grant never told me what the project was about. I told Quin that and I'm telling you the same, McCleary. The man was a friend of mine, yes. But not such a great friend that I'd lend him money."

He was so smooth McCleary could've puked. "Then how come you paid him a total of fifteen thousand over the last year?"

Holmes reminded McCleary of an actor groveling for forgotten lines, surprised they'd slipped away from him, then recouping smoothly, but not quickly enough. McCleary now had the upper hand. But before Holmes could explain, if indeed that's what he intended to do, a familiar voice behind McCleary said, "Mind if I join you?"

It was Robin.

And the solicitous expression on Holmes's face when he looked at her rubbed McCleary wrong. Very wrong.

Something odd seemed to happen in the air too. It rippled with an undercurrent, as if someone had just told a joke and McCleary had missed the punch line.

"Did the seminar break for a while?" Holmes asked.

"Yeah. I realize this guy works for you, but he's *boooring,* Paul."

Paul? Since when did Robin start calling Holmes *Paul*?

"The class is going to mutiny before the day's over." She glanced from Holmes to McCleary. "How come I feel like I'm interrupting something?"

"You're not," McCleary leaped in. "I was just asking Paul why he'd made payments to Grant Bell that totaled some fifteen thousand." Holmes opened his mouth to protest. "It's okay. Robin knows the particulars on this case."

"Not *those* particulars, I didn't." She rested her chin in the palm of her hand as she gazed at Holmes. The undercurrent quivered again. "Any explanations, Paul?"

The usually composed DA looked like a kid who was about to have a tantrum. He stabbed the tabletop with his finger. "Hey, guys, you forget I'm an attorney. I know the law. Your bullshit tactics don't intimidate me. If I don't feel like answering your questions, I won't. Unless you've got a warrant, McCleary."

"Nope."

"Yeah, that's what I figured." He pushed away from the table. "Now, if you'll excuse me," he barked, and marched off.

"Testy, testy," McCleary laughed.

Robin rolled her lower lip against her teeth. "Fifteen thousand? How'd you find that out, Mac?"

"What difference does it make." The tension in the air bled away for a moment, but returned when he realized Robin was waiting for him to refer to Saturday night. But for once he had nothing to say.

"You're still annoyed with me, aren't you?"

Her long dark lashes thicketed her eyes, which were downcast. "I don't think 'annoyed' is what I was, Robin."

"Oh."

Oh? What kind of response is that?

"So how was your Sunday?" he asked.

"Okay."

Better than his, probably. Aw hell. They could sit here all day, feinting like boxers, his mind echoing, *Who, Robin? Who is he?* What was the point. "I've got to get going."

"I'll walk out with you."

He shrugged. *Suit yourself.* She walked with him to the front door, and McCleary finally said, "I thought you had to go back to the seminar."

"Screw the class. I'm coming with you. Izzo can't expect you to work on everything by yourself."

"Forget it, Robin. I appreciate the thought, but I'm doing just fine."

Her eyes searched his as her body stiffened and seemed to take root in the floor. "You want to get together tonight, Mac? When you get off?"

"Can't. I've got a commitment." How much better that sounded than "I'm working late." It was the sort of answer she might have given him.

She realized it and smiled thinly. "Okay."

"Gotta run, Robin."

He left her standing there in the hall, gazing after him. It felt good to come out on top for once. No. It felt great, the sort of goddamned great that made him want to leap into the air and click his heels like a leprechaun.

12

1.

GINGER'S JEWELERS WAS located on Las Olas Boulevard, Lauderdale's Worth Avenue, where everything was exclusive and overpriced. Quin felt compelled to whisper when she and Rusty walked in; it was that sort of place. The salmon-colored carpet was thick, the glass cases sparkled, soft music drifted through the sweet air. The sales people were well-dressed and smiled, smiled, smiled.

They paused at one of the cases and peered through the glass at the array of jewelry. Price tags, of course, were discreetly tucked out of sight, as if to say that if you were concerned about prices, you shouldn't be in here. The surfeit of gems was impressive, winking against black velvet like multicolored stars in an August sky.

"Morning, may I help you?" asked a smiling young woman in a crisp white suit.

"We'd like to see Ginger Hale," Rusty said.

"Ms. Hale is on the phone at the moment." *Smile, smile.*

"We'll wait."

"Who can I say would like to speak to her?" *Still smiling.*

"Private investigators," Rusty replied.

Now the polite smile strained a bit. "Do you have names?"

"We'll give them to Ms. Hale, if you don't mind," Rusty replied, his smile matching hers.

"I'll tell her."

A few minutes later, the woman returned and informed them that Ms. Hale couldn't see them right now, but suggested they call for an appointment. "I'm sorry, that won't do," Rusty said.

"Excuse me?" said the woman.

Rusty rocked forward on the balls of his feet and leaned across the counter toward the woman. "Tell her that this concerns Grant Bell, and better that she sees us than the po-lice. Tell her that, if you please."

Her hesitation was the sort, Quin thought, that indicated Ms. Ginger Hale had probably said, *Get rid of them.* "Okay. I'll tell her."

"I already don't like her," Quin whispered.

A few mintues later, they were in Ginger Hale's office. The room was neat, orderly, and small, with posters of gems covering the walls: rubies like glistening, bloody suns, sapphires as blue as the Mediterranean, emeralds, diamonds, each of them caught at a different angle. The photograph on the wall calendar was of a pearl the size of a child's fist. It seemed to be simply floating in the bruised blue of space like a planet. A ceramic dolphin that looked achingly familiar, Quin thought, was at the edge of the desk with shoots of ivy billowing from the creature's blowhole.

"Ah'm sorry to keep you waiting," said Ginger Hale as she swept into the room, trailing perfume. She moved with quick, short steps, the gold bracelets on her arms dancing together, creating a sound like shattering glass. She was short, petite, with long, straight hair the color of sand, which she wore pulled back with barrettes. She reminded Quin of a Barbie doll. She didn't seem Grant's type. But then, Quin was no longer sure what Grant's type had been. Or if there had even been a type.

Although she was rather ordinary looking, there was certainly nothing ordinary about her jewelry. Besides the bracelets, she wore a deep green emerald ring set in a double tiered band of gold. From her gold necklace hung a delicate gold heart with an emerald in the center. Her earrings matched. On her other hand was a tiny star sapphire ring. In fact, she wore so much stuff that it was a wonder she could move beneath the weight.

Rusty introduced himself and referred to Quin as Sally Jacobs. "Pleased to meet y'all." She had a thick Southern drawl that for Quin became a scent: the sickeningly sweet fragrance of magnolia blossoms. "Would y'all like coffee? A soft drink? Anything to drink?" she asked.

"No, thanks. We'd just like to ask you a few questions," Quin replied.

"About Grant." Her tone became appropriately bereaved. "Ah read 'bout it in the paper. A terrible thing, absolutely horrible. Makes me want to move out of South Florida, ah can tell you that." She sat down, crossing her legs demurely at the knees, tugging at the hem of her skirt. "What can ah do to help y'all, anyway?"

"Do you have any idea what Mr. Bell was doing in the Amazon?" Quin asked, taking a soft and easy tack with Miss Magnolia Blossom.

"Promotional photography, that was mah understanding. For some big company that was doing research with plants down there."

"How well did you know him?" Rusty asked.

"We'd been good friends for about three years."

"How good?"

She took umbrage at the question, because when she spoke again, her voice was punctuated with indignity. "Well, we dated from time to time, if that's what you're asking. It was sort of serious for a while, then he started traveling more and ah got a little tired waitin' around, if you know what ah mean."

"When was the last time you saw him?" Quin asked.

"Oh, about a month ago, ah guess it was. We met at Marina Bay for a few drinks, then went out to dinner."

"And then back to his place," Quin blurted, thinking of the size 3 panties, and wondering where *she* had been that night.

Ginger's eyes strolled toward Quin, as if considering her for the first time. There was nothing shy in her voice when she said, "Yes, and then back to his place."

She reached for the Styrofoam Cup on her desk. Her nails, painted the color of raspberries, were so long they curled over the tips of her fingers like a witch's. Her

110

gold bracelets danced together again. The emerald on her finger caught the glare of the overhead light, fracturing it.

"But you can be sure ah was jus' one of *several* women he saw," she added quietly. "He was the sort of man you could love real easily. But if you did, it was like a . . . a curse. So you were better off jus' taking the relationship for what it was worth and falling in love elsewhere."

As she spoke, Quin thought of the women's clothes she'd found in Grant's closet, the note from the Dutch woman about the romantic cruise on the Amazon, and that kid, Pete Gilbert, saying, *Were you one of his girlfriends?* How many secrets had there been? Was every clue going to lead to another stratum of his dual life? It was like peeling away layers of an onion. Next week or next month she would reach the inner core, but suppose that even the core had layers?

"In the beginning," Ms. Magnolia added, "that was a tough thing for me to understand."

Yeah, you look like you suffered. "Did you know he was living with someone?"

"No. No, ah didn't. But ah can't say that ah'm s'prised. He had that . . . charisma, I guess, about him that women love."

"Ever heard of something called greenfire?" Quin asked.

The effect the word had on Ms. Magnolia was almost comical. Her face puckered at the seams, her mouth flattened out in a pale line, and she was suddenly very busy stirring her coffee, tugging at her hem, flicking bits of lint from her blouse. When she spoke, her voice momentarily lost its sweet Southern drawl. "No, no, I can't say that I have." She stood then, all five feet of her. "You're going to have to excuse me. Ah'm due at a sales meeting in about two minutes. If y'all would like to meet again, just give me a call, hmm?"

Her discomfort was so obvious that Quin felt like seizing her by those thin little shoulders and wagging her note to Grant in her face. *Ever seen this note, honey? Your name is Ginger, isn't it?*

"We'll do that," Rusty replied. He took Quin's arm. "Let's have a look at the gems, sweet lady."

Ms. Magnolia followed them to the doorway. "By the way, ah didn't think Grant had any family. Who hired you?"

"Someone who's interested in the twelve million," Rusty said quickly. "We'll be in touch, Ms. Hale."

2.

Paul Holmes and Bob Izzo sat outside by the pool in the condominium complex where the chief of police lived with his wife and daughter. Izzo's muscular chest was pink from sunburn, his nose glowed red as a radish, his thinning hair was still damp from swimming. "I always try to get in a four-mile swim in the pool and then a heavy workout in the gym every morning," he explained, as a waiter brought their drinks.

Fruit juice, Holmes thought distastefully.

"They've proven that swimming is the most efficient all-around exercise," Izzo continued.

"Perish the thought," Holmes drolled.

"Oh, you should try some sort of exercise, Paul, if only to ward off heart attack country."

Holmes rested his hand on the folder beside him. Izzo was going to have a lot more to worry about than heart attacks, he thought. "There's something I'd like to talk to you about, Bob."

"What's that."

"The Bell homicide."

"Right. McCleary's case. What about it?"

Holmes opened the folder. "I want the investigation dropped."

Izzo bent his straw at the top and sucked at it noisily. "It's a clear-cut homicide, Paul. It can't be dropped. Now what's this all about?"

He removed the photographs from the folder and passed them to Izzo. "I have copies of these, naturally, but I think you'll be interested in looking through them before you make your final decision."

Frowning, Izzo looked at the photos, saying nothing, color seeming to spill from his face. There were six photographs of the captain with a young man, the two of them in various lewd positions. They'd been taken in an apartment about two hundred miles up the coast, far enough away so that Izzo could indulge in anonymity. They'd been worth every penny Holmes had paid for them.

Izzo turned the stack of photos over. His eyes were like granite. "You're a fuck, Paul." His voice was quiet, even, and shot through with hatred.

The tone, of course, was one Holmes had grown accustomed to over the years. A man did not get to be DA without stepping on a few toes, especially a man who had designs on the governor's mansion. Or Congress. Or maybe the Senate. He folded his hands on the table. He had nothing against Izzo personally and said as much. "But I want the investigation dropped. You've got twenty-four hours."

"Just how the hell do you expect me to do that?" he hissed.

"For starters, you can take McCleary off the case."

Izzo's wide blue eyes skewed scornfully. "You don't seem to understand the logistics, Paul. There's more involved to killing an investigation than just taking an officer off the goddamned case. Especially McCleary, for Christ's sake. He's head of the homicide division."

"I don't care how you do it, just do it."

Izzo's gaze didn't flinch. "You killed him, didn't you. You killed that sucker Bell."

"No, I didn't kill him. But that asshole McCleary is going to twist certain facts and try to pin this on me. I've got too much to lose." He paused. "Just like you."

Izzo shook his head and murmured, "Jesus." He folded the photos in half, ran his fingertip along the crease until it squeaked, folded them again, then ripped them in two. "I could have you arrested for attempted extortion, Holmes."

"But you won't. Your wife and daughter would have copies of these before the warrant was issued, and your career in the department, friend, would be shit, despite gay liberation and all the rest of it. Think about *that*."

For a long moment, Izzo didn't move. He just continued to stare at his hands, resting on the torn photographs. Big hands, Holmes thought absently, muscular, the kind of hands that could pulverize a man's Adam's apple.

"All right." His voice was acquiescent, defeated. "I can't do everything at once without arousing suspicion, so I'll start with McCleary. I'll call you after I've spoken to him." He lifted his gaze then. "How do I know you won't release these?"

"You have my word."

"Your *word*?" Izzo threw his head back and laughed. "Oh, man. Your fucking word. Wonderful."

"It's the best I can do."

When he got up to leave, Izzo was still sitting at the table, the corners of the torn photos rusting in the breeze.

13

1.

WISHOD PHARMACEUTICALS WAS a privately owned company whose products included over-the-counter remedies for things like headaches and upset stomachs, diarrhea and constipation, pulled muscles and sprained ankles. In short, McCleary thought, Wishod dealt with the aches and pains of being human. It also manufactured more esoteric products like blood coagulants, a certain type of suture used in surgery, a host of downers and uppers, painkillers and antibiotics. Although he was disinclined to believe anything Paul Holmes said, he wondered if it was true that Wishod had paid off a group of independent researchers, and if so, what kind of drug was involved.

McCleary stood in front of a tremendous wall map with little red flags marking Wishod's other offices and distributors. Besides the home office in Fort Lauderdale, there were five other branches in the U.S. and distributors in fifteen foreign countries, including Brazil and Peru. Not bad for a company started only twenty-five years ago by a man who was now said to be as reclusive as Howard Hughes.

"Detective McCleary?"

He looked around. "Hi."

"I apologize for making you wait like this. Mondays around here are never good."

Everything about Killington was big. He stood well over six feet, his hand nearly dwarfed McCleary's when he shook it, his voice seemed to boom. One article McCleary had read pegged Killington's age at forty-five, but he looked ten years younger. Good genes or good living or both, McCleary thought with a touch of envy. But whatever his age, he was indeed Wishod's visionary, just as Quin had said. Killington was the entrepreneur who had expanded the company's holdings to radio and TV stations, land, banks and also the man who had conceived the Amazon research project. And for an instant, McCleary felt small and inadequate in his presence.

"I just heard about Grant's death last night. I imagine you've got a lot of questions. I sure do."

McCleary asked about Wishod's research in the Amazon, and Killington told him basically the same thing everyone else had, but in more detail. "The thrust of our Amazon project is to test as many plants as we can for pharmaceutical use and set aside those that show promise. Both Brazil and Peru have much less stringent regulations for experimentation than the FDA imposes, so we'll be trying out certain drug derivatives on the local populace."

"What kind of derivatives?"

"We've found one type of herb which may be effective in halting the progress of leprosy, which is still a problem in certain areas in South America. Another looks promising for the treatment of schistosomiasis, a disease caused by the larva of the schistosoma flatworm that lives in freshwater rivers in many Third World countries."

"So you're concentrating mainly on diseases found outside the U.S.?"

"No. We're looking for anything that can be of possible benefit. See, one reason Grant was so valuable to us was his ability to mingle with local people. He would talk to them about their myths, their folklore, question them about herbs indigenous to the region, he'd even visit village shamans." Killington's smile reminded McCleary of Robin's—so quick, so radiant, it dispelled dark clouds, gloom. "He was extraordinary in that respect. I admit I was one of the first to scoff when he

116

started following leads he'd gotten from some of the folklore. But when those leads resulted in the harvest of a native plant we're testing now with leprosy, I stopped scoffing mighty quick.''

"Does the word 'Greenfire' mean anything to you?"

"Greenfire." He was sitting on the couch beneath the window, and now his long arms rested along the back. Everything about him was open, but pensive. "No, I don't think so." Then he snapped his fingers. "Wait a minute. *Fuego verde*. Sure. I remember. It's one of those folktales.''

Bingo. "About what?"

"Well, let's see. My memory's a bit rusty when it comes to this stuff." His brows furrowed. "If I remember correctly, the legend says that the El Dorado Pizarro was searching for wasn't a city of gold, but of emeralds." He paused. "I think there was supposed to have been a tribe of Indians who smuggled huge quantities of emeralds out of Colombia and hid them somewhere in the jungles of Peru. Part of the legend is that this tribe supposedly possessed the secret of immortality.''

"How were they supposed to gain immortality?"

"Good question. I don't know.''

"So then this greenfire myth was something Grant pursued.''

"No, not really. It was just one of the myths he collected and passed on to our men at the research site. Besides, we're a pharmaceutical company, not gem hunters.'' He flashed his brilliant smile again.

"Exactly where was Bell doing work for you?" McCleary asked.

Killington got up and walked over to the wall map. He pointed at Belem in northeastern Brazil on the Atlantic coast. "Here's the mouth of the Amazon." McCleary followed Killington's finger west along the Amazon. "Here's Manaus, a thousand miles upstream." It was marked with a tiny red flag. "That was one area. Then there's Leticia, Colombia, and three hundred and fifty miles farther, Iquitos, Peru. Those three sites.''

McCleary nodded and Killington stepped away from the map. For a few moments, he spoke loquaciously about Grant, the tragedy of his death, the personal and professional loss he felt. He said all the right things and he seemed sincere, but McCleary wondered why he felt that Killington was holding back.

But at least the man had told him something about greenfire and that was more than McCleary had been able to find out elsewhere.

2.

Trevor waddled into Quin's office and, without saying a word, set his Bible in front of her. She looked at it, squashing the impulse to laugh, and then glanced up at him.

"What's this for, Trevor?"

"You look like you could use a few words from the Good Book, Quin."

She pushed it back across the desk toward him. "Thanks, but I wouldn't even know where to begin to look."

"Oh, that's easy." He picked up the book and began paging through it, his expression earnest and somehow pathetic.

"Trevor, it really isn't necessary."

"It might be when you hear what I've got to tell you, Quin."

"It couldn't be any worse than anything else I've found out today," she replied, thinking of Ginger Hale and the size 3 panties.

"We're losing money."

It was the last thing she ever expected Trevor to say. She thought he was joking and burst out laughing. "What're you talking about, Trevor?"

"God's testing me."

"No, that's not what I mean. How the hell can we be losing money?"

"IBM decided they don't want the land."

"So? Why should that mean we're losing money?"

"Well, I also made some unwise investments."

"What kind of unwise investments?"

"I'm not sure. The accountant's coming over this afternoon and we're going to review the books."

"Then sell some of our property."

"I'm going to, starting with the two empty duplexes."
He was thumbing quickly through the Bible now, perspiration beading thinly across his upper lip. " 'And though I shall walk through the valley of the shadow of death—' "

"*Please*. Not that one."

He slapped the Bible shut. "You know why I'm fat, Quin?"

Because you eat too much, Trevor.

"Why?"

"Because I never should have left the Catholic Church for the Church of the Good Faith. This is God's way of punishing me."

"I thought you said He was testing you, not punishing you."

"Both. He's doing both."

He looked so miserable that she didn't have the heart to tell him what she thought of religion. "How much are we losing?"

"What?" He blinked.

"How much money is the firm losing?"

"We're in the hole, but I don't know by how much."

"How come you didn't let me know before now, Trevor? I mean, you must've known."

"Look, Quin, you just handle the investigative stuff and I'll do the financial end, okay?" The misery in his face had been replaced by the old resentment about her 49 percent. She felt like pointing out that in light of what he'd just told her, it appeared she was doing a better job of holding up *her* end than he was at holding up *his*. But the truth was, she just didn't feel like arguing.

"I'm going home for the rest of the day," she said, getting up.

"Okay." His voice had turned listless. She looked at him oddly, sensing that he wanted to say something more. She had no way of knowing that Trevor was seeing Grant's face impaled against hers, and thinking that the bastard was grinning like Satan.

3.

Shortly before McCleary left Wishod, he called Detective Ron Valencia in Lauderdale homicide, who agreed to meet him at the Bon Soir Motel just south of Oakland Park Boulevard on U.S. 1. McCleary knew the area. At one time there'd been little else here but strip joints and bars, most of them owned by organized crime. In recent years, the city had cracked down on the strip joints, forcing them farther west of town, but somehow the Bon Soir had escaped the purge. It catered mostly to local hookers and, during the tourist season, to college kids looking for cheap places to stay.

He met Valencia in the lobby. The man reminded McCleary of a bear—short, plump, with a soft, round face, watery dark eyes, and a porous nose like a wedge of Gouda cheese. "When I walked in here this morning and saw this guy, I immediately thought of the stabbing the other night in Miami," Valencia said, his Hispanic accent so slight, it was barely noticeable. "We've had people here most of the day, dusting the room, taking pictures, going over the place with a fine tooth comb." As he spoke, he kept fiddling with the waistband on his slacks, hoisting them up on his hips. He patted his stomach. "I'm on this diet, see, and none of my clothes fit. C'mon, the room's right down the hall here."

"Did anyone see who he was with?"

"No. The man, Jake Wilford, came in and registered for the room himself, and the clerk claims he never saw who he was with. Maybe what we're dealing with is a hooker."

There was a lot of blood, more than they'd found in the tennis pro's apartment. It had smeared against the side of the bed, streaked across the rug in patterns that reminded McCleary of an aerial view of a macadam of highways, it had stained the sheets. "When we found Wilford, it looked like there'd been some sort of struggle," Valencia explained.

"What time did he check in?" McCleary asked.

"Around one-thirty. I spoke to his ex-wife and got a photo of him which I'm going to have circulated at some of the local watering holes. It'd help if we could pin down where he was."

McCleary asked if it was okay to touch the TV knob, and Valencia nodded. When he turned the set on, the screen filled with a lurid scene. "I can't believe this stuff's legal," McCleary mumbled, and switched the set off.

He walked into the bathroom, noted that the towels were missing and the wastebasket was empty. Valencia's men had no doubt hauled off anything that might have provided clues. They went back outside, into the afternoon heat. The distant sound of sirens pricked the air. The rush of traffic beyond them on U.S. 1 made a noise like wind through a tunnel. Now that he was outside, McCleary realized there was something about the odor in the room that had been nagging at him since he'd walked in. But damned if he knew what it was. Maybe nothing more than the smell of death, an odor you never got used to. McCleary inhaled deeply; the air escaped as a sigh.

Valencia chuckled. "I know, that's exactly how I feel. It's funny, you read these statistics that three quarters of homicides are committed by people who knew the victim. What I'd like to know is how come I always seem to get those in the other twenty-five percent?"

"You, too, huh."

"I'd been keeping tabs on those knifings in Dade. They tapered off for a while, until that tennis pro the other night."

"Yeah." McCleary looked over at Valencia. "Why do you think Wilford was killed by the same person?"

"Don't know exactly. Just a hunch, I guess."

"How old was he?"

"According to his license, he was forty-four. That makes him older than the others. But I figure that maybe our little lady has decided that what's good in the twenties and thirties must be good in the forties, too."

"Was there any sort of mark on this guy's head, like an X or a cross in blood?"

Valencia's dark eyes widened. "Well, yeah, there was." Goosebumps rose along McCleary's arms as he explained what they'd found on Tom Darcy's forehead. "A signature," Valencia breathed, jamming his hands in his pockets.

"It's beginning to look that way."

Signatures ranged from the astrological connections the Zodiac killer had used to the sexual mutilations that had marked the victims of the Boston Strangler to names scrawled in blood at the scene of a crime or initials carved into a person's body. They were as diverse as the lunatics who committed such crimes.

"And it wasn't on the other five guys?"

"No."

"So either we've got two sickos now—the new one with a religious quirk who prefers slightly older men—or something weird is happening in our little lady's head." Valencia reached into his pocket and brought out a pack of gum. He offered McCleary a stick. McCleary shook his head and watched as Valencia skinned it, then carefully doubled the stick and popped it in his mouth. "Food substitute," he murmured, and McCleary thought suddenly of Quin, who ate enough for two Ron Valencias and was about a third his size. "Listen, I've contacted a cop out in Oregon, Lance Wright, who specializes in unsolved murders. I've asked him to look through his records and see if he's got anything that fits this stabbing and the one in Miami. It might give us some leads."

"If you think it'll help, I'll send you the reports on the other stabbings and you can forward them to him."

"Okay. It's worth a try. Wright's solved about a hundred old murders, and one of those was twenty-four years old."

There it was again, McCleary thought, dark fields penetrated by someone not as close to the cases. The possibility that clues to these murders might be right in front of him was damned unsettling.

4.

The long afternoon shadows shot across the grass to the beginning of Grant's garden, where Quin now walked. She was tired, and she wasn't sure whether it was physical or mental or if the difference even mattered. When she'd left work, she'd taken a long, hot bath, she'd read, she'd watched the soaps, she'd done everything she could to keep from thinking. She'd slept for a while, but not well because first there was Trevor with his Bible and his grim announcement. Then Ms. Magnolia's face kept floating around inside her head, loose, disembod-

122

ied, bumping up against the walls of her dreams like the beginning of a nightmare. *Ms. Magnolia, one secret among many.*

And yet now there was something relaxing about the slippery moss against her bare feet and the fragrance of perpetual summer that clung to the shade among the plants and trees. The sprinklers came on; drops of water struck her skin like rain. No wonder Grant had taken refuge in his private forest. The fecund odors of earth and dampness possessed an elemental, timeless quality, perhaps stirring some deeply buried racial memory of when man lived and foraged in the forest.

It had taken them half a dozen trips to transport the plants from the townhouse, she remembered. That very afternoon, Grant had begun replanting everything. She could almost see him, pruning roots and leaves, digging holes, piling stones along the edge of the garden, his bare chest damp with perspiration. The way he'd carved a private world through the trees and foliage on the property had been a labor of love. It was as if his little Amazon had provided him with roots, a foundation, an identity that his nomadic life might have otherwise stripped from him.

She stopped at the pond. He'd dug the hole, poured the concrete, had bought the goldfish that now swam through shadows dappling the water. Dried leaves and twigs floated on the top like toy ships. She tried not to think about the impending funeral. Or about Ginger Hale. Or about duplicity and deceit. Instead, she imagined Grant crouched here near the pond, patting dirt at the base of a dozen shoots whose names she could never recall.

"Quin? You out here somewhere?"

"Back by the pond, Nikki." She made a mental note to feed the goldfish later, then hurried along the path. Nikki was examining one of the half-dozen or so types of orchids hanging from a wooden trellis that marked the beginning of the garden. "This is a surprise," Quin said.

"Just checking on you, kiddo. I called and called, and when you didn't answer, I started getting worried."

"I can never hear the phone out here if the windows are closed. Steve get back okay?"

"Yeah. And this morning I met him in Lauderdale and we picked up our wedding rings, Quin. Look." She paused on the stoop, opened a tiny box she brought out of her purse, and slipped the ring on her finger and held out her hand.

Quin drew in her breath. "It's gorgeous, Nikki."

The diamond, set in a simple gold band, was studded alternately with chips of sapphires and rubies like drops of blood. The waning afternoon light struck the diamond brilliantly, then seemed to snuggle down inside it so the gem sparkled with life.

"You're still going to be maid of honor, aren't you?"

"Of course I am. Why wouldn't I be?"

"Oh, I thought maybe you were irritated with me from the other night, when we went out."

"No." She felt like adding, but didn't, that she was hurt, maybe, because of what she knew Nikki wasn't telling her about Grant, but that she wasn't irritated.

They went inside. Quin fixed a pot of coffee, cut up carrots, cauliflower, and cucumbers, and made a dip as Nikki chattered away about the wedding (just family and close friends at the church Steve and Nikki attended), reception (huge and lavish), the honeymoon (Austria). Quin heard herself asking questions, laughing, felt a part of herself swept along in Nikki's excitement. But another part of her remained distant, self-contained, almost envying Nikki her happiness. *It could have been me. Grant and me.*

Except, of course, for the other women, the secrets.

"Today I met one of Grant's girlfriends," she said suddenly.

"What?"

"Her name's Ginger Hale. She owns a fancy jewelry store on Las Olas in Lauderdale." She turned, facing Nikki. "On top of it, I also talked to a kid who lives in Grant's complex who mentioned that Mr. Bell had an awful lot of girlfriends."

Nikki didn't say anything.

That wall again, Quin thought. Here it was. The silence filled with the ticking of the clock, burps from the coffeepot, Nikki shifting around at the table. *Tell me, damn it, just tell me.*

124

Quin got out two mugs, set the munchies on the table, sat down. The wall thickened in proportion to the silence, like a mathematical equation. Quin ate several carrots, wanted to get up and start dinner because her hunger was a black gulf inside her begging to be satiated, but she wanted to break through Nikki's wall worse than she wanted food. So she stayed where she was. "What is it, Nikki? What is it you know that you're not saying?"

"I told you what I know, Quin." A cool voice, distant and growing more so. *Drop it, Quin, back off. Some secrets are meant to be kept.* That's what Nikki's voice was really saying.

She didn't pursue it. For a few minutes, they busied themselves with the veggies and the dip and their coffee. Nikki lit a cigarette, and Quin wished she still smoked. She wanted to chatter idly, chatter to bridge the gulf, but found that she couldn't. She and Nikki, who'd been her closest friend for nine years, had absolutely nothing to say to each other. And it was the specter of Grant who stood between them.

14

MY FINGERS FLEW across the keyboard, words tumbled like acrobats through my head, I was back in that dingy room in the Bon Soir, back in that bed that quivered like something living. Swept along in a kind of feverish passion, I wrote until the scene bled dry. Then I sat back and reached for the last sheet:

He seemed a pathetic creature now, white, thin, his body like a stalk of stripped sugarcane. His legs were splayed as indelicately as a frog's, his vapid eyes skimmed some inner dimension of space, time. Her gaze fixed on the knife in his chest, and she was afraid to pull it out, afraid that when she did, the blood would spurt.

She stepped toward him, holding her breath. Suppose he wasn't really dead and suddenly bolted forward, perky as a puppet? But she couldn't leave the knife in him. She couldn't. She gripped the pearl handle, and the muscles that held the blade in place made sounds like smacking lips as she pulled. And pulled.

The knife popped free, and she stumbled back with a startled gasp. His head lolled to one side. She thought she was going to be sick, so she squeezed her eyes shut and fell forward at the waist, letting the blood flow to her head.

The blood rushed, and with it came the past, the

*boy who'd raped her. This man was that boy. Or
would have been if the boy had grown up.*

Was that possible?

*How had everything gotten so mixed up? How? '
How?*

How? I knew how. And it frightened me. The words
breathed, they had fire, life. I was there in the dirty old
motel where the man's spidery hands groped and caressed and probed. I felt the tug of the muscles in his
chest when my protagonist pulled the blade out. A pos-
sessive tug, almost, yes, and I understood her awe when
she touched her knuckle to her tongue and tasted the
salt of his blood.

My hand trembled as I dropped the sheet on the desk.
Billy Hendrix was the black bird of my childhood, the
black hole I twisted around inside me until light penetrated. Now the tennis pro, Jake Wilford, the others,
would shine from the pages of this new book, stamping
it with that ineluctable imprint which *Black Bird* possessed, that imprint that screamed, *This is real, this
happened, but we've labeled it fiction.*

And it scared me bone deep. The tremors of my fear
sent me out of the room, into the kitchen to execute
more mundane chores. I would make something to eat,
wash dishes, read, water the plants, do anything but
peek behind the veil that separated *me* from *her*, from
Kara Newman, mind of my mind, flesh of my flesh.

She wanted me, she wanted all of me. I could feel her
sometimes, deep inside me, waiting, laughing, her cruel
fluttering touch the tongue of death. Kara Newman—
muse, devil, creator.

15

ROBIN WAS WHISPERING to him, laughing softly, her breath like summer against his cheek, his neck. In the dream, McCleary reached for her, his hands touching the curve of her waist, and then she danced away from him, quick as sunlight on water. She was a mute; she had to speak with her eyes, her hands, her body. She undulated in a lazy, slow-motion freedom, her head thrown back as if she were anguished, as if pain seeped through the soles of her feet and braided through her bones. He moved toward her, but it was too late. She snuggled up to Paul Holmes like a cat in heat, and he laughed cruelly, with triumph, his laughter pursuing McCleary out of the dream.

He awakened four minutes before the alarm went off, feeling grumpy and out of sorts. Why was it only the bad dreams stayed with him? Then he thought of Robin in the courthouse cafeteria, Robin zipped into her languid body like a cat's, calling Holmes "Paul," and how Holmes had looked at her. Maybe the dream had a message he didn't want to examine too closely. Maybe Holmes was the person she'd spent Sunday with. If so, if Robin were actually having an affair with that horse's ass, McCleary thought, then it meant he knew absolutely nothing about her at all.

But by the time he got out of the elevator on the third floor of the station, the reality of the dream had receded and he was whistling a tune from *Hair*. It dated him, but his taste in music had been eclipsed in the late sixties and early seventies. Except for some instrumental pieces, he hadn't bought a new record in at least ten years, maybe more. Robin had occasionally poked fun at him for it, telling him he was stalled in the past.

Well, what of it?

He rounded the corner into his office, astonished to see Robin, as if she'd popped full-blown from his dream. At the window, bird arms folded at her waist, stood Treena Esposito. Robin rose a shade too quickly, hands brushing nervously at her skirt. "Uh, Mac, Mrs. Esposito insisted on waiting for you. Now that you're here, I've got to get back to the courthouse, okay?"

She looked anxious as hell to get away from the other woman, whose fury was evident in the flash of her green eyes. "Hi, Mrs. Esposito," McCleary said pleasantly.

"I'd like to talk to you," she snapped.

"I'll be with you in a minute." He took Robin by the arm and led her into the hall, shutting the door after them. "What is her goddamn problem, anyway?" McCleary barked.

" 'Tis the wrath of a woman scorned, Mac."

"C'mon, Robin."

"How the hell should I know what her problem is? She storms in here before I've even had my coffee, for Christ's sakes, and makes herself right at home in your office. I told her to wait in the staff kitchen, and she flatly refused. What was I going to do, have her hauled away bodily? So I sat with her." Then she smiled sweetly and patted his arm. "Better you than me, Mac. I'd wring her chicken neck inside of two minutes. "

McCleary laughed in spite of himself. "Okay. Thanks for waiting with her."

"Sure thing."

He watched her glide back down the hall, greeting other investigators as she passed. He couldn't help but notice how men always took a second look at her, a longing look, despite the fact that her face has graced these halls for two years. Then he returned to his office and Treena Esposito.

"What seems to be the problem?" he asked.

"The problem, Detective McCleary, is that I do not appreciate your speaking to my principal behind my back and intimating that I killed Grant."

She really *did* remind him of an exotic bird. He could almost see the ruffling of her colorful plumage as she folded her skinny arms and waited for him to respond. Instead of saying anything, he decided to disarm her. He poured a cup of coffee from the percolator on the bookshelf and walked over to the window. He felt her following him with her eyes. *The seas today are stormy, Mac, just look at those whitecaps*.

"Do you like the view?" he asked, turning to face her.

"What?"

"The view. It's nice, isn't it?"

"Look, I didn't come here to discuss the view. I want to know why you went to my principal. It was unnecessary. I told you what you wanted to know about Grant. I could sue you and your department for what you did. For . . . for maligning me. Especially if I lose my job."

He wanted to laugh. But the irony was that with a clever attorney, she could do exactly that and probably win. It wouldn't matter that he'd just been doing his job. In McCleary's mind, this perversion of the judicial system was equated with Paul Holmes. The thought of Holmes brought back his dream about Robin, and suddenly his patience snapped.

"Let me tell you something, Mrs. Esposito. I don't appreciate people barging into my office. Second, I did not *intimate* anything to your principal. I'm doing my job. Your ex-husband was shot, and probably by someone who knew him. Since you happened to be married to him for five years and have sufficient reason to be bitter, that makes you a suspect. And another thing. You told me you were at a faculty meeting the night Grant was killed. It so happens you *left* that faculty meeting and didn't return until an hour later."

"My husband had locked himself out of the house."

"I suppose he'll be willing to talk to me and tell me that himself."

Her deep green eyes shifted. She folded and unfolded her skinny hands in her lap, then swept her fingers through her hair. "I, uh, would rather you not discuss this with him."

McCleary shoved his hands in his pockets and looked

down at the floor. Sunlight, muted from the tinted glass, gobbled up most of Treena Esposito's insubstantial shadow. "Apparently you don't understand what's going on. Grant Bell was murdered. Not in a script, not on TV, but in real life."

"Don't patronize me," she barked.

"Then don't give me that horseshit about not talking to your husband. At the moment, he's the only alibi you've got."

"You honestly think I could drive from Kendall High School to Grant's townhouse, shoot him, and then return to the school in an hour, Detective McCleary?" Her face, etched with its odd eccentricity, now struck him as homely, mean. "In traffic, that drive alone would take me an hour."

"During rush-hour traffic, yeah. But not at eight o'clock in the evening. And while we're at it, who did you call when you ducked out of the meeting? Grant? Were you just checking to make sure he was home?"

She stood then, and if there had been any truth to the adage that looks could kill, he would've been dead. "I don't have to sit here and listen to this."

"Fine, don't. But I'll be speaking to your husband."

"He's out of town," she said quickly. Too quickly.

"How convenient."

She moved toward the door.

"Mrs. Esposito. Don't think about leaving town." It was the sort of line she would understand.

"I told you before, Detective McCleary. I'm teaching summer school."

"But just in case you decide to get away for a weekend, make sure you check with me first."

"This isn't a police state, you know."

"Look, all you have to do to clear yourself is have someone confirm where you were for that hour. It's simple."

She made a derisive sound like a snort. "Nothing is ever simple, Detective McCleary."

Amen, he thought, and winced as she slammed the door behind her.

As Quin was about to turn right toward the interstate, she decided to swing by *Siete Mangos* first, a small Colombian restaurant where she and Grant had eaten frequently. The Guzmans, the owners, were an elderly couple who had left Colombia during the late seventies, when terrorism became rampant, and settled in Miami, where more than a hundred thousand other Colombians now lived. They'd been fond of Grant, and she wondered if either of them knew he was dead.

Although it was early, the restaurant was open and packed. They began serving breakfast at six and didn't close their doors until nine at night. While fifteen-hour days hadn't made Camilo Guzman a rich man, they'd made him comfortable enough to retire, but he refused to consider it. In fact, when Quin walked in, Camilo was standing at the door with menus, greeting people. He knew most everyone—the neighborhood locals who stopped by daily for the breakfast buffet, the smartly dressed young women here for a *cafecito* before hitting the expressway, the businessmen who preferred making deals the Latin way, over a good meal with espresso.

When he saw Quin, he murmured, *"Díos mio,"* and they brushed cheeks. He squeezed her shoulder. "I read it in the paper, *mi cielo.*"

"I was afraid you didn't know."

He motioned for the woman behind the counter to take his place at the door, and guided Quin to a table in the next room. "You have eaten?"

She nodded. "Just finished."

"Café, then, you will have a coffee, no?"

"Okay. Thanks, Camilo."

"I will tell Tinita that you're here. One minute."

He was a short, quick-moving man with thick white hair, hair like Paul Holmes would have in twenty years, she thought, watching him as he hurried into the kitchen. A few moments later, he and his wife appeared.

Although Tinita was in her early sixties, she had that lovely olive complexion that seemed to be the birthright of Hispanics. She fussed over Quin, hugging her hello, asking how she was getting along, finally sitting down when Camilo brought over an extra chair.

Quin's coffee arrived, with a pastry on a plate next to it, and a slice of fresh papaya. "Please, you eat," Tinita said. "You are much too thin, Quin. I do not like to see you so . . ." She paused, touched her own face, drawing her fingers down toward her chin, forming a point. "I do not know the word in English." Her eyes darted toward her husband's. *"La dijo?"*

Quin looked from Tinita to Camilo. "What?"

He patted the air with his hands. *"Un momento,* give me a chance, Tinita." He sat at the edge of his chair, his thick fingers intertwined on the table. When he spoke again, his voice was lower. "Quin, *mira.* The night Grant . . . was killed, he came in here."

I'm not going to like this. The thought made her hungry, and she dug her spoon into the papaya. "What time was he here?"

"I think about seven-thirty," Tinita replied. "Grant, he sat at the bar and ordered black beans and rice. But he was very nervous, Quin. He ate so little. He moved around on the bar stool"—and she shifted her buttocks, imitating his movements—"and he laughed like a goat. And I tell Camilo he should talk to Grant, to see if he was okay. I tell him that Grant, he needs a father, no?"

She began to switch tenses, and Quin could almost see Grant on the bar stool, see him squirming, picking at his food the way he used to do when something disturbed him. She scraped her spoon across the bottom of the papaya rind, finished it off. She was aware of its cold sweetness against her tongue, but couldn't taste it. "So I sit with him," Camilo said, picking up the thread of the story, "and I ask him where you are, and his face, it becomes . . . like a shadow, Quin. He says he hasn't seen you since he came back from his trip and that he believes he has . . . *como se dice* . . ." He looked to his wife for help.

"Made a mess of things," Tinita said. "That is his expression."

"How?" Quin asked.

Camilo shrugged. "This he did not tell me. But he gave me something for you."

"I will get it." Tinita rose quickly.

Camilo rubbed his thick hand over a side of his face.

"Grant, he says that if he does not come back for it by the end of the week, I should give it to you, Quin. It is not the end of the week, but he is dead, so I do not believe he would think I have broken my word, eh?"

"No, I don't think so, Camilo," she replied, her voice soft, quavering.

"Here." Tinita set a package the size of a shoebox on the table. It had been wrapped sloppily in brown paper and bound with string. Quin yanked at the string, tore off the paper. When she removed the lid, cotton that had been jammed inside spilled out. And there, against a field of white like snow, were a dozen emeralds. Big emeralds.

Camilo murmured something in Spanish as Quin reached into the box. Tinita touched Quin's arm. "Not here. Too many people."

She quickly removed her hand from the box, glanced at Camilo, Tinita, then back at the gems. *Greenfire?* Was this it? The myth? Was this the El Dorado Pizarro had been looking for? Couldn't be, she decided. These emeralds weren't worth anything close to ten or twelve million. No, they were appetizers, teasers. She wiped her hands against her skirt. Sat back. Looked inside the box again. Her fingers stepped through the cotton, seeking a note, an explanation, something. All she found was a key—small, rusting, with no identifying marks on it. She slipped the lid back on the box.

"Did Grant say anything else to you, Camilo?"

"Only that you would know where it fits."

"Then he told you about the key?"

"No, nothing. He just gives me the box and says that you will know where it fits. Then he said he had to meet someone and he left."

Meet who? Which woman?

And how was she supposed to know where the bloody key fit?

Tinita frowned. "I remember something, Quin. Some months past, Grant, he came in here one night alone. We were talking, the three of us. You remember, Camilo?"

"*Sí, sí.* He tells us he is going to be in Leticia and asks if we can give him the name of someone who knows the river."

134

"She doesn't know about Leticia, Camilo," Tinita told her husband, and looked at Quin. "Leticia is in a corner of Colombia at the edge of Brazil and Peru, Quin. It is on the Amazon."

Quin nodded, and Camilo continued. "So I tell Grant to contact my cousin, Raul, who owns a hotel in Leticia and knows everyone."

"Did he?"

"Sí, Raul, he writes me that Grant visited him and hired a Peruvian man . . ." He hesitated, rubbed his fingers against his forehead. "I cannot remember his name, but it is in the letter. You want that I get the letter, Quin?"

She rubbed a hand over her face, remembering another letter, the one Rusty Johnson had translated for her. The man's name, she knew, would be Felix Mendez, who was supposed to meet Grant in Iquitos, Peru, on July 4.

"Was his name Mendez? Felix Mendez?"

"Sí," Tinita replied, her voice excited. "Sí, I think that was the name, Quin."

3.

McCleary read through Doc Smithers's autopsy reports on Grant Bell and Dade County's latest serial victim, Tom Darcy, but found nothing unusual. Bell had died of a gunshot wound and Darcy had bled to death: simple. Smithers, however, had noted that the knife used on Darcy was most likely the same type used on the other five victims. And like the other men, the alcohol content in Darcy's blood was elevated.

So far, he'd received exactly two phone calls on Tom Darcy—one from the woman who'd found him and another from the manager of the Coral Gables Country Club, where Darcy had worked. Neither had offered any clues. Like the other men, Darcy had been a transient, one of Miami's numerous northern transplants. In fact, the only victim that had not been a transient was Jake Wilford, and he didn't really count, since his death fell under Broward County's jurisdiction.

Doesn't really count: was that the point you invariably reached in this business? Were the only corpses that counted the ones in his jurisdiction?

McCleary tossed the autopsy reports aside and strolled over to the window, the bow of his ship. The sea of light below had gone from stormy, when Treena Esposito was here, to a sort of smoldering gray that fit his mood.

"Is it burnout or indigestion?" asked a voice from the doorway.

McCleary glanced around at Wayne O'Donald, the department psychologist, and chuckled. "Neither. Both. I don't know."

"Just as I suspected," the little man said, pushing his glasses back onto his head as he came into the office. "Indecision caused by fatigue, frustration, and bullshit. Other than that, you're in fine shape, Mac." O'Donald sighed as he sat down. He had an odd, pinched face that gave him a predatory look, and huge Coke-brown eyes that were so dark it was hard to tell where the pupils ended and the irises began. The resident eccentric, that was O'Donald.

"So your professional opinion is that I'm doing great, huh." McCleary walked over to his desk, sat down, got up again, and returned to the windowsill. O'Donald's eyes followed him, silently assessing. McCleary imagined his conclusions: *Reaching burnout after a decade in Miami homicide. Inability to maintain emotional relationships to his satisfaction. Recommended sex therapy and psychiatric counseling.*

"Oh, absolutely. *If* you get outa homicide before you're forty."

"Thanks."

He dropped his glasses back on his nose; his eyes shrank. "I've prepared a little something for you: a profile on our serial murderer. I think you might find it illuminating, even if I do say so myself." He tossed it on McCleary's desk.

Dark field illuminations, here we come. "How about giving me a synopsis?"

O'Donald sat primly, an elbow resting on either armrest, fingers laced together. "Well, first off, I think it's a woman. And there're some distinctive patterns. Our lady here chooses men of a certain physical type, men she

136

doesn't know, whom she meets impersonally, probably in a bar. More often than not, she has sex with them. And recently, of course, she's been leaving her little signature. My feeling is that she's externalizing hatred toward a particular man who is physically like the men she kills. Because of the sex angle in this, Mike, I believe she was abused when she was younger, maybe by her father, maybe by another man. But definitely abused. Raped. Maybe more than once. So she has sex with these guys, then kills them. It's her way of striking back, of getting even."

"But if this happened when she was younger, why would she suddenly start killing these guys eight months ago? I don't get it."

"Something may have set her off. Or"—he sat forward, bending at the waist like puppet—"there may be other murders in other places that we don't know about."

"What about the mark on Darcy and Wilford's foreheads?"

O'Donald shifted in his chair. "I call 'em the mark of Cain. It's like she's telling us—and herself—that these men sinned, so she had to kill them."

"Religious hangups."

"That'd be my guess. What bothers me about all this, though, is how methodical she's been about not leaving any fingerprints. There's a sharp intelligence behind the lunacy. I mean, put yourself in her place, Mike. You've just slit someone's throat, you're probably covered with blood, the stink of blood is everywhere, but hey, you stop to think about what you've touched in the apartment or wherever you are. And then you very methodically go around wiping away traces."

McCleary nodded. "Yeah, I see your point."

"Now the other thing. I know you've got that Bell homicide, so I went through your file."

"And?"

"Well, so far you've been assuming he falls into the seventy-five percent bracket, that he was killed by someone who knew him well."

"And you don't think he was?"

"I'm saying it's open to question because of this guy's lifestyle, okay? In fact, his murder may not have a damn thing to do with his Amazon treks or anything else. It might just be his lifestyle that killed him. So just don't box yourself in. In fact, don't entirely discount the possibility that Bell falls into the same physical framework as the knifing victims, Mike."

"At forty-three, he was older than the others."

"Not so. You're forgetting Jake Wilford, the real estate broker. He was forty-four. And both he and Bell looked much younger than they were."

"But Bell was shot with a .45."

O'Donald held up his hand. "With someone as methodical as this woman's been, that could've been an attempt to mislead investigators, Mike, so they wouldn't be connecting Bell's death with the others. Or it could've been that she actually felt something for Bell and the impersonal use of a gun was substituted for the intimacy of a knife."

McCleary's fingers played with a pencil, tapping the eraser against the desk, slowly, rhythmically. "It sounds like a long shot to me."

"Maybe. But anything's possible when you're dealing with a lunatic. Anything."

"I'll keep that in mind." But the dozens of variables in any case had to be shuffled and reshuffled until you found the picture that seemed most accurate, McCleary thought. And at the moment, the Holmes variable looked more promising.

O'Donald started to say something, but McCleary's phone rang. It was Quin. And she was babbling.

4.

She didn't know what was more disconcerting—the ride across town with a dozen emeralds, or walking into McCleary's office and meeting his partner. Robin Peters was a knockout, and Quin sensed immediately that her relationship with McCleary was not merely a professional one. Her hand was soft and cool in Quin's when McCleary introduced them, and her grip was firm. A little too firm. A grip that communicated a *Don't get any ideas about him, Sweetie*. Or maybe that was her imagination.

138

"That's the last time I ride across town with emeralds," she said, setting the box on McCleary's desk and lifting the lid.

He let out a soft whistle; Robin murmured something inane like *incredible*.

McCleary picked one up, held it to the light. A star burst in its center. "I don't know too much about emeralds," Robin began, "except their value is partially determined by the color. The deeper the green, the better. Look at it, look at all of them." She was right, Quin thought. The green was so deep it was nearly blue. "I bet the gal with the jewelry store would be interested in these, Mac."

Mac: just the way she'd utttered that single word smacked of intimacy. And her remark annoyed Quin. Robin had spoken as though Quin weren't in the room. Yet Quin had the feeling she was making it perfectly clear that McCleary kept her informed about their cases despite her training seminar. *We're quite close, sweetie:* yeah, it was that sort of remark. Quin wished she'd go away, back to her seminar or wherever she'd come from. But Robin settled comfortably into one of the chairs, everything about her suggesting that, for the moment, she wasn't going anywhere.

She'd slipped her shoes off now, and the balls of her feet were pressing against the side of McCleary's desk. She locked her hands behind her head and tipped back in her chair until its edge rested against the wall. Yeah, she was definitely not going anywhere fast, Quin decided. But why should it bother her? For that matter, why should the woman's relationship with McCleary, whatever it was, be any concern of hers?

"You don't know what the key goes to?" Robin asked.

"Nope." But she had a few ideas. She plucked the key from the box, slipped it in her wallet. "But I will." Quin made reference to the several hours she, McCleary, and Rusty Johnson had spent last night going through Grant's articles and computer files. She said it, she knew, just to show Robin that her rights to McCleary were by no means exclusive. But Robin just sat there, smiling, lovely, and completely unthreatened. "Well, I gotta run," Quin said, glancing at her watch. "Take care of those gems, McCleary."

139

"They're going in the department safe. Where that key should go too, Quin."

"I'll return it when I've tried it out." She glanced at Robin. "Nice meeting you." *Sort of.*

When she'd gone just a few steps down the hall, Quin heard Robin Peters's throaty laugh, a sensual laugh. It seemed to echo among the sounds of typewriters and voices, nipping at her, curling around the edges of her mind, whispering, *Back off, lady, he's mine.*

5.

Izzo ambushed McCleary and Robin as they got off the elevator after depositing the gems in the department safe. "Mike. Robin. You two have a couple minutes?" He reminded McCleary of a wrestler as he strolled toward them. There was a definite sidle to his walk, as if he were stalking them, circling them.

"Do we have a choice?" McCleary replied.

"No." Izzo didn't chuckle. He didn't even smile. That meant it was serious.

They followed him to his office at the end of the hall. Izzo sat behind his tremendous desk, flicking at something on its surface, hesitating. It was going to be unpleasant, McCleary decided.

"Mike, I'm removing you from the Bell case and you're going on this serial murder thing full time."

"I've been on it full time for eight months."

"I mean you'll be working on it exclusively. Robin, I tried to pull a few strings to get this seminar business canceled for at least the next month so you could help Mike out. But since it's required for county cops who've been with us less than ten years, I doubt I'm going to get the okay unless something drastic happens."

Like what? McCcleary wondered. An invasion by aliens? A tidal wave? What?

"Chief, Mike can't be expected to work on this thing alone," Robin argued.

"He won't be alone. I'm pulling Benson out of the training seminar, since he's only a month shy of his ten years. And I've got a few people who're going to be pulled from other cases to help out as well."

"Who's going to take the Bell case?"

"I'll assign it to someone else, Mike."

The "hunch spot" between his eyes suddenly burned and McCleary knew Izzo was lying. He intended to put the whole thing on a back burner for a while because he was getting pressure from somewhere. *Pressure from Holmes?* "Look," McCleary said, "we've followed every lead and have gotten exactly nowhere. What makes you think that by shelving everything else, we're suddenly going to find something?"

Izzo unwrapped a pack of cigarettes and lit one of the five smokes a day he allotted himself. "Because, McCleary, you and Benson are going to work the singles bars, following up old leads."

"So there'll still be time to work on the Bell case," McCleary said.

Izzo's eyes narrowed. "Maybe you didn't understand me. This takes priority. Otherwise, we're going to have the mayor and every other bureacratic politician in this city on our asses. So as of now, you're off the case."

Off the case: just like that. "O'Donald thinks Bell's death and the serial murders may be connected," McCleary said.

"O'Donald," Izzo snorted, "reads too many mysteries." A dozen arguments leaped into McCleary's head, but he quickly discarded them all. He'd worked for Izzo long enough to know that once the man's mind was made up about something, it took an act of God to change it. But as he got up, he couldn't resist having the final word.

"Look, there's a lead pointing straight to the DA's office, Bob."

"So your replacement can follow it up."

"I hope to Christ you don't regret this."

"What the hell's that supposed to mean?"

My, my, aren't we defensive. "If O'Donald's right, we may all regret it."

When they were outside a few minutes later, McCleary took a deep breath. The air was so still, so hot, it seemed to singe the inside of his lungs. "What's this obsession you've got with Grant Bell?" Robin asked.

"It's called Paul Holmes. I know that shit's behind this."

"Oh c'mon, Mac. A fifteen-thousand-dollar loan doesn't constitute a motive."

Is she defending him? "I don't buy that story."

"Maybe not. But until you come up with something better, it's all you've got."

"And now Izzo's making sure I *don't* get anything better."

"Mac, you're getting paranoid in your old age, you know that? I think you're making too big a deal outa this." She smiled, then brushed her mouth to his cheek. "I've got to get back to the seminar."

McCleary watched her hurrying through the crowd, hands tucked in her jacket pockets, light braiding through her hair. His cheek tingled where her mouth had touched. He wondered why he still cared. There had been a lot of women through the years, some whom he'd loved, some whom he'd left, some who had left him. But there had been none like Robin, none who had claimed some essential part of him. She was an allergy he couldn't conquer.

He thought of his dream again, of Robin and Holmes close as twin yolks in an eggshell. Christ, that would certainly count as one of life's grossest little ironies. He supposed there was a moral in that—there seemed to be morals in most everything where Robin was concerned— but he didn't have the faintest idea what it might be.

PART TWO

Webs

"Life is the art of being well-deceived."
—William Hazlitt

16

It was a soft sound, a whisper of air. It rippled the darkness like a stone thrown into a pond, radiating outward from its source in concentric circles. Quin, still drowsy as she lifted up, thought it was Grant, that he'd just gotten home. Any minute now, she'd hear the fridge sigh open, Saran wrap or aluminum foil crinkling as he found a snack, then his footfalls on the stairs.

She lay back, closing her eyes, drifting . . . *Grant?*

She bolted forward and tried to remember where she'd put her gun. Someone was downstairs, and it sure wasn't Grant.

Her heart raced as she swung her legs over the side of the bed. Her bare feet landed silently against the cool floor. The four glasses of wine she'd consumed earlier had spun cobwebs in her head. She couldn't remember what day it was, why she'd had so much to drink, where her purse was. The gun was in it.

Merlin leaped from the end of the bed and scampered off. Quin groped at the air, blinking quickly, seeking something to root her. Then her fingers brushed the edge of the wall. She leaned into it, as though a violent wind were pushing her. Blood rushed through her head, and behind it came the pounding of her heart. She drew in a breath, listening for the noise.

She heard nothing.

Quin squeezed her eyes shut, wondering if she'd imagined it. Hadn't people warned her about exactly this?

You'll think you hear him in the house, Quin, that he isn't really dead, that he's on his way home. . . . And now, for the last ten days, since his funeral, that sense of unreality had worsened.

Since McCleary had been taken off the case, nothing had gone right. Nothing. The firm was in deep financial trouble, she hadn't seen McCleary, she'd been drinking too much. She slept and ate and went in to work, she'd written Felix Mendez and told him about Grant, she mulled things over with Rusty, she argued with Trevor. But she did these things by rote. In truth, her life spun like a dying planet at the outer limits of a dying sun.

She pressed both hands against the wall, pushing herself back. For a moment, she swayed uncertainly in the dark. The room was so black, she had to look obliquely at the door to see it, a shadow against deeper shadows. Out there, then downstairs. Her purse was on the couch where she'd left it. How could she have been so careless?

Wine, all the wine.

Too much of that.

She padded quietly over to the door, reached for her robe hanging on the back of it, slipped it on as she listened, waited, still not entirely certain she'd imagined the noise. The air conditioner clicked on, making it harder to hear anything. Her stomach rumbled as she stepped through the door and into the hall, feeling her way in the dark.

At the end of the wall, she paused. She could just make out the silhouette of the banister. She pressed her hands to her heart, willing it to quiet. And then she heard it, that soft *rippling* again in the air, that tangible something, the heaviness of another presence.

Easy, Quin. Easy.

She moved back a step, away from the stairwell. Then another step. Another. She passed the bedrooms, the bath. She felt a draft from the back stairs tickling her legs. Her foot dangled for a moment above the top step. *Don't squeak. Please don't squeak.* Then her foot came down, toes, arch, heel, twist; toes, arch, heel, an intricate dance. She grasped the railing with both hands, negotiated two more steps, stopped, listened.

Her senses had expanded, thinned out, seemed to cover

146

the house like a net: the intruder had stopped as well. Frustration swelled like bile in her throat. *Never act quickly; always give the other guy enough rope to hang himself.* Old Sammy Forsythe had told her that. She waited, gripping the railing, not moving, barely breathing.

After a while, she didn't know how long, she heard a noise again, a scratching sound like a mouse. By the time she'd realized it was the drawers being opened in Grant's den, she was at the bottom of the stairs with no clear memory of getting there. Since the intruder was in the den, she couldn't get to either exit or to her purse, her weapon, without being detected. The utility room, where she might have found a weapon or been able to get through to the garage, was directly across from the den, and the door was closed. *Never act quickly:* she'd just blown the first rule by hastily retreating to the back stairs.

The person in Grant's den was flustered, hurried, perhaps even frantic. Quin could tell by the way he breathed, quick, sharp breaths that slapped at the silence in the house. But she couldn't just stand here, at the bottom of the stairs, hidden at the edge of the wall. She needed a weapon, something to protect herself with. Had Grant finally stored his baseball bat behind the back stairs? Or had it gone into the attic? Before she could remember, the intruder's breathing pattern changed. Quin sensed rather than saw him coming from the den, moving toward her. She pulled back behind the wall, knowing if she scampered up the back stairs she might be shot, but knowing just as well that if the man continued coming toward her, she would be seen. Nothing to lose.

Her nostrils flared as she breathed in once, deeply. She poised on the balls of her feet, and as the intruder approached, Quin suddenly lunged, head lowered like a bull's, and propelled herself forward, aimed at what she hoped was the intruder's stomach.

The impact jarred her to the bone. Her teeth slammed down over her tongue. A searing pain burned through her neck. She tasted blood. But the intruder grunted, stumbled back, his weapon clattered against the floor. Quin was thrown off balance and fell with him. They grappled blindly for the weapon. His skin was like rubber. No, his body was covered with something. And he wore gloves. He shoved her away from him; she came back flailing her arms, kicking. But he was stronger, quicker. Something hard came down over her head, she struggled to hold off the black miasma that swarmed through her like angry bees, but it fastened over her, and she sank.

She was with her dad. He was telling her a story about an enchanted forest as they strolled along a beach in a sunlit past of thirty years ago. A stranger joined them. He spoke only to her father at first, his voice soft, gravelly, his footprints in the sand filling quickly with light. Then she looked at him. It was Grant.

Don't you recognize me?

But he frowned and looked at her dad. *What's wrong with her, with your daughter?*

She has the key, her father replied, then hugged her.

Quin came to in the dark, her cheeks damp with tears, her mouth filled with blood, her head aching so badly that when she moved, she thought she would pass out again. But the intruder was gone; she felt the emptiness in the house. She coughed, spit, coughed again as she pushed herself to a sitting position. Her tongue ached, felt thick and swollen. She'd bitten it when she'd fallen.

She heard Merlin nearby, purring, meowing, purring again. His cold nose touched her leg, and Quin reached for him, hugging him, pressing her face to his fur.

She didn't want to move.

She waited until the pain in her head seemed to have slid off to one side, just above her left ear, then she let go of Merlin and pressed her back to the wall. Slowly, she moved upward, wincing as the pain unfocused, spread. Her hands grappled at the walls for the switch, and the overhead light flared. She moved quickly to the couch, to her purse, found it overturned, the gun on the floor. She scooped it up, then made her way slowly into the kitchen and dialed McCleary's number. He answered on the first ring, his voice fogged with sleep. She'd never been so glad to hear anyone, not even the operator the night she'd found Grant. As she spoke, she grabbed a paper towel and wiped it across her mouth. It came away spotted with blood.

"I'll be there in ten minutes, Quin."

She hung up the receiver, reached for more paper towels, ran them under the sink faucet. She pressed them to her face, the back of her neck, her face again. Then she touched her head where the pain was. Her hair was matted; her fingers came away bloody. She held the cool compress to her head, glanced at the back door, saw the snipped chain, wondered dimly why the dead bolt hadn't held. She weaved like a drunk toward the refrigerator, opened it, reached for a can of apricot juice. Her stomach screamed for something more, but she ached too much to eat. Then she made her way into the living room, sipping from the can, the juice coating her sore tongue, and fell onto the couch. There, it was better when she didn't move. The gun was a lead weight in her hand.

She watched the clock and waited.

McCleary made it in twelve and a half minutes. She heard him screech into the driveway and pushed herself heavily to her feet to unlock the front door. As she got up, she hit the end table and the can of juice toppled. She left it. Her tongue ached where she'd bitten it; the pain in her head had diminished to a dull, heavy throb. When she opened the door, the room tilted to the left and she leaned against him, leaned into the smell of him, a scent of wind and sleep and darkness. He helped her to the couch and examined the back of her head. "You're going to have one hell of a knot, but the bleeding seems to have stopped. Let me make an ice pack for the swelling."

She nodded. The effort to speak proved too much. She closed her eyes, lifted her legs onto the couch. Her thoughts wandered like orphans through the past few weeks. There, Trevor in his grimmest face, saying, *We're going to have to sell all the property, Quin;* Nikki inside her wall of secrets; Paul Holmes telling her the money he'd given Grant was to repay a debt from some years ago and what business did Quin have blabbing to McCleary? And Grant's secret life, spinning webs around her, tricking her.

She felt like weeping. Worse than the great, yawning hole Grant's death had torn in her life was the way it seemed to be sucking everything around her into it. Relationships she'd taken for granted now seemed fragile, riddled with distrust, her financial security had been threatened by Trevor's mysterious "unwise investments," and the man she'd loved for a year had turned out to be an illusion. Then there was McCleary, whom she hadn't stopped thinking about, and who'd become as elusive as Grant.

She dozed off, and her father was saying, *C'mon now, Quin, remember. I know you can remember where the key fits.* When she opened her eyes, she thought it was her father hovering over her. She wondered how he and her mother had heard, when they'd flown in from Europe. She started to ask where her sister was, then realized it was McCleary, murmuring something about going to the emergency room.

"Hospital? What're they going to do, McCleary, put my head in a cast? No, thanks."

He gave a soft, quick chuckle and rocked back on his heels. "You're definitely going to be okay."

She sat up, drank the water. Part of her wanted to sleep, to dream of her dad and Grant on the beach, talking about the enchanted place. *I have the key to it.* She knew where it fit, she did, but it had just slipped her mind. "McCleary, listen." Quin sat up, crossed her legs at the ankles. "He came in the back door."

"I know. I saw it. How do you feel, Quin?" He handed her ice wrapped in a dish towel and she touched it to the back of her ear.

"My head hurts, but otherwise I think I'm okay."

"Then tell me where the linens are, so I can make up the couch in the den. I'm staying here."

She told him. His shadow as he ascended the stairs made him look taller, thinner than he was. She wondered why she'd called him, why he'd come. When he returned, the linens were draped over his arm. "The upstairs is . . . shit. You'll have to sleep down here."

"The upstairs is what, McCleary? What happened?" She spoke to his back. He stopped, turned. She'd never seen him look quite like he did, there in the exiguous

150

light from the hallway. There were deep shadows around his eyes. A line jutted from one nostril to the corner of his mouth.

"It's a goddamned mess, okay? You're sleeping down here."

He walked off toward the den. Quin dropped the ice pack, was momentarily dizzy when she stood. She went upstairs, barely noticing that sheets had been swept out of the linen closet, her dresser drawers had been yanked out and overturned, that boxes had been tossed from her closet shelves: a repeat of the mess Nikki's maid had cleaned up in Grant's townhouse. *You bastard,* she thought. *You dirty bastard, whoever you are.*

"Quin?"

"I'm upstairs," she called.

She reached for her pillow and ripped off the case. Then she turned it inside out with a laugh and tore away the strip of masking tape that held the key to the fabric.

When she returned downstairs, McCleary was in the kitchen, examining the back door. It seemed right, somehow, that he was here, she thought. "You need a dead bolt that goes into the wood about four inches, Quin."

She held up the key. "He didn't get what he came for, McCleary. It was in my pillowcase."

His eyes darted from the key to her face, then he laughed. "Neat trick, Quin."

"The late movies."

He shook his head as if he didn't quite know what to make of her. "You want me to hang on to it?"

She looked at it, thought of Grant's footlocker in the attic that the key hadn't fit, and nodded. "Yeah, maybe you should. Thanks." She dropped it on the counter, put on the tea kettle, brought several cold rolls from the fridge, and stuck them in the microwave. She couldn't wait for hers to get warm, so she removed it. The first bite was possibly the best of anything she'd ever tasted.

McCleary shut the kitchen door, wedged the back of a wooden chair under the doorknob. "If this guy's crazy enough to come back tonight, which I doubt, we'll hear him."

"How about some tea," she said. "And rolls."

"The lady who's always hungry," he said with a

laugh. "I forgot. Sure. Tea and rolls. Why not." He came up behind her. "You ought to keep that ice pack on your head so it doesn't swell any more, Quin. Here, let me take a look at it."

Although he touched her head with an almost clinical detachment, she couldn't breathe properly when he was this close to her. "Ouch," she said as his fingers touched the place her head was most tender.

"Oops. Sorry." His hand dropped away. And she turned around. "Quin, I . . ."

He was going to apologize. She could almost see the words forming, slipping down the length of his tongue. But what did he have to apologize for? It wasn't his fault Izzo had removed him from the case. But she heard herself saying, "Forget it, McCleary. No apology need- ed," and he touched her chin, lifted it. *Eyes like blue smoke; face it, Quin, cool you are not.*

"Yeah, it does. It matters. Some partner I turned out to be. I let Izzo intimidate me, for Christ's sake." Be- fore she could argue, he rocked forward and kissed her gently. The pain in her head shrank. She heard a train hurtling through the distant dark, the clock ticking. Then he pulled back just a little and traced his finger along the curve of her neck and chin, electrifying her skin.

She whispered, "You're giving me goosebumps, McCleary," and thought of lovely Robin.

He laughed, rubbed his hands on her arms. It was such a familiar sound, his laughter, warm and close. It stirred a suppressed hunger in Quin to be touched, held, a hunger she'd been denying for weeks. Then he cradled her face in his hands, kissing her again, and the hunger drank in the sensation of his mouth, the scent of his hair, his skin. His hands slid along her back, around to her ribs, to the swell of her breasts, making her catch her breath. And suddenly she wanted him, wanted him as she knew she had since that day in his office when Robin Bird's presence had unsettled her so much.

The bell on the microwave rang, and a moment later the tea kettle whistled, startling her. She removed it from the burner. "You want tea?" she asked, regarding him across the several feet that separated them.

"Do you?"

"No."

"Good." He smiled. Neither of them moved or spoke. Quin felt as if the director of the scene had stopped for a coffee break. She reached for McCleary's hand, his fingers tightened on hers, an arm went around her waist. They were nearly eye to eye.

"C'mon, you," she said quietly. "If we're going to do this, let's do it right."

"Subtle Quin," he intoned.

He'd already unfolded the couch and made up the bed. The sheets were turned back, the pillows had been fluffed up, light splashed over them. He kissed her again there in the doorway. Her hunger leaped across her skin. How long had it been since she'd felt like this? *How long?*

Quin had always found undressing to be the most awkward part of lovemaking. But this time it was slow, a dance of anticipation which they prolonged. She experienced a momentary sense of déjà vu when she lifted her arms and he drew her gown over her head. Then she shivered as a burst of air from the overhead vent slipped down her spine. She crept under the covers, noticing how McCleary scooped up his clothes and draped them over the back of the chair. *Different from Grant, who left his clothes wherever they fell.* As he stepped into the light, nearing the bed, she liked the sight of his body— the burly shoulders, the dark tone of his skin, flat stomach, his muscular legs. In this way, too, he was different from Grant, who was taller, thinner, hirsute. She expected her clear recollection of Grant's body to distress her, but it didn't. The light winked out, and McCleary rolled in beside her. He just lay there for a moment, not touching her, saying nothing. Her heart seemed to cry out in the stillness as he reached for her hand. Just her hand.

"I've missed you," he whispered, his thumb making lazy circles across her knuckles. Then his fingers moved lightly along the underside of her wrist, her arm. It was almost too tender to bear. It made her ache inside, ache all over.

"That tickles, McCleary," she said softly.

She felt rather than saw his face lowering to hers. It

153

occurred to her that Grant had not been much of a kisser. But McCleary was. His hand moved along her waist, across her thighs. He touched her like a blind man, learning the contours of her bones, her muscles, her joints, charting her as she was him. He kissed her again; their tongues danced. His mouth traveled along the slope of her shoulders, back up the curve of her neck. His hair smelled faintly of shampoo, smoke. Everything about him was gentle, slow, but mixed with a bristling intensity that excited her. The ache became focalized wherever he touched her, smoldering, then spreading out across her skin like a brushfire. With Grant, it had never been like this, never so slow. There had always been an exigency about him, as though he were pressed for time. With McCleary, there was no time, space dipped and curved and twisted like a Möbius strip, and now and then they would pause as if to surface for air.

After a while, Quin couldn't tell whether his mouth or his hands were touching her, she couldn't tell where his body ended and her own began. The ache was everywhere, then localized across her breasts, her throat, between her thighs. Then he was inside her, his voice a husky whisper, their bodies fitting together rib to rib, thigh to thigh, the ache a white cocoon of pleasure.

Afterward, they talked about everything except murder. He handed her his childhood as the only boy in a family of women, and she spoke of her sister, her parents. He'd majored in art, he said, but realized early on he wouldn't be able to make a living at it, so he'd sold insurance for several years in Syracuse, and hated it. His career, like hers, was an accidental profession.

As they talked, he began to caress her again, gently, slowly, as though he were memorizing the texture of her skin, her hair. She hadn't expected him to be so gentle. It was almost as if, because of his work, the tender side of him had been locked up in a back room of his life. And now, released, it flowed with unhampered emotion. With it came a compulsion to explain why he hadn't spoken to her since the day after Izzo had removed him

154

from the case. "I kept wanting to call, Quin, I kept feeling that I owed you an explanation, but . . ."

"Look, McCleary, it's not your fault that you were taken off the case, okay?"

"You don't understand. I think Izzo removed me from the case because Paul Holmes is blackmailing him, but I haven't done a damned thing to prove it."

The pronouncement about Paul didn't surprise her. She'd almost expected something like this. "What good will it do to prove it?"

"As long as I'm officially off the case, it means I can't put anyone in homicide on it without Izzo knowing about it. And to investigate Grant's death thoroughly, Quin, I need help. This serial killing stuff has kept me tied up twelve hours a day."

"What about Robin, can't she help?"

"Paul Holmes made sure she wouldn't be able to. He extended the seminar. And since the seminar is required by the county for all cops with less than ten years, Izzo supposedly can't do anything. So it's just been Benson and me."

"Where does Robin fit, McCleary? I mean, with you?"

He didn't answer immediately. But when he did, his voice was different, injured. "I don't know. We aren't seeing each other anymore." He paused. The sound of his breathing was like a pulse. "How'd you know, anyway?"

"That day I met her in your office. I sensed it, I guess.

"I think she's screwing Holmes, but that's only part of it. Things haven't been very good for a long time between us."

"Are you in love with her?" *And suppose he says yes, Quin? Then what?* She held her breath until he spoke.

"I don't know."

Quin let out her breath. *I don't know* was a whole lot better than a flat, irrevocable, *Yes.*

He lifted up on an elbow and gazed down at her, hand resting in the curve of her waist. "Are you still in love with Grant?"

"Grant's dead."

"Well, the Robin I knew is dead too."

It wasn't quite the same thing, Quin thought, but at least he'd been honest with her, which was more than she could say for Grant. "Let's just do one thing, okay, McCleary?"

"What's that."

"Be up front with each other. I'm sort of sick of lies."

He made a soft sound, not quite a laugh. "I can't imagine being anything but with you, Quin." He lowered his face toward hers, his hand slipped from her waist, along her thighs, and between her legs. He rubbed gently, his finger slid in, out, the movement slow, lazy, then he was inside her again and Quin floated out into the deep, wet dark of desire.

17

THE WARM WIND embraced me, slid along my bare arms as the man and I walked through Coconut Grove toward the bay. He had eyes like a cocker spaniel's, watery and sad, and a mouth that drooped like a flower.

He hadn't said much—not since we'd left Richard's, where we'd met, and not now. His loneliness was like a shield. He was just the sort of man my protagonist would like. His name was Elton. "As in Elton John?" I'd asked, and he'd laughed.

The moon was bright in the sky, and beams of milky light shot across the still bay waters. We sat in the grass under a banyan tree. Its roots had erupted through the ground and meandered like backcountry roads beneath its massive canopy. It was late; the Grove was empty-ing. Except for music from one of the bars, music that skimmed the dark like the beginning of a dream, it was peaceful here, quiet. I was content to just sit and think of how I would write this scene: Elton leaning back on his hands, legs stretched out in front of him, the rich scent of the air, the strains of music, a hesitant peace.

He was maybe twenty-five, fit, tall, with curly blond hair that kept falling to his forehead. "I just found out today that I wasn't approved for the loan I needed for graduate school," he said.

"Why not?"

"Because the feds have cut back on educational loans for graduate students." He reached into his back pocket,

157

pulled out his wallet and a joint. He lit it, puffed, passed it to me. The first hit made me cough.

"Hey, go easy. That stuff's been treated with something, I think."

"With what? Paraquat?"

"I hope not."

We finished the joint, and I felt like I'd slipped inside the folds of time. Sensations turned lazily, like a fan, each of its bones a separate world: there, the prickly textures of grass against my hands, the sweet fragrance from the bay tickling my nostrils, the way the ground cushioned my head and molded itself to my body as I stretched out. I gazed up through the trees into the black underside of the sky. The stars seemed close enough to touch. But when I lifted my arm, I seized only air. Elton leaned over me, smiling. He smelled faintly of freshly mown grass, summer. "Good stuff, huh."

"I'm hungry," I told him.

He pulled me to my feet. "C'mon, I live near here. I'll make us sandwiches or something."

I didn't like to go anywhere without my car. "How far?"

"Just two blocks. Short blocks."

"Okay."

He lived on the second floor of an old building with a wraparound porch. My eye for detail had sharpened since that night at the Bon Soir. I noted the way the porch sagged in a corner like a fat belly over a belt, the sticky, dirty dishes stacked in the kitchen sink, the worn look of the creaky wooden floor.

Elton made us submarine sandwiches. He served them on paper plates, apologizing profusely that all the other plates in the house were in the sink. The bread was stale, but the sauce and trimmings were delicious. It reminded me of the barbecues my parents used to have before Daddy died, before the business with Billy.

I sat with my legs propped against the porch railing, my toes curling over the rough wood, bits of the sauce dribbling onto my chin. It was peaceful here on Elton's porch, where I could see the rising moon squatting between the branches of a pine tree, and the shadows of clouds scudding the horizon.

158

Once, while he was telling me a story about something, he flicked at the tomato sauce on my chin, then leaned forward and kissed me. Gently. "You're not a student, are you?" he asked, touching my hair as he pulled away.

"No. A writer."

"What kind of writing?"

"Novels."

"Neat," he said, and that was that.

He was the first man I'd met in a long time who wasn't impressed with that word, *writer*. I didn't know whether it made me like him more—or less.

We smoked a second joint and I wanted to curl up somewhere and go to sleep. I imagined I was at home in my parent's yard, swinging in a hammock in summer heat. The netting held me, kept me safe, and when I opened my eyes, Elton and I were lying in a hammock strung between two poles on the porch. "How'd we get here?"

He laughed softly. "We climbed in, how else?"

And any minute now, I thought, Billy would come along and overturn the hammock and down I'd tumble. That had happened . . . *when?*

The day he died, yes, now I remembered. The day he'd died, he'd thrown me out of the hammock, and that was a few days after the incident when he and his friends had held me down and . . .

I didn't mean to hurt Billy, I really didn't. I found the knife in the kitchen drawer. It was one of those big butcher knives Mama kept around for carving roasts. I took it because I needed some sort of protection while I said what I had to say to him. I marched across the field by the lake where he and his stupid friends drank beer and found him alone, propped up against a tree, reading. I told him in my nicest, calmest voice that I would report him to the police for what he and his friends had done to me if he ever so much as looked at me funny again. He started to laugh. *You loved it, you know you did. That's why you haven't told anyone.*

The words yanked at something inside me and I lunged at him with the knife.

After, when he lay there in the grass, bleeding all over

his books, I pulled him by the arms to the edge of the lake. I was so afraid someone would come, that someone would find us, I removed my clothes and pulled him into the water. I paddled clear out to the center of the lake, pulling him alongside me in a neck lock like I'd learned in lifesaving class, and then I let go of him and he sank. Sank like a stone.

I washed myself, but the sensation of blood was still on my skin. So I rubbed mud all over myself, rubbed and rubbed until my skin was nearly raw. And then I dug a hole with my fingers, the black earth backing painfully up under my nails, and I buried the knife, deep. I covered the spot with leaves.

Elton's tongue was in my mouth and I couldn't breathe. I pushed him away, sat up, the hammock rocking, Elton murmuring, "Kara, what's wrong?"

"I'm okay, I'm okay." Breathless, my voice. "I've got a real bad headache."

"It's probably the grass. You want some aspirin?"

"Yeah, okay, thanks."

The screen door squeaked when he went into the apartment. I swung my legs over the edge of the hammock, breathing deeply, pushing at the sharp pain in my temples, my neck. For some reason, I thought of Quin, and knew she was responsible for my discomfort. It was as if her indomitable pursuit of the truth about Grant left tiny marks like bites along my neck, my shoulders. In fact, when Elton returned with aspirin and a glass of water, I asked him if there was anything on my neck. I lifted my hair so he could look.

"I don't see anything, Kara," he said, then pressed his mouth to the nape of my neck, gently. I took the aspirin, and he began to knead my sore muscles gently.

"Better?"

"Much, thanks." But I could still feel Quin beyond us in the darkness, Quin digging away for her stupid clues, and I hated her.

"Just relax."

So I did. I rested my cheek against his shoulder, remembering a night when Grant and I had sat on a porch somewhere, maybe in Key West. He'd asked if I was jealous of the other women in his life, and I'd laughed and asked if he was jealous of my other men. It was a ridiculous conversation in many ways. But it was as if we both understood that our relationship, brief as it was, couldn't have existed without the others, circling us like planets. From that day on, there'd been no mention of others.

Why should I think of that now?

Because of Quin. That weekend, Quin had been out of town. Yes, Grant had said as much. *My other lady's gone for the weekend.*

When Elton began to caress me again, I felt the stirring of desire. A nice man, Elton. He kissed me, gently; probed me with his fingers, gently. We made love, gently, so gently, beneath the milky eyes of the stars, and funny, but inside my head, across the dark screen of my lids, a whole section of my next chapter was suddenly there:

When she woke up, the moon was no longer visible, the stars had slid down through the cleavage of the clouds, into the inky sky. Insects buzzed at her ears, the man was snoring. She dressed, started down the steps, but the circuit breaker in her head slammed into place and pain whipped through her skull. It nearly knocked her off her feet. She gripped the railing, eyes squeezed shut as she whimpered, as the pain climbed and dug and worked its way down into her spine, her heart.

Panic clawed at her throat. Why should she go back? He wasn't Billy. Billy was dead, buried at the bottom of the lake with her past

Which lake?

The lake in . . . she couldn't remember.

Was he really dead?

She moved back to the hammock, feeling as if she were gliding over water and . . .

I looked down at him. He wasn't Billy Hendrix. He was . . . Elton. My character wanted to kill him, needed to, but I didn't want to hurt him. He'd been gentle with me. I stepped away from the hammock, my back against the rough wood of the wall.

I stared at the knife's sleek, sharp lines, the way the pearl handle fit my hand. It seemed to shimmer, as if lit from within like Excalibur, like . . . I wanted to shout at him, wake him up as I moved toward him. *Run, Elton, run.* But my teeth bit down over my lips, sealing them.

I paused at the edge of the hammock, noting the soft, serene smile on his face. A cherubic face. And because he'd been gentle with me, I killed him as he slept. The knife slid through his skin, into his heart, his eyes fluttered open, and then he was dead. A swift, painless death.

Afterward, I cried and made a tiny cross on his forehead with my knuckle. I drew it gently, and then, because the sight of his wide, dead eyes hurt me, I touched his lids, closing them.

Closing them gently.

18

1.

SCRAMBLED EGGS, BACON, whole-wheat rolls, baked plantains, coffee: Quin's appetite swelled huge as Texas as
she joined McCleary at the kitchen table. "*Platanos,*"
he exclaimed, tapping his plantain with the tip of his
fork. "I love these things."

"Grant used to fry them, but I like them baked. Oh, I
forgot the butter."

"I'll get it," McCleary said. But a moment later, he
turned away from the fridge and announced he couldn't
find any.

Quin's cheeks flushed with embarrassment. *Not the
drawer, oh please don't be in the drawer.* She opened it:
no butter, no ants.

McCleary stood to the side, watching her, smiling.
"You keep the butter in a drawer?"

"It ends up there sometimes."

She expected a snide remark. Instead, he threw his
head back and laughed. "Well, in that case, I guess I
should check the pantry." Quin looked through the cabinet next to the stove as McCleary padded over to the
pantry door. "Here it is." He held the container in the
palm of his hand like an offering, and he was still smiling. Quin took it, lifted off the top, stared with dismay at
the goo left inside. But there weren't any ants.

"So much for the butter," she said. "But now your

163

food's cold. I'll warm your plate in the microwave." But as she reached for his plate, he took her hand, uncurled her fingers, and kissed the center of her palm. His smoky eyes were laughing.

"I like my food cold," he said.

No nasty comments, he didn't want his breakfast warmed up, he didn't seem to give a damn whether the butter was in the pantry or the hall closet: Quin was delighted. They ate in silence for a few minutes, and she watched him furtively. It was her contention that you could tell a lot about a person from the way he ate. Grant, for instance, had been a gobbler, eating in much the same way that he'd made love—quickly, carelessly, as though his mind were already ruminating on the next task. But McCleary ate slowly, with the same careful, pensive absorption she'd noticed about him last night. He surrendered himself so completely to the pleasure of eating that, looking at him, you wouldn't guess he carried the weight of a slew of serial murders on his shoulders.

He glanced up at her, then leaned across the table, touched her chin, and kissed the tip of her nose. Then he sat back and said, "Where all did you try that key, Quin?"

She was trying to think of a subtle way to suggest they continue what they'd started last night, and it took her a moment to realize what he was referring to. "Grant's footlocker in the attic and his fishing tackle box. It didn't fit either one."

"I think I'll take the emeralds over to Ginger's Jewelers to be appraised."

"Why, honey chile, you'll find Ms. Magnolia jus' the sweetest little thing on two feet," Quin drawled, and McCleary laughed.

"That bad?"

"Worse. Don't go as a cop, though. You'll probably get more out of her that way. What's going to happen to the emeralds, McCleary? I mean, legally?"

"Well, they're part of Grant's estate, so they'll go into probate, then probably to you, since he willed you most everything else." He paused. "Assuming that your intruder last night was after the key, who all knew about it?"

She thought about it, then counted off nearly a dozen names: Nikki and Steve Killington, Robin and Benson, Izzo, the Colombian couple, Trevor Forsythe, Rusty, Treena Esposito, and Paul Holmes.

McCleary's face tightened. "Holmes and Treena? How'd *they* find out?"

"Treena called me a few days ago, supposedly to see how I was doing. I told her about the emeralds and the key. I didn't know then about her visit to you."

"And Holmes?"

"I don't know. He called to tell me Grant's attorney would be getting in touch and mentioned it then."

McCleary leaned forward. "Mentioned it how?"

"You want it verbatim?"

McCleary nodded.

She put herself in her I-am-Holmes-the-DA frame of mind and, in her most arrogant voice, let the words roll: " 'Hey, Quin, I heard something about a key and emeralds that belonged to Grant. That true?' "

McCleary laughed again. "So what'd you say?"

"Instead of giving him a straight answer like I probably would've done two weeks ago, I asked him what the fifteen grand was for. He went into this routine about it being a repayment on a loan. Hell, Grant never had that kind of money. At least, I don't *think* he did. So then I asked him what his connection was to Ginger Hale, and he laughed in that irritating way he has and said he was taking the fifth on that one. So maybe we should add Ginger Hale to the list too, McCleary."

His expression had changed; his skin suddenly seemed pale, pasty.

"How do you think Paul found out about the emeralds and the key?" she asked.

He averted his gaze. "Robin," he replied, and she understood his expression. The tone of his voice indicated he'd drawn the same conclusion she had the moment he'd uttered Robin Bird's name.

"Oh." She reached for her coffee cup. "Is that, uh, what you meant last night when you said things hadn't been good between you two for a long time?"

As his eyes slid back to her face, she saw injury, the cicatrices of betrayal. "Yeah, I guess that's part of it."

He sat back with a sigh. "I've suspected for a while that something was going on. I just wasn't sure what."

So, Quin thought, here was another secret uncovered in the wake of Grant's death, another intimate web of deception. She could pat his hand and tell him she knew how he felt, which was true, but that wasn't the point. If Robin actually preferred Holmes over McCleary, then she had a brain the size of a pea and deserved whatever she got. *That* was the point. But how could she say that without it sounding like a diatribe against the woman? Best to say nothing at all, she decided, and got up to clear the table.

A while later, after McCleary had left and Quin was waiting for the locksmith to arrive, Nikki dropped by. She swept into the house in a wave of expensive perfume, dressed to utter perfection. She chattered about the engagement party she and Steve were giving this weekend, ticking off the words like seconds on a clock that had been wound too tightly. "So can you come, Quin? It'll be at Steve's." Then she picked up the cup of coffee Quin had poured her and leaned into the counter as though she'd just run out of breath.

"You mind if I bring a date?"

"A date?" The word rolled pinched into the air, incomplete. Implicit in the question was a judgmental undercurrent that whispered, *A date so soon after Grant's death?* "No, of course not. Uh, who's the man? Anyone I know?"

Before Quin could answer, the doorbell rang. She excused herself and returned several moments later with the locksmith. She pointed at the back door. "There. I need a dead bolt that's going to hold and locks on all the windows. Good locks."

Nikki, who'd been too involved with what she'd been saying to notice the door, now frowned at it, and the frown deepened when the locksmith whistled. "B and E?" he asked. Quin nodded. "Well, I hope you're having a burglar alarm system installed."

"That's next on my agenda. You know of anyone good?"

"Sure, remind me before I leave and I'll give you the guy's number. Excuse me, gotta get my stuff outa the truck."

"What's going on, Quin?" Nikki asked.

"I had a break-in last night and got smacked over the head."

"*What?* Are you okay? Did you call the cops? Was anything taken? How can you be so bloody calm about this?"

"Because it's over," she replied, and told her briefly what had happened, but deleted the part about McCleary.

"I wish you'd leave town or something until Grant's killer's been found, Quin, that's what I wish."

"No way. That'd be too convenient."

"Then get a gun."

"I have a gun."

"What kind?"

"A thirty-eight."

"Get a forty-five, Quin. I mean it. You have an intruder and he's looking into the nose of a forty-five, he's going to think twice about doing anything to you."

"I didn't realize you knew anything about guns."

Nikki laughed. "You must be kidding. Any woman living alone in this area who *doesn't* have a gun is just asking for it. Believe me." She made an impatient gesture with her hand. "I wish you'd called me. I would've come over and stayed. I hate the thought of your having been here alone after it happened."

"I wasn't alone. McCleary stayed."

"So he's your date?" Her smile was odd—slow, almost sly.

"If he can come, yes."

"I hope you know what you're doing, Quin."

She detected that judgmental tone again. "What's *that* supposed to mean?"

"Didn't you tell me he was involved with another cop?"

"*Was.* Not anymore."

"Look, I think it's great you're trying to put all of this behind you as quickly as possible, Quin. But don't get hurt." *By falling for a guy who may have a roving eye like Grant:* that was the parenthetical phrase left unstated.

"I didn't say I was in love with the man, Nikki."

"Just be careful, Quin, that's all, okay?" Then, as if sensing Quin was about to ask her again what it was she hadn't told her about Grant, Nikki glanced at her watch. "Gotta run, honey. I've got a client coming in about half an hour who's *badly* in need of color advice. The party's going to be at Steve's. Or did I already tell you that?" She laughed gaily. "Nine Friday. Bring McCleary. Be happy."

At the door, she hugged Quin, then she was gone. For several moments afterward, *Be happy, be happy,* rang in her mind's ears like a mindless nursery rhyme.

2.

Eight-fifteen, McCleary thought, and it must've been ninety-eight in the shade. As he strode toward the station from the parking lot, the air quivered with heat that seemed to rise in thin waves toward the membrane of lapis sky overhead. His eyes felt huge and swollen in his face from lack of sleep, and he knew it would take one foul look from Izzo to set him off.

Izzo: who'd been been assuming McCleary wouldn't defy orders when he'd removed him from the Bell case. Izzo: who'd been banking on the *honor system,* for Christ's sake. So what had the honor system done for him? For Quin? All it had done was buy Paul Holmes time. Yes siree, Holmes the Whore had probably spent the last two weeks laughing from breakfast to dinner, certain he'd gotten away with something. Which, until now, he had. Well, no more, McCleary decided, and wondered when Robin had told Holmes about the emeralds and the mysterious key. Maybe over an intimate dinner, thrown in with wine and pâté. It was one thing to lose Robin, but quite another to lose her to Holmes, with whom she'd no doubt discussed everything from their sex lives to their cases.

He thought of Robin's dark beauty, of Quin's lightness. She was sunlight, Robin was the moon. It was that simple, that complex. Christ, but he was a mess.

As he stepped off the elevator, McCleary sensed something was wrong. You didn't work in a place for ten years without becoming attuned to its subtle nuances, its moods. The large outer room where most of the secretaries worked sang with busy sounds: typewriters, com-

168

puter keys, voices, but no idle chatter. The air stretched thinly and tightly, like a rubber band that was going to snap at any moment.

McCleary walked into the staff kitchen for coffee and Benson was in there, idly stirring sugar into a steaming Styrofoam cup. His shoulders weren't slumped so much as huddled, as if he were battling a strong wind, and when he glanced up, he looked angry. No, rabid. His eyes seemed magnified behind his glasses, like huge dark pools.

"What's going on, Tim?" McCleary asked.

"You missed the goddamned show, Mike. Lucky you."

"What show?"

"The Bob Izzo get-your-asses-in-gear show, because there's been another knifing."

McCleary's insides shriveled. For two weeks, nothing, then the lady descended like a guillotine, as if to warn them not to kick up their feet and think they'd won. "Who was it this time?"

Benson pushed away from the table. "C'mon, I'll give you the rundown on the way there."

McCleary's RX7 hugged the interstate like a lover, negotiating rapid lane switches, ducks, quick retreats. Opened up, Lady would do a hundred and twenty-five comfortably, but now she cruised between seventy and seventy-five, with McCleary and Benson sealed almost soundlessly inside.

"Uh, aren't you kinda pushing it, Mac?" Benson asked, leaning forward in his seat, growing paler by the minute.

McCleary slowed to sixty-five and Benson smiled thinly. "Thanks. Now I won't lose my breakfast."

The thought of Benson throwing up on Lady's leather seats made McCleary slow to sixty. "So who was it?"

"A grad student at the University of Miami who lives in the Grove. A woman who lives downstairs found him. She said he was going out to a place called Richard's last night. He asked her to come, but she had to study. She didn't hear him come home, and when she didn't hear him leave this morning, she went upstairs. He'd been stabbed in his hammock. He was bare ass naked."

"Did you call Doc Smithers?"

"Yeah. He's probably already there."

169

The body was gone when McCleary and Benson arrived, but the lab crew was dusting the apartment for prints and Doc Smithers was propped on the porch railing, talking to one of the neighbors. There was a dried pool of blood beneath the hammock, a paper cup lying on its side, two paper plates with something crusted on them. Flies buzzed over the plates. McCleary felt a sudden, sickening loss. While he was making love to Quin and scheming how to nail Paul Holmes, the poor schmuck who lived here had already met his untimely demise. *And for what?*

Over the years, McCleary had thought a lot about death. You tended to when you worked homicide. What puzzled him most was that even if some part of man survived, maybe nothing more than a fluff of energy, what possible cosmic lesson was there to be learned through a violent death? Did it make you more humane the next time around—if there *was* a next time? Did it teach your soul the value of love? Just what the hell was the point?

The problem with all the cosmic questions, he decided, was that they suffered from the same thing that afflicted homicide investigators: the dark field, that impenetrable veil.

He and Benson spent most of the morning talking to neighbors in the building and to the manager of Richard's, the bar where Elton Higgins had met his lady, his nemesis. But it was the same story as every other bar where they'd interviewed people the last two weeks: Richard's was too large for anyone to have noticed a guy who'd left with a killer. That was South Florida, impersonal to the bitter end.

They returned to Higgins's apartment despite Benson's protests that it would just be a waste of time. McCleary looked through the rooms, closets, the wastebaskets, under the beds. He sat for a few moments on the porch near the hammock, trying to visualize Elton Higgins as he must've been when he was here with the knife lady. He even closed his eyes and listened to the crescive sounds of traffic, people, the busy, busy shuffle of life in the Grove, and then tried to blot it out, to bring back the night noises. He sat absolutely motionless, pushing until his mind was a soft, pink blank that might absorb something of what had happened here last night. But of course it was an exercise in futility.

When he got back to his office, he stood at the bow of his private ship, gazing into the sea that was Miami, wondering when it had all started to go sour for him. Ten years ago, it was almost paradise compared to Syracuse with its ten-foot snowdrifts and months when the sun didn't shine. Now it was . . . bad, that was all. Just bad.

"Mike?"

He stiffened at the sound of Izzo's voice. *Not now, Izzo. Don't bug me now.* "Yeah."

Izzo came in and shut the door. "You've got to speed things up with these knifings. I mean it. I got a call from the mayor this morning, and he—"

McCleary spun around. "How about telling the mayor we need more men, Bob. More resources. More of everything. Tell him we're already working fourteen-hour days and making about a quarter of what he pulls in a year. Tell him that."

Izzo's tanned jowls went rigid. "What the fuck's your problem?"

I want out, a voice screamed in McCleary's head. I *just want out.* "I've gotta get some air."

As he started past Izzo, the chief caught his arm. "Hold on, boy, now just hold on," Izzo said, slipping back into his home boy routine.

McCleary stared at Izzo's fingers on his arm, thick, tanned, then he lifted his eyes. "Let go of my goddamned arm."

The chief's fingers slipped away. "You're under some serious pressure, Mike."

"Oh Christ. Now you're an armchair Freud?" His fist ached to connect with Izzo's jaw.

"Just an opinion."

"Well, let me tell you *my* opinion for a change." *Asshole.* "I think Paul Holmes has got something on you and that's why you've put the Bell case on what looks like a permanent back burner. That fucker's a damned good contender for having killed Bell, and you, friend, are preventing an investigation to save your own ass from who the hell knows what."

Blood rushed into Izzo's face. He lifted up on the balls of his feet so he was exactly eye-level with McCleary. "Watch it, boy, just watch it. Or you may find yourself outa here this quick." He snapped his fingers in McCleary's face and stormed out of the office.

McCleary stared after him and then burst out laughing. *Suspension, Izzo? About now, it would be a blessing.*

3.

Quin stopped in Trevor's office when she got to work, but he was gone. She asked Ruth Grimes, his secretary, where he was. "Church," she said, as if it were the normal place to be at this time of day.

Quin rolled her eyes. *"Now?* He's in church now?"

Ruth fingered the gold necklace at her wrinkled throat. Her tanned and leathery face, the result of decades of weekends baking on Florida beaches, showed disapproval of Quin's attitude. "The accountant was here earlier, and right after that, he left."

"And Trevor said he was going to church."

"That's right."

"This is getting ridiculous. Last week, that Reverend John from that Church of the Holy Rollers or whatever it is—"

"Church of the Good Faith, I think it's called," Ruth intoned with a glare. Her expression said she would fiercely defend Trevor and his church.

"Well, whatever. That reverend was in here last week, and he and Trevor were closed up in his office for more than two hours."

Ruth smiled tightly, but the fight seemed to trickle from her eyes. "Uh, Quin, I was wondering. Is it true the firm's losing money?"

"So Trevor tells me."

"Hmm." She grew pensive for a moment. When she spoke again, he voice was lower, confidential. "Look, I think you should know that when the reverend left last week, he had a check for two thousand that Trevor had given him."

"Two *thousand*? You're sure?" Of course she was sure. If nothing else, Ruth knew what was going on in this office.

"Yeah, I saw the entry in the checkbook. I mean, I wouldn't normally have said anything, Quin." She whispered now. "But if the company's losing money, it, uh, seems to me that—"

"You wouldn't have the checkbook handy, would you, Ruth?"

"Until this morning, I did. But the accountant took it along with all the records." She leaned forward. "I've been a little concerned, to be quite honest with you. I can't afford to lose this job."

"You're not going to lose your job, Ruth." Quin paused. "Would you do me a favor? As soon as the records are brought back, let me know, okay? I think it's time I started paying attention to the financial wheeling and dealings around here."

"Good for you, honey. I mean, two thousand dollars . . ."

Yeah: two grand when Trevor was screaming about selling every bit of property the firm owned. There was something stinky about this, she decided. Something very stinky, indeed.

"Well, if Trevor comes back, Ruth, tell him I'm out for the day, okay?"

"Any place he can reach you?"

"No, I don't think so." She rubbed at the knot over her ear. The weird ex–Mrs. Bell had some questions to answer.

19

1.

GINGER HALE REMINDED McCleary of a little wind-up doll, the kind that talked and laughed and pooped if you pushed the right buttons. She didn't seem bright enough to run a jewelry store—or any kind of business, for that matter. She was petite, looked taller than she actually was because of her two-inch heels, and her drawl was definitely acquired. She was initially somewhat cool and distant toward him, her pert nose just as high in the air as it could go without throwing her off balance. But as soon as he told her he wanted to have some gems appraised that a relative had willed him, she bubbled like soda water and smothered him in Southern hospitality.

She had coffee and a plate of fingertip sandwiches brought in. The sandwiches, delicate things minus the crust, oozed a green substance that looked suspiciously like avocado mixed with mayonnaise. He passed on those, but accepted the coffee. When he brought out the shoebox and lifted the lid, her eyes widened, but only momentarily. She made a soft, sniffling sound, as if to show him she was only mildly interested. Scratch the wind-up doll routine, he thought. The woman wasn't stupid.

"Emeralds are one of mah specialities, you know."

She was turning a stone against the light from the window. "In fact, these are Colombian emeralds, and judging from the bluish green color, ah'd say they're from the Chivor mine."

"You can tell just from the color?" McCleary exclaimed.

"Honey, ah can even give you a good guess about how deep in a mine an emerald is found." She'd popped something in her eye to examine the stone more closely, and when she glanced up, she looked like an alien with a distended black eye shaped like a cone. "During Pizarro's time, you see, the Muzo and Chivor mines in Colombia were producing, but they were covered up and hidden by the Indians before the Spaniards could seize them. Just before the turn of the century, the mine at Muzo was reopened, and in the 1920s, the Chivor mine was rediscovered. But judging from the crystallization on these gems, ah would venture to say that what you have here, Mr. McCleary, are emeralds from a time much earlier than the twenties." She removed the object from her eye. There was a subtle shift in her expression that might've been suspicion, McCleary couldn't be sure. "Would you happen to know how your, uh, relative obtained these?"

"All I know was that they've been in the family for a long time. When my uncle died, he left them to me. Why do you think these are from an earlier time?"

Her smile was a bit strained now as she picked up another emerald. "Like I said, the crystallization. You see, the first precious stones found in a mine tend to be the largest and most beautiful. The deeper you go into a mine, the less perfect the color and the crystallization. Ah've seen gems from the Chivor mine, and they weren't nearly as beautiful as these, with crystallization as finely hewn." She plucked another emerald from the box. "We'd have to do further testing, of course, but ah suspect these emeralds are from Pizarro's time, Mr. McCleary, the early 1500s."

It was beginning to look as if part of the greenfire myth was true, he thought, the part about Pizarro's El Dorado being emeralds, not gold.

"Also, there are two stones here that are over ten

carats. That's a great rarity.'' She picked up the largest emerald, examined it, exhaled her breath so that it almost sounded like a whistle. "Every emerald has inclusions, but this one is as near perfect as anything ah've ever seen."

"What value would you place on these?" McCleary asked.

"Offhand? Oh, my." She sat back, the large emerald still in her hand. "Gems like this one often sell to collectors, Mr. McCleary. But just to give you an example of what you might pay in a store . . ." She opened her desk drawer and brought out an unset emerald about the size of a typed "O." "This sells for about eighty dollars, as is. And it's nowhere near the color or the beauty of even a single one of these stones." She replaced the emerald in the drawer and turned her attention back to the largest stone. "Ah would have to say this is worth between twelve and twenty thousand."

"Just this one stone?"

"Yes. Ah would be pleased to, uh, negotiate for you on these, since our services include finding buyers for collections such as these."

"Is that what you were going to do for Grant Bell, Ms. Hale?" The best offense lay in surprise: if there were any rules McCleary had learned over the years, that one was paramount. He removed his ID from his pocket and tossed it on the desk. She glanced at it, placed the gem back with the others.

"Ah see." With just those two words, all her Southern hospitality went out the window.

"No, I don't think you do."

Her face was paler, but she held her own nicely, McCleary thought.

"Is it a crime to have known the man?"

"No. But it *is* a crime to withhold information during a murder investigation."

She studied him a moment, evidently weighing the possible consequences of her various options. "What, exactly, would you like to know, anyway? Did ah know him? Yes. Were we lovers? Yes. Did ah kill him? Of course not." She moved stiffly to her chair, sat down.

"What percentage did he offer you for finding a buyer for his little collection here?"

Her hand flicked at the lapel of her jacket, which was turned up in back. "Thirty percent."

"On how many emeralds?"

"That ah don't know."

She wasn't looking at him now. She was staring at her kneecap, which poked out from the hem of her skirt. "Let me phrase it this way. Did he mention figures between ten and twelve million?"

"Actually, it was more like twenty or twenty-five million."

Interesting, McCleary thought. That figure was twice what Felix Mendez had mentioned in his letter, and he wondered if Bell had intended to cut Mendez in on only half. "Stolen emeralds?"

"Ah should say not, Mr. McCleary." Her eyes darted to his, and her voice was weighted with indignity. "The emeralds were supposed to have been from the Chivor and Muzo mines." She made an abrupt, impatient gesture with her hand. "Like those pretty ole things you've got. Ah presume that by now you've heard of the Greenfire myth."

"Yeah. So it's true."

She reached for one of the fingertip sandwiches. "Absolutely. It's a story that's been circulating for years." She took a dainty bite from the end of the sandwich, then patted her mouth with a cocktail napkin. "About eighteen months ago, ah made a trip to the Amazon with Grant, you see. He and one of the men he worked with had found about half a dozen very small emeralds—but of the same quality as those you have—and ah appraised them."

"Found them where?"

"Somewhere in the jungle. Ah don't know the specifics."

McCleary thought of the oxbow Felix Mendez had referred to in his letter.

"Ah told him if he found more of the same, ah would be most happy to find a buyer for the gems." She took another dainty bite at her sandwich.

"Was the man who worked with Grant a Peruvian named Felix Mendez?"

She wasn't able to cover her surprise this time. "Well, you *have* done your homework."

"Did you meet a man named Jason?"

"The only man I met was Mendez."

"How many gems did he bring back to the States?"

"Ah couldn't say, Mr. McCleary. These are the first ah've seen."

"Gems worth enough to kill for, wouldn't you say?"

She looked at him with contempt. "Mr. McCleary, ah am a businesswoman. Ah do not have to kill for jewels or anything else, you understand?" She came forward in her chair now, tapping a nail against the desk. A long red nail, like the Wicked Witch of the West. "Now if you want mah honest opinion, ah think you're barking up the wrong tree. Grant Bell was not killed for his gems or whatever other schemes he was involved in, ah can tell you that. He was probably done in by one of the sweet young things he so enjoyed bedding down."

"How about some names, Ms. Hale. The names of these sweet young things."

"Ah did not keep track of the riffraff, Mr. McCleary. In fact—not that it's any of your business—ah began to see, uh, less and less of Grant on a personal basis. With all the diseases going around now, you can't be too careful." She brushed a hand under her hair, and the sudden movement made her gold bracelets dance. "Ah do know that he'd met someone new shortly before he died, because he mentioned it on the phone one day."

"Do you know her name?"

"No, ah can't say that I do." She tugged at the hem of her skirt. "Now, if you don't have any more questions, Mr. McCleary, ah have a store to run."

McCleary picked up the box of emeralds. "If you're planning on leaving town, Ms. Hale, please get in touch with me first."

Her smile was derisive. "Ah certainly will, but ah don't anticipate going anywhere, Mr. McCleary."

As McCleary left the store, he was smiling. "Ah do declare, we may have to put a tail on you, honey chile," he drawled.

2.

As Quin drove south to Kendall, she kept thinking of the night she'd met Treena. She and Grant had gone over to the townhouse, where he was still living, to watch a movie on his VCR. A few minutes after they'd arrived, Treena had banged on the door, almost as if she'd been sitting in the parking lot, waiting for them. Quin, wanting to avoid an ugly scene, had gone upstairs to the bedroom.

Although she'd closed the door, she'd still heard Treena blowing into the townhouse like a foul wind, shouting her accusations. Grant, with his usual aplomb, had calmed her down, speaking to her in a voice a parent might use with a recalcitrant child. Quin kept waiting for the sound of the front door opening and closing, for the sound of Treena's car. Instead, she'd heard footfalls on the stairs, voices. Then the door had opened.

They'd stood there, the two of them, framed in the doorway. Treena had blinked her puffy red eyes, and Grant had smiled as if there were nothing at all strange about introducing your ex-wife to your current lady. Treena had managed a nod, Quin had muttered a greeting, then they'd both looked at Grant as though he were crazy. There had been a distended, embarrassed silence until Grant had begun to chatter about how Quin and Treena had something in common, since Quin used to be a teacher. She couldn't remember how long his monologue had gone on, but she recalled the way Treena's face had caved in bit by sorrowful bit. She'd finally just turned around and walked out. Quin had remained in the room, stupefied by Grant's cruelty.

Don't look at me that way, Quin. It's the only way she'll ever leave me alone. You don't know what she's like. Two years we've been divorced and she's still pulling this crap, and I'm sick of it.

Grant had alluded to similar incidents, Quin recalled. Perhaps those cruelties had been more subtle, but they'd left scars on Treena nonetheless. If anyone had a motive for killing Grant, Treena did, Quin decided. The question, though, was why would she go to such great lengths to obtain the key? Whatever it fit didn't necessarily contain more emeralds. But if not emeralds, then what?

Quin timed her arrival just right. Treena Esposito had apparently just gotten home from summer school, because she was walking toward the house, glancing through her mail, as Quin drove up. She parked behind Treena's Honda and got out.

"Hi."

"Quin." She dropped the mail in her purse, ran a hand through her thick blond hair. "This *is* unexpected."

"You have a few minutes?"

"Yeah, sure. C'mon inside."

The house was something of a surprise. Quin had expected disorder—dishes stacked in the sink, shoes left wherever they'd been removed, magazines spilling out of their containers. She'd expected evidence of the frenzy she'd seen the night she'd met Treena. Instead, the rooms were meticulous, everything in its place, the floors as glossy as mirrors. It looked like a cleaning service had swept through the night before. But there was something wrong, a kind of incompleteness about the rooms, as though Treena and her husband had just moved in, and Quin knew that wasn't the case.

For the first few minutes, as Treena poured them glasses of cold lemonade, their conversation was little more than empty chatter, filler. They talked about Hurricane Ingrid, churning restlessly in the Atlantic, undecided about her direction. They talked about teaching, the Latin American debt crisis, about everything except Grant. It was as if he were incidental to their acquaintance and had nothing at all to do with why Quin was there.

When they moved out onto the patio, Treena suddenly said, "I had a little run-in with that bastard detective."

"McCleary?"

Her sharp green eyes skewed with scorn. "You know what he did, Quin? He actually called up my principal, for Christ's sake, and implied that I'd killed Grant!"

"Oh, c'mon, Treena. Maybe you misunderstood." McCleary might be guilty of any number of things, Quin

180

mused, but accusing people behind their backs wasn't one of them.

"Misunderstood?" She laughed. "Hardly. My principal called me into his office and started this very subtle line of questioning, until I asked him point blank what he was getting at. He told me. I saw red, Quin, I mean it. I literally saw red."

"But you have an alibi, right?"

"Well . . . yeah." She hesitated, then lowered her eyes and ran her fingers down the sweating sides of her glass. "I mean, I was at the faculty meeting, just like I told McCleary. Unfortunately, I neglected to mention that I had to leave the meeting because Benny had locked himself out of the house and I had to come back here to let him in."

No wonder McCleary was suspicious, Quin thought, and noticed how Treena quickly changed the subject. She asked Quin how she was getting along, how the firm was doing, and on and on. Quin interrupted her when Treena finally paused to sip from her glass. "Someone broke into my place last night and hit me over the head." She expelled the words, she didn't just say them, and she could tell from the expression on Treena's face that she'd understood the implication.

She sighed—heavily, ruefully—and sat back in her chair. "Jesus, Quin. Jesus." was all she said. Her startling eyes deepened in color, then lightened. One moment they were stormy seas, and the next they turned the translucent green of a wind-torn pasture, a field.

"You were one of the people who knew about the key, Treena," Quin said, speaking quietly, carefully.

Treena folded her hands around her glass, looked at Quin, smiled, shook her head, then laughed. "There are days, Quin, many, many, days, when I wish I'd never met Grant." Her voice cracked and was laced with despair. Quin squirmed. She wasn't sure she wanted to hear more about Grant's dark side, his little cruelties. But she couldn't just get up and leave. No, that wasn't quite right: she didn't *want* to just get up and leave.

"It's gotten so that I can't even have a normal relationship with a man because of him, because of those five goddamned years we were married," Treena continued. "Do you know what that's like? Do you know . . . oh hell. What difference does it make. He's dead. And you know what? I'm not sorry. Sad, yes, but not sorry. My marriage to Benny has turned to shit. Did I tell you that? No, I guess I didn't. But we're separating. We've been separated for six weeks. We . . ." She stopped, evidently realizing, as Quin had, that if she and Benny had separated six weeks ago, that meant he wasn't living here. So how could Treena have returned to the house to let Benny in because he'd gotten locked out?

Quin blinked. The heat in the patio clamped down over her, and within the dome of its stillness she heard Treena shouting at Grant that night: *I wish I'd never met you. I wish you were dead.*

"Quin, listen, please. It isn't what you think. It—"

"Then what, Treena? Why lie about it if you don't have anything to hide?"

"I . . ." She rolled her lip against her teeth.

Quin saw the anguish of a struggle in Treena's eyes, then anger.

"It's none of your business. It's not anyone's business. I don't have to tell you or that jerk McCleary anything. Just leave me alone, Quin. I mean it."

Quin didn't realize she'd pushed away from the table until she was standing. "I'm sorry Grant hurt you so deeply, Treena, but I hope to God you didn't kill him."

"Get out, Quin," Treena hissed, not looking at her. "Just get the hell out."

3.

Henry Mulhollen looked like a bartender, McCleary decided. He had a beer belly he tried to hide beneath a loose shirt, a macadam of telltale veins at the end of his bulbous nose, and a graying beard that he scratched every few minutes. He'd called McCleary nearly an hour ago, claiming that Tom Darcy, the tennis pro, had been drinking at the Green Olive, where Mulhollen tended bar, the night he'd been killed.

McCleary asked him why it had taken him so long to call.

182

"I've been on vacation, that's why. You wanna beer?"

"No, thanks. You have any coffee?"

"Coming up."

He shuffled to the bar and a few minutes later returned with McCleary's coffee and a draft for himself. "Tom Darcy used to come in here pretty regular, maybe once or twice during the week and at least once on the weekends. Sometimes he had a date with him, sometimes he didn't. The night he was here, he was alone. I wasn't on till seven or so, and we played a couple games of pool, then I went to work.

"This woman comes in. When I first saw her, I thought, shit, she's got class. But then after a while, I decided there was something . . . I don't know, weird about her, man, like she wasn't all there or something. Tending bar, you see all types, and you get so you can read people pretty well."

"Weird how?" McCleary asked.

"Well, she never looked me directly in the eyes, see. I mean, when she ordered her Dewar's, she was lookin' at herself in the mirror behind the bar there."

"Describe her."

Mulhollen's hesitation didn't bode well, McCleary thought.

" 'Bout average height, but she might've been wearing high heels, so I don't know how accurate that is. Her hair was reddish—"

"How reddish? Real red, like Lucille Ball?"

"No. Coppery like. Tinted, yeah, her hair was tinted."

"Was her hair long? Short? What?"

Mulhollen frowned, scratched his beard, shook his head. "I think it was short. But maybe it was long and she was wearing it up. I honestly can't remember, Mr. McCleary."

Great. Drinkers rarely made good witnesses. "What else can you remember about her?"

"She wore a lot of makeup and had blue eyes, these incredible blue eyes like you see on TV commercials sometimes, you know the kind I mean?"

Yeah, McCleary thought. The kind of blue that contact lenses gave you.

"Anyways, Tom he was sitting at the booth, see, and after a while, he came up to the bar. He's always had a

183

thing about good-lookin' women, and that night he'd been puttin' away a lotta beers. So he sits down and he buys her a drink and I could see they were gettin' real chummy. I heard her say she was a writer, and bein' in the bar was her research. Later, I heard Tom call her Karen or Kathy or—"

"Which one? Karen or Kathy?"

He snapped his fingers. "Kara, that was it. Anyway, they left together."

"You didn't hear her last name?" Mulhollen shook his head. "What time did they leave?"

"Between one-thirty and two."

Doc Smithers had placed Darcy's death at between one and five in the morning, McCleary remembered, so that much fit. "Was she driving her own car?"

"I don't know."

"Did you overheard her say anything about what kind of writing she does?"

Mulhollen grew pensive. His eyes took on a gloss, as though he were trying to pierce the barrier of the last few weeks and put himself back in the bar that night. "Books," he exclaimed proudly. "That was it. Books."

"What kind of books?"

He sat back, dejected. "Hell, I don't know. I mean, this place was pretty full, Detective McCleary."

Kara who wrote books: it was more than he'd hoped for. "Would you be able to come down to the station and talk to one of our artists?"

"Could he come here? My car's in the shop."

"Yeah, I guess I could arrange that. When's a good time for you?"

"I'm here usually from noon until closing."

"Long hours."

"Free booze," Mulhollen grinned, and downed the last of his beer.

McCleary stopped by the Dade County Library on his way back to the station. There were five librarians behind the reference desk and at least half a dozen people waiting for help. He took a number and got in line, wondering when libraries had become like deli counters.

"Number nine," said a short woman with stiff gray

hair and a pair of bifocals that rode low on her nose. McCleary gave her his plastic number. "Yes, what do you need?"

Ham and cheese on rye to go. He felt a bit intimidated by the air of sharp impatience about her. "Some information."

Drumming her fingers now: "That's what *reference* means, sir."

"How can I find out about an author?"

She shifted her weight to her other foot and peered at him over the bifocals. "That depends on what you want to know."

"What books a particular author has written."

"Well, sir, there's *Books in Print*. There you'll find every book currently in print in this country, listed by author, title, and subject."

"Listed by the author's last name?"

The corner of her mouth dimpled as she made a sound of exasperation. "Of course by the last name."

"Suppose I've only got the author's first name?"

"The author's first name," she repeated, a hand on her hip as she tilted to the side like a teapot. He thought she was going to scream at him and felt like he was twelve years old again and had just farted in class. Then, unexpectedly, she laughed. "As far as I know, there's no reference book that lists authors by their first names."

"Look," he went on, encouraged by her laugher, "I'm in something of a jam." He handed her his ID. They moved to the end of the counter, away from the people behind McCleary, and he explained his dilemma.

"Oh. My. Kara certainly isn't much to go on, Mr. McCleary. Even though you've narrowed it to books, what kind of books? Fiction or nonfiction?"

"I don't know."

She pushed her bifocals back into her stiff hair. They reminded him of aviator's goggles now. "If you could somehow narrow it down further, to the *type* of fiction or nonfiction book, we might have a better chance."

Now what? "I'm afraid that's all the information I've got, but I appreciate your help"—he glanced at her nametag—"Mrs. Dobbs."

"You say she identified herself as a writer doing research. And this was in a bar. Right?"

"Yes. The same night the tennis pro was killed."

"Why don't we do this. Leave me your number and I'll see what I can do. I'm not promising anything, mind you, but if I come up with something, I'll let you know. Or if you get any more information"—and she smiled now, a lovely, simple smile—"like a last name, you call me, okay?"

As he talked to Quin, McCleary swiveled around in his chair, watching the day's demise over Miami. Sunlight danced red and gold against windows in the distance and splashed into the crowded street below. The blaring of horns was audible, but barely.

As they swapped stories about the day's events, he thought of last night, of Quin's funny laugh and her sharp tongue and her frankness. Yes, most of all that, which was so different from what he'd grown to expect with Robin. He didn't hear the door to his office open, but he saw Robin's reflection in the glass as she entered and sat down.

She tipped back in her chair, smiling in that way that always did something to his insides. He asked Quin if he could call her back, asked without saying her name, then rang off.

"You look beat," he remarked.

"I was just going to say the same thing about you, Mac."

"How's the seminar?"

"Oh, about the same. Today we had shooting practice."

"I've got a question."

"What's that."

The smile was still there, but growing smaller, almost as if part of her sensed what he was going to ask. He thought of how his hands had traced her face, the contours in the hollow of her neck. He remembered the raw sensations of Robin's body, its unrestrained pleasure, and Jesus, he felt like part of him was dying, shriveling up like some dried prairie bush to be blown away in the next strong wind.

186

"Why'd you tell Paul Holmes about the key, Robin?"

"What key?"

"The key Quin St. James brought in with the emeralds. That key."

"What're you talking about, Mac?" The smile vanished, and it was like being cast into a sudden, inky blackness.

"I'm talking about the little intimacies you and Paul Holmes share in bed. The small confidences about cases; in particular, the Bell case. More specifically, the key, Robin."

He expected her to deny that she was sleeping with him, deny that they discussed cases, deny everything. Instead, she came forward in her chair, frowning a little, her expressive mouth tightening. "Mac, you're becoming obsessed, you know that? Obsessed and paranoid."

"You're sleeping with that bastard, aren't you?" he blurted, forgetting suddenly about the key, Quin, all of it. He kept seeing Robin and Holmes in his dream, the way she'd rubbed up against him, and how Holmes had laughed.

"Look, Mac. What I do with my life is *my* business. I don't give you the third degree. I don't sit here asking you questions about what you're doing with Quin St. James."

"Robin, I'm talking about your giving information to a primary suspect in a homicide investigation, for Christ's sake." He was practically shouting, and Robin flinched, as if deflecting a blow.

"That's *not* what you're talking about at all, and you know it. And besides, you're referring to an investigation that has been shelved, Mac: S-H-E-L-V-E-D."

"Shelved, maybe, but not closed. And as long as it's not closed, what the hell business do you have giving that shit information, Robin?"

She got up, hands slipping into the pockets of her slacks. "I don't know where you got that idea, but I don't have to sit here and listen to this from you or anyone else. You know what your problem is, Mac? You've wanted to get Holmes for something—*anything*—ever since he got your two suspects off. And you don't give a good goddamn how you do it, either. Instead of

187

pointing the finger at me, examine your own motives for a change."

Then she spun around and left. McCleary sat there, enveloped in the trail of her perfume, her words pounding against the inside of his head like a wild surf. *Is it true? Is that what I'm doing?*

No. There was only one way Holmes could have found out about the key. Robin was lying. She was screwing that bastard and lying to protect herself—and him. But even as he thought it, a tiny voice in the back of his mind whispered, *Is it true? Is it?*

20

1.

QUIN POLISHED OFF her apple as she trotted up the front steps of the building and stopped herself just before her shoe came down over the welcome mat. FORSYTHE & ST. JAMES, PRIVATE DETECTIVES: the words mocked her now, challenged her. After all, the last time she'd treaded on the damned thing, Grant had been shot. *Step on the mat, and watch your life go flat.*

She walked around it and into the reception area, where Ruth Grimes's radio broadcasted the latest coordinates for Hurricane Ingrid. A *hurricane*, for God's sake, just what Miami needed. When Hurricane David had threatened the Florida coast in 1979, Dade, Broward, and Palm Beach counties had been sealed up like coffins. But the storm had tricked everyone and hit farther up the coast instead. A hurricane warning this time would probably be ignored by the general populace, and then McCleary would have a lot more to worry about than a few homicides.

Your friend Ms. Magnolia said Grant had been seeing someone new shortly before he died, Quin, McCleary had said yesterday afternoon on the phone. *Did you notice anything different about him? Or in your relationship?* Different how? she wondered. That he was crazier, moodier? That he hadn't been as interested in sex?

Yes to all of the above. Yes, yes, yes.

One night when he'd come in late, she'd asked him what was wrong with them these days. Her voice had held what Grant called "that hysterical edge," and he'd turned to her with fury in his eyes. *What! Why! Where! When! You're always asking me so many questions, Quin. I'm sick of questions.*

Grant Bell: forty-three-year-old misfit, seducer of young women, emerald hunter. An inscrutable man, his quintessence a mystery, a secret.

Grant Bell: shithead.

She dropped her apple core into the wastebasket next to the water fountain and went into the staff room for coffee. Someone had spilled a condiment on the table—either salt or sugar, she couldn't tell which. But it didn't matter. She pinched the white stuff between her thumb and forefinger and tossed it over her shoulder. She heard the echo of Grant's voice saying, *I suppose you even throw spilled salt over your shoulder, huh.* "I do now, sucker," she muttered.

"You do what now?"

She glanced around. Rusty Johnson leaned against the door, his wide smile as white as the crest of a wave. "Toss salt over my shoulder," she said, and he laughed.

"I won't even ask what that's supposed to mean."

"Good. I've decided what I don't want to be when I grow up, Rusty."

"What's that."

"A private eye who investigates malpractice and insurance claims."

"Oh-oh, a professional crisis. My office awaits you when you care to discuss it."

"Got to figure it all out first."

"Then what I need from you is McCleary's number. I've got some information that may interest him."

She reeled off the number, wondering what the information was. But before she could ask, Rusty smiled and said, "Well, well, Quin. Good for you. You have my one-hundred-percent approval on that man." Then he bussed her on the cheek and danced out of the room with a snap of his fingers and a click of his heels.

Oddly enough, Quin was pleased that Rusty Johnson—who had not cared much for Grant—evidently liked Mike McCleary.

When his phone rang at nine, McCleary expected it to be Izzo. He was pleasantly surprised to hear Rusty Johnson's voice.

"Hey, my man, how are you?"

"Rusty. Good to hear from you. What's up?"

"Well, for starters, 'member my mentioning that friend of mine who worked over in the courthouse?"

"Sure." The one who considered Holmes a prick. "What about him?"

Johnson hesitated. "I hear a beep. The phones there are bugged?"

"Right."

"Okay, I asked my friend to keep an eye on the interested party, you dig?"

"Right."

"He called me yesterday and said he had some mighty interesting information. I thought it'd be best if he talked to you directly, and said I'd give you a call. His name's Joe. Joe Bean. He works in the traffic division, you know, where you pay for speeding tickets."

McCleary leaned against his desk. "Did he tell you what it was about?"

"He did, indeed, my man, which is why I think you should get over there posthaste."

"I will. And thanks for the tip, Rusty."

"Gotcha. See you soon, McCleary."

David Ruskin sang an old Temptations tune as the black man at the adding machine drummed his fingers against the side of the desk, then punched in the number without losing a beat. The nameplate on his desk said JOE BEAN, TD, BHM.

"What do the initials stand for?" McCleary asked.

Bean looked up. "Which initials?"

McCleary pointed at the nameplate. "Those."

"Ah, right. The way I figure it, see, everyone around here's got initials after their names, right? You got AA, BA, MA, Ph.D., and of course we've got plenty of BS, too. Now this here"—he pointed at the TD—"means Traffic Division. And that"—his long black finger slid to BHM—"stands for black heterosexual male."

191

McCleary laughed and introduced himself. "I'm MM from Metro-Dade PD."

Bean grinned. "C'mon, let's go someplace where we can talk private like." He pushed away from his desk, and McCleary decided his name fit him. He was tall and thin as a string bean, with a long face and huge soulful eyes. He was dressed impeccably in navy slacks and a *guayabera* shirt the color of butter and nearly put McCleary, dressed in jeans, to shame.

They left the traffic division and took the elevator to the fourth floor of the courthouse. At the end of the hall, Bean pulled out a set of keys, inserted one into a keyhole in the fire door, and opened it. "Through here. Safest place in Miami to talk."

The door closed behind them. They were on a balcony shaded by an awning that jutted from the roof. Ficus and palm trees in tremendous clay pots along the railing swayed in a stray breeze. The blue waters of Biscayne Bay shimmered in the distance like a mirage. If a man wore blinders, McCleary thought, it would be possible to shut out the worst of the climbing concrete atrocities and to see the Miami skyline as it must have existed thirty years ago.

Bean gestured to an old aluminum table with four chairs at the left corner of the balcony. "No service, but what the hell. When I brown-bag it, this is where I come," Bean explained. "You gotta have someplace like this to hide out. Otherwise you go nuts, working down there in traffic, man. You think you got weirdos in homicide, MM, but I tell you they ain't nothin' compared to what I deal with in traffic."

It wasn't traffic or homicide, McCleary thought. It was just Miami, melting pot of Latin America and the Caribbean. But who was complaining. "So tell me about Paul Holmes."

Bean sat back in his chair and propped his feet at the edge of one of the clay pots. "That, friend, will be a pleasure."

About four years ago, Bean began, Holmes had gotten a ticket for DWI that came through the traffic division, just like any other ticket for a moving violation. "He was in private practice then, and of course I knew who

192

he was, because he was always struttin' his stuff here in the courthouse. The hot-shot attorney routine.

"Anyway, it was my job back then to enter the moving violations that came through our office onto the computer and pass the tickets on to my supervisor. I remember thinking that the DWI charge would be a black mark on Holmes's record when he made his pitch for the DA's office. Everyone knew that was what he had in mind, see. Well, as it turned out, he never went to court for the ticket, never even got fined. In fact, when I went back through the computer records, there wasn't even a goddamned entry.

"I shoulda kept my mouth shut, MM. Hell, Holmes knew every judge in the system, and I shoulda figured he'd managed to get the thing removed. But I went to my supervisor, and she was a real honest sort, you know, and looked into it. Three days later, she was fired. So I got real curious. I kept my eye on Holmes, and when he got to be DA, it was just that much easier."

"Do you know which judge he bought off?" McCleary asked.

"Yeah, I'm gettin' to that. Now I know a DWI isn't that big a deal, okay? But it was the fact that my supervisor got fired, that's what really pissed me off. I mean, Holmes just stomped all over this lady's life like she didn't exist. And she wasn't any young thing, MM. Anyways, so I started watching this dude real close like, and I made a point of getting to know a couple of the ladies in his office. Most of them don't like him any better than I do, and it was this one woman, Darlene, who told me Holmes's secret."

"His secret?"

"Yeah. She says he's got this little cache of photos and shit that he keeps in his office safe." Bean reached into his shirt pocket for a cigarette, tapped it against the table, and leaned forward. His motions were smooth, fluid, agile. He reminded McCleary of Jimmy Olsen as the Elastic Man in the old Superman comics. "All kinds of incriminating evidence on people ranging from Mr. Mayor of Miami himself to that shit Judge Parker who fixed his DWI to the chief of police."

McCleary gazed at a point just beyond Bean's shoulder, where the light struck a concrete beam. It seemed to burn through his retinas to the back of his brain. "How'd he get this stuff?"

"Well. That was just the question this lady Darlene was askin'. So she snooped," he said, lighting his cigarette with a quick flourish of his hand. "For a man who's so careful about some things, Holmes is pretty careless about other things. He keeps his checkbook in his desk drawer, and one day while he was out to lunch, Darlene went through it. And funny thing, MM, she found monthly checks for a bunch of moola made out to a dude named Juan L. Valdez. You know, just like the coffee farmer in the commercial. So I decided to look up this Juan L. Valdez in the phone book. He lives just east of Calle Ocho. When I called there, I said he'd been recommended by Paul Holmes. He tells me right off that he doesn't do no killing, that his specialty is getting info. 'If you wanna me to cripple someone, that is extra,' he says."

McCleary sat forward, arms folded at the edge of the old table. "Joe Bean, I think you missed your calling in life."

Bean waved a hand through the air, the smoke from his skinny brown cigarette curling like a pretzel. "Uh-uh, McCleary. I am the world's biggest coward. I don't like guns. I don't like blood." Then he sat back, grinning. "But oh, man, how I love a mystery. And how I would love to see this fucker Holmes pay. Pay big."

"How difficult would it be to get into the safe?"

Bean rocked his hand. Smoke curled drunkenly around his hand. "Depends."

"On what?"

"On whether I can be a part of it."

"Frankly," McCleary said with a chuckle, "I've just decided you're indispensable."

Bean's smile seemed to curl his earlobes. "Then here's my plan, MM."

3.

Why was it she kept returning here like some lost homing pigeon? Quin wondered as she let herself into Grant's

194

townhouse. She had a stack of files on her desk at work that had been multiplying like mutant cells since Grant's death, yet here she was, looking for . . . she didn't know. She'd been picking up his mail, she'd gone through his bank statements, his old income tax forms, his file of travel receipts. Where else could she look for clues?

She walked into his den, sat at his desk, stared at the blowgun attached to the wall at an angle. She swiveled around, yanked open the top drawer of the filing cabinet, her fingers stepped through the folders. *Nothing*. She jerked open the second drawer. At the back, she found two things of interest and wondered how she'd missed them before. The first folder was labeled "Telephone Bills" and the second wasn't labeled at all. Grant had been too organized not to label something, she thought, and opened the second folder.

There was only a single sheet of paper inside that listed several dates, followed by a note:

APRIL 23: I feel like a prospector, panning for secrets rather than gold. There's something about her that doesn't set right with me, but I don't know what it is.

MAY 4: We went to Key West this weekend, while Q. was away on a case. It was crazy and glorious and she makes me feel like I'm 18 again. But the other thing still bothers me.

MAY 12: She won't let me photograph her. It's weird. I've never met a woman who didn't want her picture taken. This evening we met here, & she nearly went manic on me when I got out my camera. She left in a huff.

MAY 22: She says, "Look, I think you'd be better off without me. I don't want to hurt you." And I had the eerie feeling she wasn't talking about emotional hurts, but that's crazy, isn't it?

JUNE 2: This afternoon, we screwed at the Holiday Inn on Lauderdale Beach. She told me that her

195

mother lost her mind because her father took a bunch of pictures of her when he'd bought a camera. She was absolutely serious. She's got this idea, see, that if a person's image is captured on film or on a canvas, the soul is imprisoned or some such shit, and the artist or photographer then controls the soul. I can't figure her out. Sometimes she scares me.

June 8: *I know her secret, I know, damnit, I know.*

Quin read the page several times. Except for certain parts, these might have been the journal entries of an adolescent, writing about his junior high crush. They might even have been pathetic, except for the funny ache she felt when she re-read the line about the Holiday Inn. Certain words leaped off the page at her, words like *secret, sometimes she scares me,* and the stuff about the soul being imprisoned.

Judging by the dates, the woman he'd written about could have been the new woman Ginger Hale said Grant had been seeing shortly before his death. Did that mean this woman, whoever she was, had killed him? Or was Ginger Hale just covering up?

Quin dropped the page in the folder, shut it. *Here, Quin, it happened here, in these rooms.* And suddenly she could feel the dark derangement of the killer's mind twisting through the air like smoke signals. *I was here, I killed him, and I'll kill you, too, if you get in my way.* She tried to shove the thought aside so she could go through the phone bills, but her terror undulated through her in waves. She pressed the heels of her hands against her eyes, and in the black within, tiny stars exploded. Their dust swirled, forming faces and shapes that rushed toward her, locking her in a struggle of wills. She leaped up so quickly the folders slid off the desk. Grant's notes and phone bills skittered across the floor, her heart pounded as if she'd been running, she couldn't catch her breath. The room slid sideways like a tilt-a-whirl, sucking away the scattered papers, the light, her life. Her arms shot out, grappling blindly for the edge of the desk so she could steady herself. *I'm a threat:* the thought careened wildly through her head, bouncing like an echo against the walls of her skull. *Threatthreatthreat.* Quin slapped her hands over her ears and squeezed her eyes shut. She was a threat because the killer understood her determination to ferret out the truth.

The echo gradually diminished and she opened her eyes and the world came back into focus again. There: the smooth dark wood of Grant's desk, his file cabinets, the pine floors strewn with papers. Her stomach cramped with hunger, her knees felt weak, but the worst was over. She scooped up the folders, slammed the file drawer shut, and fled the townhouse.

4.

As McCleary descended from the fourth floor, he felt like he was floating on a cushion of air. If Bean's plan worked, and McCleary felt sure that it would, he'd give Izzo whatever it was Holmes had on him, inform him he was back on the Bell case and to assign the serial murder cases to someone else. And then, one way or another, he'd nail Holmes for Bell's murder.

You so sure he killed Bell, Mac? Or is this because of Robin?

"Pick, pick, pick," he said to himself.

He was still smiling as he got out of the elevator, as he ducked into the men's room. The smile became a grimace when he saw Paul Holmes standing at the mirror, drawing a comb through his thick salt-and-pepper hair with the vanity of a little Caesar.

"Mike McCleary. I haven't seen you in a while. What brings you to the courthouse?"

"Fame and fortune, what else."

Holmes guffawed; McCleary felt like slugging him.

The DA slipped his comb into his back pocket and patted the side of his hair once, fixing several errant strands back in place. An image of Holmes and Robin together insinuated itself into McCleary's thoughts, sprouting like a weed, catching fire. *It has nothing to do with*

Robin, Nothing, Nothing. . . . But the afferent pathways in his brain were blocked, and all he saw was the two of them coupling in a frenzy. *You'll get yours, Holmes.*

"So how's it going on the investigation, Mike?" An unctuous smile now, and Holmes giving his hair one last pat.

"On the serial killings?"

"No, Grant Bell's."

"Izzo temporarily shelved that, but I don't suppose you know anything about that."

"No, I don't suppose I do."

Now, in that bright, lucid spot in McCleary's mind where Robin lived, where Robin breathed, he could see Holmes kissing her, nibbling at her ear like a little fish, and it hurt, God, how it hurt. The words rolled off his tongue: "And I don't suppose your wife knows anything about you and Robin, either."

Holmes's look was accusatory and direct, as if, for the first time, he actually understood that McCleary might be a formidable threat. His usually mellifluous voice, a voice as smooth as twelve-year-old Scotch, turned mean. "McCleary, let me give you some advice. Don't fuck with me. I'll ruin you. And that's a promise."

"You might." McCleary smiled. "But the difference between you and me, Paul, is that I'm willing to risk that to see your ass in prison." Then he slipped his hands in his pockets and shuffled past Holmes and into the hall, grinning so widely his teeth grew cold.

21

". . . HURRICANE INGRID, now about four hundred miles southeast of Puerto Rico, is packing winds of a hundred and fifty miles per hour, making it a category-four hurricane. Dr. Neil Frank, at the Hurricane Center in Miami, says that Ingrid is an extremely well-organized storm and one of the fifteen most powerful hurricanes of the century. He . . ."

"Blah, blah," muttered Paul Holmes, and switched off the radio as he pulled up in front of the apartment building. He reached for the flowers, bottle of wine, and two pounds of shrimp on the seat beside him. He whistled as he walked briskly into the building and rang Robin's doorbell. This, he thought smugly, would be a landmark evening, a celebration of sorts.

Robin opened the door wearing a cotton blouse with tiny flowers on it, and jeans. She looked at him blankly, as though she didn't know him. He was a little chagrined at her reaction. He'd expected her to be more demonstrative, more . . . well, more something. After all, in the four months they'd been seeing each other, he'd been here only once, and none of those meetings had been spontaneous. "Can I come in, Robin?"

"Paul. Sure." She stepped back, admitting him.

"Dinner," he said, indicating his package, and then passed her the flowers—several roses, baby's breath, and in the center, a bird of paradise. She inhaled the fragrance, her eyes watching him over the top of the bouquet, smiling a little now.

"Are we celebrating something I forgot about?" she asked as he followed her back into the kitchen.

"Maybe." He came up behind her as she stood at the counter arranging the flowers in a vase. He inhaled the scent of her hair, her skin, wondering why his wife never smelled as fragrant as Robin. His hands slid over her hips, and for a moment she seemed to tense. Then she covered his hands with her own and turned in the circle of his arms. Her mouth was warm and dry when he kissed her.

"You feel like you've got a fever."

"It's called burnout, I think."

"Too much seminar?" he chuckled.

"No, I think I'm just sick of police work." She turned back to the flowers and finished arranging them in the vase. She emptied the bag of shrimp into a cauldron and ran cold water over them.

He enjoyed watching her, the way she moved with an instinctive grace, her snug jeans accentuating her leanness, her long legs.

"So where's Miriam this evening?"

"Out with the ladies at a bridge tournament or something."

The way he said it made Robin laugh. She passed him the corkscrew, turned off the water. She leaned lazily against the counter, arms folded at her waist as he opened the bottle of wine.

"If you're sick of homicide, you can always go back to law, Robin."

"Yeah, except that I got sick of practicing law, too."

She was like a precocious child, he thought, tackling something with a passion until the fascination wore off and boredom set in. "Personally, I don't see how anyone could stomach being a homicide investigator, Robin. And if you're serious about returning to law, you know you've got a job any time you want in the DA's office."

She twirled a strand of hair at her neck around her index finger. "I may just take you up on that."

The cork popped from the bottle. He got down two wine glasses, filled them. "Okay, a toast." She was smiling. Her dark hair fell loosely around her face, onto her forehead. Sunlight from the window over the sink swam against her collarbone. Holmes leaned forward, brushing his mouth against her neck. She giggled; it was a playful sound. Wholly Robin.

"What're we toasting?"

"The demise of your relationship with McCleary."

Her smile flattened out, and Holmes noted the pulse at her throat. "What're you talking about, Paul?" She set the wine glass on the counter, her arms returned to her waist, everything about her became defensive.

"I ran into him in the men's room at the courthouse. Appropriate place for a gutter conversation, now that I think about it." Holmes sipped at the wine. The tang made the tip of his tongue tingle. "He wanted to know if my wife knew about us. About you and me. I was under the impression that he didn't know about our arrangement."

"I never told him, if that's what you're asking."

"You wouldn't lie to me, now would you, Robin?"

She scratched her head, glanced away from him, picked up the wine glass. When she finally laughed, it was a strange sound, utterly devoid of amusement. "Let me get this straight, okay? You're married. I'm single. Now correct me if I'm wrong, Paul, but I think the way this kind of thing works is that what I do on my own time is my business. Not yours. *You're* the one sneaking around. Not me. It so happens I did not and have never said anything to Mac about you. It might be that he just put two and two together, I don't know. At this point, I don't much care, to tell you the truth." Then she tipped her head back, drained the glass, set it back on the counter. Her fingers closed around the bottle and she held it out. "I would greatly appreciate it if you would take your wine—and your shrimp"—her hand swooped for the cauldron with the shrimp in it and shoved it toward him— "and get outa here. *This* I do not need."

So many surprises, he thought. She was the brightly wrapped gift beneath a Christmas tree, the surprise you held to your ear and shook, the surprise you tore into and didn't understand when it was finally exposed. He didn't know what to make of her. Perhaps he never had.

He took the bottle and the shrimp from her, placed them on the counter. She stood with a hand on her hip, glaring at him. He stepped toward her, touched his hand to her face. "I'm sorry," he said.

"Yeah, so am I."

As she started to move past him, Holmes caught her hand, spun her around, crushed her against him. For a moment, just a moment, she struggled. Then she went limp in his arms, making a soft sound like laughter. "You don't understand, do you," she whispered. "You'll never understand. You're just like Mac. You want to own me, and I'm not for sale."

The sun had gone down, the room smelled thickly of perfume, smoke from Robin's cigarette, of deep July. They were lying in the dark, the vestiges of passion strewn like memories around them. Holmes said, "I was serious about the position with the DA's office, Robin. You're licensed in Florida. The move wouldn't entail anything more than a two-week notice at the department."

The tip of her glowing cigarette was a beacon in the dark. "How do you know I'm licensed in Florida?"

"I found out, that's how."

Her laugh smoldered, then burst with delight. "Spying on me, you shit." She turned, stabbing out the cigarette. "I've got to think about it."

Holmes turned on the lamp. The light burnished Robin's skin a soft gold. "McCleary's going to try to nail me for Grant Bell's murder." Now why had he said *that*?

"He just doesn't buy your story about that fifteen-thousand-dollar payment, Paul."

"I was repaying a loan."

"According to Quin, Grant Bell didn't have that kind of money to lend."

It was a not very subtle way of telling him she thought he was lying. "You talked to Quin?"

"I talk to Mac. He talks to Quin." She moved the pillow against the headboard and sat back again. "Actually, I think he's screwing her, so he's really in a pretty good position to get information."

Her tone was dispassionate, as if McCleary were nothing but a postscript. "How do you know that?"

202

She shrugged. The light slid from her shoulder to her collarbone. "She came into the office one day when I was there and I just had the feeling something was going on. You can tell. At least I can."

"And it doesn't bother you?"

"No more than it does when you go home to your wife."

It wasn't natural. It seemed that certain vital emotional links were altogether absent in Robin. Of course, there were plenty of people who probably thought that of him. But it wasn't the same thing, not at all.

"You changed the subject," she said with a smile, nudging him in the ribs. "Where'd Grant Bell get fifteen thousand to lend you, Paul?"

"Forget it. This is going to place both of us in a compromising position, Robin." He threw back the sheet, swung his legs over the side of the bed.

She touched his back, a soft, cool touch. "We've never let cases come between us before, and there are some that could have, you know that."

"We've never had a case where I was one of the primary suspects, either, Robin."

"It doesn't change anything. Work is one thing, this is another. I'm concerned about you. That's all."

He said nothing, but neither did he move from the bed, from her touch. He wanted to believe she was sincere. He wanted to, really.

"Why's it so difficult for you to believe I might actually care about you, Paul?"

"I guess because you've got McCleary on the sidelines."

"How's that any different from you having your wife?"

"It just is." Because of a legal document, he thought, which bound them even though little else did. *Which doesn't mean shit, and you know it.*

"Things with Mac haven't been too great since I got back from my vacation." An annoyed voice now, almost brittle, he noticed. She got out of bed, walked over to the chair where her robe was, slipped it on. "Anyway," she continued, strolling back to the bed, "*If* you were responsible for having him removed from the case, it's just going to make him all that more determined to try to pin something on you."

"Why're you telling me all this?"

She sighed. "Someone needs to, that's for sure."

She moved restlessly on the bed, as if to find a more comfortable position. Heat emanated from her body, the same dry heat he'd felt earlier when he'd kissed her. Her voice, when she spoke again, had a disembodied quality to it, as though she weren't really in the room but were speaking to him through the marvel of electronics from another place. "Paul, you sit up there in your little ivory tower, believing you're immune just because you've got connections or some little blackmail scheme going, and it isn't going to work with Mac. I know him." An exhalation of smoke, then, "I know how he thinks."

"He's off the case, Robin."

"Don't kid yourself. He's been biding his time. Whatever you've got on Izzo, it isn't enough, Paul. The man could fire Mac and it wouldn't make any difference."

Holmes had a quick, sharp visage of himself in prison. And not one of the lush federal places, either. No, one of the state facilities overrun by queers, drug dealers, and murderers, and governed by guards who were mentally defective. He knew what those places were like; he'd never live through it.

The room suddenly seemed too warm, too small, closed. *Like a room in a prison. If you go to prison, you'll die, Paul, count on it.* He rubbed his hands over his face. "You have no idea what a bastard Grant Bell was," he spat.

"I thought you were friends."

He snorted. "He didn't know the meaning of the word."

When he thought of Grant now, there was a hollow ache where the good memories should have been. He wished he could peel away the sins of the past, efface the stains the friendship had left, or better yet, that he could rearrange events altogether. He felt the story slither like moss down his tongue, pressing against the back of his teeth. He wanted to clamp his mouth shut, but the words had assumed a force of their own, the secret was begging to be told, shared.

"When we were freshmen in college, I was accused of

204

raping a woman. Fortunately, it didn't hit the papers, because I was still a minor, just a few weeks away from turning eighteen. My folks hired a good lawyer, and he convinced the judge that the offense should remain in the juvenile courts. He would've gotten me off altogether, but there was a witness. So he gave me five hundred hours of community service and agreed to bury the case once I'd complied. The woman was black, too, which was another factor in my favor.''

In the ensuing silence, he felt her stiffen beside him. "So did you do it, Paul? Did you actually rape her?"

He hated the accusatory tone of her voice. "Look, Robin, Grant and I were at a party and this woman came on to us, for Christ's sakes. She wanted it. It was only afterwards that she started screaming rape."

"Us? She came on to both of you? Grant was the winess?"

"Witness, shit, he was just as much a part of it as I was. The fucker turned on me to save his own ass."

"Then why did you stay friends?"

Holmes ran a hand through his hair. "We didn't. Not for a long time. Then . . ." He shrugged. "I don't know. About five years ago we ran into each other in a bar one afternoon and started talking and . . . hell, it's hard to hold a grudge for twenty years." He paused. "But I shouldn't have had anything to do with him again. When he realized he was going to need money for this Amazon project of his, he started blackmailing me. Five grand here, five grand there, and suddenly, over a two-year period, I'd paid the sucker close to twenty-two thousand dollars.''

Holmes slipped down between the sheets, feeling empty now, empty and exonerated. He wanted to sleep, to forget. Maybe when he woke up, the world would be a different sort of place, a place where friendship mattered.

But Robin was sucking noisily on another cigarette and speaking again. "Someone who knew about the emeralds and the mysterious key broke into Quin St. James's house the other night and assaulted her in the process."

He didn't like the way she said that. "It wasn't me, if that's what you're asking, Robin."

"I wasn't accusing you."

No, you were testing me. "What's the key to?"

She hugged her legs against her, rested her chin on her knees. "More emeralds, probably.

Yeah, great. While Bell was sucking him dry, he was hauling emeralds out of South America. Holmes laughed, a dry laugh that quickly turned salty and wet as he began to sob—with remorse, relief, bitterness. After a time, Robin took him in her arms like an infant or a broken doll, rocking him back and forth, whispering to him in a singsong voice. He fell asleep in the net of her embrace, a sleep as abrupt and deep as death.

When he awakened, he saw ice chips of stars glimmering through the window. Robin's breath warmed his shoulder, her hand cooled his chest, the bed had molded itself to his body. He didn't want to get up. Ever.

"You never asked me if I killed him." His voice rang plaintively in the quiet.

She stirred, her fingers stroked his chin. "I don't have to ask. I know."

She didn't elaborate; he didn't ask her to. But in the coming days, this small omission would eat away at him like cancer.

22

"Mama?" I blinked against the dark. "Mama? Is that you?"

I'd heard a noise in the front room. It was Mama, wasn't it? She always had trouble sleeping. Some nights she roamed the house like a possessed witch, murmuring her prayers, her invocations, lighting candles to the saints. But that was after . . .

No, I didn't want to think about it now. The past was a murky pool, as bottomless as the lake where Billy lay. Big Billy, who wanted to play pro ball and probably would have. *If he'd lived.*

I turned my face into the pillow and giggled. *Fly away, black bird, fly away.* But the black bird always sang in the dead of night. I would hear it sometimes, singing, singing until its song shattered the thin line between the past and present, singing . . .

Then I heard the noise again. Maybe Mama was drunk. That happened sometimes, too. She would pour a glass of wine, red wine, always red wine like the blood of Christ. Next, she would cut out circles of Wonder bread with cookie cutters and take communion. But she always drank more than a sip of the wine; sometimes she drank the whole bottle. My Mama, the lunatic.

But wouldn't she say I had made her that way? Wouldn't she say she'd fallen into madness, the way other people fall into love, after she'd guessed about Billy and kept the secret to herself?

It was a lie. I didn't make her crazy. I didn't, I . . .

Why did the room smell funny? I sat up. The room smelled thick, hot, the man next to me was so still. What was his name, anyway? Sam? Gary? Sonny? Well, it would come to me. I had met him . . . that would come to me also. My head ached from all the Dewar's I'd put away, my tongue felt thick and dry, I wanted to go back to sleep. But Mama was drunk in the front room, and pretty soon she'd start stumbling over things and . . .

There: the noise again. It wasn't Mama. Couldn't be. She was in a home. It wasn't a car going by, either. I got out of bed, quietly, ever so quietly, surprised to see I was still dressed. *Why? Why do I still have my clothes on?* There was something wrong with this. Where did this scene fit?

Maybe I'd already written the scene and had tumbled into it as if into a house of mirrors, and any minute now I would meet my protagonist and we . . .

I needed my purse. I patted the floor at the side of the bed until I found it. I slung it over my shoulder, reached inside for the knife. As my fingers closed around it, I heard footsteps in the hall outside the door. "Gary? Gary, hon, you here?" A soft voice, hesitant, a woman's voice.

My insides twisted. Spears of pain jabbed at my temples. I backed up to the wall, wishing the man, Gary, would wake up and make the woman go away. I felt the cool wall through my blouse, smelled the flash of sweat on my skin as the door opened a crack and admitted a slice of light.

"Honey? C'mon, I know you're here because I saw your car outside."

Now the door opened a little wider, the woman's breathing was like a mare's on a cold morning, light splashed umber across the bed. "Gary?" Her voice hissed as she stepped into the room.

She made a strangled sound, as if she'd suddenly drawn in poisoned air. She kept making the sound, pulling in more and more of the air as she stumbled back.

My head jerked toward the bed. Where had all the blood come from? Why had I been lying in it? Sleeping in it? Why were my clothes covered with it? The woman seemed to be trying to scream, to form words. For one long and terrible instant I had visions of her tearing through the halls of the building, screeching, and of people descending on the apartment in droves, and then the police would come and . . .

I shoved the door, hard. It slammed into the woman, knocking her to the floor, robbing her of breath. I sprang from the shadows, voices screeching in my head like metal against concrete. How had everything veered out of control like this? How? But the woman stared at me in lugubrious horror, eyes bulging from her young and pretty face that was blotched with red like she had measles. "No, no, don't make any sound, please, I don't want to hurt you, I don't . . . it's just the men, see, the ones like Billy who . . ."

I moved steadily toward her. She scooted along the floor on her buttocks, the tendons in her neck so tight they were like thick vines just beneath her skin. And the sounds, God, she emitted horrid little noises—incomplete shrieks that died in whistles of indrawn breath. The end had already been determined, just as it had been with Billy. Yes, oh God, yes, I was sorry, very sorry, I hadn't wanted to hurt her.

"You mustn't scream," I told her, even as she was scrambling to her feet and tearing toward the front of the apartment. A pinched sound dribbled from her mouth like saliva.

I raced after the woman, threw myself at her legs. She fell like an antelope in mid-flight, kicking, screeching once before I brought the knife down hard, again and again. The blade sank into her flesh as if it were dough, striking bone, several bones. Then I yanked it out, knowing I should annoint her head, but there wasn't time. Everything had slid away from me, as if I were slopping through mud. I jumped up, a sob swimming in my throat, and ran toward the back bedroom. How had this happened? How? But the question circled lazily in my mind, like a buzzard.

Fingerprints: had I touched anything? I didn't think so, but there wasn't time to check. Too late, oh Christ, too late for everything. I kicked out the screen in the bedroom, scrambled through the window, dropped to the ground. My car was on the street. I remembered parking it there, taking up two spaces so no one could pen me in.

I bit down on my lip to keep from sobbing.

My heart thudded against my ribs, my legs itched to run, but I forced myself to walk. Was anyone watching from the windows? My neck twitched, wanting to turn, to look. My hand trembled as I unlocked the car, slid in. My foot ached to press the accelerator to the floor as I pulled away from the curb. Twitches, tremor, aches: my body begged to betray me.

Eyes darting now to the rearview mirror: no one had come out of the building yet. At the end of the street, I jerked the wheel violently to the left and turned. Trees along the side of the road bent toward me as I passed, nodding their heads. Lights from houses winked through branches. My hands sweated, my eyes burned, the stink of blood filled the car.

Music, I would listen to music. My fingers fumbled for the radio dial. The car purred as it gathered speed, then seemed to break loose beneath my hands as I drove onto the interstate.

I didn't remember the drive home. I didn't recall walking into my familiar rooms. But the moment I opened the closet in my bedroom and saw my typewriter on the floor, I knew what I had to do.

I brought the typewriter from its hiding place and set it up on the desk. I was covered with blood, I stank of blood, but I typed the scene. Oh, how the words flowed, tumbling madly, beautifully, frantically, like impatient children. This was how I'd written *Black Bird*, in frenzied spurts over a period of six weeks. I even felt the same: the metallic taste in my mouth, the heightened emotion, the sharp edge of my perceptions. When I was finished and read the scene over, I knew it was perfect. *Perfect.*

A bone fatigue settled through me as I rose from the desk. My bloodstained hands cut into my vision, then my clothes. I hurried into the bathroom, shucked my clothes, stepped into a shower so hot the water nearly burned my skin. But there went the blood, swirling pink down the drain as I scrubbed and scrubbed. . . . For just an instant, I was in the lake again, scouring myself with mud, the odor of Billy's death thick in the autumn air.

When I got out of the shower, I slumped to the bathroom floor and began cutting my clothes into strips, the strips into squares, the squares into halves. My eyes burned with weariness, my fingers were wrinkled from the water, but I worked deftly, diligently, cutting, cutting, cutting.

I was afraid to flush the pieces down the toilet because suppose the pipes clogged? So I put everything into a bag and walked outside, where the moon lay impaled against a cloud shaped like a scythe. I dug a deep hole in the sandy earth. Nothing had changed, nothing in all those years since I was seventeen and digging a hole to bury Mama's butcher knife.

23

1.

QUIN ASKED THE operator for the area code for Cartagena, Colombia, then dialed the number listed three times on Grant's April phone bill. Two rings and a woman answered. She sounded as close as next door.

"Good morning, Fuego Verde. This is Louise Fuentes speaking, may I help you?"

"Uh, yes. Is this a private home?"

"No, it isn't ma'am. It's an emerald shop."

Quin sucked in her breath. *Fuego Verde: Greenfire.* "My name's Quin St. James. I'm calling from Miami. I need some information and was wondering if you might be able to help me."

"I'll certainly try."

"I'm investigating the death of a friend of mine, and the number of your shop was listed on his phone bill. His name was Grant Bell."

The woman made an odd sound, as if she'd just been kicked in the solar plexus. "I . . . I'm sorry, I don't know anyone by that name," she said and hung up.

Quin replaced the receiver and sat there a moment. Then she dialed the number again. It was busy. She waited five minutes, tried the number once more. This time, a man answered.

"Good morning, *Fuego Verde.* This is Carlos Fuentes. May I help you?"

"Yes, may I speak to Louise, please?"

"I'm sorry, Louise is with a customer. Is there anything I can help you with?"

Quin started to ask *him* if he knew Grant, but some small alarm sounded in her head. "Could you have Louise call me at her convenience? I'll leave you my name and number. She can call collect. It's about the, uh, purchase of some emeralds."

"Certainly." Quin gave him her office and home number. "I'll give my wife the message, Miss St. James."

Wife, Quin thought as she thanked him and hung up. Suppose, just suppose, the woman had been one of Grant's little secrets? A month ago, the notion would've struck her as preposterous. Now it not only seemed plausible, but a reasonable explanation for why she'd hung up on Quin. An emerald shop, a husband who didn't know anything about his wife's infidelities, an American adventurer who no doubt swept Louise Fuentes off her feet.

Quin would give her forty-eight hours to call back, and if she didn't, then she'd start making a pest of herself. She wanted answers, and she no longer cared how she got them.

2.

McCleary stood at the painting in his office, puzzling over what was different about it. He'd bought it at an art show in the Grove last year because it possessed that certain something that had the power to transport him. It depicted an old fisherman in denim coveralls, arms raised as he cast his line into a lake. The surface of the water caught the autumnal reflection of the surrounding foliage and trees, as well as the arch of lapis sky. The artist had layered the colors cleverly, so that sometimes he couldn't really tell where the reflection ended and the reality began.

As McCleary studied it, he realized he'd never noticed the way the water had also captured the wisps of cirrus clouds in the sky. The clouds, interfaced with the other reflections, seemed to create faces in the water—

faces with mustaches, bushy eyebrows, faces with wide, sensuous mouths, startled eyes, dimpled chins. The images had always been there, of course, but he'd never looked at the painting at this particular angle, in such pale morning light. Like the dark fields, he thought. It was all a matter of perspective.

"Mike?"

His shoulders tensed at the sound of Izzo's voice. He reluctantly turned away from the painting. "Morning."

McCleary noticed that Izzo's tan was fading now that he'd been on the seven-to-three shift for the last week, which robbed him of his daily swims during the heat of the day. Funny, but with his muscular chest and the way he carried his arms, the chief looked slightly simian. McCleary wondered if the man had always looked that way or if, through some twist of cosmic justice, he was regressing on the evolutionary scale.

"You have any luck with the composite Jean Zavik drew up from Mulhollen's description?"

McCleary shook his head. "Nope." He'd made the rounds of half a dozen local bars last night with the composite drawing of their knife-wielding lady, but to no avail. He blamed Henry Mulhollen's lousy description rather than the artist. Mulhollen had been unable to provide vital details: what a difference a hairstyle made in a woman's appearance or the length of a nose or the fullness of a mouth. He said as much to Izzo. "I was told the face could've belonged to a hundred women in Dade. I think she disguises herself somehow, Bob."

Izzo sighed. "Well, it looks like she got two more. A man and woman out in the university area."

"A *woman*?"

"Yeah. The neighbor who called said the woman was a girlfriend. The call came through about five minutes ago. The receptionist buzzed you, but no one answered."

McCleary bristled at the accusatory tone in Izzo's voice. He hadn't fallen into bed until two last night, and he'd been up by six. What the hell did Izzo expect, anyway? "I was taking a piss," he snapped. "I'll get

214

Benson and we'll take a ride over there. Let me have the address."

Izzo gave it to him. "I already called Doc Smithers."

"Okay, thanks."

McCleary turned his back on Izzo and poured a mug of coffee from the percolator, hoping the chief would get the hint and vanish. But he felt the skin at his temples tightening as if the barometric pressure in the room had suddenly dropped. *What's it going to be this morning, Bob? More threats? Maybe a show of remorse?*

He stirred Cremora into the mug, then glanced around to offer Izzo a cup. But surprisingly, the chief had left. McCleary stood there, gazing into the hall through the open doorway, his thoughts fixed on the enigma of Bob Izzo and whatever it was Holmes had on him. Then he called Benson.

The building was like hundreds of others in Dade, a concrete monster. But at least the developer had seen fit to plant a few olive trees around it and to landscape the front yard. There was, in fact, enough greenery to have tricked the birds. As they got out of the cruiser, he actually heard bluejays and sparrows. Even Benson commented on it, and they paused for a moment on the walk to listen as though the birdsongs were a symphony.

"God, look at us," Benson murmured. "We're on our way to a double homicide where neither of us wants to be."

Birdsongs and murder: the mind divided itself right down the middle, neat as an apple. Yeah, McCleary understood it, all right. And as if to deny the truth of what Benson had just said, they hurried into the building.

The apartment was the first one on the bottom floor. The door was open, and before they entered, the odor of urine and fecal matter made McCleary grimace. Then he saw the woman. Her cheek was flattened against the rug, her wide, dark eyes were fixed in abject terror, her gaze created an invisible line that shot toward the tip of his shoe.

He stepped back quickly, as though her gaze had burned him.

She was young, maybe nineteen, and had been stabbed repeatedly through the back. Doc Smithers crouched beside her, feeling her neck for a pulse McCleary knew wasn't there. Her purse had been tossed into a nearby chair, tossed carelessly, and her car keys were on the coffee table. McCleary started down the hall, toward the open door at the end.

The detachment he was usually able to muster deserted him when he stepped into the room. It was not just the sight of the man, lying nude on his back, stabbed through the throat, the chest, or the crimson sheet that partially covered him, or the blood smeared on the rug and the headboard. That was bad, yes. But the evidence of derangement sickened him, *frightened* him, at a level beyond words. The gaping wounds in the mattress looked like the killer had been gutting a chicken. The headboard had been punctured multiple times. And when he pulled back the sheet and saw the man had been stabbed repeatedly in the groin, the penis attached by only a thread of skin, his knees nearly buckled. The coffee churning in his empty stomach bit into the lining of his gut like acid.

"My God," Benson whispered behind him.

McCleary pushed past him and hurried into the front room, grateful that someone had opened the porch doors. He took great gulps of the hot morning air.

"That bad?" Doc Smithers asked, coming up behind him.

Bad? "It looks like the woman arrived unexpectedly, and after killing her, the murderer escaped through the window," McCleary said as he turned away from the porch. "The screen's been knocked out." Which probably explained why there were no crosses on the victims' foreheads this time.

"The people from the lab should be here any minute," Smithers noted. Anxious to get out of the apartment, away from its odors, McCleary nodded, stepped over the woman's legs, and walked across the hall to talk with Marcy Landers, the woman who'd called. She jabbered like she'd been on speed for three days, but McCleary was able to glean a few facts: Gary Heinich, twenty-seven years old, was a computer salesman who frequently argued with his twenty-year-old girlfriend, the dead woman. The half-dozen tenants McCleary spoke to agreed they'd heard the screams between one and one-thirty this morning but believed the couple had been fighting, so they hadn't interfered. No, they hadn't seen anyone leaving the apartment. No, they hadn't heard Heinich come home. Yes, he sometimes hit the singles bars, notably Murphy's, in the Grove. The girl, Katherine Moseley, was a student at the University of Miami. No, she and Heinich weren't living together, but she did spend a lot of time at his apartment. Yes, no, yes, no, yes. *Eeny, Meeny, Miney, Moe. . . .*

He knew he was on automatic, that the scene in the bedroom was making predatory circles at the edge of his mind. In some solitary moment it would descend in its full-blown horror, captured in the sort of detail that only memory provided. But for the moment, there was a small comfort in these familiar routines—questions, the scratch of his pen across the page of his notebook.

When McCleary left, he made his way through traffic to Coconut Grove. Murphy's, open only a few months, had once been a boutique called Adam's Apple. Then Eddie Murphy, the actor, and his manager had come along, bought the place for nearly a half-million dollars, added a second floor, and turned it into a restaurant and disco. When McCleary arrived, only the restaurant was open. McCleary told a waiter what he wanted and the man led him into the manager's office.

Jack DuProi managed both the restaurant and Delirious, the disco. A husky guy in his early thirties, he grinned a lot and looked like he'd probably played pro ball. He grinned when McCleary introduced himself, grinned when McCleary mentioned a double homicide, but stopped grinning when he said Gary Heinich.

"Heinich. Sure, I knew him. He got bounced outa here a couple of times. Big troublemaker. I'm sorry he got killed, but I'll tell you something, Detective McCleary, this guy was a bastard. Some people just get mellow when they drink, you know what I mean? Other guys, like Heinich, get mean."

"Was he in here last night?"

"He was in here probably four nights a week, and yeah, he was here last night."

McCleary removed a copy of Jean Zavik's drawing. "With her?"

Jack frowned as he examined the drawing. He swiveled his chair around and held it under a bright desk lamp, then shook his head. "I hate to tell you this, but she looks like half the women who come in here."

Thanks, Henry Mulhollen.

"Sorry I couldn't be of more help."

Me too, friend. Me too.

Ron Valencia gazed at the drawing, then tugged at his waistband and glanced at McCleary. The corners of his mouth turned down. "Shit, Mike, I could say my daughter looks like this drawing."

"Yeah, that's what I was afraid of. The bartender who gave me the description doesn't exactly have an eye for detail."

Valencia chuckled. "Hell, when I'm shitfaced, I'm not even sure I know what my *wife* looks like."

The two men were in a restaurant near the Metro-Dade station. Valencia, grasping for any shred of evidence, just like McCleary, had driven down from Lauderdale to pick up copies of Jean Zavik's drawing.

"Any word from your Oregon guy?"

"Yeah. He hasn't found anything yet that matches the MO I gave him." Valencia stabbed a leaf of lettuce in his salad bowl. "You think this woman's really a writer?"

"I guess it's possible."

"And Mulhollen claims he heard her say she was doing research?" McCleary nodded and Valencia sat back. His fork clattered against the bowl. "God, this whole peninsula's filled with sickos, Mike."

"Our department shrink thinks there's a possibility that the knife lady also killed Grant Bell, the shooting I told you about."

"Well, anything's possible."

But then how did Treena Esposito fit? She'd lied to Quin to cover up something, and she'd lied to him. And what about Ginger Hale? And what did Kara Someone do to his Paul Holmes theory?

No, he knew Holmes had to be involved. Why else would a man go to the lengths he had to get the investigation dropped? But that tiny, niggling voice that was Robin's whispered, *You don't care how you nail him, Mac, as long as you do.*

And for the first time, he admitted to himself that, yes, maybe it was true.

3.

When Quin sliced into her filet mignon, it bled. She grimaced and sent it back. Nikki said, "What's wrong with a little pink meat, Quin? You're acting like the damned thing's alive or something."

They were sitting in the patio of a restaurant on Calle Ocho. Hispanic music, weaving a subtle spell through the scent of gardenias and jasmine, made Quin wish she could walk out of here and into the bustling night of a Latin American city. *Any* Latin American city, it wouldn't matter, as long as it was hundreds of miles from Miami. *A city like Cartagena, where Louise Fuentes lived?* She pushed the thought aside.

She hadn't wanted to go out to dinner. But Nikki had insisted, Nikki who was alone for the evening—as she was for many evenings—because Steve had to work late.

"I think I may become a vegetarian," Quin remarked, picking at her salad. "Do you know, I have an aunt who refuses to eat anything that has eyes?"

"What?" Nikki laughed.

"That includes shellfish; eggs, because they come from chickens, which have eyes; and meat, naturally. Even fowl. She says that at the moment an animal is killed, its fear is so great it releases poisons. Then we eat those poisons."

Nikki's elbows rested against the edge of the table, and she folded her lovely hands together. Evidently she wasn't going to dig into her lobster until Quin's filet mignon had returned. "God, I never pay any attention to all the stuff you hear about food. If I did, I'd never get *any* pleasure from eating."

Quin impaled a radish at the end of her fork, thinking about pleasure. If she were playing a word-association game and someone said *Nikki,* her immediate response would be *pleasure.* No, that wasn't quite right. For the last few weeks, her response would have been *secrets.*

And tonight those secrets separated them like the Pacific, and had, really, since the evening they'd gone to see the movie in the Grove.

"If you were thinking of yourself in terms of an animal, what would it be?" Quin asked suddenly.

"What're you talking about, Quin?"

"C'mon, this is a game. What animal, Nikki?"

She sat back with a patronizing smile. "Okay. An animal. Can I name a bird?"

Quin nodded.

"Okay, a hawk."

"What's your favorite color?"

Nikki laughed. "This sounds like those things we used to do in junior high, Quin."

"Just humor me, c'mon."

"Okay, my favorite color's red. A blood red."

"If you thought of yourself as a body of water, what would it be?"

"Ocean."

"What does a small, black room with no windows and no doors represent to you? Just one or two words."

Quin could see the little wheels turning in Nikki's head as she ruminated. "The end," she said softly.

The waiter returned with Quin's filet mignon. When he'd left, Nikki sat forward, arms resting parallel to the edge of the table. "Well? So what's it mean?"

"The bird or animal is how you see yourself. " *Hawk: Predatory. But preying on what or who?* "Your favorite color is how you think other people see you." *Red: Vibrant? Energetic? Overwhelming?* "The body of water is how you perceive yourself sexually." *Ocean: Vast, practically infinite. Maybe promiscuous?* "And the small black room is how you perceive death." *The end.*

The brief silence between them was punctuated by the

220

sounds around them: guitar music, traffic, the pop from a bottle of champagne. Nikki finally laughed, but it was strained. "Where'd you learn that, anyway? Psych one-oh-one?" And she tore into her lobster with a vengeance.

"It's just a silly game," Quin said, and wished she believed it.

24

THE WEATHER EXPERTS claimed the thunderstorm was nothing more than the result of a high pressure system, but McCleary wasn't buying it. He blamed the hurricane, swirling like a dervish somewhere north of Puerto Rico, for screwing up the beginning of his weekend. Wind whistled as it whipped sheets of rain against his office windows. Traffic three stories down was snarled and ugly. It was already five-thirty, he was supposed to be at Quin's by seven-thirty, and he still had to go home to shower and change. Yeah, it was Hurricane Ingrid, all right, conspiring, teasing South Florida with a taste of what her fury—if she struck—might bring.

He glanced at his daily list. The only items that hadn't been crossed out were: party with Quin, call Rob Valencia, check with Millie Dobbs on Monday. He was reaching for the phone to call Quin to tell her he'd probably be late when his phone rang. He debated not answering it. But if it were Bob Izzo, who expected him to eat and sleep in his office and work fourteen-hour days, seven days a week, then he'd be starting Monday with an altercation. He reached for the phone.

"Homicide."

"Mr. McCleary, this is Millie Dobbs. At the Dade County library?"

"Mrs. Dobbs, right. How're you?"

"Just fine, thanks. I was wondering, Detective Mc-Cleary, if you had any more information. I read about the double homicide in the paper."

"Nothing yet." The blaring of horns drifted up from the street.

"I, uh, just wanted you to know I've been giving your little problem a great deal of thought. I realize it's Friday and rather late, but I was wondering if you might be able to drop by? I think I've found something."

I love you, Mrs. Dobbs, he thought. "I'll be there in twenty minutes."

His estimate turned out to be optimistic. Rain made Miami drivers neurotic. There were numerous fender-benders, stalled cars, and some of the streets had inadequate drainage and were already flooding. In several spots the flooding was so bad waves undulated over the curbs. More than once he patted Lady's dash and murmured words of affection and appreciation. If coy little Ingrid *did* hit, he thought uncomfortably, Miami was going to be in a world of trouble.

By the time he reached the library forty minutes later, he was afraid Mrs. Dobbs might already have left. He parked Lady and darted through the rain toward the building. The library was practically empty, and Mrs. Dobbs was the only person behind the reference desk, standing there like a fixture, her fingers poised on the computer keyboard. She smiled when she saw him and suggested they talk in the back office.

The room was small, and it seemed that every available space was crammed with books. There were books jammed every which way on a cart, books piled in chairs, stacked on the desk, books on top of a computer. She cleared space for them both, served him a mug of coffee from the pot brewing between stacks of books, then brought out a bottle of anisette. "A splash, Mr. McCleary?"

He chuckled. "Sure."

"Friday evenings are always slow, so I make sure I have something to help pass the time. Now. . . ." She sat down, the cart overflowing with books between them. She sipped primly from her coffee laced with anisette. "I was trying to put myself in this woman's place, based on what you'd told me. I said, 'Okay, Millie, now if you were an honest-to-God writer doing research in a bar, just what in the dickens kind of books would you be writing?' Well, that helped narrow the choice, somewhat: maybe she was doing some sort of exposé on the Miami singles scene. But that didn't feel right, if you know what I mean. After all, she's presumably been killing these men she met in the bars, right?''

Another sip at the anisette, and now she removed her glasses from the stiff nest of her hair and set them aside.

For a moment, McCleary could imagine her as she must have been thirty years ago, a slender, pretty woman with a soft, crisp Midwestern accent who loved her anisette, her beaus, but was forever temperate. "And?" McCleary asked.

"And what I concluded, Mr. McCleary, is that she writes about murder."

"How'd you decide murder instead of something else?"

"Well, I'm not sure exactly. I just was trying to slip into her skin, and that's what I came up with. She writes about murder, see, because she knows what she's writing about."

"You mean she goes into the bars with the intention of picking up someone to kill."

"My theory is that she may not think of it that way at the time, since it comes under the research heading, but it amounts to the same thing." She stood, set her mug aside, and walked over to a cart against the far wall. "Now, granted she might never have been published, that this writer routine was just that. A routine. But I took my chances." She touched a hand almost lovingly to the stack of books on the cart. "So I started combing through our mystery collection. It's quite extensive, you know, which is partially my fault. I've been doing a lot of the ordering for the last five years, and I happen to have a weakness for mysteries." She paused. "I don't know whether you realize it, but mysteries comprise thirty percent of the market."

He shook his head, feeling small and ignorant. Listening to her was like stumbling blind into another world. Homicide had taken up so much of his life for so many years that he couldn't remember the last time he'd read anything more than a book on art.

"Anyhow, I started going through our mystery collection, as I said, looking for any author whose first name started with a K or a C or was Kara or Karen, since that's close. . . ." She gestured to the overflowing cart. McCleary swallowed hard.

"*All* those?"

Millie Dobbs let out a soft, delighted laugh. "Oh, no. First, I divided them into piles by five-year periods. These"—she swept her hand over the books on the first shelf—"are murder mysteries published within the last five years. Of these, I looked for stories set entirely or partially in Florida. Now that might've been a mistake. Just because the lady lives in the area doesn't necessarily mean she wrote about the area. But writers generally seem to stick to areas they know well. Anyway, then I narrowed that group down to six whose authors' first names begin with K or C, Kara or Karen, as I said before." She lifted the small pile, set it at the edge of her desk. "They're all murder mysteries, Mr. McCleary, and the authors first names run the gamut from K to Karen to Kara to Christine."

McCleary looked from the books to Mrs. Dobbs, then back to the books again. He felt overwhelmed that this little old lady with her bifocals and her coffee sprinkled with anisette who didn't know him from Adam had taken the time. This was Miami: people here weren't supposed to do things like that.

He started to thank her, but she waved it aside and said, "A toast, Mr. McCleary? And then we'll get these books checked out."

He laughed and held out his mug.

2.

Quin estimated that there were seventy-five to a hundred people at Steve and Nikki's engagement party. They spilled out of his spacious home into the patio by the pool and then into the yard, which backed up to the intracoastal waterway. Music and laughter floated out over the dark waters, where now and then a boat slipped past. Waiters and waitresses moved silently among the guests with trays of drinks and hors d'oeuvres. The redolence of the air stirred memories of other sea-swollen nights, of smoother, less complicated times, before she'd known the truth about Grant.

She and McCleary made their way through the crowd to the patio and then outside into the warm, damp darkness. She drew in a deep breath, grateful to be away from the din. The rain had stopped an hour ago, and the night smelled like spring. They walked over to some vacant chairs at a corner of the yard, beneath the umbrella of a willow tree. McCleary whipped a handkerchief out of his pocket and wiped off the chairs. Then he bowed deeply at the waist. "Madam," he said, and Quin laughed. For a while, they sat silently, watching the moon in its solitary passage, playing hide-and-seek with a narrow band of clouds. A cabin cruiser, lit up with colorful globes of light, drifted by.

"I've always wondered what it would be like to be that rich," Quin remarked, motioning toward the cruiser.

"Or *this* rich," McCleary replied.

"I think we're in the wrong professions, you know?"

McCleary chuckled. "I think we'd had this conversation before."

She told him about the page of notes she'd found at Grant's, the phone bills, and her call to Cartagena. "If the woman hasn't called back by tomorrow, I'll call her again."

"And then what? Suppose she hangs up on you again?"

"You playing devil's advocate, McCleary?"

"No, not really. But if the woman hung up on you once, she'll probably do it again."

"Then I'll fly to Cartagena," Quin replied, and knew suddenly that she would do exactly that if she had to.

"Let's exhaust our leads here, first, okay? If those don't turn up anything, then I'll go to Cartagena with you."

"I'm sure Izzo would love that," she remarked.

He didn't say anything. Quin fished around in her purse until she found the notes Grant had made, and handed them to McCleary. He slipped the page in his coat pocket. "I'll read it later." She nodded, noticing the way the milky light created a softness to his face that was absent during the day, as if there were parts of him

226

which emerged only after the sun had gone down. A secret McCleary, sublime. And tonight, somewhat reticent, after quickly perusing the half-dozen murder mysteries the librarian had given him. He reached for her hand. "Tell me about Grant."

"What do you want to know? I think I've told you most everything."

"What sort of relationship did you have?"

It wasn't an idle question. She sensed purpose behind it, a purpose that was only partly professional. His thumb moved across her knuckles, slowly, almost absently, dipping into the tiny valleys, rising the knobby hills. "In the beginning, it was good. It's always good in the beginning." *Like now*, she thought, but didn't say it. "And toward the end, it was strained. Everything else in between seems vague, like it didn't really happen."

She could almost feel him relating what she'd said to the puzzle of Grant's murder as well as to something in his own life. "You know, in homicide, there's a phenomena we call dark fields. They're like blind spots that develop when you're too close to a case and can't see the answer even though it's staring you in the face." His gaze fixed on the reflection of the moon in the water as he spoke. She had the distinct impression he wasn't speaking to her so much as to himself. "I used to believe dark fields were confined to homicide, but not anymore. I think our lives are permeated by them, Quin. They're a kind of defense mechanism or something that sustains illusions and makes emotional involvement a dangerous pursuit."

A magma of clouds had drifted over the moon. His thumb lay motionless now on the back of her hand. Despite the heat, she shivered. "What're you trying to say, anyway, McCleary? You think I've got secrets?" She laughed to keep the conversation light, because she was afraid it would veer into darkness—suddenly, irrevocably.

"I'm not sure." He turned his head. Moonlight, dimmed by the passing clouds, illuminated only one side of his face and mustache. The other side was thrown into shadow. He wasn't returning her banter.

"Oh c'mon." Her voice was quiet, soft, like his, and

she withdrew her hand. The abrupt absence of the connection between them was like having the floor yanked out from under her. She felt as if she were tumbling in slow motion toward the bottom of a dream.

"I guess I'm afraid of caring too much, Quin."

"And you think I'm not?"

His smoky eyes fixed on hers, and she couldn't read them. For a long moment there was only the dark, the sound of water lapping against the sea wall, and the whispering of their separate pasts. Then he reached out and touched her face. She lowered her eyes because the intensity of his gaze hurt her.

"Well, well, this *is* cozy."

The nerves in her neck tingled, McCleary jerked around, and Paul Holmes was smiling, thoroughly enjoying his intrusion. He was with Miriam, his diminutive wife, who seemed thoroughly embarrassed. Her glazed eyes screamed that she'd had too much to drink, didn't understand what her husband was doing, and that she just wanted to crawl into bed and wipe out tonight.

"Paul, Miriam, hi," Quin stammered.

McCleary said nothing.

Miriam gulped from her glass and drew in her shoulders as if pressing herself back against the dark.

"So how've you been, Quin?"

He smiled widely, and she realized Holmes wasn't just drunk, he was blasted. Beside her, McCleary was stiff as a corpse, not looking at Holmes as the man went on about how pleased he was to see that she'd so quickly realized life was for the living. Liquid spilled from Holmes's glass as he leaned toward Quin, tapped her on the shoulder, and said, his words slurring, "I think it's wonderful that you're fucking Mike here, I do, I really do."

Quin just stared at him, at his white and perfect teeth, not sure she'd heard him correctly. Then everything happened very quickly. McCleary was on his feet, Quin saw him drawing back his arm, hand clenched at it connected with Paul Holmes's jaw. The DA's glass flew out of his hand as he stumbled back, lost his footing, and went down. Miriam let out a yelp that was drowned in the noise from the house, and her glass dropped to the ground. Then McCleary reached for Quin's arm and guided her back toward the light, music, the crowd, saying nothing. She was mildly surprised that his grasp on her arm was gentle, as though the moment they'd shared before Holmes had intruded had been redeemed and now continued. When she glanced back, Holmes was getting to his feet, rubbing his jaw, and Miriam was backing away from him.

As they stepped into the patio, where the orbs of colorful lights were reflected incompletely on the surface of the pool, Quin reclaimed her arm. "I'd like a drink," she said.

The softness in McCleary's face that the moonlight had created earlier was gone. In its place she saw pain, hardness, incredulity, each emotion like a separate wave trying to absorb the other.

"A drink. Yeah, I think I could use a drink too." He squeezed her hand and vanished in the crowd.

Quin stood there, staring at her shoes, wondering what she was doing here. When she glanced up, Nikki was coming toward her, wearing a red silk dress, Nikki with her hair like a whiskey river in the light, Nikki who saw herself as a predator.

"Quin, I didn't think you were going to come." Her cool cheek brushed Quin's, her hands took hold of Quin's. She was high, and not on booze.

I don't know you, I really don't know you anymore, Nikki.

"Where's this Mike McClerchy I've heard so much about, hmm?"

McCleary, not McClerchy.

Nikki's glossy eyes slid about like mounds of Jell-O as people stopped to say hello, to offer congratulations. Her practiced smile slipped in and out of place, then she tugged at Quin's arm and drew her outside the patio. "He *did* come, didn't he?"

"He's getting us drinks," Quin said.

"Quin, listen. There's something that's been bothering me." While one hand flicked her hair from her neck, the other reached into the pocket of her dress and brought out a cigarette. "I want you to know this. I want you to know because Grant was truly a shit, honey,

229

and it's all in the past and I want you to be happy with this McClerchy."

"McCleary," Quin corrected.

"Right." She took a deep breath, raised her eyes, and for a moment, some of the steam and ersatz gaity seemed to bleed from her face. "Remember I told you about seeing Grant in the mall that evening with the girl?"

Quin nodded.

"Not long after that, I ran into him in one of the bars in the Grove, and I was pretty out of it, Quin, and so was he, and, uh, we went back to his townhouse. He admitted later that he'd brought me back there as a sort of insurance, knowing that if I said anything to you about the girl, Quin, he would tell you . . . about me. That's what kind of man he was. He . . ."

Certain things immediately penetrated Quin's awareness: the texture of her dress against her clammy hands, the din around them, the perspiration pimpling Nikki's face. She was still talking, but Quin had ceased to hear her. She simply walked away, her legs stiff as planks as McCleary's voice pounded in her ears: *They're like blind spots . . . they sustain illusions*. . . . Then one day the dark fields are lit up, Quin thought, burning the illusions away.

"Didn't you say Nikki owns a .45, Quin?"

"What I said, McCleary, was that she suggested I buy a forty-five." It was late, she was tired, and barely an hour ago, the woman she'd considered her closest friend had admitted that she'd slept with Grant.

They were sitting in McCleary's kitchen, and his voice leaped and sank in the space between them. Beyond the room, she heard nothing, as if the world outside of them had caved in, been buried in the moonlight, and tomorrow they would awaken to a civilization entombed in rubble.

"But didn't she intimate that *she* owned one?"

"Yes." Quin rubbed her eyes. "But I don't know if it's a .45."

"Besides the fact that she admitted she'd slept with Grant, didn't you say she also thought he was a bastard?"

What was wrong with his voice, anyway? Why was it

so cold, so utterly distant? "I don't want to talk about it, McCleary. Let's go watch TV or something."

He looked like he was about to say something, but then he apparently changed his mind and just nodded. He picked up the plate of cheese and crackers, set the last half of her tuna fish sandwich on the edge. Quin reached for their glasses of orange juice and followed him into the living room. It, like the rest of the apartment, was spacious, neat, and possessed that particular feel of a man who lived alone. The white-tiled floor stretched like a field of clouds to the porch doors that opened into the night. It was broken up by colorful throw rugs which he referred to as his "magic carpets." The wicker furniture with its plump dove gray and magenta cushions conferred a beach house ambience. It was a comfortable place where you could kick off your shoes and settle in for a while.

But what had surprised her most of all were McCleary's paintings. They filled the walls—sketches, watercolors, acrylics, an assortment of rural scenes, a few portraits. Some were awkward, almost diffident, others possessed a professionalism and sensitivity that astonished her. Among his own paintings hung works by other artists. There was, for instance, a strange print by M.C. Escher of flying geese emerging from other geese that were mirror images, a watercolor of an Oriental woman by Edna Hibel—a West Palm Beach artist—oils that evoked a gamut of moods. His penchant for art smacked of the sublime McCleary, she thought, the man hidden behind the cop facade.

Quin plopped on the couch and set the glasses of juice on coasters on the cherry-wood table. The half-dozen books the librarian had given McCleary slid toward her, and she finally set them on the floor. He switched on the overhead fan and slid a wall panel aside. Within was a TV, an elaborate stereo system, and a VCR. Simple tastes, but expensive.

McCleary sank onto the cushion beside her, munching on cheese and crackers as she polished off the rest of her sandwich. She was still hungry; the thought of the ice cream in McCleary's freezer tempted her, but not enough to get up and walk into the kitchen. Her stomach growled in protest. McCleary heard it and glanced at her. "You want something else to eat? I've got a fridge filled with food, Quin."

"No, it's okay."

They watched David Letterman, laughing at the right moments, groaning at some of his silly jokes, acting as though nothing was wrong. But between them hovered their unfinished conversation. And Quin, who hated loose ends, finally couldn't stand it anymore. "Look, Nikki didn't kill Grant. She didn't. I would know it if she had."

His response was quick; he'd been waiting for her to broach the subject again. "How? How would you know, Quin?"

How? "I just would, that's all." Her voice held a defensive edge, and she hated it. She slid off her shoes and drew her legs up against her.

"Quin, I'm just trying to get things straight, that's all."

"Yeah, I know you are." She didn't look at him; she stared at Letterman making chopped liver of his guest.

"Has Nikki ever mentioned anything to you about wanting to write?"

Her head snapped toward him. Light from the lamp splashed onto his forehead, slid the length of his nose, and nestled finally in his mustache. "McCleary, she's not a murderess. Or a writer. As far as I know, she's never had any *desire* to write. You can't know someone for nine years and not know something like that, you can't."

"But you lived with Grant for a year, never knowing he was seeing other women, Quin."

"I *chose* not to know it," she corrected. "It's called brain censorship." As soon as she'd said it, she realized the same could easily apply to Nikki. More brain censorship. She reached for a cracker, jammed it in her mouth, washed it down with the rest of her juice. "I thought you were convinced that Paul Holmes killed Grant."

"I don't know anymore where he fits."

Indignant and annoyed now, she snapped, "Well, it's

232

easy for you to point the finger at me. But what about Robin and Paul? You didn't know about them, either."

"That was different. We weren't living together, we. . ."

Something soft and strange flickered across his face, some emotion she couldn't read, maybe pain, maybe something deeper than pain. He smiled, but it didn't touch his eyes. "Dark fields, these are the dark fields I was talking about, Quin."

It wasn't funny, but she let out a weird, clipped laugh that sounded like the call of a bird felled in mid-flight. She wrapped her arms around her legs and rested her chin on her knee. Letterman ended. A movie came on. They didn't speak. But after a while, she took one of the magenta pillows, dropped it in McCleary's lap, and stretched out. Her head sank into the feathery softness. Her eyes closed as McCleary massaged her neck. She saw Nikki on the dark screen of her lids, Nikki aiming a .45 at Grant Bell and pulling the trigger.

25

I ROLLED A clean sheet of paper into the typewriter and typed my name at the top: Kara Newman. No, not my name, but Mama's mother's maiden name. I forgot that sometimes. I chose Nana's name because she wasn't crazy. My fingers tingled, then suddenly they were off, dancing across the keyboard like tiny ballerinas, executing pirouettes and splits and impossible leaps:

> She dug up the clothes she'd cut into strips, squares, and rectangles. The stink of the old blood mixed with the uberty of the earth, nearly gagging her. In the gray wash of pre-dawn light, her dirt-spotted fingers seemed grotesque, combing the pieces into a neat pile, scooping the pile into a paper bag. Like a dog with a bone, she buried her treasure, her secret, in another part of the yard, near the hedge, in the shade. Then she covered it with dried leaves.
> It wouldn't do for the spot to get too much sun. The bits of clothing might take root like seedlings and grow. And suppose the sprouts had the faces of a man and woman? Suppose they developed vocal chords and learned to speak? They would tell the story of their deaths and then everyone would know she was as crazy as Mama, that she

I dropped the sheet on my desk. A spot of dirt stained the corner, and I went to wash my hands again. And again. Mama would say I was worse than Pontius Pilate. I could still see her, washing her hands the day her mind broke forever, murmuring she could no longer be responsible for what she knew, for the secret. Now she lay listlessly in a nursing home, cooing like an infant. People fed her, walked her, spoke to her, changed her clothes when she wet herself.

And my secret was safe because Mama was crazy and Grant was dead.

As I started typing again, I thought of the young woman who'd gotten in the way, remembered how the knife had sung when I'd plunged it through her back. I hadn't wanted to hurt her, hadn't meant to. But I liked it, I liked the power that had imbued me as the woman's life had winked out like a star. Murder is a cultivated taste, like anchovies.

My fingers paused, I looked at what I'd written: *I am doing something wrong.*

I need help.

Help.

Hel.

He.

H.

(please)

PART THREE

Illumination

"We are all born mad. Some remain so."
—Samuel Beckett

26

1.

EARLY SATURDAY MORNING, Quin and McCleary sped along the Palmetto Expressway as Roy Orbison crooned from Lady's tape deck. It was going to be a good day, McCleary decided. They'd started it off with coffee on the porch, the two of them as comfortable together as an old married couple. Now they were on their way to breakfast, a special place McCleary had frequented in the past with Robin. Later, they would tackle the books Millie Dobbs had given him. An orderly progression, A to Z: he liked that. Even the soreness in his knuckles from decking Holmes couldn't daunt his mood. In fact, the pain was almost exquisite, since no single act in his life had given him such pleasure.

"Hey, McCleary," Quin said, eyeing the side mirror. "I hate to mention this, but there's a silver Caddy back there that's been tailing us ever since we got on the ramp."

McCleary glanced in the rearview mirror. The Caddy's windows were too darkly tinted to catch a glimpse of who was inside. "Well, there's one way to find out." He pressed his foot to the accelerator, watching the speedometer climb: 60, 68, 75. The Caddy kept pace, but at a respectful distance. He spotted the sign for 836 West and, half a mile later, whipped into the left lane and sailed up the ramp. It would take them out by

Florida International University and to the no-man's-land farther west.

As soon as they were on the open highway, he floored Lady. She took off like a shot, engine purring, the landscape blurring, the deep blue sky in front of them dipping so low to the ground it swallowed the treetops. When he glanced in the mirror, the Caddy was keeping pace like a silver bullet.

So much for his perfect Saturday. "I think it's official. You have a weapon on you?"

"In my purse."

"Would you reach in the glove compartment and get my gun?"

The glove compartment fell open with a click, and Quin drew in her breath. "God, what do you do with *this* thing? Hunt elephants? What is it?"

"A .357." She passed it to him, took out her own. He flicked off the safety, set the magnum in his lap, tried to concentrate on the road. When he saw the turnoff for the university, he held to the center lane until the last possible moment, then swerved sharply. The RX7 fishtailed, the tires screeched, he gripped the steering wheel, grinding his teeth. Then the car swept down the ramp, and in the mirror he saw the Cadillac burning rubber. He took the curve at sixty, slowed as the traffic began to logjam, looked anxiously in the rearview mirror. The Caddy wasn't in sight. Not yet.

Ahead, the light was red and cars whizzed through the intersection. He slammed the heel of his hand against the horn, sailed through the light as several cars braked, then nearly sideswiped a van that had zipped out of nowhere.

Quin, gripping the seat, said nothing.

He headed toward the FIU campus. When he looked in the mirror, the Caddy was bearing down, graced with a green light. McCleary veered sharply right, negotiating the turn onto the campus with less dexterity than he would have liked, but who could be picky?

Since it was Saturday, there weren't as many cars around as there would've been otherwise. At least something was in their favor. He also knew the campus. Five years ago, a kid had drowned in the shallow manmade lake in front of the administration building and everyone but the fellow's sister assumed it was suicide. She'd alerted the police, and McCleary had gotten the case, and he'd been bitten bad by the kid's sociology professor. Lanie. Lanie Sellers. But that was another story.

The point was, cops as well as the campus security force patrolled here regularly, and he suspected they were going to need help. When the Caddy had rounded that last corner, sunlight had struck the back window, silhouetting five men inside.

Lady screeched past the anthropology building, past Languages, Foreign Relations, and Law, that great bastion of bullshit. He kept his hand on the horn, and students leaped back onto the curb, hurling invectives at him, and nowhere was there a security car. The Caddy was directly behind him, and one of the back windows was coming down, and fuck oh fuck, McCleary thought, the weapon looked like an Uzi. *Not here, not here with so many people around.*

"Get down!" he shouted. Quin slid down in the seat, gun frozen in her hand.

He opened Lady up wide as he hit a dirt road that angled off toward the string of bleached, half-finished buildings in the distance. They were additions to the medical school or social sciences or something, and beyond them lay no-man's land. The Uzis opened fire.

Lady's back window shattered.

Quin gasped sharply, and a moment later she threw herself toward the window and started firing. A flying shard had nicked McCleary in the neck, and when his hand darted to it, his fingers came away bloody. Quin tossed him a handkerchief which he pressed to the wound, then she slid down in the seat and reloaded her weapon. He glanced quickly at her, and in one of those brief, pellucid moments, noted how her singular purpose had hardened her features.

McCleary swerved recklessly across the old road, toward a space that loomed as vast and barren as a desert. Heat shimmered in waves above the sand ahead of him. Hot air whipped through the broken back window. The Mazda leaped from the packed dirt to white sand, tires spinning, then catching and thrusting them forward. The

Uzis fired another round, he could hear the shots, but Lady had too much of a lead.

Several half-completed buildings rushed toward him, the structures so white they were blinding. Dust flew up around the car and settled through his open window, stinging his eyes, clogging his throat. He coughed. He heard another round of shots, but by then he was on the far side of the buildings, flying, flying, lunging for the speed of sound. In between the buildings he caught glimpses of the Caddy on the other side. The men took potshots at the car, bullets spraying the buildings, knocking out the few windows.

His tongue darted along his lower lip and tasted of dust. The glare hurt his eyes, making him squint until he felt the grit in the wrinkles at the corners. He grabbed for his sunglasses on the dash, slipped them on. The Mazda bounced and jimmied, splashed through a deep puddle from last night's rain. His teeth clattered until his head ached. Quin was at the window again, about to shoot when he turned wide and headed back in the other direction. It threw her off balance.

"What're you *doing*?" she shouted.

"We're splitting."

He was close to the end of the buildings where he'd started before the Caddy swerved. Lady jumped the curb, banged as she hit the street, lost speed. He slammed her into third gear, fourth, then raced toward no-man's-land west of campus.

He sped down the second side street he came to. A dirt road. Dust flew. The Mazda swiped a garbage can that was at the side of a hidden driveway for Monday's pickup. It lifted the can about five feet and garbage rained through the air. There had to be more side roads in here, he thought frantically.

Quin's face was milky as her head jerked around. "I don't see them. Maybe we've lost them."

"I'm not taking any chances."

Right, left, then he was on one of the narrow little roads. He saw a junkyard ahead. He bore down on it, his eyes darted once to the mirror, the Caddy was no-where in sight. He screeched into the yard, slowed so the dust would settle, and finally came to a halt behind a wall of old tires. Even a .357 wouldn't be much help against Uzis, but just the same, he reached into the glove compartment for his extra ammo, and he and Quin leaped out of the car. The silence, the heat and desolation clamped down over them.

They ran straight for a wire mesh fence covered with vines of ivy and hibiscus and scrambled over it. His sleeve caught on the end of a wire and ripped, but he fell softly to the ground, landing on both feet. A moment later, Quin landed beside him, but she came down hard on one ankle and grimaced.

He pulled her to her feet. "Can you walk okay?"

"With a bunch of crazy whatever those people are behind us? You bet I can."

They were in a lot covered with weeds and mango trees. Beyond the lot was another fence and then some mini warehouses rising from the concrete like space stations on a lunar landscape. No place to hide.

He winced as he heard tires screeching somewhere nearby. These suckers were crazy enough to come after them on foot with their goddamned Uzis because there wasn't a soul for miles and what were a few shots on a bright Saturday morning in the city that led the nation in homicide, right?

He grabbed Quin's hand, and the tall grass scratched at them as they raced through it. McCleary stopped at the thickest mango tree—tall, but not so tall that it stood out. The branches were bushy, the leaves thick, and hey, guess what? They weren't going to starve to death. There were fat, ripe mangoes hanging from the branches like balls on a bull.

"Go," he said, and Quin scrambled up the thick trunk, her dexterity suprising him. He followed, grateful he was wearing sneakers, remembering the morning not so long ago he'd done exactly this to escape the pit bull. They stopped finally when the branches looked too thin to support their weight. Below them, the thick leaves offered adequate cover. By ducking his head just a little, he could see the junkyard. Where the Caddy was. Where men were scuttling out of it. Five men, and Christ, all of them were armed.

He and Quin exchanged a glance. Her face was

sheathed in sweat, and she hugged the nearest limb so hard her cheek pressed against it. "Nice friends you've got," she whispered.

He rubbed the knuckles on his right hand, thinking of Holmes, certain he was behind this.

Quin, interpreting the gesture correctly, lifted her brows. "Paul? You're sure?"

"Who else?" he hissed, and then they fell silent as one of the men in the junkyard shouted, "*Epa, patrón! Por aquí! El carro está aquí!*"

Aw shit, McCleary thought. They were going to waste Lady. *Better her than you, friend.*

But even so, when the shots rang out, McCleary squeezed his eyes shut and gripped the branch with both hands to keep from falling. Around them, birds—startled by the gunfire—rose in clusters, their wings beating the hot air like a single, frenzied heart.

2.

For nearly two hours the five men fanned out from the field like a special forces batallion. Quin watched them darting about, scurrying like fat, exotic roaches intent on a new cache of food. The muscles in her legs, which were drawn tighty against her, screamed for movement. The air beneath the canopy of leaves and branches was hot, still. Sweat trickled along the sides of her face and between her breasts.

The heat, combined with her hunger, brought on a wave of dizziness, and she finally rested her forehead against her knees and closed her eyes. Once, her sense of equilibrium deserted her and she felt herself toppling. McCleary grabbed her arm, steadying her, then shifted his position so she could lean against his shoulder. "I won't let you fall, Quin," he whispered.

She thought of Lady, wasted in the junkyard, and, reaching out, touched her hand to his face, which was shiny with sweat. *Are we gonna get outa here, McCleary?* her mind shouted. He squeezed her hand, then turned so he could peer through the branches to the mini warehouses, where the Caddy and the men were.

Even if they were both crack shots, she thought, the

chances of their making it out of here alive if they opened fire were slim. And since there was no place to hide on the ground, they were stuck in the tree as long as the men were in the vicinity.

A shudder chattered along her spine as she heard voices. McCleary took out the .357 again. Quin, purse still slung over her shoulder and pressed to her side hugged the trunk as three men stopped in the shade of the tree, *their* tree. Her heart hammered. If any one of the men dropped his head back, that was it. Don't move, Quin, she told herself. Don't sneeze, cough, don't breathe too hard, and oh God, stomach, please don't growl.

The men were speaking Spanish. Two of them were armed, Uzis resting snug as infants in the crooks of their arms. The third man was plump, short, balding. When one of the men referred to him as Señor Valdez, McCleary's spine went rigid. The Cuban that Joe Bean had told McCleary about, she thought, and McCleary's link to Paul Holmes. Her eyes watered as she continued to stare at the three men, willing them not to look up. She could see the bald spot on the crown of Valdez's head, the triangle his arm made as he slid a hand into the pocket of his slacks. Their voices seemed abnormally loud, trapped beneath the canopy of the tree with the breathless air.

Suddenly, someone shouted, "*Patrón, creo que se fueron por aquí!*" The two armed men took off across the lot at a sprint. Valdez remained in the shade of the tree for a moment, fingering a fat cigar still wrapped in cellophane. One quick glance at McCleary told her he was just itching to drop from the branches onto Valdez's shoulders and ride him like a monkey demon. He probably would have, too, Quin decided, except that Valdez strolled away from the shade toward the Caddy. A few moments later, Quin spotted the Cadillac moving slowly past the mini warehouses.

They remained in the tree another fifteen minutes, then McCleary whispered, "Let's make a break for it, Quin."

She glanced at her ankle, which was swelling, then back at McCleary and nodded. "Which direction?"

"Through the junkyard and back the way we came."

Her ankle ached every time she put pressure on it, but they made it safely through the junkyard and to one of the side roads. Branches from the banyan trees knitted together, forming an awning of shade, and a blessed breeze licked at their damp clothes. She asked how far it was to the campus. "Four miles."

In four miles, she thought, she was going to need medical attention for dehydration, not to mention her ankle. Or her hunger. "I've got to rest a minute, okay?"

He paused, wiped his arm across his forehead. The expression on his face was odd; she didn't think he'd heard her. "A car." He grabbed her hand, pulled her along after him as he pounded into the thick scrub brush to the left of the road, then hit the ground.

A twig poked her in the ribs, dust swirled up her nose, she stared at a spider perched on a blade of grass not six inches in front of her. She heard the car roaring past, felt McCleary lift up to take a look. "Was it the Caddy?"

"Yes."

He waited another moment, then straightened. Quin sat back on her heels, picking stickers off her clothes. McCleary stood and helped her to her feet. "I'm sorry I got you into this," he said, still holding on to her hand.

"Just get me to a water fountain, McCleary, and all's forgiven."

He chuckled and hugged her quickly. "If I ever have to get stuck in a disaster, Quin, I hope it's with you."

It was the nicest compliment she'd had in years.

3.

Three hours later, after Quin had taken a cab home to nurse her swollen ankle, McCleary hopped out of a Triple A truck in front of the police station. A white ball of fury had taken root in his brain like a tumor. His car, which resembled a prop from a war film, had been towed to a gas station five miles from his apartment. The windows and windshield had been shot out, the doors riddled with holes, the tires were flat. But Lady hadn't exploded, the bastards had made sure of that. After all, even in Miami, an exploding vehicle would've drawn too much attention. If there'd been any doubt in his mind before about Joe Bean's plan, there wasn't now. Holmes was going to pay; McCleary intended to get even.

The front room in the homicide department was empty. Not surprising, since it was Saturday. But he heard a radio. In the quiet, it seemed an isolated, almost lonesome sound. It was coming from Robin's office.

He stopped in the doorway. She was scribbling away at her desk and didn't notice him immediately. Her shoulders hunched, she rolled her lower lip against her teeth. She was wearing jeans and a cotton print shirt cut low enough so it showed off her long neck. Her painted toenails peeked out from under the desk.

"You work on Saturdays now?"

Her head snapped up. "Mac."

"Writing up your resignation?"

She managed a tight, nervous laugh, then motioned toward his torn shirt. "What happened to *you*?"

"I had a run-in with a mango tree."

"What?" she laughed.

He closed the door and leaned against it, hands in his pockets. "A bunch of Hispanics in a silver Cadillac opened fire on me with some goddamned Uzis, that's what happened. They also wasted my car. I suspect your friend Paul Holmes is behind it."

He noted how her expression began to close off. "Why do you think Paul's behind it?"

"That's how he operates, Robin, in case you haven't figured it out yet. He plays dirty, and when he can't find dirt, he plays for keeps." McCleary had been moving steadily toward her. Now he knocked his knuckles against the desk, hard. "But I don't suppose you've seen that side of him yet, have you?"

She got up, moved to the window. She stood there with her fingers tucked in her back pockets, gazing out, then she turned. With two fingers, she rubbed a spot between her eyes. "Paul Holmes wouldn't kill anyone. And he certainly wouldn't hire someone to kill you."

McCleary laughed; he couldn't believe what he was hearing. "You *are* screwing that asshole. You're not only *screwing* him, you've been talking to him about this case and he's one of the primary suspects."

Her laugh was quick, brittle. "Suspects? Why? Because of the fifteen grand he paid to Bell? He gave you an adequate explanation for that, Mac. I was there the day he gave it, remember?"

Yeah. It was the same day some small detail had clicked in his mind about Robin and Holmes being lovers. He noticed how she'd once again deftly sidestepped his accusation that they were.

"I didn't find his explanation satisfactory."

"Only because you've had a vendetta against the man since he was in private practice."

"We've had *this* conversation before," he said. "And as far as a vendetta is concerned, you're way off base."

Her spine stiffened, her jaw had an obdurate thrust, the steady gaze of her eyes was hard, mean. "Bullshit, Mac. You've had it in for Paul for years."

Here we go again, he thought wearily. "Even if that were true, it doesn't change the fact that Holmes knew about the key Quin brought in here that day, Robin. And there's only one way he could've known."

He waited for the brick wall to go up. He expected her to deny it; she didn't. But there was a subtle shift in her expression. She ran a hand over her face, and after a long, hollow moment, said, "You're right. It . . . it slipped out and I . . . oh hell." She sighed as she sat back in the windowsill, looking at her hands.

Slipped out when? In the sack? "You're a cop, Robin. Since when does confidential information just *slip* out?"

"Mac, Bell was blackmailing Paul. That's what the fifteen grand was about." She said it softly, her forehead lowered so he couldn't see her eyes.

"Blackmailing him." Oh sweet Christ, he thought, and started to laugh. Maybe there was justice in the universe, after all.

"Why?"

"Because he needed money for his little Amazon project, I guess."

"And that doesn't constitute a motive for murder, Robin?"

Her lip quivered. Tears swelled in her eyes. Then she covered her face with her hands and began to cry. "I . . . I don't know what I'm doing anymore." She waved

248

a hand toward her desk. "I've been sitting here all morning, and the only thing I've been able to think about is resigning. I don't know how . . . how I got into this goddamned mess. It wasn't supposed to get complicated, Mac. None of it."

Complicated, McCleary thought. *Yeah, it was definitely that.* He jammed his hands in his pockets, wished he had a cup of coffee. But he knew if he went over to the coffee maker on the shelf, he'd find mold growing in the grounds. Little details like that always escaped Robin.

He heard himself talking again, about the emeralds, the key, the break-in to Quin's house, all things Robin knew about already. Why was he bothering to reiterate? Why bother at all? "Who else has a motive like blackmail, huh?"

"Mac, there were other people who knew about the gems and the key."

"Yeah, but no one with as clear-cut a motive for killing the man, Robin."

She threw up her hands. "You haven't looked for motives with anyone else. Hell, maybe Trevor Forsythe's got a motive you don't even know about. Or Quin's friend, Nikki. Or . . . God, you're hopeless. It all comes back to the same thing. You want to pin this murder on him, and you don't care how you do it." She didn't raise her voice, but he felt like she had shouted it at him. how could she defend the bastard?

"What was it Bell knew that was worth fifteen thousand to Holmes, Robin?"

He could see she didn't want to tell him. But he knew she would. He knew she would because he would shake it out of her if he had to. She ran her hands along her jeans, made a soft, defeated sound. "When he was seventeen years old he was convicted of raping a black woman."

A huge, oppressive weight swelled in the center of his chest and pressed hard, as if he were trying to break free of earth's gravity. The man who'd been elected to the DA's office primarily because of the feminist groups that supported his radical punishment for rapists had raped a woman himself. McCleary didn't know what to say. It was like peering through a window at a version of the world he'd read about, seen on TV, knew existed, and had even dealt with in other cases, but had never experienced in quite this way. Robin was sleeping with this man; that made it an intimate, personal thing. *So who the fuck are you?* he wanted to shout. The difference between his situation and Quin's was one merely of degree: Robin hadn't had to die for the truth to come out.

"Terrific," he muttered and started toward the door.

"Mac."

"What."

"Just a minute." She hurried over to him, touched his arm. Her hand was cool and damp, her skin dark as a shadow against the white of his arm. Oh God, he thought, he still felt something when she touched him. In some part of himself, he still loved her.

He looked at her, thinking of the night, lifetimes ago, outside Bell's townhouse, when she'd driven up in her Buick. He remembered how she'd smelled and tasted and how he'd wanted her so badly his insides had ached. Just as they were aching now.

"Don't hate me," she whispered. "Please don't hate me. I couldn't stand it if you did."

"Hate you?" The words nearly choked him. "I could never hate you, Robin. I'm not sure I can even stop loving you." Then he stepped away from her before he did what he wanted to do, before he backed her up against the wall, ripped off her jeans, and took her just as Paul Holmes had once taken a black woman.

It wasn't until he was out in the nearly empty street that he realized he not only didn't have a car, he had nowhere to go.

27

"...I TRIED CALLING Detective McCleary at the station, but he wasn't in, and I thought I should tell you or him the truth," Treena Esposito was saying. She sat stiffly on the other side of the butcher block table in Quin's kitchen, the need for confession written all over her face.

Quin looked down at the bucket where her swollen ankle was soaking, where the water cut her leg off at the calf. The only explanation for Treena's surprise visit, she decided, and for Nikki's admission last night, was that sodium pentathol had been poured in the city water supply. It had started a truth disease. And at the moment, she didn't know how much more truth she could stand.

"The truth about what, Treena?"

She gazed at her hands, which were fumbling for a cigarette. "About why I left the faculty meeting the night Grant was killed."

Quin said nothing.

"I've been having an affair with an assistant superintendent of schools who's married. We were together the night of the faculty meeting. I didn't want Detective McCleary asking him questions, Quin. You can just imagine what sort of position that would put him in."

"Not as bad a position as it put *you* in," Quin remarked, wishing the woman would leave, wishing she could curl up like a cat here in the ribbon of light on the

251

table. "Besides, you really should be telling this to McCleary, Treena. Not to me."

"I told you, I tried to call him at the station, but he wasn't in."

Yeah, he was stuck in a mango tree.

"I've decided I just can't live like this anymore, Treena continued. "It seems like my entire adult life has been nothing but a big, fat lie. First with Grant, then Benny, and now this."

Quin removed her foot from the bucket, wondering if maybe the truth serum was able to permeate the pores of her skin. If so, then now it pulsed through her bloodstream, was playing havoc with the synapses in her brain, and any minute now she'd tell Treena exactly what she thought of her.

"How was your life with Grant a lie?"

"The same way it was for you. The only difference is that for me, it was five times as long. You're lucky you knew him only a year, Quin."

"*Lucky?* I wish I'd never met the man, Treena." *Rejection:* was that included in the stages of grief, maybe sandwiched in between *denial* and *anger?* She only half listened as Treena spoke in a halting voice about her life with Grant—the secrets, lies, the small deceits, the other women. Quin was relieved when the doorbell rang, giving her an excuse to get up.

Treena also rose, murmuring something about having overstayed her welcome. Quin didn't protest, didn't even extend Treena a cordial, *It was nice to see you again.* She limped with her to the door, watched as she brushed past the mailman who'd rung the bell.

"Got a packet of stuff for you here, Miss St. James," the mailman said. "Didn't want to jam everything in the box."

"Thanks."

She stood on the stoop until Treena and the mailman had driven off, wondering why McCleary hadn't called, where he was, what he'd done with his car. Then she went back inside, sifting through the mail. The third letter in the packet was the one she'd mailed to Felix Mendez in Iquitos, Peru. It had been stamped with what looked to be the equivalent of "Return to Sender." Quin

252

dropped it in the garbage, pushed her chair and the bucket closer to the phone and dialed the *Fuego Verde* number in Cartagena. Louise Fuentes answered. Quin recognized her voice, but this time she didn't identify herself, and there was something guarded about her tone.

"Mrs. Fuentes, this is Quin St. James, in Miami. I'm calling about Grant Bell's death."

"Look," she hissed. "Don't call me again, do you understand? Don't call." Then the connection was broken. Quin slammed the receiver down. *Okay, lady. No phones. But how about a house call, hmm?*

No, not yet. McCleary was right about exhausting leads here first. Leads, she thought, which seemed to be trailing right to Paul Holmes. It was easy enough to imagine that Paul was capable of murder, but when she tried to visualize him shooting Grant, it just didn't feel right. She knew if she closed her eyes, if she let herself come unfocused, she would feel that hard, persistent *pressure* which was the killer's psyche, and it would not be Paul Holmes.

This person, the killer, was something altogether different. A female, yes, she was almost certain. If she tried, Quin knew she would feel the woman as she had that afternoon in Grant's apartment when she'd found the phone bill. She would feel the chill nipping at the edge of her mind, her senses, a chill that whispered, *You: Stay back, stay away.* And the quiet terror would seep through her pores, infecting her.

Quin rubbed her hands along her arms, wiping away goosebumps. "You're spooking yourself, kid, and it's broad daylight." She laughed, a quick, false sound, and suddenly all she wanted to do was get out of the house.

2.

Key Biscayne on a Saturday afternoon was not the worst place to be in Miami, McCleary decided. But neither was it the best. The blustery air on the corner where he stood smelled of fried plantains and black beans from the Cuban eatery next door. Everyone who passed seemed to be speaking Spanish. The breeze did little to alleviate McCleary's discomfort. His shirt was drenched from the afternoon heat, his feet hurt from two hours of walking. A life as a starving artist, McCleary thought, would've been preferable to this. He slipped a quarter into the pay phone and dialed Joe Bean's number.

"Ayuh, this is Bean."

"Hi, Joe, it's Mike McCleary."

"MM. How goes it."

"It sucks, Joe," he said, and Bean laughed. "You free tonight?"

"You got something in mind, McCleary?"

"Yeah, you could say that. Juan Valdez and his lackeys wasted my car a few hours ago and probably would've done the same to me if they could have."

"Name the time, McCleary."

3.

As Quin limped into Ginger's Jewelers, she spotted Ms. Magnolia Blossom behind one of the counters, talking with a customer. Her soft little laugh rode the sweetly scented air like a chariot, and her Southern accent rounded off words so they seemed to bounce as she spoke. Quin tried to imagine this woman with Grant—holding him, making love with him, traveling with him to the Amazon. But it was like waiting for a child's drawing of stick figures to fatten up, fill out: it just wouldn't form.

"I'd like to talk to you," Quin said, stopping at the counter when the customer had walked away. She felt dizzy with hunger and wished she'd fixed herself breakfast before leaving the house.

"Ah've already said my piece to you *and* to the police, Miss, uh . . ." She groped for the name Rusty Johnson had used when he'd introduced Quin.

"Quin St. James."

"That wasn't the name you used the *last* time you were here," Ginger Hale drawled.

"I'll be glad to talk right here," Quin said loudly, drawing stares from several of the salespeople.

"That won't be necessary."

When they reached Ginger Hale's office, she spun

quickly, arms folded at her waist. "Now *what* is it you want, anyway? And just who *are* you?"

"I was living with Grant."

Ginger Hale looked Quin up and down, quickly, assessing who her competition had been. "Well." She fingered the gold heart with the emerald in the center which hung at her throat, then tossed her head. "Ah don't mind telling you, Miss St. James, that ah've got a business to run and ah don't appreciate your barging in here like—"

"I don't give a good goddamn what you appreciate," Quin snapped. "I want some answers."

A man appeared in the doorway, a *big* man with muscles and a face so ugly it had probably broken his mother's heart, Quin thought, stepping back. "You want that I should show the lady out, Ms. Hale?"

She waved him away and shut the door. "All right, what answers do you want, Ms. St. James? Answers about my relationship with Grant?"

"No, about the emeralds."

"I told that damned detective about the emeralds."

"Tell me," Quin said, noticing how quickly Ginger Hale's Southern accent had been sucked up in her annoyance.

"He came to me about three years ago and asked if I knew about the greenfire myth. I told him of course I did, but I didn't believe in it. He said he was going to prove it was true. It was the sort of challenge Grant liked, you know."

The remark was uttered with a proprietary air designed to get a rise out of Quin.

"And?"

"He wanted to know if I would lend him money for this little venture. I refused."

"What'd he need money for? Wishod paid his way down there, they paid his expenses."

Ginger rolled her eyes. "Mah dear," she said, dropping her hands to her sides, tugging at the hem of her blouse. "It wasn't like these gems were accessible. They had to travel three days up an Amazon tributary and then two days into the jungle. They required all sorts of supplies—boats, men, food, water, tools."

"Did you know he blackmailed someone to raise the money he needed?"

She brushed her fingers across her spotless desk. "I knew he'd obtained the money, but it wasn't my business to ask how."

"See no evil, speak no evil, hear no evil," Quin murmured.

The other woman glared at her, then slipped back into her Southern voice. "Ah can see why Grant never told you anything."

Quin managed to hold on to her temper, but barely. "What about when you went down there with him?"

"Like ah told the detective, ah only saw a half-dozen or so gems and ah appraised them."

"And offered to find buyers if they came across other emeralds."

A slight hesitation, then Ginger nodded. "Yes."

"Even though the gems would've been smuggled out of Peru."

"Listen, except for Pizarro, Grant was the only man ah know of who spent three years of his life looking for greenfire. As far as ah'm concerned, if he found them, he deserved them, and ah was willing to get him a fair price for his investment of time and money. That's business."

Quin removed a sheet of yellow paper from her purse and held it up in front of Ginger Hale. "Does this look at all familiar?"

The other woman blinked, reached for the letter, but Quin drew her hand away and quoted from it: " 'Greenfire, if you remember, is part mine.' Any comments? Observations? Maybe a defense?"

Ginger sat down with a heavy sigh, crossing her legs at the knees. Her foot moved slowly back and forth. She rubbed the back of her neck, sighed again. "Look, ah'm so tired of all this, ah just can't even tell you. You want answers? Okay, ah'll give you answers. Ah received a telegram from Grant about five days before he got back to the States after this last trip, saying he'd found a *bunch* of emeralds. But then he didn't bother getting in touch with me after he returned. Ah knew he was home, because ah'd driven by the townhouse one night. It irritated me no end. We had a verbal agreement, after all. So ah sent him the note."

"Then why did you refer to greenfire as being half yours?"

Her foot stopped moving, and she shifted in her chair. Quin expected her to say she'd financed the exploration or that she and Grant were secretly married or to spit out some other dark secret. Instead, she tapped one of her long nails against the desktop and her eyes blazed. When she spoke, her voice was a shade too loud. "Because as far as ah'm concerned, they were. *Ah* was the one who arranged for buyers. *My* reputation was on the line, *my* contacts. And that bloody bastard was going to double-cross me just like he double-crossed everyone else, and ah wasn't going to stand for it. Ah . . ." She stopped, abruptly, as if a piece of food had just gone down the wrong way and someone had slapped her on the back to dislodge it.

"You what?" Quin prodded.

She sat back; her foot began to move again. She didn't look at Quin as she spat, "Ah hated him, that's what."

4.

McCleary took a cab to Quin's, where he had an extra change of clothes. He could've gone home, but wasn't exactly enthusiastic about the idea. Juan Valdez probably knew where he lived and might decide to finish the job he'd botched.

When he realized Quin wasn't home, he settled down on the front porch with Merlin, slipped off his shoes, and examined his aching feet. No blisters, but a long, hot bath was definitely in order.

"You think she'll let me borrow Grant's Escort, Merl? Until I've got the money to get Lady fixed?"

Merlin lifted his head at the sound of his name and yawned.

"Yeah, I think she will." McCleary continued to stroke the cat's belly, trying not to think about tonight. It was too late for an attack of conscience, he admonished himself. He'd called Bean, the whole thing was set, he couldn't back out now. The only way to defeat a man like Holmes was to beat him at his own game, and if he didn't do that, what assurance did he have that Juan Valdez and his lunatic friends wouldn't be back?

He rubbed a spot between his eyes and, instead of thinking about tonight, concentrated on the white-hot pain in his chest that was Robin.

28

1.

THE COURTHOUSE LOOMED like a slumbering giant in the orange glow of sodium lights that lined the street. The orange spilled onto the neat, trim hedges along the front and made the statue of blind justice look like the overfed, jaundiced woman she was, McCleary thought.

Joe Bean was driving, and as they passed the lot on the north side of the courthouse, he gestured toward the two cars parked there. "Security guards. One of them roams the building and the other parks himself on the first floor with his portable TV."

"Are they armed?"

"Yeah." Bean slowed down and pointed at the alley in back of the courthouse. "That's where we're going in, McCleary. I've got the key to the back door. But we're going to have to break into Holmes's office."

McCleary patted the small bulge in the pocket of his dark jacket. "No problem. I came prepared."

"Me, too." Bean reached into his glove compartment. He brought out two dark hoods—*executioner hoods,* McCleary thought—with slits cut in them for nose, mouth, eyes, ears.

"Oh c'mon, man," McCleary laughed.

"I'm a great believer in redundant safety measures."

He took the hood and shoved it in his pocket. As they circled the block in silence, he heard Robin saying, *You* just want to nail him, and you don't give a damn how you do it. A long time ago, a woman had told him that his stubbornness would someday prove to be his undoing. He could no longer remember the woman's name or even what she looked like, but the remark had bothered him through the years and bothered him now. Was he that certain about Holmes? What about Ginger Hale? And the fact that Nikki Anderson owned a .45 and not only detested Bell but had also been to bed with him? Was he so damned sure about Holmes that he was willing to stoop to Holmes's level?

Yes. yes, yes, yes.

So be it.

Bean stopped the car on a dimly lit side street with a row of spavined houses. Since this area was only six blocks from the station, it was patrolled regularly. But if they got into a spot, he had his ID on him. *That low, Mac?* Yeah, that, too, he decided. He intended to get what he'd come for.

In the alley, they paused for a moment, pressed back into the bushes, and slipped on their hoods.

"Okay, Mike. I'll walt till I hear the music."

"Right."

McCleary darted out from the protection of the bushes, clutching the Japanese radio under his arm, and stopped when he reached the hedge that circumvented the building. He parted the branches with his hands and squeezed between the hedge and the side of the courthouse. Then he moved along the inside at a crouch, around to the north side of the building. Light from an upstairs window spilled onto the hedge and over into the grass, momentarily exposing him. He ignored it and continued. When he reached the corner of the building, the sodium lights gave him pause. He didn't think he could be seen from the street, as long as he kept at a crouch, but he still didn't like it.

A commando you are not, my friend.

Inside the gloves, his hands sweated, the hood seemed too small, he wanted to turn around and forget the whole thing. But then he thought of Holmes and Robin together, and he pushed forward. When he was inches away from the long picture window, he flattened out on

260

the ground. He extended his arm and positioned the radio so it was upright on the grass. He removed the remote-control device from his pocket, held it securely in his hand as he made his way back toward Bean. When he spotted his shadow like a smear next to the stoop, he hit the button.

". . .and this is A-1A, FM, Miami, and we've got a request from . . ."

When Bean leaped onto the stoop, McCleary was right behind him. He tucked the remote-control device into his jacket pocket with the plastic shopping bag. They pressed their faces to the glass door, peering down the long hall where the guard at the TV was now standing, walking away from the counter. Bean inserted the key in the lock, quietly turned it. The door opened with a nearly inaudible sigh as the strip of rubber on the bottom moved inward against the floor. They slipped inside. McCleary heard strains of a soul tune. *Yes sir, R&Bs for a night of B&Es.*

They crept through the shadows to the edge of the hall, where the guard stood at the front door, speaking into his walkie-talkie. ". . . probably those goddamned kids again, Bruce, but I'll check it out. Over."

Bean glanced at him, and even though the hood covered his face, McCleary knew his expression was saying, *I told you there'd been kids around.*

The guard stepped outside.

McCleary and Bean slid around the corner and down a second hall, past the elevator to the stairs. When they were in the stairwell, Bean whispered, "Let's hope that getting out is as easy as getting in."

McCleary wished he knew what floor the other guard was on. He didn't relish the idea of running into the man, of anyone getting hurt. As they ascended the stairs, he stopped, stepped up onto the railing, unscrewed the light bulb, and darkness settled in around them again. It struck him as odd that the very thing that had been so menacing in the past now made him feel safe, hidden. It all depended on which side of the fence you were on.

On the second-floor landing and again on the third, he did the same thing. Bean was nodding his approval just as McCleary heard static from a walkie-talkie and the door below them opening. "Bruce, this is Jimmy. What'd you find outside?"

More static. A wall of sweat moved across McCleary's back. "Just a stupid radio. It's those kids, I'm telling you."

"Well, add this to your gripes, man. The bulbs in the stairwell have burned out. If one of these prissy attorneys comes barreling through here some night and breaks his neck, we'll probably get blamed for it," Jimmy said.

"I'll add it to the repair list. Hey, Jimmy, you oughta see this radio. One of your kids would probably like it. Over."

"I'll finish checking these floors, then I'll be down."

The door closed again. McCleary let out a silent sigh of relief. He was definitely not cut out for this.

Bean tapped his shoulder. "C'mon, man, while he's still on the second floor. Get out your tools."

Then they were scurrying down the third-floor hall. McCleary felt like an insect, turned loose in a new and alien world where nothing was familiar, nothing was known. The carpet muffled their footsteps. The overhead lights were dim, but he wished for the total blackness again, the thick ink like a womb or sleep or death. As he stood at Holmes's office door, working at the lock with his tools, his senses switched to a kind of hyperalert: he heard the drone of the tv three floors down, a siren screeching in the distance, the elevator moving.

Bean's head snapped around. "It's going down," he hissed. "C'mon, man, hurry."

Hurry, hurry, hurry. . . . The door swung open and they stepped into Paul Holmes's office. McCleary switched on his flashlight and kept the beam aimed at the floor.

"The man's inner sanctum's straight ahead," Bean whispered.

The beam nipped at the walls, the desks, the couch. *Dark colors and white, a stark contrast, like the Whore himself.* McCleary thought he could even smell Holmes in the air, could hear the echo of his supercilious laughter. They stopped at the door and Bean worked at it with a credit card. After a moment, the lock clicked and they stepped in, shutting the door. The air conditioner whispered in the dark. The beams from their flashlights darted like twins toward the far wall..

"He's even got the damned thing hidden behind a painting," Bean whispered.

The painting was splashes of color which might have been anything, with no form or shape except that conferred by the onlooker's imagination. And what McCleary saw as his flashlight swept over it was a man and a woman wrapped together in an undulating dance. *Robin & Paul, sitting in a tree, kissing.* . . . Bean spun the dial on the safe.

McCleary set the painting aside as the door clicked open, as Bean reached inside. "Jesus, there's a mountain of stuff in here, McCleary."

"Just bring it all. We'll sort through it later."

Bean jammed photos and negatives, letters and reports, into McCleary's plastic shopping bag. Just as he shut the safe and McCleary thought for sure they were actually going to get away with it, he heard something. His senses strained; he heard it again. "Someone's out there," he hissed.

The room sank into total blackness again. The two men took up positions on either side of the door. McCleary could hear Bean breathing, his own heart pounding in his ears, saw his career as a cop being sucked into a vortex like dirty water down a kitchen sink.

"What the hell," a voice in the outer office muttered. The overhead light came on; the walkie-talkie crackled. "Hey, Bruce, this is Jimmy. The DA's office has been broken into, man. You wanna get up here on the double?"

When there was no response, the man, Jimmy, murmured an expletive. Sweat rolled down the sides of McCleary's face, and the hood stuck to it like adhesive. His right hand gripped his weapon, his left clutched one of the envelopes. *Go away, no one's supposed to get hurt. Just go away.* A blade of light beneath the door darkened with movement. The knob turned, the door crept open, McCleary saw a thick hand with plump fingers patting the wall for the light switch. The thought of light panicked him. He brought the butt of his gun down hard over Jimmy's fingers. The man let out a screech, and suddenly the door flew open and Bean leaped into the air, his long spider legs kicking out, connecting with Jimmy's solar plexus.

The man fell back into the office with a grunt, his fat cheeks pink from exertion, his eyes wide with surprise, fright. As he struggled to get up, McCleary grabbed him around the neck from behind, fingers around his throat, thumbs on the brainstem. The man struggled to free himself, clawing at McCleary's hands, struggling for breath. Then he went limp, and McCleary winced. *Don't be dead, Please, just don't be dead.* He let the man down gently to the floor, feeling for the guy's pulse. *Alive.* Bean brought the heel of his shoe down over the man's walkie-talkie, doused the light, picked up his weapon and dropped it in the wastebasket. "Let's get outa here."

They got as far as the second-floor landing before they heard the familiar static from a walkie-talkie. It was Bruce, trying to raise Jimmy. Bean hopped onto the railing and slid to the first floor. McCleary imitated him, but landed hard on his feet. His teeth came down over the tip of his tongue.

If the only casualty was a severed tongue tip, he could count himself lucky.

He heard the elevator starting and glanced worriedly at Bean, who was listening intently. He felt like a teenager prowling for thrills, not a detective doing this for a purpose. *Shit. Since when do you believe the end justifies the means?* He was no different from the Watergate burglars.

"It's going up, Mac, we're in luck. C'mon."

They crept out into the hall in the main lobby. The TV was still on. McCleary heard voices, laughter. At the edge of the hall, they paused. McCleary expected to hear the elevator descending again, shouts, voices, something. But there was only the perpetual drone of voices in TV land.

They moved forward. He wanted out, that was all. Out of the building, the hood, out of homicide. *And that's really the bottom line, isn't it? Out of homicide.*

A sound ripped through the silence with the force of an explosion, echoing painfully inside his skull, turning his blood cold. It took him a moment to realize it was an alarm.

"Jesus," Bean barked. "Jesus."

Hey, guess what? We're gonna get caught.

But Bean grabbed his arm and pulled him toward the door. Then they were stumbling out into the alley and flying down the street toward Bean's car. McCleary ripped the hood off his head and sucked at the air, the warm, wonderful July night air. Their feet thumped the pavement while sirens pinched the uneasy quiet beyond them. When he looked back, it seemed the courthouse was lit up like a stage prop, one-dimensional, unreal. *Did we really do it? Did we?*

They reached Bean's car and threw themselves inside. McCleary shoved the shopping bag under the seat, tore the gloves off his hands, flexed his fingers. He wanted a drink. Something cold, something that would obliterate his senses immediately and completely.

Bean pulled slowly away from the curb, turned on the radio, punched buttons until he found music. His eyes darted anxiously to the rearview mirror, then back to the road, then to the mirror again. As they turned onto I-95, heading north, Bean glanced at him, his dark face slick. "I say we have a celebration drink, Mike, and look through what we've got here."

"I say that sounds mighty good, Joe Bean. Mighty good."

Then they looked at each other and laughed.

2.

For most of the night, Quin struggled through dreams as thick as soup, dreams in which the killer broke into the house, dreams in which McCleary was caught, dreams in which she saw Grant being shot. She awakened early, exhausted, ravenous, worried that she'd heard nothing from McCleary.

She fixed breakfast, fed Merlin, kept glaring at the phone, willing it to ring. She finally couldn't stand just sitting around anymore and decided to start the Escort. Since McCleary was going to be using it, she wanted to make sure the battery wasn't dead. She started the car okay, but the gas gauge needle swung toward empty, so she drove it three blocks to the gas station. It coughed and bucked for a block, then stalled. When she restarted it, the car slid into an uneasy wheeze. She felt odd and displaced, because the Escort, like everything else, had certain memories attached to it. Distasteful memories.

She wanted to push the memories aside, but she'd been doing too much of that lately. So she let them come. They marched in like conquering tin soldiers, noisy and aggressive: there, the two of them trying to make love in the back seat, Grant's groping hands repellent to her now, the bitter smell of vodka or gin or something on his breath, her head squashed up against the edge of the seat. *Okay, you satisfied, guys?* Another exorcised memory, another part of her life with Grant sliced away and buried. She pulled into the full-service pump at the Texaco station and asked the guy to fill it up.

Before she even thought about what she was doing, she opened the glove compartment and reached for the notebook where Grant had recorded his mileage. She flipped to the right page and then stopped, suddenly, and laughed. *Old habits die hard, Quin. What difference can mileage possibly make now?*

But she paged through the notebook, noticing Grant's small, neat entries: dates, mileage at fill-up, number of gallons, the cost. Farther toward the back, he'd recorded things like oil changes and lubes. Between the fill-up and mechanical entries, she ran across a page on which a single word had been written over and over again in different types of handwriting—a precise, slanted script, a backhanded script with exotic loops, a block print. It was as if Grant had been sitting at a stoplight, expelling the thought uppermost in his mind. A woman. A woman named Kara.

It took a moment for the name to penetrate, to connect, but when it did, it suffused her senses. It blocked out sunlight, the warm haze of the July air, the man wiping down the windshield. She shivered despite the heat. She dropped the notebook as though it had burned her fingers. She started the engine, slammed the car into gear, saw the man's face peering at her through the windshield, realized she hadn't paid him.

"How . . . how much?" Her voice was not her own. It sounded like a child's who had just discovered something unspeakable in her parent's bedroom.

"Ten even, ma'am."

She fumbled through her wallet for the proper bill, thrust a five and a wad of ones at him, and took off. A nameless fear gathered momentum within her as she drove the three blocks recklessly, wanting only to get out of the car, out of her skin. *Kara, Kara,* sang in her mind, the lamentable chords of a tune that had ended— not with a knife across the throat, but with a chest full of holes and Grant bleeding on the kitchen floor.

3.

McCleary was sleeping off four gins with plenty of ice on Joe Bean's couch in the middle of Liberty City. It was an uneasy sleep, punctuated with disconnected dreams about Bob Izzo. In one, Izzo was spread-eagled on a bed, hands and legs bound with leather straps, and his face was a study in rapture as some young man leaned over him. McCleary awakened with a sour taste in his mouth and his stomach heaving and made it as far as Joe Bean's bathroom sink before he got sick.

He pressed his forehead to the cool edge of the sink and finally reached out, turned on the faucet, and splashed cold water on his face. *How was I supposed to know that was his goddamned secret?*

And how was he supposed to march into Izzo's office with those photos and toss them on the desk with an insouciance he didn't feel and demand that Holmes be arrested? For what, extortion? If a warrant for that was to be issued, the photos of Izzo, the stuff on the mayor, the letters and reports on half a dozen city officials would have to be used as evidence. McCleary's intent had never been to ruin anyone's life. All he'd wanted to do was nail Holmes for Grant Bell's murder.

"Aw shit," he groaned. "Aw shit."

He shuffled back into the living room, continued on

into the kitchen, and saw a note Bean had left him propped up between a coffee cup and the salt shaker.

Mike,

Here are the photos and all. Rusty Johnson called & said Quin's looking for you. You're sposed to get in touch. Pronto. My man, whenever you want to do business again, just holler. *I loved it.*

The Bean

McCleary looked around for the coffee and made himself a pot. He couldn't find any milk and drank two cups of very black, very strong Cuban coffee. Then he went into the living room to call Quin.

He'd never felt so miserable.

29

1.

"DURING THE THREE days Ingrid was stalled in the Atlantic, her winds increased to a hundred and fifty-five miles an hour, making her a category-five hurricane and the second most powerful this century. She's presently moving north-northeast at about ten miles an hour. If she continues in this direction, she would hit somewhere along Florida's east coast late Tuesday evening or early Wednesday morning. . . ."

The voice of Dr. Neil Frank, director of the Miami Hurricane Center, drifted in and out of Quin's awareness. She and McCleary were sprawled on the couch, where for the last hour, they'd gone through the six books Mrs. Dobbs had given him. Of the six, they'd narrowed the selection to a pair: *Killing at St. Charles* by K. L. Olson, which McCleary was reading, and *Black Bird* by Kara Newman, which she had. The book, dedicated to "Billy Hendrix, who never knew," opened in the early sixties, before the Beatles, the Pill, before the woman's movement. The rural setting was somewhere in central Florida, although an exact location was never given. The "I" voice was that of a woman in her thirties, looking back on a murder she'd committed when she was seventeen years old. It began with the crime, and drew her in like a whirlwind.

Quin was transported to the rural town with its dust

and its backwater people whose faces were "like old leaves" and whose prejudices "predated the light bulb." She squirmed with the protagonist as she was taunted by Bobby Heckler, her tormentor, her nemesis. She hated the girl's mother—a religious fanatic who said her novenas faithfully and had liquid nitrogen coursing through her veins, and pitied her father, a weak man who'd had a promising career as an engineer and lost it to the bottle.

During the rape scene, her stomach began to churn, and she had to set the book aside. "McCleary?"

"Hmm."

"You believe in hunches?"

He laughed and tapped a spot just between his brows. "Yeah. My hunches burn right here."

She nodded.

He continued to look at her. "Why?"

"Well, my hunches hit me about here." She pressed two fingers against the center of her breastbone, heartburn territory. "And it's burning like crazy there right now. I think this is the lady." She held up the book. "Kara Newman. *Black Bird*. Like the old Carly Simon song."

McCleary removed the scrap of paper he'd been using for a bookmark, the sheet she'd torn from Grant's gas mileage notebook that had *Kara* scrawled all over it. "*This* is the lady."

Quin knocked her knuckles once against the cover of *Black Bird*. "Same woman. I'm sure of it. What was it your librarian friend, Mrs. Dobbs, said? That the woman writes murders because she knows what she's writing about?"

"That's a novel, Quin, not real life."

"It was *published* as that, but it isn't. No one can write about a rape or a . . . a murder like this unless it's happened."

McCleary dropped his legs over the side of the couch, set his book aside, ran his hands through his hair. "Quin, Truman Capote wrote *In Cold Blood* after months of interviewing people who were involved in all that. He got into the killers' heads, but he wasn't the killer."

Quin shook her head. He still wanted to believe that

270

Holmes was behind it, that Holmes had killed Grant. He wanted to believe it despite the scrap of paper with *Kara* written all over it, despite everything. "McCleary, you know what? You're in the dark field. I think you want so badly for Paul Holmes to be it, you're refusing to seriously consider anything else." She said it gently, without accusation, but McCleary's expression shifted until his eyes seemed pinched, hurt. He opened his book again and stared at it.

She waited. "Yes? No? I'm way off base? What?" she said finally.

"You're probably right," he replied.

"What're you going to do with the photos of Izzo?"

"I don't know." He looked so miserable, Quin leaned toward him, reached for his hand.

"C'mon, let's go over to the station and run Kara Newman's name through the computer."

2.

He felt like the classic schmuck, if there was any such creature. Quin was right. But he wasn't just *in* the dark field, he was mired, stuck, being sucked into it as if into quicksand. And the first step to climbing out was this, tapping Kara Newman's name into the computer. He wasn't surprised, though, that nothing turned up. Nor was he surprised when, Monday morning, an editor at the paperback publishing house informed him that the editor who'd worked with Ms. Newman on *Black Bird* was now living in Europe.

But now that he was climbing out, he didn't intend to give up. He explained who he was and why he needed the information. The editor informed him she wasn't at liberty to give out any information about their authors. "I'm afraid you'll have to go through the New York Police Department, Mr. McCleary."

"But that could take weeks." A pulse of frustration throbbed at the back of his head. "Have you published any more of Ms. Newman's books?" he prodded.

"That was the only one."

"Is that her full name? Can you at least tell me that?"

The woman sighed. "If you'll hold, I'll check."

McCleary fumed to a Mozart tune that filled the empty spaces of "hold." His fingers drummed the brown envelope with the photos of Izzo in it as his temples tightened in a rising crescendo of a migraine.

"Mr. McCleary? Kara Newman is a pseudonym. But I can't tell you anything more. If you'd like to speak to our legal department, I can connect you."

More lawyers? He thanked her, hung up, and sat there at his desk in abject misery, thinking about Ginger Hale, Nikki Anderson, Treena Esposito. *Which one?* It was the old *Eeny, Meeny, Miney, Mo* game again. In the movies or the detective episodes on TV, the cop would've gotten the name and address in a flash. But then, this wasn't *Miami Vice,* and he wasn't Sonny Crockett in a white linen suit; what'd he expect for real life, anyway?

He thumbed through the book, which he'd read in one sitting last night, and stared at the dedication. His eyes dropped to the copyright and he suddenly grinned. He dialed Washington, D.C., information and asked for the number for the Library of Congress. When he called, he requested the copyright division.

"Just a minute, sir."

A young man answered.

"I need some information," McCleary said. "I've got a book which I think was written under a pseudonym, and I'd like to know the author's real name."

"The only thing I can give you is what's on the application, sir, which is part of the public record."

"Which application?"

"The copyright application. An author isn't required to give his or her real name. Who's the author?"

"Kara Newman. The title of the book is *Black Bird.*"

"I'll check."

The man returned a few moments later and informed McCleary that the only name on the application was Kara Newman. So much for his great brainstorm. He rang off and called Ron Valencia in Lauderdale, who gave several noncommittal grunts as he listened to McCleary's story.

"It sure sounds like a long shot to me, Mac. But I'll call Lance Wright in Oregon again and see if he's got anything at all that fits. What's the name of the book again?''

"*Black Bird*." He paged through the book once more, and when it fell open on the dedication, he sucked in his breath hard and rubbed the burning hunch spot between his eyes. "Ron, listen, tell Lance Wright that the victim's name may have been either William or Bill Hendrix."

"Will do. I'll call you back when I've got something."

3.

Quin got to work later than usual, but as soon as she arrived, Ruth Grimes told her Trevor was out sick. "And Quin, there's something else," she said, rocking forward in her chair, lowering her voice. "You wanted me to let you know when the accountant brought the financial records back." She swiveled around, picked up several thick files, and passed them to Quin. "He came in this morning."

"Great. Thanks. Thanks a lot, Ruth. Is the firm checkbook in here too?"

"Sure is. Right in the first file."

Ruth's finger slid along the gold chain around her neck. "I sure hope you can figure out why we're losing money, Quin." She lowered her voice. "I can't afford to lose this job."

We've gone through this once, Ruth, Quin thought, struggling to suppress her irritation. "You're not going to lose your job, Ruth. Neither am I. So don't worry about it."

It took her two pieces of fruit and several handfuls of dry roasted peanuts to wade through the year's canceled checks. But as her fingers played the adding machine, her fury mounted by the minute. Waste, all she saw here was waste: astronomical utility bills, fees to attorneys and accountants, the $2,000 check made out to the Church of the Good Faith—*from company funds*—mortgage payments on property she didn't even know the firm owned.

Halfway through the stack, she came across a check for $4,500 made out to Grant Bell. Scribbled on the memo line in the lower left-hand corner in Trevor's sloppy hand was "For professional services."

What professional services?

She sped through the remaining checks, looking for others made out to Grant, but there were none. She immediately attacked the other files with a vengeance. She'd never been very good with numbers, had nearly flunked math in high school, and barely made it through college algebra. But this was all pretty straightforward. Over a two-year period, since Sammy Forsythe's death, Trevor had paid Grant close to thirty thousand from company funds. Which meant, of course, that he'd known the man long before the firm had investigated the insurance claim he'd filed for the theft of his camera equipment. No wonder Trevor had given the case to her.

She collected the checks and copied each one. Then she dumped them into an envelope, went through the rest of the papers, and found an accounting sheet dated only last week. She copied this, too, slipped it into the envelope with the checks, put the copies in a separate envelope, and marched out to her car.

She followed the interstate until it dipped into Coral Gables, then headed along LeJeune Road to Miracle Mile. It occurred to her that she wasn't thinking clearly, that she might, in fact, have taken leave of her senses. At the end of the shopping district, she turned left toward Trevor's.

This part of the Gables reminded Quin of the Deep South, with sprawling homes set back among banyan trees so old they were probably around before the white man arrived. Trevor's house had belonged to his father, and since Sammy had died, the yard was no longer tended with the same care; the windows needed washing, cobblestones were missing from the walk. In short, the place suffered from indifference.

She stopped in the driveway. The engine clicked importantly in the silence. It started to rain, and drops tapped the Toyota's roof and windshield, and still Quin sat there. Trevor's Mercedes and Winnie's sat side by side in the driveway like two peas in a pod and slowly blurred as the rain came down hard. She was so angry she was shaking. Her damp hands left stains on the envelope as she picked it up.

She darted for the house, and for a moment, as she rang the doorbell, she thought of old Sammy Forsythe, whom she had loved like a father. Sammy was why she was here and not at the police station.

Trevor's youngest daughter, Becky, answered the door. She was wearing navy blue shorts and a bright red halter top, and she was barefoot. "Hi, Quin."

"Hi, honey, is your dad home?"

"Yeah, he's got a cold. C'mon." She reached out and Quin took her hand. A tiny, soft hand, trusting. *Oh, Jesus, I can't do this.*

But before she could turn around, there was Trevor, waddling out of the bedroom in a robe, his nose as red as a cherry. "Quin. Hi. This is a surprise." He suddenly sniffled and sneezed into a wadded Kleenex he'd brought out of his robe pocket.

"Becky, go tell Mommy that Quin's here, will you?"

"No, it's okay," Quin said quickly. The last thing she wanted was Winnie in attendance with her good intentions. "Is there someplace we can talk, Trevor? Privately?"

"Well, uh, sure, Quin. In the den here. You want something to drink?"

"No, nothing. Thanks." She followed him into his cedar-paneled den. He closed the French doors, removed several books from the bookcase, and brought out a bottle of Scotch. He poured a shot glass for himself. "I gotta hide this. Winnie gets upset. But it's the best thing ever invented for the common cold," he murmured and, tilting his head back, drained it. Roses blossomed in his cheeks. He made a funny sound deep in his chest, then coughed. She wondered how many he'd had already today. "What's wrong, Quin? Ever since you walked in here, you've looked like you lost your best friend or something."

She opened the envelope, turned it upside down over the desk. The checks rained out. Trevor stared at them, frowning at first, then he looked at her and comprehension flickered in his soft gray eyes.

"You knew him *a year* before I even met him," she

hissed. "You *knew* him. You paid him thirty thousand over two years, Trevor. *For what?*"

He turned his back on her to fiddle with his stereo. Something by Bach flooded the room. Then he went over to the desk, his fingers stepping through the canceled checks. His belly was a blob of gelatin, moving as he moved. Quin didn't know whether she hated him, pitied him, or both.

"He did a story on private eyes. Beyond that, I don't have to tell you anything, Quin."

"Trevor, I'm your *partner.* I *trusted* you."

"I did what I had to do," he said, his voice oddly strained, quiet, his fingers still stepping slowly through the checks. Then he turned away and poured himself another jigger of Scotch.

"Either you tell me, Trevor, or I'm going to McCleary. You *do* know McCleary, don't you?"

"You can't threaten me. You don't even know what the hell's going on, Quin. Shit, all these years you've been bopping around like you're some kind of *hot shot* investigator and you don't know shit." He leaned toward her, stabbing the air in front of her face with his plump finger. "You think it's easy doing the financial end of this business?" He swept the checks off his desk with a swift, abrupt twitch of his hand and drank down the jigger of Scotch. "I'd like to see *you* try what I've been doing since Pop died. You sure did a snowjob on him, didn't you, Quin? Forty-nine percent of the firm and *for what*? What the hell can you do that I can't?"

He grimaced and sneezed again into his torn Kleenex. "I know you were screwing Pop, Quin. You must've been. It's the only reason he would've given any portion of the firm to someone who wasn't family."

She thought of Sammy Forsythe with his funny face, that lump in the middle of his nose from a run-in with an ex-boxer when he worked for Pinkerton, and she wanted to cry.

"Trevor, you still haven't answered my question. What *professional services* did Grant perform for you for thirty thousand?"

"God," he laughed. "You're pathetic, Quin, you know that? You never knew what Grant was about, did you?

276

And off the record, it wasn't just thirty grand, it was more like forty, and it's still none of your goddamned business. And just for your information, if you go to the police with these checks, you're only implicating yourself, sweetheart, since you are, after all, a *partner*."

The dark fields, she thought, here they were, embracing her, squeezing her until her eyes bulged, until she was forced to *see*. When she spoke again, her voice was low, mean, and her hands were clenched in tight fists at her side. "Did you kill him, Trevor?"

The flap of skin that was his double chin seemed to tremble. He snickered. "You going to make a citizen's arrest, Quin?" He poured another jigger, wiped his hand across his mouth, and she realized he was drunk, that he'd probably been imbibing most of the day. "Let me tell you something about your precious, Grant, Quin. He could outmaneuver God, that's how slick he was. And women? Oh, man, he had women coming out the kazoo."

He knew her tender spots, all right. He was plucking them out of her like weeds, crushing them in his fat hands and tossing the dust in her face. A sob had lodged in her throat like an ice cube. She wanted to lunge for him, scratch at his plump, ugly face, and claw until she drew blood.

A knock at the door interrupted them. Winnie peeked in. "Hi, Quin. Becky said you were here. Can I get you . . ." She saw the bottle of Scotch, the jigger, and Trevor glared at her.

"Don't start, Winnie. Christ, just don't start. I've had it with—"

Quin turned quickly. She rushed past Winnie, heard Trevor barking something to his wife in a drunken voice, and then she was outside, racing through the rain to her car. She slammed the Toyota in gear, it slid across the slick pavement, coughed, then sped away.

By the time she reached the end of the block, she was sobbing.

4.

This Monday morning had all the earmarks of disaster, McCleary thought. First the phone call to New York, then rumors about a general meeting to discuss a plan of action in case Hurricane Ingrid made landfall here, and he still hadn't done anything with the photos.

Move, Mac.

But he continued to procrastinate. He removed his trusty little notebook from his pocket and flipped it open to the day's list. The only entry on it was: *The photos*. "Okay, Mac," he muttered to himself, "it can't get much clearer than that." He drew a thick dark line through it and headed downstairs.

On his way to the second floor, where O'Donald's office was, three people stopped him to ask if he'd heard about the break-in at the courthouse Saturday night. And each time, his nerves tightened like guitar strings, his bones ached with tension, his conscience rolled over in pain.

He stopped at the water fountain for a drink, and when he looked up, Benson was strolling down the hall toward him. He asked McCleary if he'd heard about the break-in, and when he nodded, Benson burst out laughing. "Oh, man, you shoulda seen him, Mac. The Whore is shitting bricks over whatever was taken outa that safe."

"Did Izzo put you on the case?"

"No, one of my other men. But I was over there this morning and all Holmes did was fret and pace, and shit, McCleary, I could smell the fear on him."

What about me, Tim? Can you smell the fear on me, too?

After all, tucked here under his little ole armpit was enough evidence to incriminate everyone from the mayor to judges to half of city hall for illegal activities of one kind or another. Corruption wasn't just a way of life in this city; people ate it for breakfast.

When he walked into O'Donald's office, the psychologist was dictating into his machine. He immediately switched it off, rocked back, grinning, and said, "Seventy-five big ones up front, Mike."

McCleary chuckled and sat down. He tossed *Black Bird* on O'Donald's desk. "There's our lady. Seems she writes murders for amusement. Under a pseudonym."

With the eraser end of a pencil, O'Donald nudged his

278

glasses farther back on the bridge of his nose, picked up the book, paged through it.

"It describes a murder committed when the protagonist was seventeen years old, Wayne. A rather heinous murder. She sliced this guy up good and lugged his body into the lake. She had a mother who was a religious fanatic." He rubbed the burning hunch spot between his eyes. "My theory is that maybe she's working on another book now, and—"

"Yeah, I get the picture, Mike."

"Where's this fit into psychology? Tell me that."

O'Donald shrugged. Behind his glasses, his eyes took on that sharp glint of intelligence that indicated McCleary now had his full attention. "Mike, a lot of things don't fit into neat categories. This lady's just one of the numerous sickos running around. Some are more dangerous that others. Some function quite normally most of the time and then, whammo, outa left field comes this compulsion. My guess is she's way above average in intelligence and probably wrote *Black Bird* here as a sort of purging. And maybe, following your hypothesis, when it came down to her next novel, the same . . . uummpphh wasn't there, you know? The same . . . drive. So she decided to add the kind of reality *Black Bird* had. Does the victim in the book have any kind of, uh, signature on his forehead?" O'Donald tapped the eraser on his pencil against the desktop slowly, rhythmically, like a drum, waiting for McCleary to answer.

"Yeah. She carved a goddamn cross into the guy's forehead."

The eraser stopped moving. O'Donald came forward, his odd face twisted in a grimace. "Christ," he murmured.

"And for a while, in the book, after his body was found, the cops thought it was some sort of ritualistic killing. The murderer—murderess—by the way, was never found. In the book."

"You said the book's written as a flashback, right?" McCleary nodded. "So what does the protagonist do for a living now?"

"A homemaker, mother of two."

The eraser began it's annoying tapping again as O'Donald mulled this over. "Uh-uh, Mike, it doesn't fit.

279

If this crime actually happened, and the author Kara Newman is actually the same woman doing these serial killings, I doubt very much she'd be married. I bet you ten to one that this woman is an educated professional who's trying desperately to form emotional, heterosexual attachments which her trauma won't allow her to do. I doubt she's married, but hell, it's not inconceivable that she *has* been married and is divorced. She may even be engaged or seriously involved with someone and the relationship is probably rife with problems."

He went through a mental list: Nikki was about to embark on her second marriage, and in McCleary's mind she definitely had problems. Treena was ending her second marriage and involved with a married man. And Ginger Hale? Aside from her admission to Quin that she detested Grant, about the only thing his tails had turned up on her was involvement with a man who was an organized crime figure. It was Rubik's cube all over again, he thought. He still wasn't able to perceive the whole, the essential pattern.

McCleary changed the subject and asked O'Donald if he knew Paul Holmes.

"Who *doesn't*? Why?"

"What's your professional opinion about him?"

O'Donald laughed. "I can't say I've ever had the pleasure of having picked the man's brain."

"From observation, then."

"All bullshit aside?"

"Yes."

He stopped rocking. His fingers swept along the edge of his desk. "I think he's a perfect politician."

"Meaning what?"

O'Donald was smiling. "Mike, the only difference between Paul Holmes and, oh, say your serial killer, is that Holmes found an outlet for his aggressions in politics. There he's got legal sanctions for things which, anywhere else, would land you in jail."

The man certainly had a gift for calling the shots, McCleary thought, as O'Donald sat forward.

The overhead light glinted against his glasses. "Why do I get the feeling you seem to be struggling with something, Mike?"

Wanna see this city's politics blow apart at the seams, Wayne, ole boy? Why, indeed. And all along, he'd wanted Holmes, just Holmes. Yet he hadn't been able to form the vital link to get him for Bell's murder—at least not a link that would hold up, considering who Holmes was. Besides, the scrap of paper Quin had found in the Escort's glove compartment sure made it look as if Kara Newman had also killed Bell. So the most he could do at the moment was use the evidence in another way to buy himself time. The same kind of time Holmes's attempted blackmail of Izzo had bought him.

"You just solved my problem, Wayne."

"I did? And free of charge? I can't believe it."

"I owe you a dinner, thanks."

"Hey, Mike," O'Donald said as McCleary got up. "Keep me posted on our friend Kara Newman."

"Count on it."

30

BOB IZZO LOOKED like he'd spent his weekend in the Caribbean, McCleary thought as he took a seat in the chief's office. His tanned face glowed, and confidence throbbed in his stride as he paced the office with the phone resting in the crook of his arm and the receiver propped between his shoulder and his cheek.

"I know, I know, Jan, just do what you can to field the calls. I don't want to talk to any more reporters." He dropped the receiver in the cradle and set the phone on the desk. "Jesus, the fucking courthouse gets broken into and you'd think Windsor Castle was robbed and the Queen was raped," he barked. "And on top of it, we've got this mother of a hurricane out there, and if it keeps coming like it is, Miami's gonna be in a shit load of trouble. Which reminds me. I need two men from your department who'll be willing to do hurricane duty."

McCleary nodded. He wasn't here to discuss a hurricane or the possible inundation of Miami.

"And now that I've got you in here, Mike, I need a report on what's happening with these stabbings."

"I've got a name, a pseudonym," he said, and explained. "But I came by to tell you I'm going back on the Bell case." He didn't bother mentioning the possible connection between Bell's death and the serial killings. First, he wanted to see how Izzo would play his hand.

"That homicide is on a back burner, Mike. I don't want to go through this again."

Predictable, McCleary thought, and tossed the manila envelope on Izzo's desk. "Take a look at this."

Izzo reached inside the envelope, and then his movements became dreamlike, as though he were moving through Jell-O. His jaw slackened. He looked up once, and in the man's eyes McCleary saw a whirlwind that was panic, astonishment, and then a flurry of luminal connections as Izzo mentally sped through his options.

"The negatives are in there too," McCleary said. Izzo seemed to be sinking into his chair as he stared at the negatives, saying nothing. His big, thick hands trembled as he slipped the photos back into the envelope. He swiveled around in his chair and gazed out the window, into the parking lot. McCleary noticed that the back of his neck was tan. He thought of the photo with Izzo on his knees like an animal, Izzo taking it in the ass.

He sat down.

"I suppose you've already reported this."

"No."

His chair squeaked as he turned toward McCleary. "Why not? I violated the law, Mike. I intended to put this Bell murder on a permanent back burner to save my ass."

"I'm not interested in what you intended to do. I did what I had to do because I honestly believed Holmes had killed Bell. Now it looks like our knife lady may have killed him, although I'm still not entirely certain he wasn't involved. But this at least relieves the pressure on you so the DA's office can be investigated. Without the negatives, Holmes can't touch you. And I don't think the bastard's going to make a stink, since right about now he's probably shitting bricks about everything else that was in that safe of his."

"Other stuff?"

"Don't think for a minute you were the only person he had information about, Bob."

"How'd you find out where the stuff was?"

"That's my business."

"An investigation of his office has got to come from a lot higher up than us."

"Is the mayor high enough?"

For the first time since McCleary had entered the office, Izzo smiled. And why not? His secret would be protected, and one way or another, Paul Holmes would pay. A wave of disgust swept through McCleary—toward Izzo, himself, Holmes, the whole rotten system. When this was over, if it ever was, he intended to shut himself in his apartment for three days and do nothing but paint and sketch.

"Yeah, I'd say the mayor's office is high enough."

"I need a couple of things."

Confidence flowed back into Izzo. McCleary could almost see it, a confidence like new blood. "Shoot."

"Twenty-four-hour surveillance on three women: Ginger Hale, Nikki Anderson, and Bell's ex-wife, Treena Esposito." Izzo, dizzy with glee, didn't bother inquiring why McCleary had drawn a connection between the serial killer and Bell's murderer. Which suited him just fine.

"Done. Anything else?"

"Yeah, I want a guy named Juan Valdez picked up for attempted murder. If he sings, which he probably will, we've got Holmes for conspiracy to commit murder."

McCleary briefly explained about the silver Cadillac, and the chief scribbled Valdez's address. "Did you run a check on his name?"

"Yeah. One arrest for assault and battery three years ago. Guess who his attorney was."

"I'll have him brought in this afternoon."

"I want to question him," McCleary said, thinking of Lady, rusting in a parking lot. "You might say I've got a personal interest in the man for wasting my car."

"You can use a department car until your car's fixed or you get a new one."

And if I ask you for a ticket to heaven, will you grant me that, too, Bob? Now that things were out in the open, Izzo was too anxious to please. It was as if he expected McCleary to renege on his word, to walk out of the office and release a statement to the press on the chief's indiscretions, his omissions. This was the sort of power over other human beings that had placed Holmes

284

where he was, and McCleary didn't like it. He didn't like it one goddamn bit.

"Thanks, but I've got a car to use." *Bell's junky Escort, Izzo, how's that for a gross irony?*

"How'd you find out Bell was blackmailing Holmes, anyway?"

Because Robin's been screwing the man, what do you think of that? But how could he, in good conscience, protect Izzo for what he'd done and snitch on Robin, his partner, and a woman he'd loved, perhaps loved still? "It doesn't matter how I found out. But just in case Holmes threatens you again, Bob, remind him that he's finished in this county if the voters find out he was convicted of rape, okay?" Then McCleary laughed. "Hell, he's finished here, anyway, even if the voters *don't* find out. I'll make sure of it."

"*Rape?* Holmes?"

"Yeah."

"Mike, I gotta ask you one more question."

"What."

"Did you have something to do with the break-in to Holmes's office? Is that where these photographs were?"

Funny, McCleary thought, but the idea of lying again, of covering up again, left a sour taste in his mouth. "Yeah, but that's all you'll ever know about it, Bob."

Izzo fingered the envelope, and for an instant pain quivered like a living being in his eyes. "Then I owe you," he said softly.

"You don't owe me shit. I didn't do it for you. I did it for me." He did it because Robin was right that he wanted to nail Holmes and it didn't make any difference how he did it. "Let me know when Valdez is brought in. I'll be back in an hour. I'm going to the mayor's office." *To shake up Holmes's little empire.*

2.

Holmes had taken a booth at the back of the restaurant, where it was quiet and he could keep an eye on the front door. He'd canceled the seminar for today. There was only a week left, and besides, he had more pressing things on his mind.

Like the courthouse break-in.

And the possible repercussions for him.

And . . .

The door opened and he saw Robin as soon as she stepped inside. The first sight of her never failed to stir something deep inside him. He enjoyed watching the way her eyes slid around the room, looking for him, how she ran her fingers through her thick hair, then the quick smile when she spotted him. It was as if her mere presence connected with the more primitive part of his brain, bypassing logic, reason, diving straight for the murky pool of his emotions. As she joined him in the booth, he wanted to submerge his face in her hair.

"I saw you on TV this morning," she said, then cocked her head, her eyes fixing on the straw-colored bruise that had spread across his jaw since Friday evening. "What happened to you?"

"I ran into your friend, Mike McCleary," he replied, and explained. He omitted his remark to Quin, of course, because it had nothing whatsoever to do with why McCleary had decked him. "I think he's taking the demise of your affair rather hard, Robin."

She lowered her eyes, fished around in her purse for a cigarette, lit it. "I doubt that he'd slug you because of me, Paul. Mac obviously isn't pining away for me if he was with Quin." She paused. "Is your offer still open?"

It took him a moment to realize what she was referring to, because he was distracted by the dark storm brewing in her eyes. There was something unsettling about her, Holmes decided, and wondered if it had always been there or if he were just noticing it for the first time.

"I thought you didn't want to practice law again, Robin." *And why did you pick today to discuss it? Why not next week? Or next year?* Why today when all he could think about was his empty safe and the possible repercussions?

"I've changed my mind."

"Why?"

She looked at him blankly, as though she'd never considered the question. "I don't know, I just have."

The waitress came over to the table. Robin ordered a

sandwich and coffee and Holmes said he'd have the same.

"What happened?" He sensed something had, and that it involved McCleary, but he should've known better than to prod.

"Nothing *happened*, Paul. I'm just fed up with police work, okay? Now is the offer still open or not? I can give a two-week notice at work today if it is."

"Testy, testy," he murmured.

She stabbed out her cigarette, sat back, then came forward again, glaring at him. "I'm not in the mood for games, all right? Either yes or no."

"Of course it's still open. It'll take some bureaucratic shuffling, though, so give me a month."

"Paul, I don't want to spend another month working with Mac, do you understand? He . . . I can't stand it."

The tone of despair or desperation in her voice startled him. "Okay, give your notice, then. Tomorrow, okay? You can start two weeks tomorrow. I'll make a slot for you. My personal assistant or something."

"I don't want to be your goddamned lackey, that isn't what you offered."

"I didn't mean it that way. You'll be an attorney, Robin, not anyone's gofer."

The waitress returned with their lunch. Now that the issue of her future had been settled, she seemed relaxed, Holmes thought, more like the same slick, self-contained Robin he was used to. For a few minutes they discussed the break-in at the courthouse. "One of Benson's men is in charge of the investigation, so I don't expect anything to be resolved."

"I like Benson," she remarked.

Holmes rolled his eyes. "God, you *should* get out of there, Robin. Benson's a pansy." She ignored the remark and asked what had been taken from the safe. "Mostly just papers and cases," he lied.

"But how'd they get into the safe?"

"No safe's impenetrable."

She nodded.

He had a feeling she wanted to say something more, but she didn't. "How about if we get together tomorrow night?" he asked.

A slow smile worked at her mouth. She regarded him beneath her thick, dark lashes. "That must mean Miriam's got bridge or tennis or something." Any other time, the sarcastic edge to her voice would have annoyed him. But today he had other things on his mind.

"Actually, she's going to her sister's again. She'll be gone overnight. We'll have a celebration dinner. I'll even cook for you."

She laughed. "Boy, that's a switch."

"I'll bet McCleary never cooked for you."

Her laughter vanished so quickly it still echoed in the air. "Did you hire a Cuban hit man named Juan Valdez to shake Mac up, Paul?"

The way she just slipped the question in, between one breath and another, so unobtrusively, startled him. She would be a formidable opponent in *any* courtroom, he decided, with more tricks up her sleeve that Houdini. He washed down his bite of sandwich with coffee, reminding himself she was still a cop, and McCleary's partner. *But she wants out.* Since she was going to work for him, she would have to learn the ropes.

"C'mon, Paul, it's a simple question. If we're going to work together, you're going to have to trust me. I know about Bell and I know about the rape. What could be worse than that?"

He didn't appreciate the way she put it, and he didn't like the expression on her face, as though she'd just bitten into something bitter. But she had a point. "Yeah. I did." Actually, his instructions to Valdez were to do more than just shake McCleary up, but he didn't tell Robin that.

She took a deep breath and nodded. "I warned you about him, Paul."

"What're you talking about?" She rubbed a hand across the back of her neck, as if to knead away tension. Holmes's gut tightened. "Robin?"

She exhaled as she looked up at him. "I told you, and you didn't listen. Now you're going to be in a heap of trouble, Paul. I think it was McCleary who broke into your safe."

3.

Guillermo Sandez had been mayor of Miami for nearly five years. His longevity in office wasn't the result of visionary campaigns or even political acumen. His secret, McCleary decided, was much simpler. He believed in Miami, and he possessed an almost fanatical appeal in the way he presented the city to outsiders. He'd been instrumental in drawing conventions and filmmakers when tourism had begun to drop off. He'd cleaned up the beaches, the parks, and had stirred public passion for a mass transit system, the Metrorail, which had been suffering like a handicapped child since its birth. But the people liked Sandez because he possessed a magical capacity for juggling the needs of Miami's three ethnic groups—blacks, Latins, and Anglos.

He was an attractive Hispanic, which was probably part of his appeal: average height, thick, dark hair, dark eyes, an amiable smile, lean, a sharp dresser. He welcomed McCleary after only a five-minute wait and gestured magnanimously to one of the large, comfortable chairs around a coffee table near the window.

He crossed his legs at the knees; his arm rested across the back of the chair. His body language screamed that he was a man who had nothing to hide. Nothing, McCleary thought, but the acceptance of a $55,000 bribe from a building contractor to change a zoning ordinance. "What can I do for you, Detective McCleary."

"I think after you glance through these," McCleary said, indicating the envelope he placed on the mayor's desk, "you'll agree that the DA's office should be investigated for, uh, questionable practices, Mr. Mayor."

Sandez's smile was still in place as he opened the envelope, as he removed the papers. Then it shrank. It was like watching an abrupt eclipse of the sun. McCleary felt a sickening knot in his stomach as he realized that Sandez was going to react just as Izzo had. He had a sharp, hurtful visage of himself on a throne, with Izzo and Sandez bowing deeply, murmuring, *Oh bwana, thank you for not telling.* . . .

The mayor glanced up, his eyes pinched, haunted. When he spoke, his lips pursed, as though the very words were distasteful. But he didn't question how McCleary had gotten the information. The ins and outs of politics had at least endowed him with a certain grace. "I think I see what you mean, Detective McCleary. Yes, I certainly do."

"Good. I'll hang on to these, Mr. Mayor, until the investigation's under way, and then I'll mail you the package."

This definitely wasn't to Sandez's liking, but he was polished enough in these matters to accept McCleary's decision without protest. "I, uh, presume there are other papers similar to these?"

"Not on you." McCleary got up. "Thank you for your time, Mr. Mayor."

When McCleary was outside again, the knot in his stomach had turned tough and hard as leather. Was this the only way to win? Were winners determined by who played the dirtiest? He was no different from Holmes, who had used these same documents to get *his* way. He felt as he had that day the men in the silver Caddy had wasted his car and Robin had admitted she'd been discussing the Bell case with Holmes. Betrayed. But this time, he was also the betrayer. He'd not only stooped to Holmes's level, he'd sold out.

31

I STOOD IN A corner of the room, spinning like a ballerina. Colorful scarves and nightgowns, blouses and dresses and underwear littered the floor, the bed, the chair near the window. Drawers lolled from the bureau like tongues, other drawers had been overturned. One, which I'd shoved across the floor, had a crack through the heart of it. I fell to my knees in the closet doorway, dizzy from spinning, and tossed aside boxes, shoes, the laundry basket, digging to the back for the manuscript. I knew I'd put it in here somewhere.

I knew.

I remembered laying it there, on the top shelf, until I would have time to get back to it, edit it, decide what was lacking. I remembered moving it, too, but to where? The den? Was it in the den?

I pressed my fists into my eyes until I saw stars, until the tiny stars imploded and dust filled my vision. This wasn't in the book, *Was it?*

Which book?

The missing one, the second one. Right, of course. I was looking for the missing manuscript which was about . . . *what?*

I crawled over to the bed, into the stack of gowns and scarves. The soft, silky fabric of a nightgown brushed my bare leg. My hands dropped from my face and I stared at the gown, an orphaned memory flickering off and on like a faulty light bulb. Something about the gown.

I reached for the gown, pressed it against my cheek. Flutters of memories, now, like the urgent beating of wings, stirred the air in the room, making me dizzier. I rushed into the den, still holding the gown, and sat at the typewriter. After a moment, my fingers remembered what my brain could not:

> She could still see him, sitting at the edge of the bed as she danced toward him, holding the gown at the sides like a skirt. She twirled, he caught her around the waist and twirled with her, just the two of them, spinning like planets locked in a singular orbit. Then they fell, still spinning, onto the bed.
>
> "Let me see what you're writing. C'mon, let me see," he whispered into her hair.
>
> "No." She sat up, running her hand down the front of the gown, smoothing it. "No. It's private."
>
> "You don't trust me." Petulant now, his lip thrust out, he moved away from her. She could feel him withdrawing the net of his emotions, and it hurt her. Hurt bad.
>
> "I've got to shower." She left him alone in the bedroom and . . .

And he'd taken the manuscript. Grant had rummaged through my closet and had taken the manuscript, and that was how he knew the truth. About me, about Billy, all the Billy truths, about everything. That was how he'd known about *Black Bird*. I squeezed my eyes shut and there was his face, his grin, the night he'd waved *Black Bird* at me and said, "See? I know, I know who and what you are. What do you think of that?"

He'd taken the manuscript, and Quin had the key to wherever Grant had hidden it. Quin, who hadn't been able to leave any of this alone, Quin, Quin, Quin.

Now I knew what I had to do. I knew it as if the knowledge had always been buried somewhere inside me, superimposed over other memories. And after, when

I was done, I would bury the knife in the yard with the shredded clothes. I would bury Kara and her typewriter, I would burn the manuscripts—the one Grant took and this one. Then I would rise—cleaned, reborn, a phoenix.

32

1.

AFTER HIS RUN early Tuesday morning, McCleary brought in the porch furniture and put up hurricane shutters in preparation for Ingrid's arrival. The National Hurricane Center estimated the storm would make landfall a hundred miles up the coast about three tomorrow morning. But since Ingrid was two hundred miles wide with winds of a hundred and thirty, the mayor had recommended evacuation from low-lying areas in Miami. Areas like those where McCleary lived.

He loaded most of his valuables, including his extra canvases and paints, into Bell's Escort and drove over to Quin's place, which was inland and on higher ground. She'd left him a note on the front door, saying she'd driven to work to make sure the building was secure. *See you tonight, but call as soon as you've spoken to Trevor, okay?* He folded the note and slipped it in his pocket, thinking that Trevor Forsythe fell about third on his list of things to do today.

On his way across town in the rain, McCleary saw ample evidence that residents were battening down the hatches. Buildings were being boarded up, there were long lines at gas stations, and the parking lot of the grocery store he passed was jammed with cars. As soon as he walked into the station, Benson informed him that Izzo's men had finally caught up with Juan Valdez and had just brought him in. McCleary grinned. *Goodbye, Paul Holmes*.

It took two hours, but Juan Valdez sang and sang, spilling his guts into a tape recorder while McCleary and Benson sat on either side of him. Throughout, McCleary kept remembering how this fucker and his men had wasted Lady and hunted him and Quin. It took every bit of self-control he possessed not to grab the Cuban by the lapels of his expensive jacket and shove his fist down the man's throat. When it was over, Valdez's moon face shone with sweat and he began to cry. McCleary leaned so close to Valdez, he could smell the stink of his fear. "One question. What were Holmes's exact orders, Valdez?"

The Cuban blew his nose into a monogrammed handkerchief the color of eggshells. "He says to me that I am to get rid of you, *sí*, that is exactly what he tells me to do. But then when you and the señorita got away, I tol' him I quit." He made a gesture like an umpire, crossing his hands through the air. "No more, I feenished."

"You killed my fucking car," he spat, and marched out of the room.

McCleary went over to the courthouse to see fat Judge Parker, who'd been in cahoots with Holmes for years. He informed His Honor that he would turn over certain incriminating evidence on him unless he issued a subpoena for Holmes's arrest. His Honor stammered and his pudgy cheeks grew as pink as a baby's rump and his nostrils flared like a rabbit's. He lacked the mayor's grace, but he nodded, *Yes oh yes*, and McCleary nearly laughed in his face. It was easier than saying the alphabet or taking a crap. It was all so bloody easy when you held the trump cards.

By the time McCleary returned to the station, rain battered Miami. He dropped the subpoena on Izzo's desk. "Do it tomorrow." He had someone else to see, and at the moment, he didn't think he could stomach Holmes.

Izzo looked at the subpoena and laughed. "It'll be a pleasure." He slipped the subpoena in a drawer and locked it. "I've put Robin on hurricane patrol tonight,

Mike. But once this goddamned storm's moved on, you'll have her back."

"I don't want her back."

"I thought you two worked well together."

"We used to, but not anymore." He could see Izzo was about to question him, but he just shook his head. "Find her some other partner." It no longer hurt to think of not working with Robin; in fact, it didn't much matter.

Before he left the station, he called a florist shop near the library and ordered a bouquet of flowers for Millie Dobbs. "And when would you like these delivered, sir?" the woman asked.

"As soon as possible."

"What would you like the card to say?"

He thought a moment. " 'You were right. Many thanks, Mike McCleary.' "

On the way to the Gables, Bell's Escort wheezed at a stoplight and stalled. He got the car started again, but for a moment mourned Lady who'd never failed him, never died in traffic, never had anything wrong with her except a flat tire. As stupid as it seemed, the blasted car had been a constant in his life, one thing he could count on when all else failed. Now he didn't even have that.

Quin, there's Quin: the thought flew through his mind as he exited the interstate and headed toward Trevor's. Yeah, there was Quin whom he loved, but not with the passion, the blindness, that he did Robin.

Robin. His mood had something to do with her. But just the thought of her brought oppression, a sort of breathlessness. *You're on the edge, Mac. You are.* In fact, with very little effort, he could peer over the precipice and glimpse the swirling dark on the other side which was everything that had gone wrong in his life. The failed relationships, the search for an ideal which he suspected didn't exist, the suppressed bitterness that had accrued over the years without his realizing it. The dark, he thought, which would ultimately end in madness.

A little girl answered the door. She peered at him with a face that was Trevor's, minus the fat. "Is your dad home?"

"Sure. Who're you?"

"Who is it, Becky?" Forsythe called from inside the house.

"Detective McCleary," he said, and walked inside. Forsythe stood in the hallway, and he looked like hell. "I've got some questions for you."

His eyes darted to his daughter. "Honey, go make some coffee, will you?"

She hesitated, then smiled uncertainly at McCleary. "Okay. I'll tell Mommy we have company."

As she walked off, Forsythe hissed, "I don't have anything to say to you."

"Wrong, Mr. Forsythe. You either say it to me or you're going to be saying it to a judge, take your pick."

Forsythe sneezed into a tissue and backed down the hall. "I want to call my attorney. I know my rights, McCleary. I can call my goddamned attorney."

McCleary walked up to him, grabbed him by the robe, and pushed him up against the wall. "I'm a bit short on patience, Mr. Forsythe, and I've got just one thing to say to you. Tell me about the night you killed Grant Bell."

Forsythe's hands, which had been clutching McCleary's arms, trying to push him away, went slack. He turned his head to the side and squeezed his eyes shut. Tears rolled from beneath his thick lashes, onto his plump cheeks, and he nodded, once, weakly. "I didn't kill him," he whispered. "I swear I didn't."

McCleary stepped away from him. As Forsythe moved into the den, McCleary followed. Forsythe shut the French doors, walked over to the bar against the wall, brought out a bottle of Scotch, and poured two jiggers. He offered one to McCleary, but he shook his head. "Was he blackmailing you?"

Forsythe nodded again and sniffled.

"For what?"

"I . . . I don't have to tell you that. I want to call my attorney."

McCleary's patience broke. He rushed toward Forsythe, who grabbed the bottle of Scotch by the neck and shouted, "*No!* Don't come near me!"

"Trevor? Trevor, honey?" The French doors opened.

A woman who McCleary presumed was Mrs. Forsythe stood there, blinking as she looked from her husband to McCleary. "Who're you?"

"Get outa here, Winnie."

She stepped into the room, her young daughter behind her. "I said, Who are you?"

"Detective McCleary, homicide." He passed her his ID.

"Homicide? What . . .?"

"Get out, Winnie. I mean it," Forsythe said through clenched teeth, lowering the bottle of Scotch to the bar again. "And take Becky with you."

The girl began to cry. As Mrs. Forsythe took her daughter's hand and stomped out of the den, Trevor's plump face squashed together like an accordion and he started to weep again. McCleary just stared at him, feeling absolutely nothing.

"Look," McCleary said finally, his voice surprisingly calm. "I don't think you killed him. But tell me what you know. I need to know what you know."

"Sure," Forsythe said, his voice ragged. "And then I suppose you'll offer me immunity, huh?"

"No."

Forsythe blew his nose, looked down at his hands, which were still clutching the jigger, clutching it as though it were the last thing in the world he owned. "The fucker was blackmailing me, but I won't tell you for what. I won't incriminate myself."

So Bell had blackmailed Trevor just as he'd blackmailed Holmes to finance his Amazon project, his search for greenfire. "And?"

"And . . . the night he was killed, I . . . I went by his townhouse. I . . . I was going to plead with him. I mean, the fucker was sucking me dry, McCleary. And . . . and when I got there, I . . . I found him. Dead. In the kitchen. Just lying there on the floor in all this blood and—"

"What time was this, do you remember?"

Another sniffle, then he downed the jigger of Scotch. "Around eight-thirty, I think."

"What'd you do?"

"I left."

"You didn't ransack the townhouse?"

"No." His voice had fallen to a hoarse whisper.

"Okay. Here's another question. Did you break into Quin's house? Hit her over the head, Trevor?"

The fat man raised his eyes. McCleary knew—knew in that inviolate place within himself where he had always known such things—that Trevor was responsible and was going to deny it.

"No."

A rage nearly blinded McCleary as he grabbed Forsythe by the robe, yanked him to his feet. "You could've killed her, you shit. Were you looking for whatever Bell had on you? Is that it?" Then his rage receded like a wave as he saw what he was doing, saw as if a part of him had stepped back from the scene. He dropped his hands.

Forsythe's swollen cheeks were pink as if with sunburn. He stabbed the air with a pudgy finger and shouted, "You'll pay for that, McCleary. I'll sue your ass but good!"

McCleary just looked at him—at his trembling double chin, his gray and angry eyes, at his belly bulging against the robe. He felt nothing but disgust. He turned and walked out of the den, the house, out of Trevor Forsythe's life.

2.

Quin was surprised to see Nikki's car in her driveway. She hadn't spoken with her since the night of the engagement party. She opened the trunk of the Toyota to get the groceries and hurricane supplies just as Rusty Johnson's car stopped on the grass.

"Hey," he said, hurrying through the drizzle, the wind flapping at the edges of his raincoat. "You lost me in traffic there for a few minutes. Here, let me help you with that stuff." He jerked a thumb toward Nikki's Volvo as they hurried up the walk. "Whose car is that?"

"It belongs to my friend Nikki." She fished around in her bag until she found a package of sesame breadsticks. Any minute now, her stomach would make an awful fuss if she didn't get something inside it. She punched her

299

nail through the cellophane over the breadsticks and propped one between her teeth like a Groucho Marx cigar as she opened the front door. She saw McCleary's stuff stacked neatly against the far wall. "Nikki's probably out back in the patio. Let me see what she wants, then we'll get started on those storm shutters." They set the bags on the kitchen counter. "I really appreciate your coming over here to help me put up these storm shutters, Rusty."

"You're not weathering the storm here alone, are you?"

"No, McCleary'll be over later tonight."

Through the window, Quin saw Nikki on the patio at the edge of the awning, staring out into Grant's garden, her shoulders slumped, her spine curved against the gray light.

"I'll be back in a second, Rusty." Quin nibbled at her breadstick as she stepped outside. "Nikki?" She was alarmed when Nikki didn't turn, didn't move, didn't even seem aware of her presence. It was like looking at a statue, Quin thought dully, then repeated her name.

Nikki turned. Her eyes were swollen from crying, rain had misted in her hair.

"What's wrong? What's happened?" Quin asked gently.

"Steve. I told him. He couldn't accept the truth."

She laughed; it was a shallow sound, riddled with despair, cynicism, bitterness, Quin couldn't tell which, maybe all. An image of Grant and Nikki together in the townhouse crept into her thoughts; Quin shook it away. "What truth? What're you talking about?"

Nikki dropped her head back. Gray light shot across her cheeks. One hand slipped into the pocket of her jacket and the other into her purse. for a moment, Quin froze. She stared at Nikki's hand in the purse. *A gun? Does she have a gun?* A gust of wind blew the drizzle in her face. She shuddered.

Then Nikki said, "The truth about Grant."

From the back door, Rusty Johnson called, "Hey, Quin, phone. It's Mike."

Quin didn't look away from Nikki's hand. "Tell him I'll call back in a minute."

Nikki whipped her head around, evidently surprised

there was someone in the house. "Who's that?" She brought her hand out of her purse, tapped her finger against the top of a pack of cigarettes, lit one.

NO GUN. Jesus, no gun, Quin thought, and bit down hard on the breadstick. It tasted like dust in her mouth. "He's one of our investigators. Nikki, what about Grant? What did you tell Steve?"

"Hell, we were having one of those I'll-tell-you-if-you-tell-me-talks. Clearing the air before marriage, Quin, that sort of stuff, you know?"

She nodded stiffly. But all she could think of was no gun.

"So he told me about this brief affair he'd had with a Peruvian woman shortly before Grant introduced us. And I told him about Grant."

Oh brother. The last thing Steve would've been able to accept was Nikki sleeping with a man he'd considered a friend. "What'd he say?"

"He did what you did. He just walked out. That was yesterday. I haven't heard a thing from him." Her lower lip trembled. "Quin, can you forgive me? I don't know why I do things sometimes," she said as she cried. Her mascara ran; smears shaped like moths smudged her cheeks.

Quin hugged her. *No gun, no knife.* "Look, there's nothing to forgive, okay? Come on inside and I'll introduce you to Rusty and we'll have dinner."

Nikki shook her head. "No. Thanks, Quin, but I feel better. Really." She managed a thin smile. "I may even go home and call Steve and ask him to stay with me during the storm."

"You're sure?"

"Positive."

Quin walked with her around the side of the house, disturbed by her own suspicion. *Nikki isn't a killer. She isn't.* It was just the intrusion of the past again. *And again. How many agains are there going to be?*

She stood in the driveway while Nikki backed out, waved, watching Nikki whom she'd loved like a sister, and whom she'd never really known. Before she turned away, she saw a car coming toward the house, then past it. Perhaps it was the car's shape or its color, maybe it was just some sixth sense falling into place. But she knew the car was following Nikki.

3.

McCleary stood at the bow of his private ship, where the windows were smeared with rain. Below, some of the streets had already flooded. In less than six hours, Ingrid would bear down on the Florida coast, wreaking havoc. He knew he should leave, drive over to Quin's, but suppose he was needed here during the storm? Just two floors below, an evacuation center had been set up, and he could feel the pulse of activity. And somewhere in the wet dark, Robin was on duty, alone, probably at one of the other evacuation centers.

The back of his neck bristled and he spun around. Robin was framed in the doorway, illuminated from behind by the hall light. "Hi, Mac." She came into the office.

He turned on the light and found it hurt him to look at her, to remember. But as always, he couldn't *stop* looking at her. She seemed more remote than usual, her dark eyes hooded, hair pulled back from her face with barrettes or combs and tumbling across her shoulders. He noticed it glistened with raindrops. "I thought you were on duty tonight."

She dropped an envelope on his desk. "I'd appreciate it if you'd give this to Izzo."

"What's in the envelope?"

"My resignation."

It seemed to McCleary that only a moment passed before he breathed, "Oh," but it might have been longer. Either way, it was pathetic that the only thing he could muster at the end of a two-year partnership—and a yearlong affair—was *Oh*. "What're you going to do?"

She rubbed her hands together as if for warmth. Her cheeks burned with color. "Going back to law." She paused, averted her eyes toward the window, then looked at him again. "I'm going to practice with Paul Holmes."

The words seemed to echo in the strained silence between them, then suddenly blazed like Christmas lights and blinked on, off, on again. McCleary leaned against

302

the edge of the desk. "You may be practicing alone, Robin, since Paul will probably be in custody tomorrow."

Her eyes moved, but slowly, as though she were drugged or coming out of a deep sleep. "So you won, didn't you, Mac? You finally got your man." She shook her head, looked down at the floor, her smile the most surfeit of smiles.

"But not for murder."

"But for something, and that was always the point." Another hesitation. "The courthouse, I knew you were responsible for that."

"He had enough information in that goddamn safe, Robin, to blackmail half the city of Miami. Is that the kind of law you want to practice?"

The corners of her mouth turned down scornfully. "Don't give me *that*," she snapped. "What the hell do you know about the practice of law?" And more softly, she added, "What the hell do you know about anything? Grant Bell knew more than you did, for God's sake."

McCleary barely heard her. He made a strangled, pathetic sound as he said, "God, and I wanted to marry you."

Her head jerked up. "You wanted to own me, Mac, *own* me, that's all you wanted." It wasn't until he stepped toward her that he saw the tears in her eyes, quivering, threatening to spill. "I . . . wanted so much to love you," she whispered, "and you just never gave me the chance." Then she turned and was gone before McCleary could even react. When he did, when he finally moved, feeling as though he were uprooting himself from the floor, she was nowhere in sight. At the end of the hall, he heard the elevator descending.

33

THE THRILLING FLUSH of noise: tonight I needed it. Music, the dance of ice in glasses, the rise and fall of laughter, voices. Although the place wasn't crowded, because of the impending storm, I needed the noise and the hot press of bodies that stung the air with the scent of booze and perfume, after-shave and decadence. I needed the assurance that I was human, still, that I wasn't suspended in some hot nude pearl sky like vapors waiting to become a cloud.

Was I mad?

Yes, oh yes, mad as a hatter, crazy as a loon, all the clichés fit me, just as they had fit my mother.

I wandered through the bar, watching, watching, watching: the bartenders madly mixing drinks, their blenders whirring until the contents were foam; the waitresses in their blinding white smiles; and then everyone else, men in suits, men in jeans, women in slacks gathered at the ankles.

I gulped at my Dewar's as I neared the table where I'd been standing the night I'd met Grant. I saw his reflection in the darkened window, imagined that he floated there behind the glass, a tiny orb of light, a presence, still conscious. *Would death be so bad, really?*

A cessation, a respite, a deep sleep, and then rebirth: he'd believed that death, like life, was a progression.

Toward what?

Toward nothing.

I giggled.

Beyond the room, I heard the wind, rain, the anger of the approaching storm. It seemed right that tonight nature's fury and I would be companions, partners that whipped through the dark streets, purging.

Then I turned from the window where I thought for sure I'd seen an orb of light that was Grant Bell, and realized I was crying.

34

1.

SHE HAD ENOUGH ice in the freezer so that if the electricity went off, she could dump it in the cooler and store perishables inside. She had two flashlights, a supply of extra batteries, candles, a manual can opener, five gallons of drinking water, extra food for Merlin, a transistor radio. Quin also had plenty of fruit, cold chicken, and canned goods. She wouldn't starve to death just in case Ingrid pulled a fast one and slammed into Miami. The only thing she lacked was the presence of another person—specifically, McCleary.

Her sister, Ellen, had called, because she'd heard about the storm on the news. She wanted to know if Quin was okay, where the investigation stood on Grant's murder, and who was this guy McCleary she'd mentioned in her latest letter? McCleary, who hadn't arrived, Quin thought, listening as rain drummed against the shutters Rusty had helped her put up. Already the power had gone out twice. All right, the blackouts had been brief. But each time, she'd spiraled into a deep panic in which she could *feel* something out there in the dark. Now she sat at the edge of the couch in the living room, cleaning her gun, reloading it, knowing she was being ridiculously paranoid. When she'd loaded the gun, she went into the kitchen, peeled an orange, helped herself to a piece of cold chicken. She leaned against the counter as she nibbled at it, and wished she had company—Ellen, McCleary, even Nikki. As if to assure her she wasn't alone, Merlin padded into the kitchen and sat at her feet. She tossed him a piece of chicken, then shredded some pieces in his bowl.

Ants paraded between his bowl and his water dish, carrying bits of Little Friskies. She followed them with her eyes to a crack between the tile and the wall. She thought about giving them a little pep talk, then decided what the hell. At least they weren't palmetto bugs, and on a night like this, where would they go?

Mush head.

She stared at the phone, rubbing her hands along her arms. *C'mon, McCleary. You're late. Call me and tell me you're on your way. I don't want to go through this storm with just a cat and ants for company. Call.*

2.

As McCleary was leaving his office, the phone rang. He snatched it up, heard Ron Valencia's voice swimming in a sea of static. ". . . McCleary . . . heard from . . . Wright. . . ."

"I can't hear you, Ron," McCleary shouted into the phone.

". . . now? Can you hear me now? It's about Lance Wright. He . . .." Another burst of static. ". . . a Billy Hendrix out in . . .." The line went dead. When he tried to call Valencia back, he couldn't get a dial tone, then the power shut down. For a moment in the thick, black silence, he heard the rage of the approaching storm and the cackle of the wind like a coven of witches, clawing at the glass. He glanced once at the windows, where Miami had sunk into darkness, and a shiver sped through him. He fumbled in his pocket for matches, lit one, and went through his drawers until he found a flashlight.

In the hallway, beams of lights snipped away at the heavy blackness as other people made their way toward the stairs and the evacuation center set up on the first floor. All McCleary wanted to do was get out of the building and over to Quin's. But on the first floor, where transistors blared, where families were settling down for the night with blankets, pillows, and belongings, some-one asked him to help replace a piece of plywood that had been ripped off one of the windows. He couldn't refuse, but first he patted his way along the wall to Izzo's office to see if the phone was working. It seemed imperative that he call Quin. A sense of urgency shud-dered along his spine as he lifted the receiver. *Please be working.*

The phone here was also dead.

3.

The wind shrieked, its velocity augmenting with each gust. Rain pounded the shutters on the east side of the house. Candles flickered in the bedroom, where Holmes and Robin were, and created ghastly elongated shadows on the walls. The transistor on the nightstand crackled with static as the newscaster reported power outages all over the city.

"Wind gusts of seventy have been clocked at Miami International Airport as the outer bands of the storm move in closer to shore. Ingrid is moving to the north-northwest at about twenty miles an hour. This puts landfall about two hours earlier than anticipated, with the eye expected to hit between Fort Pierce and Mel-bourne. . . ."

Holmes shut off the transistor with an angry flick of his wrist and sat up in bed. The storm had made him restless as a ghost. "Let's have a drink," he suggested, glancing at Robin. The lambent light from the candles played havoc with her face, throwing one side com-pletely into shadow and washing out her features on the other. "We'll celebrate your resignation."

"Sounds good to me." She tossed back the covers, her long legs swinging over the side of the bed. She reached for her clothes. Holmes watched as her shoul-ders and breasts vanished beneath her blouse. He pulled on his jeans, picked up one of the candles, stared at their reflections in the sliding glass doors that led to the patio. The glass was covered by storm shutters, so their reflections seemed to sink into a space between them and the doors. It gave him a claustrophobic feeling, as if he'd been buried alive and the oxygen was slowly being gobbled up.

"Paul, I'm kinda curious about something," Robin said as he started to the door.

"What."

"Why'd you rape that woman?"

He rolled his eyes. "We've been through this before."

"But you *raped* her."

Jesus, he thought. What was wrong with her, anyway? He'd explained it all to her. She was the only person he'd ever trusted enough to tell. He hadn't even told Miriam, whom he'd been married to for fifteen years. Didn't that mean *anything* to her? "And I atoned for it, Robin. Who do you think got county funds diverted to the Rape Crisis Center? Until I got into office, the people who worked there did so on a volunteer basis, for Christ's sake. And I had funds allotted for speakers, hot lines, and to expand the special rape task force in the police department. None of that existed two years ago."

The flame on his candle flickered, and for a moment the wind, the rain, the din of the storm seemed to pause as if for breath. In the sudden quiet, he could hear Robin sighing as she stood, as she reached for her purse. Apprehension prickled his arms; he felt the room closing in.

"Now c'mon, let's have that drink. You want the usual?"

Behind him, she giggled. "Yes."

Now *that* was a familiar sound, wholly Robin. "Kahlua coming up," he said.

"No, not Kahlua. A Dewar's. A Dewar's on the rocks, Paul."

4.

People were still scurrying into the evacuation center as McCleary drove out of the station lot. Wind and rain buffeted the Escort. The windshield wipers weren't worth a shit, he thought, rolling the window down and sticking his head out so he could see the road. The sense of urgency that had seized him earlier now surged, as though it were connected with the power of the storm. But it was more than the hurricane, he thought, rubbing the burning hunch spot between his eyes. It was . . . what? He could feel it, whatever it was, just beyond him. But when he reached for it, the thing vanished like a dream.

He switched on the radio as he slowly negotiated the flooded roads, taking an alternate route toward Quin's so he wouldn't have to venture the interstate.

". . . all residents in low-lying areas should now be evacuated," the radio announcer said. "There is severe flooding on Key Biscayne. Seas are about eight feet above normal. Precautions should be—"

McCleary shut the radio off.

The buildings on either side helped buffer the car from the wind, but there was no protection from the lashing rain. As he moved through an intersection, the streetlight overhead swung, a howl of wind smashed against the car, the Escort fishtailed and nearly stalled.

"C'mon, you piece of shit," he whispered, "just get me to Quin's, then you never have to do anything else again."

He'd never seen the roads so empty. He felt as if he'd been catapulted into a Fifties science fiction scenario: last man on Earth and all that. Now and then, a still functioning streetlight cast an eerie glow through the torrent. The steadily dropping barometric pressure had created a tightening band of pain across his temples. His fingers ached from gripping the steering wheel so hard, and his damp clothes had given him a chill.

The Escort waded through about two feet of water and suddenly coughed, bucked, and refused to gather speed. McCleary pressed his foot to the accelerator, swearing at the car, at Grant Bell whom he knew was chuckling in his grave, and swerved the wheel violently to the left, into a deserted shopping center. The car wheezed. McCleary kept his foot on the accelerator, muttering to the car, coaxing it forward just a little farther. Wind thrashed across the asphalt desert of the parking lot, slamming against the Ford as it sputtered on. It finally died as McCleary coasted into a narrow alley between the backs of two buildings. The wind still whistled through the opening at either end, but it was manageable.

He had two options. He could look for a phone and call Triple A or he could attempt to fix the car enough so it would at least get him to Quin's. He doubted that even Triple A would be out in a mess like this and had no assurance that when he found a phone, it would work. "So that leaves plan B, buddy," he murmured. He slid on his poncho, which he'd been carrying around in the car with him all day, slipped the hood over his head, and got out of the car with the flashlight.

He threw up the Escort's hood, checked the belts and hoses. The fan belt was loose, the battery cables were caked, an alternator wire hung by a thread. "Christ," he muttered, and ran to the trunk. Quin had mentioned that Grant kept a tool box in here. He was no mechanical whiz, but maybe if he tightened the damned fan belt and secured the alternator wire the car would move.

The spare tire lay loose in the trunk, and when he flipped back the worn carpeting, he found the tool box embedded in the place where the tire should've been. It was locked. He slammed his fist against it, then ran back to the front of the car for his Magnum. He brought the butt of the .357 down hard over the lock several times. The lid gave as the look came loose. He flung it open. No tools, no goddamned tools at all, just a bunch of papers. He set the flashlight down, so light splashed on the box, and shoved the papers aside. The wind lifted some of the sheets and they sailed off into the rain like kites, only to tumble, waterlogged, a few moments later. Maybe beneath all this stuff there was at least a wrench or a pair of pliers, *something*, he thought frantically, digging through the sheaf.

As he leaned closer to the tool box, isolated words on the papers seemed to quiver in the glow of the flashlight, then leap out at him. He stopped moving, then suddenly his arms lashed out, trying to hold the papers down. McCleary hugged the sheaf of papers to him, gathering them up in his arms, protecting them with a flap on the poncho. He rushed to the front of the car and threw himself inside. The papers slid across the seat and onto the floor. He grabbed them at random, shining the light on one after another, perusing them madly, water dripping from his hair and poncho, onto the papers. This was it, he thought wildly, Grant Bell's cache of secrets, the evidence Trevor had been looking for the night he broke into Quin's house. *The tool box, that's what the key fits.*

There was something about a piece of commercial property Trevor Forsythe had been given in return for terminating an insurance investigation. He found the disposition of Paul Holmes's rape charge. The last item was a manuscript entitled *Mac* by Kara Newman. As he paged through it, his hands shook so violently the beam from the flashlight hopped and danced across sentences, paragraphs, chapters which were himself and Robin, the tumults and twists of their affair. With every page he turned, his heart was pulverized bit by terrible bit, the grains blown into the tempest. *I wanted so much to love you, and you just never gave me the chance.*

McCleary finally pressed his forehead to the steering wheel, squeezed his eyes shut against the pain, the dark fields, the past, and wept.

5.

Paul turned, stirring her drink with a skewer, tucking a cocktail napkin around the bottom of Robin's glass. "I didn't know you drank Dewar's."

"There're a lot of things you don't know about me."

She watched him over the rim of her glass as she sipped at her drink, candlelight splashing onto her auburn hair, her cheeks. Shadows like smudges snuggled beneath her eyes, and there was a certain numinous quality about her that disturbed him. Holmes lit a cigarette and another candle and another until the room in the mirror over the bar threw back all the light. In the mirror, he saw Robin reach into her purse; her mouth twisted into a smile as he turned around.

"You going somewhere?" he asked.

"Not just yet. I still need one more scene for the book."

"The book? What book?" Why was he suddenly sweating? Why did the room seem so hot? Christ, he felt like they were in the middle of Africa at high noon.

"Oh, that's right. You don't know about my books, do you, Paul? But Grant did. Yeah, he found out in a real sneaky way."

His gut tightened with a spasm that might've been the beginning of laughter but quickly became an almost exquisite pain, like the onset of food poisoning. He had no idea what she was talking about. "Grant?" You knew Grant?" A frown burrowed down between his eyes like a tiny mole.

She dipped her finger into her glass, sucked off the Scotch, smiled wryly, secretly.

"Oh sure, we were friends. Old friends. At least for seven, eight, maybe nine weeks. I forget."

Holmes blinked. Beyond the room, the storm shrieked like a shrew. He gave a quick, sharp laugh. "What're you talking about, anyway, Robin?"

"Grant took my manuscript, about Mac, and then he found out my secrets, and then he read *Black Bird*, so he also knew about Billy. Did I ever tell you about Billy, Paul? Billy the rapist?" Her hand eased down into her purse, and he stared at it so hard he thought he could see the veins, the sinews and muscles beneath her soft, flawless skin. "Billy was soooo bad to me, so bad." She shook her head once, twice. "He . . . he made two of his friends hold me down when he . . . when he did it, and then . . . they laughed, all three of them. They laughed and they took turns with me and . . ."

He saw her hand whip out of her purse and sucked in his breath. The gun with its pearl handle glinted in the candlelight. He knew he was saying something to her as he backed slowly away from the bar, toward the kitchen.

"You shouldn't have told me about the black woman, Paul. You shouldn't have. I'm almost sorry that you did." Her smile was languid, crazy. He continued to back away from her, blowing out the candles, eyes fixed on her finger against the trigger, his mind grappling for a way out.

"Robin, we can talk about this, we can, you know, it doesn't have to . . ." He no longer heard his words, only the practiced murmur of his voice. His voice that had swayed juries and struck deals, his voice that had bargained and bartered and—

She fired.

His hands flew up as he stumbled back, into the table. One of the lit candles tumbled to the floor. The flame flickered, caught at the hem of the curtains drawn across the sliding glass door. It flared, it scampered up the fabric like a frantic rodent, and Holmes heard screaming. Oh God, it was a horrible sound, the sound of someone being eaten alive, and it was coming from him.

6.

McCleary sprinted along the walkways of the deserted shopping center, rain lashing his face, his mind crying out, *But she said she couldn't type. How could I not have seen it? How, why, when* . . . The dark field had been illuminated, and now it galloped through his head like a primeval creature, roaring, kicking, as he tossed his mind like a net into the past, seeking answers.

He ran past Publix, sale banners plastered in its taped windows, past a pastry shop, a pizza joint, all of them shut down, their windows crossed by huge Xs of masking tape. Pain curled through his lungs and what was left of his heart. The wind battered him, rain dripped down inside the poncho. In his mind, he kept seeing *Mac* by *Kara Newman*, and knew it would brand his vision like a curse for the remainder of his life.

As he rounded the corner of a building, he plastered himself against the wall to catch his breath. Then he saw the four cars parked outside the bar directly across the alley from him, the bar whose windows flickered with candlelight. He tore across the alley, loving whoever the fools were inside, daring Ingrid's wrath with a hurricane party.

7.

". . . we're feeling the eastern edge of the storm right now as she nears landfall about a hundred and fifty miles up the coast. Ingrid's maximum sustained winds are

314

about a hundred and ten miles an hour. Dr. Neil Frank from the National Hurricane Center doesn't expect gusts in Miami to reach more than seventy and says we've been spared the western edge of the storm, which is considered the more dangerous. . . ."

"Terrific," Quin grumbled, and shut off the transistor. She slumped down against the couch, worried that something had happened to McCleary, hating her imprisonment here without power or phone. With the air off, the house was stifling, and she walked over to the front window to crack it open.

The warm, wet air felt good against her skin. Wind whistled along the crack; rain stung her forehead. Merlin leaped into the windowsill, nuzzling her with his cool, damp nose, and Quin pressed her face against her fur.

"It'll be over soon, Merl," she whispered, and wondered why she didn't believe it, why it was so easy to imagine that the sun would never shine again, that the rain would just keeping coming and coming, forty days and nights of it.

Just then, headlights swam through the rain, struck the windows, and a car pulled into the driveway behind her Toyota. Certain it was McCleary, she ran to the front door and threw it open.

"Hurry!" she shouted.

He raced into the house. As he brushed back the hood of his yellow slicker, Quin frowned. Robin Peters shook out her long, thick hair and smiled softly. "Hi, Quin."

35

1.

MCCLEARY BURST INTO the bar with a rush of wind and rain
that snapped up heads, blew napkins and empty bags of
potato chips off the counter, and extinguished nearly
every candle. He slammed the door shut, and in the
ensuing brief silence, the five pairs of eyes at the round
table in the center of the room scrutinized him. The air
smelled of spilled booze and dope.

"What the hell you doin' out in this storm, boy?"
asked an old bearded fellow who'd gotten to his feet and
shuffled toward McCleary.

"Is your phone working?"

"Don't rightly know. You'll have to try it." He waved
toward the phone on the bar. "Want somethin' to drink?"

"Yeah, a beer. Thanks."

"How's it lookin' outside?" called one of the men
from the table.

"Like shit," McCleary mumbled and lifted the receiver. He didn't realize he'd been holding his breath
until he heard the tone and exhaled. He dialed Quin's
number, but there was no ringing, no busy signal, nothing. He tried the number again, the same thing occurred,
and he slammed the receiver down and dialed the dispatcher. The number was busy, but since the phones at
the station hadn't been working earlier, maybe that meant
the lines were still out of order. He sat for a moment,

rubbing the hot burning spot between his eyes. The old fellow set the beer on the counter in front of him.

"Want me to hang up that there wet poncho for you, son?"

"Thanks." He shucked the poncho, and the old man hung it on a wooden coatrack behind the bar with four other raincoats. McCleary paid for the beer and downed half of it. "My car died. Out there. In the lot." *And Robin, oh Jesus, Robin.* The man's eyes were the sort of timeless blue that encouraged talk, and McCleary felt the rest of the story sliding down his tongue like some premature infant who couldn't wait to be born. He clamped his mouth shut.

"Ain't suprised. Winds are past seventy, and that rain's coming down somethin' fierce. But the brunt of the 'cane done missed us."

McCleary picked up the phone again and dialed Quin's number. It rang once, there was a click as if it had been picked up, but that must've been a trick of the storm because no one spoke. "Quin? Quin, it's me, McCleary."

He heard someone breathing, then: "Hi, Mac. Quin's in the bathroom."

He suddenly understood the phrase *blood turning cold.* Except that it was worse than that. He felt as if he'd been injected with curare, and slowly, very slowly, his organs were shutting down. Air froze in his lungs, his heartbeat slowed, nerves short-circuited. His brain was being deprived of oxygen, and he couldn't think straight, couldn't make the necessary connections. When he finally realized he was actually responding, it was as if another McCleary had taken over. He heard himself telling Robin he'd wait for Quin to come to the phone. He said it like there was nothing at all unusual about Robin being at Quin's, Robin who had killed nearly a dozen men in the last eight months, Robin—his nemesis.

"Okay. Sure. You been out in this storm, Mac? It's a mess, I'll tell you, a real mess." her voice was strangely soft, dreamy, childlike. *Deranged.* McCleary dropped his ID on the counter and motioned toward the old bearded fellow. On a cocktail napkin, he wrote: *If there's another phone, call 555-1342 and tell them to dispatch a cruiser immediately to 1754 Andalucia Drive. It's an emergency.*

The old fellow took one look at McCleary's ID and the note and rushed into a back room. Robin was still speaking in that soft, dreamy voice, telling him about her trip across town.

"What're you doing out in the storm, Robin?"

"Oh, I had to go see a friend. My friend Paul. But I think everything sort of got out of control, Mac. He isn't a very nice man and I had to shoot him and then . . . then this candle fell over and . . . well, I *had* to do it, Mac. He . . . he was just like Grant, he was, really, maybe worse than Grant. Do you think his house burned down?"

Keep her talking. As long as she's talking, Quin is safe. "I don't know. Why do you think the house might've burned down?"

"The flame caught on the curtain and . . ."

Aw Christ, he thought. "Why was Grant bad, Robin?"

"He . . . he stole the manuscript . . . and he . . . he found out about *Black Bird* and he . . . Oh, Mac," she whispered. Those two words, uttered with such black despair, nearly ripped him apart. "How did everything get so complicated? Kara's so mean."

"Robin, is Quin out of the bathroom yet?"

"Yeah, but she can't come to the phone, Mac. I need the key and she knows where it is and she won't tell me. I . . . I had to hurt her. I didn't want to hurt her, but she. . ."

ShekilledQuinkilledQuin. . . . The words rang in his ears. "Why do you need the key, Robin?"

"My manuscript's wherever that key fits, Mac. Grant hid it, I know he did."

Perspiration trickled along the sides of his face. His heart hammered. "Robin, Quin doesn't have the key. I do. I have the key. It fits the tool box in Grant's car, and I've got Grant's car."

Another giggle. "You're fooling, Mac. I know you are. I remember how you used to fool me sometimes."

"How's Quin hurt, Robin?"

"She . . ." A long hesitation. When she spoke again, the dreaminess was gone. "Fuck you, Mac, you weren't

318

very nice to me, either, so fuck you and your stupid Quin." She hung up. McCleary dialed the number again, his hand trembling, bile turning the inside of his mouth sour, but the phone was busy.

"Mr. McCleary," the old man said, hurrying out of the back room, "I got through. The dispatcher said she'd try to get a car over there pronto, but there ain't any cruisers in that neighborhood."

"I need a car. I need a car fast."

The old man motioned to one of the men at the table. "Pete's got a four-wheel drive that sits about eight feet off the road."

A chair scraped against the floor and the man named Pete lumbered over. He had a thick beard, a cigar stuck in one side of his mouth, and he was *big*. He also looked loaded. "Got the jeep out back."

"I appreciate this," McCleary said.

"No problem, man. The way I figure it, you cops are the ones who make Miami halfway civilized."

Whether Miami was civilized, McCleary thought, was open to debate.

2.

Quin, lying on her side on the living room floor, hands and legs bound with cord, heard Robin's conversation with McCleary. Her shoulder stung where Robin had sliced her with the knife, but despite the blood, she knew instinctively the cut wasn't deep. She worked her wrists frantically until the cords were loose enough to slip off, but before she could untie her ankles, Robin slammed down the phone.

Quin shut her eyes and said a silent prayer to God or whoever else might be listening. She took several deep breaths, forcing her fear to the back of her mind. When she opened her eyes, she was staring at the tips of Robin's soiled shoes. But her thoughts were lucid.

Robin shone the flashlight on Quin's face. "That was Mac. He tried to trick me. He said he has the key, Quin. But I know you do." She crouched, touched the tip of her knife to Quin's neck. "Where's the key?" The knife pricked the skin, and Quin winced, felt her fear pounding at that back door in her mind.

"It's hidden upstairs," she said quickly.

"Where upstairs?"

"In my pillowcase."

Robin grinned. *This is what madness looks like. If you live, remember it.* Robin took her by the shoulders and moved her to a sitting position. Quin kept her wrists clamped together behind her back, as though they were still tied. "Well, we'll just see about that." The knife trailed across Quin's neck, the touch as light as a feather, then moved across her cheek, stopping just below her right eye. Quin sucked in her breath sharply, and Robin smiled. "I know you'll wait right here like a good girl, Quin." Then she leaned close. "And don't get any ideas about Mac saving you, honey, not in *this* storm."

Quin nodded. Tears sprang into her eyes. She watched Robin pick up the candle again, saw Merlin peek out from under the couch, then the light disappeared from the room. Robin's shadow on the wall loomed erratically, smearing when the candlelight flickered, vanishing as Robin reached the top of the stairs. Quin scooted back farther into the shadows, rubbing her wrists, working at the cords around her ankles until they were loose, then she patted the coffee table behind her for the letter opener.

3.

The flames had swept through the kitchen, igniting anything that was flammable, and set off the sprinkler system. Now smoke curled thickly in the air around Holmes, and he tried to keep his face close to the floor, where there was more oxygen. He was bleeding profusely from the wound in his leg, and the white, angry pain there had spread throughout the rest of his body. He could hear his flesh and muscles and nerves screeching with agony, falling in on themselves, dying, as he crawled toward the garage door. But the exertion brought on more bleeding, and he had to stop.

He groped blindly for the phone, grabbed the cord, jerked it off the table. It smacked the floor. When he pressed the receiver to his ear, there was no dial tone. He dropped the receiver and pulled himself across the floor again, dragging his wounded leg, trying to ignore the pain and the sticky blood oozing against his skin.

So much blood, he thought dimly, and the image of Robin aiming the gun flared again in his head.

In the family room, there was less smoke. He gulped at the air, crawled the remaining few feet to the door, and sat up. His eyes burned terribly from the smoke, he was weak from loss of blood, and for an instant, he nearly passed out. His hands groped for the knob. He pulled himself up and pain shot through his leg, making him gasp.

He managed to open the door and pull himself into the garage. For several long moments, he simply sat with his back against the wall, drawing great, heaping lungfuls of air, his eyes closed. He couldn't see in here, but when his hands touched his leg, he felt the soaked, sticky fabric. His stomach cramped; he turned his head to the side and threw up.

Smoke wafted into the garage, he could smell it, he would smell it for the rest of his life. If he lived. This thought galvanized him. He pressed his hands against the cool concrete, flattened his back to the wall, and slowly pushed himself up. The pain, oh Jesus, the pain struck him fiercely, and he fell toward the button that would open the garage door.

He leaned against it, pressing, pressing. Why wasn't the door rising? The power, of course; the door was electric and the power had gone off. The only other exits were the front door and the one off the utility room.

Holmes patted his way along the wall, back into the family room, the smoke singeing the inside of his nose, his mouth, burning his eyes. He could no longer feel his leg. He thought he heard music, yes, somewhere there was music, and it was a lovely, comforting sound. He wasn't alone, he wasn't going to die here, like this. No, the person playing the music was coming for him.

"*Here!*" he shouted. "*I'm here!*"

Then his hot, sticky hands seized a knob and he turned it and fell out into the storm. Wind raged into the house, rain sliced his face and hands, but he didn't care, out here the air was cool and clean and forever, and the music, the lovely music was louder. It seemed to slip in around him, each note a separate world, each bar a pair of hands that lifted him, soothed the pain in his leg.

He turned his head and felt the cool, wet grass against his cheek, and then, in his mind, the music pushed the storm away and the sun came out. And slowly, Paul Holmes bled to death.

4.

Quin got shakily to her feet, felt Merlin rub against her leg, and scooped him up in her arms. She could hear Robin upstairs, tearing the bedroom apart, and then her voice shouting, *"Quin, you lied, there's no key up here!"* She ran to the front door, Merlin scrambling in her arms now to escape. Quin threw it open, stumbled out into the storm. The wind was a wall, pushing against her, shoving the biting rain into her face. She leaped from the porch and pushed herself into the hollow space beneath it. A moment later, Robin raced out onto the stoop, shouting Quin's name, her voice quickly gobbled up by the wind.

Another moment passed. The front door slammed. Merlin stopped trying to escape, but embedded his claws deeply in Quin's thighs. She rubbed her aching shoulder, blinked away water dripping into her eyes, winced as Robin's flashlight combed through the driveway. It skimmed the roofs of their cars, which looked like great sweating prehistoric creatures in the glow of the light, then flew across the front hedge. Robin ran down the steps to the edge of the driveway. Quin stared at her figure, sheathed in the yellow slicker, willing her to get in her car and leave. Instead, she turned, flashed the beam around the yard. Quin pushed back against the concrete as far as she could as the beam inched closer. And closer. *No, not here, Robin. I'm not here.* She held her breath. The beam paused, illuminating her.

She scrambled out of the hollow, Merlin leaped off into the dark, and she ran through the water puddled in the grass, Robin shouting at her. As she flew around the corner of the house, the wind slammed into her, nearly knocking her to the ground. Robin fired, missed, and Quin raced on, straight for the two acres of pines and citrus, right into the heart of Grant's labyrinthian garden.

5.

Some of the roads were completely submerged, as if the mighty Atlantic herself had reared up and crashed over Florida's peninsula. More than once, McCleary held his breath as Pete swerved the four-wheel drive up onto a sidewalk, a lawn, and then into the street again.

Traffic lights were down in some places, floating like exotic aquatic creatures in small lakes, and in one spot, a ficus had simply broken in the middle and fallen across the road. Pete slowed as they aproached, rubbed his beard thoughtfully, then threw the jeep into reverse. He backed up several feet, slammed the jeep into first, and drove it over the top of the tree.

When they were finally barreling down an open stretch of road, the wind hammered them, the jeep skidded, and a sharp, hurtful image of Quin dug into McCleary's brain. *If she's dead, if Robin killed her, if . . .*

He checked the .357 to make sure it was loaded, patted his pocket for the extra ammo, and swallowed hard. "Who're we after, anyway?" Pete shouted over the din.

"A woman," McCleary replied. *A woman I wanted to marry.*

6.

The canopy of trees and vines protected her somewhat from the storm, but it was too black to see anything and too noisy to hear Robin. Stripped of the two senses she relied on the most, Quin shut her eyes for a moment, trying to visualize the garden. She'd entered from the east side, and now lay in about six inches of water to the west, not far from the path and the goldfish pool. She didn't know what she was going to do now that she'd oriented herself, but she would think of something.

She opened her eyes, peering through the brush that

323

covered her, waiting for a glimpse of Robin's flashlight. Her arm flared with pain as she moved slightly, but she took comfort in the fact that the cut wasn't deep, that she wasn't going to bleed to death. But she was ravenous enough to begin gnawing on branches, ravenous enough to shove a handful of mud in her mouth, to . . .

The beam of light cut suddenly into her vision, illuminating the driving rain, the slant of the foliage, and Robin's yellow slicker. She was almost directly in front of Quin, near the pool. The light darted about.

Robin shouted, "Quin, c'mon now, I'm sick of these games. You can't get away, you know you can't. Just tell me where the goddamned key is. When I have the key, and my manuscript, then I'll go."

What difference does the key make now? She nearly yelled it, but bit down on her lip and moved steadily back through the water and muck until she was out from under the bush. She gripped her arm just beneath the cut, rocked back on her heels, and moved around behind a cluster of bushes.

"You shouldn't have taken Mac away," Robin shouted. "You shouldn't have. He was mine. He's always been mine. And . . . and I want Grant's cameras. Those are mine, too."

Quin shut out the sound of her voice. Her bare feet sank into mud, she felt something slither across the top of her foot and almost screamed. A gust of wind hammered against her spine, forcing her to a crouch. She locked her arms around her knees and pressed her forehead to her thighs until the gust had diminished somewhat, then crept along the bushes toward the path.

Suddenly, a crash resounded in the din. *The trellis, the wind just blew down the trellis.* Robin's light danced toward the end of the path, and Quin squashed back against a bush as it pierced the dark only a few inches from her. The light closed in on her. *Now or never, Quin. Nothing to lose.* And when Robin started past her, Quin threw herself forward and leaped into the air. Her feet struck Robin in the small of the back, knocking her down. The impact catapulted Quin back. She smacked the ground on her wounded arm and cried out. Stars winked on and off in her head as she scrambled to her feet a moment before Robin did.

7.

McCleary was out of the jeep and running before it had even stopped. He raced toward the house, rain biting at his face, drumming the hood of his poncho. He saw Robin's car parked behind Quin's, but there were no lights in the window. So either Robin was waiting for him inside, in the dark, or Quin had somehow managed to escape. *Or she's dead.*

He hesitated at the porch, torn with uncertainty.

The spot between his eyes burned. He looked down and saw Merlin peeking from beneath the porch. He raced around the side of the house, Pete behind him now with a powerful flashlight.

For a moment, McCleary saw nothing but the shattered trellis, the branch that had fallen across it, and a tangle of plants and vines the wind had twisted. Then Pete's light homed in on Robin and Quin. Robin had her backed up to a thicket, and he saw the sharp glint of her knife, jabbing at the air inches in front of Quin's face, taunting her, the rain pouring over them. For a moment, the light froze the expression on Quin's face, blazed it into his vision. Then he shouted, "*Robin!*"

She spun around, her wet face encased in the hood of a yellow slicker, then she lunged toward Quin, grabbing her around the neck. "*Get away from me or I'll kill her, I swear I'll kill her,*" she screamed.

"Just let her go, Robin, c'mon," he called, moving slowly toward her, the .357 aimed at her head.

"*Don't come any closer, Mac.*"

He stopped as he saw the knife pressing into Quin's neck. Blood ran down her arm, a river of blood. Pete towered beside him, just holding the powerful light nice and steady, so steady McCleary could see the trickle of blood on Quin's neck now. She was sobbing.

"Let her go, Robin," he shouted.

But she backed away, toward the brush, moving slowly, carefully, the knife still poking Quin's neck. Then everything happened very quickly. Quin brought her elbow back hard into Robin's ribs, wiggled free, and tore away, holding her arm. Robin simply stood there, staring at her knife as though she didn't know quite what to make of it. The light glowed against her face, slid over her slicker, then she lifted her head, blinked away the water clustered on her lashes. Her mouth formed words: *Mac, oh Mac, you wouldn't let me love you.* Then she was nothing but a blur, rushing toward him with that knife, and God help him, he lifted his gun and fired.

Epilogue

October 3

QUIN PARKED AT the curb behind McCleary's car and rummaged through her stash of munchies in the glove compartment. She settled on the mixture of raisins and dry-roasted peanuts, perfect for a mid-morning snack, and probably about three hundred calories.

She got out and walked over to the metallic blue RX7. Lady Two seemed sleeker somehow than her predecessor, sitting low against the road, her finish polished to a perfect sheen that looked impervious to the hot Florida sun. Quin ran her hand over the roof, smiling, and hurried toward the front of the building. She paused at the top step and looked down at the welcome mat in the center of the stoop. McCleary had designed the logo: a rising gold sun, plump as a grapefruit, with a wavy ribbon of cloud right through the middle. Above it was ST. JAMES & McCLEARY and just below the horizon, in small letters, PRIVATE EYES.

She stepped around it, nibbled at a handful of raisins, and walked inside. Ruth Grimes was on the phone, but smiled cheerfully as Quin swept by. The air in the hall swelled with the tapping of computers and typewriters, the sound of laughter, the pealing of phones. These sweet songs of prosperity had been wrenched from the sale of the firm's duplexes, office buildings, and property, because Trevor had been desperate for cash. After paying off outstanding debts, Quin had used most of her share of the money to buy out Trevor's fifty-one percent. The last she'd heard, he and Winnie had sold their twin Mercedeses and refinanced their house to pay his legal expenses, which would be considerable, if he intended to stay out of jail.

But Trevor was no longer her problem.

She left her lunch in the staff room fridge, polished off the rest of her raisins and peanuts, and walked into McCleary's office. He, Joe Bean, and Rusty Johnson were huddled around McCleary's desk, perusing photographs from one of the old cases. All three men glanced up. "Good news, guys," she said. "It looks like the state's going to let me keep the emeralds."

"I thought they were still in probate," remarked Rusty.

"They are. But it looks encouraging. Which means that once we find a buyer, we can expand. Maybe buy the place next door like Trevor planned."

"What about Ginger Hale?" McCleary asked with a grin. "I'm sure she'd be glad to find a buyer."

"Sure thing, McCleary," she laughed, making a face.

"Hey, you're forgetting something, Quin. What about Louise Fuentes in Cartagena?" asked Bean. "Aren't you going to pursue that?"

Her eyes met McCleary's; he rocked back in his chair. "Bell's dead, Robin's dead, the case is closed. What's the point of dredging it all up again?"

"My man," Rusty said, running a finger alongside his nose, "nothing is ever that simple."

"This is, Rusty," Quin replied, and wondered how come she didn't really believe it.

About the Author

T. J. MacGregor lives in South Florida. She is also the author of two other books in the Quin St. James/Mike McCleary series: KILL FLASH and DEATH SWEET.

The T.J MacGregor series continues as St. James and McCleary join forces again.